**If your whole life
is a mystery,
can the love you feel
be real?**

Fate has robbed Stephanie Marsh, Mat Cruz and
Paige Winston of their memories. But it hasn't
taken away their capacity for passion. Can they
trust their hearts to take them where their minds
cannot? And will they ever regain their

missing
memories

Relive the romance...

Three complete novels by your favorite authors!

About the Authors

MARY LYNN BAXTER
knew books would occupy an important place in her
life long before she began to write them. After
graduating from college with a degree in Library
Science, Mary Lynn became a school librarian
before opening the D & B Bookstore in her
hometown of Lufkin, Texas, where she lives with
her husband, Leonard. She has written twenty-eight
books and is a frequent Waldenbooks bestseller; her
book *Tall in the Saddle* captured #1 on their
bestseller list.

PAULA DETMER RIGGS
discovers material for her writing in her varied life
experiences. During her first five years of marriage
to a naval officer, she lived in nineteen locations on
the West Coast, gaining familiarity with places as
diverse as San Diego and Seattle. The two-time
RITA award finalist has received four awards from
Romantic Times, including a Career Achievement
Award for *Forgotten Dream.*

ANNETTE BROADRICK
believes in romance and the magic of life. Since
1984, when her first book was published, Annette
has shared her view of life and love with readers all
over the world. In addition to being nominated by
Romantic Times as one of the best new authors of
that year, she has also won the *Romantic Times*
Reviewer's Choice Award for *Heat of the Night,*
Mystery Lover and *Irresistible;* the *Romantic Times*
WISH Award for her heroes in *Strange Enchantment,*
Marriage, Texas Style! and *Impromptu Bride;* and the
Romantic Times Lifetime Achievement Awards for
Series Romance and Series Romantic Fantasy.

missing **memories**

Mary Lynn Baxter
Paula Detmer Riggs
Annette Broadrick

MISSING MEMORIES

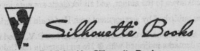

Silhouette Books

Published by Silhouette Books
America's Publisher of Contemporary Romance

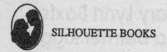

SILHOUETTE BOOKS

by Request

MISSING MEMORIES

ISBN 0-373-20110-9

TALL IN THE SADDLE
Copyright © 1991 by Mary Lynn Baxter
FORGOTTEN DREAM
Copyright © 1990 by Paula Detmer Riggs
HAWK'S FLIGHT
Copyright © 1985 by Annette Broadrick

CONTENTS

A Note from Mary Lynn Baxter

I loved writing this book because it's about something near and dear to my heart—Texas. I'm a Texan born and bred, and proud of it. Texas is synonymous with cowboys and ranches.

Tall in the Saddle is about a lonely cowboy who unwittingly becomes involved with a classy city girl. Following a plane crash near his ranch, Flint Carson carries amnesia victim Stephanie Marsh home to the Diamond A Ranch, hoping her memory will soon be restored, thus ending his Good Samaritan stint.

The best intentions take a twisted turn when sexual sparks fly and they find that they are not only attracted to each other, but are falling in love. However, these two strong-willed people fight their feelings, further complicated by the fact that she hasn't recovered from her amnesia. Only after many bumps and bruises does their love grow into something as lasting and enduring as the Lone Star state itself.

I hope you, as a reader, receive as much pleasure from reading *Tall in the Saddle* as I did from writing it.

Mary Lynn Baxter

TALL IN THE SADDLE

Mary Lynn Baxter

Special thanks to Troy Hill for all of his help

One

From afar a baby screamed. Closer, two teenagers exchanged a passionate kiss. A bored voice droned over the intercom, announcing flight information.

Flint Carson paid scant attention to the sights and sounds around him. He was too intent on making his way through the airport concourse in Little Rock, Arkansas. For the first time in months, if not years, there was a spring to his gait.

Hours in the saddle and manual labor had supplied him with a wealth of energy, yet his movements were economical and purposeful. He never seemed in a hurry. At six foot three, he towered over the average citizen. His weight was adequate where it ought to be; life had given him a lean hardness.

Thank God, the trip to the Diamond A Ranch had paid off, he thought. He'd gotten confirmation that he was on the right track with his breeding of the Brahngus cattle. He was hell-bent on building them into a profitable herd.

And to think he hadn't wanted to make the trip. Flint had felt he couldn't be away from his struggling ranch in East Texas for a day, much less several. But if he were to cross-breed any more stock, he'd have no choice, especially with money being in such short supply. With no guarantees, he'd already used what little cash he had.

"Hey, mister, watch where you're goin', will ya?"

Flint paused, realizing he'd unconsciously sideswiped a fellow passenger with his duffel bag. "Sorry," he muttered.

The man glowered at him. "Yeah, me, too."

For an instant Flint felt himself bristle, but then sound judgment took over and he merely shrugged, turned his back and walked off. One smart-mouth kook wasn't worth getting riled over. He didn't stop again until he'd reached the gate that posted his Houston flight.

He dropped his duffel bag in a deserted corner and leaned against the wall. But it was almost impossible for him to remain idle. Impatiently he removed his Stetson hat and ran his hand through his thick chestnut-colored hair. When that gesture failed to calm his restlessness, he shoved the hat back on his head and let his thoughts wander back to his project.

This Brahngus line could be the break he'd been waiting for. Even at that, he couldn't allow himself to get too excited or optimistic. He'd failed at so much lately. In fact, failure had been such a part of his life that he'd gotten used to it, like an old pair of boots.

Flint had never known complete security or lasting solace. So he had a habit of accepting the brief moments of comfort as exactly that—brief. As a precaution against the anxiety, chaos and defeat he knew were sure to follow, he readied himself.

Flint had found out at an early age that life was not fair, that only the tough survived. A change-of-life baby, he'd been neglected more often than not. His mother had been lazy, and his daddy had worked all the time. Yet money had always been scarce.

His daddy had hounded him to go to work as soon as he was old enough, but Flint had wanted to participate in school sports. Somehow he'd managed to juggle both successfully. In the end, sports had been his salvation. They'd gotten him a college scholarship.

During his college years, Flint had developed a fascination with law enforcement and worked toward making that a career. He'd also worked at overcoming the shock and loss of his parents. They were killed when a tornado ripped through their mobile home.

Upon graduation Flint had gone to work for the Houston Police Department. He'd been recruited by the Drug Enforcement Agency after special training and had worked there until a drug bust went sour and he was injured, forcing him into a leave of absence.

But dredging up thoughts of his ill-fated childhood and perils on the job was a waste of time and good energy. The problems he faced now had nothing to do with the past. The way he looked at it, he'd been given a clean slate, and he aimed to make the best of it or die trying.

The overhead intercom screeched in Flint's ear. He frowned and at the same time reached for a cigarette only to remember with disgust that he'd given up the nasty habit months ago. He settled for a piece of gum while his eyes wandered around the waiting area. It teemed with people of all sizes, ages and nationalities. Instead of being fascinated, he was repulsed. He hated crowded flights. He hated crowds period. Give him the wide open spaces and his privacy anytime.

Only after Flint slapped his pocket again and looked back up did he see her. A woman, who looked to be in her late twenties, was laughing at something someone was saying to her. She was in his direct line of vision, and for a moment Flint was held by the sound of her husky laughter.

She was a real looker to boot. Her milk-white skin and gently curving mouth were perfect foils for curly black hair that framed her face and shone like black silk. And she had the body to match the face. She was dressed in an off-white suit. Her blouse was silk and her high, firm breasts molded the soft fabric in a way that confirmed his guess that she didn't have on a bra.

He turned his gaze, but not before shifting uncomfortably. He fared no better, however, when he concentrated on her legs. They seemed endless. And her derriere was round and tight.

"Damn," he muttered, then slapped his empty pocket again for a cigarette, all without taking his eyes off her. It wasn't so much her beauty that mesmerized Flint, as it was her total unawareness of it. Or, he corrected himself, her calm acceptance of it as a God-given right.

Again he realized he was staring, and cursed vehemently. Still, he didn't turn away, watching as a stocky, sour-faced man approached her. If her reaction was anything to judge by, she wasn't glad to see him. Her face lost its color, and her mouth tightened into a straight line.

His curiosity more than a little aroused, Flint propped a booted foot against the wall and watched as the man closed the distance between him and the woman. He was handsome enough, all right, Flint thought, sizing him up. But there was something about him that didn't ring true.

Right off, he couldn't put his finger on the reason for that feeling. It wasn't because the man was dressed flamboyantly and expensively, though Flint did have a tendency to scoff at such attire. Nor was it because he had a receding hairline that he tried to cover up by combing too much hair to one side. That merely drew a cynical smile from Flint. His attitude. Yeah, that was it. He thought he was better than the average person.

The woman stiffened suddenly and edged backward, but not before a heated argument had ignited. Mere snatches of their conversation reached Flint's ears, but it was obvious they were both upset, especially the woman.

Only after the man raised his voice did Flint realize just how volatile the exchange was.

"I'm warning you," the man hissed.

Although color surged into the woman's cheeks, she didn't back down. Instead, she straightened to her full height, which Flint judged to be about five foot eight, and looked at the man eye-to-eye. But her comeback was lost on Flint as the voice on the intercom chose that moment to announce another flight.

Whatever she said caused the man's sour face to turn even sourer. After glaring at each other for another long moment, the man pivoted on the soles of his highly polished shoes and stamped off.

The woman seemed to wilt, but then she regained her composure and arranged her features to show none of the turmoil that Flint was certain roiled inside her.

And still he continued his perusal. How long had it been since a woman had piqued his interest? he asked himself with contemptuous amusement. He knew the answer. Not since his wife had walked into the hospital, after he'd been stabbed in the gut, and announced she was leaving him.

Muttering another colorful expletive, Flint tried to shift his thoughts to something more pleasant. He didn't want to think about that time in his life, about how he'd nearly lost his mind and had turned to the bottle to forget he'd failed at both his job and his marriage. The scar tissue inside his heart hadn't toughened nearly enough to allow him that luxury. He doubted it ever would.

But neither did he want to dwell on that lovely woman across the way, who had apparently recovered from her verbal skirmish and once again held court.

In many ways she was like the pompous creep who had just left her. The world and everyone in it revolved around her. Why hadn't he picked up on that before? He'd thought

he was a master at spotting her type. He'd lived with one
just like her. Yeah, on closer observation, she reminded him
of his ex-wife, Madge.

He turned away. He would not let her interest him. He
didn't need a woman. Not now—when it had been a year
and a half since he'd beaten his drinking problem and taken
over the dilapidated ranch his uncle left him. The ranch had
given him a new lease on life. Satisfaction swelled in his
chest, and holding back a grin, he turned to face the woman
again.

As if she sensed she was being scrutinized, she looked
abruptly in Flint's direction. Furious at being caught, he
tried to avoid her gaze. He wasn't quick enough. Their eyes
met and clung. For a moment it was as if a hot current had
cut through a formidable ice flow. The atmosphere sizzled.

She smiled. He did not. Jerking his head, Flint forced his
attention to the loudspeaker announcing his flight.

"'Bout time," he said under his breath as he reached for
his bag and hoisted it onto one shoulder.

Once on board, Flint located his seat next to the aisle
without any trouble. He buckled up and tried not to think
about how much he'd give for a cigarette. That thought
magnified when he looked up and saw the dark-haired
woman staring down at him.

"Excuse me," she said. "I think that's my seat next to
you."

Two

Cursing silently, Flint stood. Of all the passengers who could have been his seating companion, why did it have to be *her*?

While she passed in front of him, he stood rigid, careful their bodies didn't touch. Still, in the process her perfume assaulted his nostrils and her hair grazed his face. He jerked back as if he'd been slapped by a rude hand. But the damage had been done.

"Sorry," she murmured breathlessly before dropping into her seat.

Once seated, she kept her eyes averted. His tension seemed to have communicated itself to her. After fastening her seat belt, she made a big deal of reaching down and fumbling through her travel bag. Flint watched as she pulled out a magazine that had something to do with the jewelry industry and began thumbing through it.

Figures, he thought with a smirk. This lady and fancy baubles seemed to go together. Through narrowed eyes, he continued his guarded perusal of her, his curiosity heightened. A sudden intuition told him this woman represented a danger to him. He scoffed at the idea.

Disgusted with his train of thought and his absurd reaction to this woman, Flint tightened his face and turned his attention to the activities inside the cabin. The flight attendants scurried up and down the aisle checking seat belts and other things pertinent to takeoff. Many passengers were already asleep. Others were reading or chattering with fellow companions.

Flint rubbed his forehead, wishing the flight was over and he was in his truck driving to the ranch. He couldn't wait to start applying the techniques he'd learned in Little Rock. His friend and closest neighbor, Ed Liscomb, would be interested, too, as he was also dabbling with the Brahngus cattle.

More than that, Flint couldn't wait to get off this damned plane and away from this sweet-smelling woman who continued to play havoc with his hormones.

He didn't know how he knew she was looking at him, but he did. Was it because he was so aware of everything about her? Reluctantly he faced her, though he made sure there was no repeat performance of a while ago. He refused direct eye contact.

She was smiling. "I'm Stephanie Marsh."

Classy name for a classy broad, Flint thought churlishly. "Flint Carson," he muttered. Even to himself, his voice sounded rough, like sandpaper. He coughed and turned away, certain she'd get the hint that he didn't want to be disturbed.

She didn't. She leaned closer, as if lessening the distance between them would abate his obvious hostility.

"Do you think the weather will hold?"

"Couldn't say."

Much to his dismay and discomfort, his short answer still didn't give her the hint. She remained where she was, so close the elusive perfume she wore seemed to become embedded in his flesh. He squirmed in his seat.

His long legs weren't made for such close quarters. But he knew it wasn't the seats that caused his discomfort, and that made him that much madder.

"I don't know about you, but I hate the thought of taking off when the sky is overcast, like now," she said, chattering as if he were giving her his undivided attention. "How about yourself?"

Her voice sounded husky. Or was raspy a better word? He cleared his throat, then drawled, "Don't have an opinion one way or the other, ma'am."

"Am I bothering you?" she asked bluntly.

Startled, Flint brought his head up just enough so that again their eyes connected. She had the most enormous direct blue eyes he had ever seen. They crawled up and down him like live things, missing nothing.

"Are you always this outspoken?" he countered equally as bluntly.

Her delicately drawn features betrayed a curious stillness. Only her heavy-lashed eyes alluded to the fact that she was ill at ease.

"Well?"

A tinge of color surged into her face, and she gave a short laugh. "Not usually," she said, looking away, then back, clearly uncomfortable under his direct gaze.

Nothing concrete showed on his boldly carved features, but his dislike of this ongoing conversation was obvious.

With a deep sigh, he finally dragged his gaze away. What was with her, anyway? It didn't take a rocket scientist to figure out he didn't want to talk. Hell, she didn't look dense. So why didn't she just mind her own damned business?

He set his mouth and listened to the flight attendant talk on the intercom.

"Ladies and gentlemen, welcome aboard . . ."

The voice went on, but Stephanie didn't listen. Her attention was on Flint. Though his face was averted, she continued to watch him, watch the way the muscles in the back of his neck and shoulders rippled, then bunched.

He was tense and uncomfortable. Good, she thought, only to ridicule herself for such childish behavior. But that feeling of remorse was short-lived. Although she had no idea what caused this rude and surly man to feel this way, she took great pleasure in the fact that he did.

Her gaze leveled on him. He was a redneck if she'd ever seen one. He was handsome, though, albeit in a rough-and-tough sort of way. A straight nose, strong jutting chin and rigid mouth added to his aura of remote inaccessibility. He could easily qualify for the Marlboro cigarette billboards, she thought, remembering the way his green eyes had pierced hers from under thick eyebrows that almost met.

As a rule she was not drawn to the rough cowboy type. They were a turnoff. She liked her men more refined, more gentlemanly. Nevertheless, she was attracted to this one.

Why? What was so intriguing about him? Was it because he showed no interest in her? Though Stephanie was totally without conceit, she knew that no matter where she went, she drew attention. Men looked at her.

But a relationship with a man was the last thing she wanted or needed. One broken engagement was enough for her. What she wanted was to make her jewelry business successful and to maintain her hard-won independence from a domineering mother.

Having grown up in a family where money was in abundance, she'd never wanted for anything except that independence. The fact that she was an only child of divorced parents hadn't helped, either, especially as her father was now dead.

Stephanie had finished her education at an exclusive girls' school, then had gone to work for Flora in the family-owned real-estate business, a business that would one day be hers. But there was a catch; she didn't want it.

A great lover of the arts and very artistic herself, she had always wanted to work with precious stones. She'd inherited her talent from her grandmother. Only after she'd turned twenty-eight and broken off her tumultuous engagement to David Weston, handpicked by her mother, did she leave the company and pursue that dream.

That was eight months ago, and now Stephanie was riding an emotional high. She had just completed the sale of her career. Thinking about the necklace, with its old mine-cut diamonds and history that dated back to Napoleonic times, brought chill bumps to her skin.

Stephanie's future had never looked brighter. But if she was to maintain that edge and keep her store solvent in the competitive world of the jewelry business, she could not let up. That commitment left no time for personal luxuries such as pursuing another relationship.

Besides, she hadn't found a man who could make her palms sweat and her heart race. David certainly didn't. She had decided no such animal existed.

Stephanie sobered. The last person she wanted to dwell on was her ex-fiancé or rehash the conversation they'd had prior to her boarding the plane. But her mind was determined to backtrack.

She'd gone to Little Rock to conclude a small piece of business with David's elderly aunt, whom she'd come to know and love. Weeks before, at the old lady's request, she had sold several pieces of jewelry for her and had gotten a handsome price, taking no commission for herself. She'd known Cynthia was short of money because David had the nasty habit of freeloading from her.

She'd only been at the airport a short time when she'd received a shock. Seeing David make his way toward her was the last thing she'd expected, even though he was originally from Little Rock and visited his aunt often. Still, she had been certain he'd followed her there this weekend. He hadn't taken their break-up well and had been harassing her with unexpected visits and random phone calls.

"What are you doing here?" she'd demanded, her face flushed.

David's blond eyebrows had shot up. "Now, is that any way to talk to your fiancé?"

"Ex-fiancé," she snapped, wondering anew how she'd ever let her mother ramrod her into a relationship with this man. Oh, he had everything going for him: blond good looks, polished manners, education, breeding. But when it came to character and substance, he was lacking, or at least Stephanie thought so. He had fooled her for a while, but no longer. The thought of him touching her again made her cringe.

His handsome features didn't change, nor did his smooth voice. "I don't see it that way."

"Well, that's the way it is," Stephanie said flatly. Then lowering her voice, she pressed, "Why are you here?"

"In Little Rock, you mean?"

"Don't play games with me!"

"I came to see my aunt, of course."

"Liar."

That softly spoken accusation finally rattled his composure. His blue eyes narrowed in challenge. "I'd watch what I said, if I were you."

"Don't you dare threaten me." Stephanie's eyes flashed fire. "I resent you following me, and I want to know why you did."

David stepped closer. "You know why."

"No, I don't. Suppose you enlighten me."

He was so close now, Stephanie could see the tiny hair positioned in the center of the mole on his right cheek. For a moment she was mesmerized by it. She wondered if he knew it was there. No, she knew he didn't. He wouldn't allow anything to mar his looks. If the situation hadn't been so serious and she hadn't been so mad, she might have laughed.

"You're not going to get away with it, you know."

"Look, David..."

"No, you look," he countered. "I want you to return Cynthia's jewelry to her."

"What!"

"You heard me."

"I'll do no such thing."

"Oh, yes, you will. Those weren't hers to sell."

"And just whose were they?"

"Mine."

"Yours?" Her tone was incredulous.

"She promised them to me."

"Well, until she dies, they're hers to do with as she sees fit. And she saw fit to sell them."

"Unsell them."

Stephanie tossed her head. "That's crazy. *You're* crazy. Anyway, the deal I made with your aunt is none of your concern."

"That's where you're wrong."

"Go away, David." Even to her own ears, her voice sounded tired. "Leave me alone and leave your aunt alone. Haven't you put us both through enough grief already?"

His mouth curved in a sneer. "If you don't get that jewelry back, you'll really know what grief is."

"I told you—don't threaten me."

"I'm warning you!" His voice had risen, and he'd lowered it only after he'd realized everyone around him was gawking. "And you damn well better listen."

She'd stared at him coldly, then he had turned his back on her and walked away.

"You haven't heard the last of this," he had hissed to her back.

Now, as Stephanie forced her mind back to the moment at hand, back to the plane's whining engines, she was still miffed that David continued to disrupt her life. Maybe her sorority sister in Austin was right. Maybe she should put some distance between herself and David, at least for a while. The thought of visiting Amy's bed-and-breakfast retreat in the hill country was suddenly appealing. She made a mental note to call her friend when she got home, and firm up her plans.

It galled her, though, that David had any influence over her at all and that she took his threats seriously. Deciding she wasn't going to let thoughts of David further dampen her spirits, she stole a glance at the man next to her. He appeared as uptight as ever and just as mysterious.

A brief smile touched her lips, and at the same time she ignored the nervous flutter in her stomach. Why not? she thought. Why not strike up another conversation? If nothing else, it ought to be interesting.

She tapped him on the shoulder. "By the way, what did you say you do for a living?"

Three

"I didn't."

Stephanie sighed, but when she spoke, her voice was even. "No, I guess you didn't. And what's more, you don't intend to. Right?"

Something close to a scowl altered his expression. "Are you just curious, Ms. Marsh, or simply bored?"

His brusqueness seemed to have little effect on her. She smiled. "Maybe a little of both, Mr. Carson."

"Well, at least you're honest."

Her smile was disarming. "Maybe too honest for my own good."

He shrugged and turned away. What had he done to deserve this? Again, all he wanted was to be left alone. It was safer that way and much less painful. He'd learned that the hard way as a child. As the memory of those years rose to the forefront of his mind, his lips twisted into a grimace. To this day they haunted him.

He could still hear the kids in his school taunt him, call his names because his jeans were too short and too tight. And the teachers were as bad, but in a different way. Sympathy shone from their eyes when he couldn't produce the latest craze in lunch buckets filled with goodies, much less money to buy a hot lunch.

He had learned that if he kept to himself, he didn't have to endure shame and humiliation. In his solitary world, there were no peers to judge him, no class distinctions.

When he met Madge, years later, things changed. He changed. Before he realized it, she'd ripped that protective covering off him and shown him what he'd been missing. For a while he'd joined the world of the living. But when their marriage started to sour along with his job, he retreated back into himself.

And he'd be damned if he was going to let any woman, no matter how enticing, penetrate that barricade. No sir, he wasn't about to get mixed up with a woman.

"I've found that in my line of work honesty pays off," she said at last, effectively breaking into his thoughts.

He inclined his head in a mock salute. "Is that a fact?"

"If you're not honest, you don't last long in my business."

Flint felt a smile loosen his lips. He'd have to hand it to her, she had guts and determination. Most people would have given up long ago, especially after they'd received one of his cold, bitter stares. But not Stephanie Marsh. His coldness hadn't deterred her in the least. Yet he sensed her behavior was out of the norm. Gut instinct told him this. There was a nervousness about her that seemed out of place.

"It's the same in my business," he said, admiration neutralizing his tone.

"And just what would that be?" She laughed deep in her throat and angled her head. "I'm not going to let you off the hook, you know."

He permitted his droll humor to surface briefly. "I didn't imagine you would."

"So?"

"So I'm getting started in the cattle business," he added rather reluctantly.

"Oh, so you're a rancher?"

His laugh was sarcastic. "I wouldn't say that."

"I don't understand."

"No, I'm sure you don't." His voice was rough.

"I don't know anything about cattle." She gestured with her hands, then eased an errant strand of hair behind a delicate ear. Never once did she take her blue eyes off him.

"We're even. I'm sure I wouldn't know anything about what you do." His gaze fell to the magazine. "Especially if jewelry's involved."

She threw him a challenging look. "We'll just have to correct that, won't we?"

He steeled himself against the warm femininity she exuded. "I don't think that's . . ."

"Oh, come on, tell me about your cows."

The way she said *cows* made him smile.

"You ought to do that more often, you know?" Stephanie teased.

She'd caught him off guard. "What?"

"Smile. It does wonders for you."

Unsettled and disturbed, he turned away without answering.

"So, I'm waiting."

The smile no longer in place, he faced her again. "They're a cross between Black Angus and Brahman bulls."

"They sound mean," she said, shivering.

"They are."

She didn't get a chance to respond. Nor did Flint.

The pilot's voice claimed their attention. "Ladies and gentlemen, I apologize for the delay. But we've been cleared for takeoff and should be in the air momentarily. Flight attendants prepare for takeoff."

"Thank goodness," Stephanie muttered. "I'm ready to get this over with."

Flint gave her a curious look. Her face was now minus its color. "You don't like flying?"

"Let's put it this way. I feel better once we're off the ground." A half smile lengthened her lips. "What about you?"

"Same here."

"It seems that every time I get ready to take a trip, planes start to fall out of the sky."

"That's why I try to avoid the news as much as possible," Flint said, and watched her grip the arm-rest as the engines revved. Shortly, the big plane raced down the runway, then soared upward.

He kept his eyes on her and watched as she visibly relaxed. That was when he realized he'd been almost as uptight as she was, but not because of a fear of flying. Smothering an expletive, he focused his gaze on the front of the cabin.

"So where were we?" she asked.

He didn't pretend to misunderstand. "You were gonna tell me about your work."

"I'm warning you. You may get more than you bargained for."

Although he wasn't looking at her, his faint smile came and went. He couldn't believe it, but he was doing what he swore he wouldn't do. Here he was conversing civilly with a woman, something he hadn't done since Madge divorced him.

"Estate jewelry sales have come into their own of late," she said.

"Is that your business?"

"That's it. Six months ago I opened a small shop in Houston and right now I'm mostly handling antique jewelry." Her voice rose with excitement. "Later, though, I hope to add other related items such as antique dresser silver, sewing kits, which include thimbles and sterling embroidery cases." Stephanie paused. "And then there are your fine laces..."

He shook his head. "You might as well be talking Greek."

Her laugh was a free and warm sound, and for a minute his heart skipped a beat. Promptly he cursed himself for his foolishness.

"Even if I went into it, you'd still be lost. But to simplify it as best I can, I deal in antique jewelry, both costume and colored gemstones."

"I'm still lost."

"All right. See if this makes sense. Garnets, for example, are considered colored gemstones. And though the gemstones interest me the most, I sell a lot of seed pearls and sterling silver."

In spite of himself, Flint was curious, though he'd have to admit that it wasn't the details of her work that held him, but the woman herself. Every gesture, every smile, every flash of her eyes cut through him. He cleared his throat. "So do you have to wait for people to die to get that kinda stuff?"

His choice of words drew another laugh. "No. Although I do get a lot of it that way."

"Go on."

"I haunt flea markets, although there you have to be really careful. Quarterly I set up a booth at the International Show at Market Hall in Dallas. But my main sources are attorneys who settle estates and trips to the English countryside."

Flint blinked. "English as in England?"

"The same."

"Must be nice."

If she detected the sarcasm edging his tone, she didn't show it. "Oh, it is. It's great fun. You never know what you'll find, either." Her eyes mirrored the smile on her lips. "Once, in this obscure village, I came across a mother lode of great stuff. I bought a five-piece Victorian parure set for a song."

"Sounds like something to eat."

Again she laughed deep in her throat. "Far from it. Actually it's a matched set of earrings, choker, bracelets and rings made up of garnets and seed pearls. These were without exception given to the bride by a groom before the marriage. Only a fast girl would have worn them beforehand."

"Of course," he said drolly.

"As ludicrous as it sounds, it was true."

"So how do you know you're not buying junk?"

"Most of us use a loupe, which is a jeweler's eyeglass. Also, I carry a diamond probe in my purse."

"Sounds lethal."

Again she laughed. Again he shifted in his seat.

"It's a simple little electronic device that's small enough to put in your purse. It tells you if the stone's a diamond or a zircon."

"I'll be damned."

"I'm boring you to death with all this, I know, but once I get started I don't know when to quit." Her laughter tempered to a sheepish smile, and there was a faint blush at the base of her throat. He wondered what it would be like to touch that exact spot with his lips.

"Pray tell who minds the shop while you're doing all this?" He spoke brusquely to distract his thoughts from their unwelcome path.

"A dear friend who hopes to one day become a partner."

"Sounds like you've got it made."

"As a matter of fact I do." Her face shone, which made her all the more beautiful. "Recently I turned a deal that allowed me to set up shop and become truly competitive in a very cutthroat business."

When he didn't respond, she went on in that same lilting voice. "Actually I made two wonderful deals. The first one was a find of a lifetime, at an estate sale. A woman was auctioning off her grandmother's possessions. The necklace I bid on and got came with a history that dated back to Napoleon. But it was only after another jeweler confirmed my appraisal that I knew what I had.

"I went back to the woman and asked her if she'd like it back and she said no, that she was satisfied with the money I'd paid her. You can't imagine how excited I was . . ."

No, he couldn't, Flint thought, scowling silently, never having had that luxury. She was everything he wasn't. She *had* everything he *didn't*. She had class. He had none. She was high society, and he was a washed-out agent struggling to become a rancher. Resentment kicked up inside him as the string of his past failures paraded one by one through his mind, not to mention the gamble he was taking with the cattle, which had yet to pay off.

"You're not listening to me, are you?"

Through the silence that yawned between them, her voice sounded feeble.

When he didn't answer, she went on. "What's . . . the matter?" Her voice faltered again. "Did I say something wrong?"

"No," he muttered tersely, unable to meet her puzzled gaze.

Stephanie opened her mouth to speak, only to close it as a flight attendant and beverage cart stopped beside Flint.

"Would you care for something to drink?" Her glance swept both of them.

"Thanks, I'll pass."

"Water for me, please," Stephanie said.

Long after the attendant had moved on, silence prevailed. Stephanie sipped her water and ignored him. She was upset, and he didn't blame her. He'd acted like a jerk, but he sure as hell wasn't going to apologize. It was better this way, anyhow. This trip would soon end, and he would never see her again.

He stole a glance at her and watched as she tipped her head back and took another sip of water. The column of her throat was absurdly vulnerable in the sunlight.

He bit his lower lip to stop a blistering expletive from escaping his lips, just as the plane hit a pocket of air turbulence. The glass bounced off his chest, and water saturated his lap.

"Oh, no!" She raised horrified eyes to his and for a moment neither moved or spoke. Finally Flint's muttered curse forced them into action.

"Oh, God, I'm so sorry," she said, clearly rattled. "Here, let me help." She then grabbed the two napkins off her tray and dabbed at Flint's thighs.

With a sharp intake of breath, he stilled her hand. His fingers felt the fragile bones of her wrist, which were almost exposed through the screen of flesh. Then, as if he'd been stung, he dropped her hand.

Her expression was difficult to read as she lowered her flushed face and once again attacked the stain in his lap.

"Don't," he said in a strangled voice, grappling to get his handkerchief out of his back pocket.

"Please, let me help."

"No, I..." The words died in his throat as her hand accidentally encountered the hardness between his legs. They both froze. Then swearing, he pushed her hand away.

Had she felt the bulge under his fly? Of course she had, you idiot. If nothing else, her sharp, indrawn breath and wide, shocked eyes were dead giveaways.

"Look, stay the hell away from me."

"Flint?"

"Give it a rest. Just give it a rest, okay?"

Stephanie swallowed a biting retort, put her head back and squeezed her eyes shut. But she couldn't stop her face from flaming or her heart from racing. Anger as well as dismay kept it puffing like an out-of-control engine.

How could she have been so careless? But it was an accident, and no matter how well-endowed he was, it didn't excuse his rude behavior. And she wasn't entirely blameless in the charade, either. He'd made it clear from the get-go that he didn't want to be bothered. She'd kept on, though, until she'd forced him into a conversation that soon turned into a confrontation.

When had things started to go wrong? Long before the incident with the water, that for sure. What had made his face turn back to concrete and his eyes narrow into dark slits? Something she said had obviously turned him off.

The bottom line was she should have curbed her nervous chatter and labeled her fascination for him an indulgent but passing fancy and let it go at that. Only she hadn't.

Well, who cared anyway? She certainly didn't. Mr. Flint Carson wouldn't have to worry about her the remainder of the trip.

Feeling good about her decision, she willed herself to relax, determined to sleep. At that precise moment something went haywire. A loud sound assaulted her ears. An explosion? Was that it? Before she could answer the question, the plane vibrated.

A passenger screamed. Another cursed. Another stood up and yelled for the attendant.

Stephanie bolted upright in her seat and turned toward Flint. She opened her mouth, but only a squeaky sound came out. Fear, like a cold blade of steel, constricted her throat. Her mouth turned dry. Her lips went white. She could feel the hair on her neck bristle and stand on end.

"What . . . what was that?" she finally managed.

"The engine. Something's happened to the—" He got no further. Without warning, the plane took a violent nose-dive.

"Oh, my God," Stephanie cried, "we're going to crash!"

Four

Stephanie blinked, then rubbed the back of her hand across her eyes. A ball of pressure swelled inside her chest, a threatening suffocating malaise. *Help! Someone help me!* But why did she need help? The pressure built and thrust its way into her lungs until her cry came out a sob. She forced her eyes open.

At first she couldn't control her vision. But then she saw an outline of a man. He stood beside her. She blinked again, several times trying to bring his face into focus. When she succeeded, she recognized him, yet she didn't.

"Stephanie?"

Stephanie? Who is that? Was he talking to her? If so, she didn't recognize that name.

She shut her eyes again and dug her fingernails into the palms of her hands. Where was she? What was all that noise? Why was she lying down? Questions with no answers swirled through her head. They made her dizzier than ever.

If only she could *think*. But she couldn't. Her mind, in its present state, simply refused to function. Her head pounded as though someone were driving nails through it.

"Stephanie, are you awake? Can you hear me?"

Once more she slowly opened her eyes, and this time everything was focused. The tall, lean man who had been there moments before was still there. A plastic bandage covered one eyebrow, and his features were drawn and pinched.

Stephanie resisted the urge to give in to panic. Instead, she forced herself to speak. "Yes...I can hear you. But who's...who's Stephanie?"

She watched as the lines in his forehead deepened, forcing his eyebrows to point toward the center.

"You're Stephanie," he said. "Stephanie Marsh."

She licked her parched, dried lips and struggled to her elbows.

"Hey, take it easy," he cautioned, helping her until she was in a full-fledged sitting position.

Taking him at his word, she sat still and took deep gulping breaths. The silence that followed trembled with the pounding of feet against the tiled floor. The air was clogged with the smell of medicine, of burning cloth, skin. She felt her stomach turn over.

"Are you all right?" His eyes on her were disturbingly gentle.

She didn't respond. Finally, when the room settled, Stephanie realized she was in a hospital, on a stretcher in what looked to be a hallway. *And I don't know who I am!*

"What...what happened?" she whispered at last, looking at him through dazed and disoriented eyes. Then before he could answer, she hurled another question at him, "I know you, don't I?" She clutched at his hand. "Please, tell me I know you."

"Shh, take it easy," he said again. "Yes, you know me. I'm Flint Carson."

"What...what happened?" She choked on the words, unable to keep the tremor out of her voice.

Flint eased himself down beside her on the gurney, then disentangled his hand from hers. "Our plane crashed..."

Her cry was tremulous.

A spasm of emotion she couldn't identify crossed his face. "You don't remember the crash?"

"Oh my God, oh my God," she whispered. "I can't remember anything." Her voice rose several octaves. "Did... did many survive?"

"About half."

Another sob tore loose. "Where...did it happen?"

"In a pasture near Crockett."

"And this is the Crockett hospital?"

He nodded. "But it's not equipped to take care of all the injured. That's why you're in the hall."

"Why can't I remember any of this?" she wailed, and pushed a clump of hair behind one ear, only to then wince.

"Watch out," Flint said. "You hit your head."

"I...seem to be fine otherwise, though."

"True, except for the bruises on your arms and legs."

"What about yourself?" She wiped the tears from her eyes with the back of her hand, then fastened her eyes on his bandage. "Were you...hurt?"

"I'm fine," he said brusquely. "You don't worry about me."

Her lower lip began to tremble, and she looked at him with terrified eyes. "I...I can't believe I...don't know who I am...or where I live!" She grasped Flint's hand again and clung to it.

Before he could respond, a shadow fell over them. Dressed in a white coat, a short, bald-headed man with a tired-looking face stood unobtrusively beside Flint.

Flint calmly withdrew his hand from Stephanie's and stood. "Hello, Abe."

Dr. Abe Powell only had eyes for Stephanie. "Well, it's good to see you awake, young lady."

In spite of her own devastating circumstances, Stephanie's heart went out to him. Like Flint, he looked exhausted. Yet he had the kindest, most sympathetic eyes she had ever seen. "Why can't I remember anything?" she asked in a strident voice, and once again fought off the panic that churned inside her.

Dr. Powell replaced Flint beside her and took both her hands in his. "You let me worry about that. Despite our limited capabilities, we're going to do what's best for all concerned, including you."

Stephanie tried to smile her gratitude, but even that was too much of a chore. She was starting to feel as exhausted as her companions looked. To move one bone or one muscle proved excruciatingly painful.

"I think she's about to fold on us, Abe." Flint's words came out in a rush.

Stephanie raised her eyes to him. "No...I'm not. It's just that I'm . . . I'm so tired," she said, and watched his expression darken with concern. Or was it anger?

"You're suffering from amnesia more than likely caused by the lick on the head," Dr. Powell said, "but we'll know more when we do the CAT scan."

"How . . . long will it last—the amnesia, I mean?" Her voice was a mere whisper.

The doctor sighed. "I'm afraid I can't answer that. You could remember everything within the hour. Or it could be days or months or—"

"Not . . . ever," Stephanie finished for him.

"I doubt that, my dear. But for now we'll take one day at a time."

Stephanie's eyes sought Flint. "Do . . . do you know anything about me?"

"Only that you own an antique jewelry store in Houston and that you spoke with a man just before you boarded the plane." Before she could ask the questions that quivered on her lips, Flint told her everything he knew about that incident.

"There's nothing else, you're sure?"

"I'm sure." Flint's voice sounded pinched as he and the doctor exchanged looks.

Stephanie massaged her forehead, feeling her hopes fade. She had felt so confused and afraid—trapped in the body of a stranger.

"Why don't you lie back now?" Dr. Powell said. "I'll have a nurse bring you something for your head."

"What's going to happen...to me...?" Wild-eyed, she looked around. Controlled pandemonium, but pandemonium nonetheless, still ruled the day. Doctors and nurses shouted orders. Each vied to be heard over the other.

Candy stripers, office workers and what looked like every other able-bodied person in the town scurried about doing what they could to take care of the injured. And the dead— she wouldn't...couldn't bear to think about them. Not now, anyway.

"We'll take care of you, that's what," Abe said.

"But...I...I shouldn't be taking up space here."

"You let us worry about that." Dr. Powell's calm but slightly gruff voice soothed her so that she could pay attention to what else he said. "Right now, rest is the best tonic for you."

"But...but..."

Flint uncurled his body from against the wall and jumped into the conversation for the first time in a long while. "I second that motion." He jammed his hands into his pockets and transferred his gaze to Stephanie's pale face. His eyes darkened. "You took one helluva lick to the head."

"Flint's right. And while I don't think there's anything to be concerned about, you must be checked."

Stephanie nodded mutely.

"After we get the results of the tests, we'll talk." Dr. Powell stood then and gave her a reassuring nod. "In the meantime, you follow my orders."

"Abe, I'll be along in a minute to help," Flint said.

The doctor paused and brought his stooped shoulders back around. "Everything seems to be under control. Anyway, you've more than done your part."

"Doesn't matter. I'm still needed."

Abe smiled wearily. "Thanks."

Once the doctor had shuffled off, Stephanie's eyes turned to Flint. "You're . . . not leaving, are you?"

"Just to help, that's all."

"What . . . what about afterwards?"

"I suppose I'll rent a car and drive to my ranch."

"Oh, please, you can't!" Stephanie couldn't keep the desperate note out of her voice as she endeavored to stand.

Flint rushed toward her. "For crying out loud, stay put. You're not nearly as strong as you think you are."

His harsh voice had the desired effect. Stephanie fell against the pillow. "You're right," she said shakily, "I'm not."

He didn't respond.

"Will you stay with me during the test?" she asked softly, and watched again as his expression changed.

"I . . ." he began.

Sensing he was about to refuse, she cried, "Please!"

"Damn!" he muttered, clearly at a loss as to how to deal with this sudden turn of events.

Stephanie quivered. "Please?"

She knew she was being selfish and God was probably going to get her because Flint was needed. Though at the moment, he looked as if he needed a bed more than she. Still, she couldn't stand the thought of being separated from him. He was the only sane thing in all this insane mess that had suddenly become her life.

"Please, don't . . . leave me," she whispered.

He swung back around. "All right, you win," he said, sounding drained to the bone. "I won't leave you."

Flint scrutinized Abe's tired face. "You look like you've had it, man. You sure you're gonna make it?"

They had met in what was now the deserted doctors' lounge, which moments before had been occupied by several other weary doctors. They had passed them going out as they were coming in.

"No," Abe said, helping himself to a can of fruit juice in the refrigerator. "But I have no choice. I'll carry on till I drop. You know that."

Flint almost smiled. "Yeah, I know that."

He and Abe Powell had a history, not a long one, but a history nevertheless. After Flint had been released from the hospital in Houston, he'd been sent here to the Crockett hospital, which was forty miles from his ranch, to finish his recuperation. Abe had been his doctor.

The two of them had gotten into a verbal skirmish the first time they'd met because they were so much alike—bullheaded, stubborn and uncommunicative to a fault. In the end, however, Flint developed a grudging respect for the elderly man and trusted him. He knew Abe felt the same about him. Out of that trust had come friendship.

"What about you?" Abe asked, breaking into the silence. "Are *you* all right?" He cleared his throat. "According to the paramedics you wouldn't stop long enough to let them check you."

Flint shrugged. "There wasn't time. Anyway, I wasn't hurt, and others were. I did what I had to do."

Abe shook his head. "When I think of what you went through—"

"I know," Flint said, his voice unsteady. "When that plane took a nosedive, I just knew it was—" He broke off, unable to go on.

"Curtains," Abe said. "And by rights, it should've been, for all of you. Not many people walk away from a crash like that."

"Do you think she'll be all right?"

"Yes. And I think her loss of memory is only temporary, but I can't say for sure."

"I sure as hell hope so."

Abe rubbed his bald head and eyed Flint carefully. "What's she to you, anyway?"

"Nothing," Flint said flatly.

Abe gave him an odd look. "You meant it, then, when you said you didn't know her?"

"Damn straight, I meant it. Never laid eyes on her till she sat next to me on the plane."

"Holy Moses." Abe took a healthy sip of the juice. When he finished, he wiped his mouth. "All I can say is that you'd never know it by the way she's clinging to you."

Flint tightened his lips.

"So you don't know a thing about her except her name?"

"That's about the size of it. And that she lives and works in Houston."

"Along with a million other people."

"Yeah, right."

Abe sighed.

"For a while, though, I thought I'd struck paydirt. Someone handed me a purse, told me they thought it belonged to Stephanie. But later, when I opened it, it wasn't hers."

"Damn shame," Abe said, and once more rubbed his bald head. "When things settle down a bit, maybe the airline can help her out, shed some light on who she is."

"Let us pray."

A silence fell between them while Abe eased down onto the couch and closed his eyes.

"She practically begged me not to leave her."

Abe's eyes fluttered open. "Does that mean what I think it does?"

"Yeah."

"What are you going to do?"

"Stay with her."

"And later?"

Flint's features were bleak. "I wish the hell I knew."

For Stephanie, the following hours passed in somewhat of a blessed blur. She was taken to X-ray for the scan, then back to the hall where she finally fell into a deep sleep. When she awakened, Flint was sitting in a chair next to the stretcher, his head to one side, his eyes closed. In rest, the exhaustion lines on his face had relaxed.

She seized the opportunity to study him, noting the broad expanse of his forehead, the black-lashed, hooded eyes with their arched brows, the narrow straight nose, the wide mouth and the square, almost heavy jaw. And framing it all was the thick unruly hair. It was a face at once arresting and noncommittal. It demanded attention, but it gave nothing away.

As if sensing he was being scrutinized, Flint opened his eyes and straightened.

Their gazes held while the air seemed to crackle around them. As if to challenge the sensation that held them, Flint bolted out of his chair and faced the nearest window. For the first time, Stephanie felt awkward in his presence. The silence didn't help either; it seemed to gnaw at them both, leaving her to bear the brunt of her tormenting thoughts alone.

She felt empty inside, an emptiness she was powerless to fill. If only there was something she could do to trigger her memory. But how did one go about doing such a thing? Somewhere out there her family, her friends, were worried sick about her.

What about a husband? Her heart almost stopped beating. No. Something told her that she wasn't married. Her breathing returned to normal. Besides, she didn't have on a wedding ring.

So if she didn't have a husband, she surely had a job. Of course, she did. Everyone worked, didn't they? Her clothes, though soiled and rumpled, were quality goods, expensive. That could prove her point.

His low, strong voice interrupted her. "You're not helping matters by worrying."

Something inside her snapped, and because he was close, she took her frustrations out on him. "How would you know?" she lashed out.

He raked his fingers through his hair with raw impatience. "I don't, but..." Her quivering chin stopped his harsh words. "Hey, don't. Don't do that. You've done great so far."

She swallowed a sob and tried to smile. "According to whom?"

"Me."

"Oh, Flint, what am I going to do? I have no place to go—"

Abe opened the door to an adjacent room and without preamble said, "Flint, if you'll help her in here, I have the results of the test."

Once Stephanie was seated in the cubbyhole of an office, Abe smiled at her. "Just as I had hoped, there are no signs of damage, no swelling of the tissue around the brain."

"So what are you... saying?" Stephanie asked.

Abe's gaze was direct. "Your loss of memory is not the result of the blow to the head."

"Then why...?" A shiver rolled down her spine.

"Let me finish, and I think you'll understand." Abe paused and leaned against the back of a scarred desk. "You're suffering from what is known as psychogenic amnesia, which in laymen's terms is hysterical amnesia."

"And just what the hell is that?" Flint demanded from his position behind Stephanie's chair.

"The loss of memory usually occurs after some stressful episode or traumatic experience."

"Are you saying I can't recall anything because of... of fear?" Restless, Stephanie got up and crossed to the window. She stood there, fighting tears and agonizing over her helplessness.

"That's exactly what I'm saying. When one's life is in jeopardy, fear can do tremendous damage. However, with this type of amnesia, it usually disappears as suddenly as it came on, with complete recovery and only a small chance of recurrence. Meanwhile, though, your behavior will be otherwise unremarkable. You'll remember some things and can function normally."

"But isn't there something I can do... *you* can do to..." A single, choked sob tore through her throat.

"I'm afraid not, my dear. We play the time game—wait it out." Abe's eyes held sympathy. "But later, if it doesn't return just as I said, then there's hypnosis and other measures we can take."

Weakness forced Stephanie to return to her seat. From there she looked directly at Abe. "And in the meantime?"

Abe rubbed his jaw. "In the meantime, I insist you stay overnight for observation." When she would have protested, he held up his hand. "But because we do need your bed, I see no reason why you have to stay any longer, except that you don't have anyplace to go." His tone was gentle.

Stephanie's face crumpled. "I..."

"Yes, she does."

Her eyes swung from the doctor to Flint. From the concealing shadows of his Stetson, he acknowledged her shocked stare. His eyes, more black than green, bore down on her with an intensity that contrasted with his relaxed attitude.

"What . . . ?"

Ignoring her, Flint faced Abe. "I'll take her with me to the ranch."

Five

The early-morning sky was tinted a delicate shade of yellow. Frothy threads of clouds floated through it. The warm air, filled with the scent of growing things, especially flowers, perfumed the typical East Texas day.

Flint, however, was not concerned with the weather or his surroundings. He was concerned about himself, concerned that he'd truly taken leave of his senses.

Stephanie Marsh, sitting rigidly beside him, bore testimony to that.

He had just pulled the rental car onto the highway, and already he was wired so tightly that he felt he could snap the steering wheel in two with little effort.

What had he been thinking when he'd blurted that he'd take her with him? Hell, he had trouble taking care of himself, much less a woman who didn't even know her own name.

The dilapidated state of his ranch suddenly shook him. He wished now he'd taken more pride in its upkeep, especially inside. At least one bedroom was fairly decent. In his mind's eye, though, he pictured the rest of the house, the mess he'd left—papers strewn everywhere, clothes scattered about, rinsed but unwashed dishes in the sink... He grimaced, wondering what she'd think, only to mentally kick himself. What did it matter what *she* thought?

It didn't. But he'd opened his mouth and committed himself, and that was what he cared about, what he was going to have to deal with. But how? He cast a sidelong glance at her and felt that same unidentifiable emotion that had caused him to bring her home.

She had looked lost, alone, vulnerable. But beautiful. If anything, the white cast to her face, the weary droop to her full lower lip, the violet circles under her eyes, added to her beauty, made her look ethereal.

Yet that didn't excuse his actions. Nothing could do that. God, what a mess.

Stephanie moved abruptly. Her thin silk blouse revealed the fragile bones in her shoulders. And again Flint was aware of the nipples pressing pointedly against the fabric. He averted his gaze.

Had his actions stemmed from lust? No. Of course not. He hadn't wanted a woman in a long time, and he didn't want one now. So why the swell under his fly when he'd stared at her breast? His own shame and mortification almost made him curse aloud.

Flint was a man who lived by his instincts. They had kept him alive on the job when by all rights he should have been dead. But this crazy impulse scared him. He had avoided a lot of traps in his life, but now he had plunged into one with his eyes wide open. One that he would surely regret.

"Flint?"

The soft-spoken use of his name brought him around to face her.

"Yeah."

"Why...why are you doing this? Why did you agree to take me home with you? Granted, I couldn't stand the thought of staying alone at that hospital, but..."

"I wish to God I knew."

She was clearly hurt by his terse response. "You can stop the car right now, and I'll get out."

"And go where?"

Her chin jutted. "I...don't know."

He watched her silently, put out at his rough handling of her, but shaken by the effect she had on him. She hadn't asked to go home with him. That had been his own dim-witted idea, and it wasn't fair to take his anger out on her.

"Look...forget I said that. Sure it'll be awkward, as I'm certainly not set up for guests, but we'll manage."

"What...about clothes?" she asked hesitantly "I need other things, too."

She didn't look at him, and her face was flushed as if she was embarrassed to ask him for anything. He sympathized with her; he'd hate having to depend on someone else for his livelihood. He'd been down that road. And once was enough.

"You aren't up to shopping, are you?"

"No, not really, but I could try."

"No need. I'll take care of it."

"You will?"

Her tone implied she couldn't imagine him taking care of such things. He cast her a mocking glance. "I will."

"I guess I'll have to trust you, won't I?"

"I guess you will, at that," he said sarcastically.

Another silence.

"As soon as we get to your place, I want to contact the airlines."

The urgency behind her words penetrated the fog in his brain. "I've already thought of that. I also think we should call the jewelry stores in Houston, all of them if we have to." He watched her face brighten. "But, only after you rest and your head stops pounding. Right now you don't need the added stress, unless you want to end up back in the hospital."

Her eyebrows peaked into a troubled frown. "No, of course I don't, only—"

"That settles it, then."

"What's your ranch like?" she asked suddenly, sounding desperate again.

"Run-down. But I'm working like hell to fix that."

"Are you having any luck?"

He shrugged. "The new breed of cattle I'm experimenting with will tell the tale."

"I see."

"No, you don't." He bit out the words. "Your life is so far removed from mine that you don't see a damn thing and never will."

She sucked in her breath before throwing him a fulminating glance.

Cursing silently, he said, "Look...I didn't mean that the way it sounded."

"Forget it," she said tersely. "I realize we're both under pressure."

A waiting, uneasy silence came between them.

"Why don't you put your head back and rest," Flint said awkwardly. "You're going to be fine. Just give it time. And stop worrying."

With that he dragged his gaze off her and back onto the road, while asking himself why he didn't take his own advice.

She wished she could stop worrying. But that was impossible. Until she got her memory back, her mind and heart would remain in turmoil.

She had so much to be thankful for, though. How many people lived through plane crashes? She forced herself to concentrate on the beauty around her, something she was certain she had heretofore taken for granted.

She didn't think she'd ever seen anything as beautiful as the blaze of wildflowers. Bluebonnets, crimson clover, Indian paintbrushes, buttercups and black-eyed Susans grew alongside the highway. And lurking among those were the shocking yellow senecio. No artist's brush, no matter how talented, could capture this beauty. For a while it brought her the peace of mind she so badly needed.

That feeling of tranquility disappeared the minute she stole a glance at the man beside her. Cold reality set in once again. Not only did she not know who she was, but she was dependent on this stranger.

For some crazy reason she trusted him. And Dr. Abe Powell trusted him. For now that was good enough for her. What she couldn't figure out was why he had offered to let her stay at his ranch.

He regretted it; that was obvious. He was the type of man who liked his privacy. She had sensed that about him in the hospital room, and she sensed it more now. Even so, she knew he wouldn't go back on his word.

Why did that offer her so little comfort? Was it because he seemed so intense, as if he were charged with too much angry energy and was looking for an outlet?

Like herself, he wore the same clothes he'd had on yesterday. She watched the muscles flex in his arms as he skillfully maneuvered the car. His skin was a warm honey color and sprinkled liberally with fine dark hair. She was intensely aware of him as a man. She shouldn't be, but she was.

She turned and saw Flint watching her from beneath lowered lids. "Are you . . . married?" she asked, not thinking.

He turned white. "No."

"Have you ever been?" She knew she should leave well enough alone, especially as he looked as if he were about ready to explode. But something she couldn't put her finger on drove her to delve further.

"I don't think that's any of your business."

"No, I guess it's not," she said, hearing the tremor in her voice and hating herself for it.

A sardonic smile thinned his lips. "I was married once."

"Divorce?"

"Yes."

"I'm sorry."

"Why? I'm not."

An awkward silence ensued.

"Do...do you think I'm married?"

The car swerved slightly. "What makes you think that?" he asked, when the vehicle was once more in control.

"Maybe that man in the airport was my husband."

"No way." The reply came in a strained growl.

"You say that with such conviction."

He shrugged. "Instinct tells me I'm right."

"Is that all?"

"Let's just say I give you more credit."

She puzzled over that, then said, "It sounds like something was wrong with him."

"There was. He's a first-class jerk. And he's not your husband. Just trust me on that."

A short, but seemingly final silence fell between them.

"How much farther?" she asked dejectedly, realizing he wasn't going to say anything else. But then, she knew there was nothing else to say. He'd already told her everything he knew.

"A few yards up the road is the turn to my place," he said.

Feeling her insides constrict, Stephanie closed her eyes. When she opened them, Flint was braking in front of a white frame house that looked badly in need of repair. Her heart gave a decided lurch at the same time she shifted her gaze to Flint.

Reading her reaction, his features turned cold and unbending. "You wished you'd stayed in the hospital, don't you?"

She forced herself to look into that dark face. "No... I—"

"Ah, save it," he said savagely, and opened the door.

She took several deep breaths. They didn't help. Nothing would help except the return of her memory. She couldn't bear to think about the consequences if that didn't happen.

Six

"Well?"

"Well, what?"

Ed Liscomb snorted. "Ah, hell, boy, don't give me that song and dance."

The corners of Flint's eyes crinkled. Ed was the only person he knew who could call him boy and get away with it.

"I'm not going to let you off the hook this time, either," Mary, his wife, put in softly.

Flint rested his mellowed gaze on her. "You mean you're going to side with this old codger?"

Mary smiled, but her eyes were serious. "In this instance yes. When you phoned and told me you had a guest, a woman you didn't even know, I was too stunned to ask questions, but not now."

Besides Lee Holt, his ex-partner at the agency, Ed and Mary Liscomb were the only friends Flint claimed. Generally he didn't like people poking in his business.

But with Ed and Mary, the rules didn't apply. He tolerated their meddling because they were fine people and genuinely cared about him, as much as he'd let anyone care, that is. Two days after he'd taken over the ranch, they had come over and welcomed him. Their spread of several hundred acres lay two miles south of his.

While he was struggling to get started, Ed had it made. Flint suspected his neighbor was actually a millionaire. He'd become successful in oil before the market collapsed. Damned shame they didn't have any children to carry on, their only son having lost his life in a car accident. You would never know they were wealthy, though. There was not a pretentious bone in either of them.

Ed was as tall as Mary was short. Both, however were slender, except for Ed's pot belly. At sixty, his gray beard was full. And his whiskey-toned, boisterous voice evinced his love for beer. Mary, on the other hand, was soft-spoken and attractive with a clear complexion and short hair flecked with gray.

They were kind and generous to a fault. Whether Flint liked it or not, they had taken him under their wing. Mary kept harping, "We're going to humanize you, force you to join the land of the living."

Flint doubted that. He liked his life the way it was and saw no reason to change it. The sooner he rid himself of his guest, the sooner he could get on with it. First, however, he had to explain who his guest was and why she was here.

But simply thinking about Stephanie and her reaction when they had arrived earlier caused his heart to hammer violently. In spite of his vow not to give a damn about what she thought about his place, he found that he did. The living room had looked like a pigsty—worse than he'd remembered. But Stephanie hadn't seemed to notice, or if she had she didn't comment. Fatigue was written on her face, and the top priority had been getting her to the spare bedroom so that she could lie down.

He'd stood awkwardly just inside the door and stared at her. "Er...is there anything you need? How 'bout a cup of coffee?"

A semblance of a smile relaxed her lips, but he noticed she wouldn't look at him. She sensed the strain in the air as much as he did. "No, I'm fine. I just want to rest for a while." He shifted from one foot to the other. "Sure, but if you need anything..."

"Thank you," she had whispered.

That had been several hours ago, and she was still sleeping. Meanwhile he'd called Ed and Mary to let them know he was all right and to ask Mary to purchase a couple of changes of clothes for Stephanie, as well as other items pertinent to a woman's needs. He'd planned to buy the things, but he hated to leave her. She looked so frail, as if a brisk wind could blow her away.

Ed finally broke the lengthy silence. "By the way," he said gruffly, "we're glad you're all right."

"God, yes," Mary added softly. "When we heard about the crash and realized it was your plane...well, I don't have to tell you what went through our minds." She broke off with a shudder.

Flint's eyes were bleak. "I sure as hell thought we were goners."

Ed took a seat beside his wife on the couch and crossed his arms over his belly. He stared at Flint, who leaned against the mantel, his features grim. "Well, all I can say is it wasn't time for your number to be punched."

"I don't ever want to live through it again," Flint said roughly.

"What really happened?" Mary asked. "The news said it was birds, but I find that hard to believe."

"Well, believe it," Flint said tightly. "When the plane hit them, the fan cut loose from the right engine and ripped a hole in the wing." He snapped his fingers. "After that, it was quick and devastating."

"Damn!" Ed's voice boomed. "No wonder the thing went down. It's a miracle anyone survived."

"Only those of us in the front did." Flint's eyes were suddenly as hollow as his voice.

Mary's eyes were wet. "So...so it was those poor souls in the rear who...who died."

"Most of 'em, yes," Flint said.

"How you were able to function enough to help is beyond me," Mary put in. "I'd have been so shaken up, I would've been paralyzed."

"No, you wouldn't, hon," Ed said, facing his wife. "You'd have rolled up your sleeves and pitched right in, just as Flint did, and helped as many people as you could."

Mary wiped a tear off her cheek. "Maybe...I don't know."

"Well, it was a few hours out of hell, I can assure you," Flint said. He took his Stetson off and tossed it onto the back of the nearest chair. "I worked on pure adrenaline, but I've never felt so useless or frustrated." He paused. "Or seen so much suffering."

Again Mary shuddered, and the room fell silent. "So is that why you brought this woman here?" she asked at last.

Ed stood and joined Flint at the fireplace, propping a booted foot on the hearth alongside Flint's. "Yeah, back to your...er...house guest. It's obvious she wasn't seriously hurt..."

Flint released a pent-up sigh, then answered reluctantly, "No, not too bad."

"So why is she here?" Mary was clearly baffled, and it showed in both her face and her voice.

"She took a lick on the head," Flint said, his gaze including them both, "which caused temporary amnesia."

"Oh, no," Mary said with a frown. "That poor woman."

"That still doesn't tell why she's here." Ed's tone was brisk and not nearly as understanding.

"She was sitting next to me on the plane, and I guess she saw me as her savior." Flint's attempt at humor failed. His smile came out a smirk. "Hell, how should I know? It just happened, that's all."

Ed and Mary looked at each other and then back at Flint. They seemed dumbfounded by his actions. But after seeing the dark, closed expression on Flint's face, they realized it was no use questioning him further. He'd said all he was going to say.

"Well, if I... we can be of any help," Mary said, "don't hesitate to ask."

"You've already helped," Flint said. "By the way, I need to pay you for the clothes."

Mary stood. "Don't worry about that now."

"I insist," Flint countered, pulling his billfold out of his back pocket and handing Mary several bills. "Does that cover it?" Mary nodded. "Thanks again."

Ed cleared his throat, and when he spoke, his voice was uncharacteristically subdued. "Well, boy, we'd best go now and let you get on with your business. But if you need us, just holler."

"Will do," Flint said.

"Let's get together as soon as you can. I wanna hear about your trip and what you found out."

"I'll get with you in a day or so," Flint said, following them to the door. "Thanks again for everything."

He had just closed the door when he heard the noise. At first he didn't know what it was. But then he heard it again. This time he knew. *Stephanie!*

"Now what?" he muttered, hearing her cry again as if in pain.

With his heart in his throat, he bounded down the hall. The instant he crossed the threshold, he pulled up short.

The moonlight, streaming through the window, allowed him to see every detail of her as she sat in the middle of the bed. Her face, ravaged with tears, looked starkly white under the cloud of dark hair. But it was her body silhouetted underneath the shirt he'd given her to sleep in that drew his attention and held it.

Her shoulders were bare, and he pictured what it would be like to hold her and swallow her up. He gripped the knob, momentarily robbed of his breath. Her beauty took it away.

"Stephanie?" he finally croaked, unable to move. "What's the matter?"

"Oh, please, help me," she cried, turning glazed, feverish eyes on him. But he knew she wasn't actually seeing him. She was in the throes of a nightmare.

"Help me—I'm on fire," she whispered, her shoulders quivering.

He quickly strode to the bed and paused at the edge, near enough to touch her, to smell her. The scent filled his nostrils with a renewed awareness that shocked him. That awareness knocked his relationship to her completely off center. Alarm rose in him.

"Please," she cried, holding her arms up to him.

Blocking out his thoughts, he sat down and pulled her toward him. She latched on to him and placed her fragile body against the rock-hard solidity of his.

"Shh," he began awkwardly, "everything's going to be all right."

Only it wasn't, not for him. Sweat collected, then ran down his body like rain. He shouldn't be holding her like this. With superhuman effort he tried to disentangle himself.

"No," she pleaded, and looked up at him. "Don't leave me."

He didn't want to. Oh, God, he didn't want to. She felt so good, so right. But it wasn't right. It was wrong, wrong, wrong! Cursing silently, he tried once again to put distance between them.

She clung that much tighter and pressed her breasts deeper into his chest.

"No," he said thickly. Even through his shirt, her nipples felt like points of fire. He ached to lick them with his tongue.... His body turned hot with shame. Only his iron will curbed that impulse.

A coldness feathered down his neck, while another wave of heat washed over him so intense it stopped his breath in his throat. He tightened his jaws until the muscles clenched into white ridges, while he placed both hands on either side of her shoulders and gently, but firmly, pushed her back against the pillow.

Mercifully, she had fallen back to sleep.

He didn't get up. He couldn't. He'd have to wait out the damage done to his own body. Hot blood had rushed to his groin when she'd pressed against him. He could scarcely move or breathe.

Flint didn't know how long he remained there before he dragged himself to his feet. He trudged to the door where he turned and watched the steady rise and fall of her chest.

In his own room, a few minutes later, he eyed the bed as if it were something menacing. He might as well not even bother, he thought with a curse.

It was going to be a long night, a very long night indeed.

The sun poked through the flimsy curtains and directly into Stephanie's face. What had awakened her? She shifted positions, only to flinch. Why was she so stiff? So sore?

Gingerly she opened her eyes and without moving, stared at her surroundings. They meant nothing to her. The room had all the personality and warmth of a hospital room, she thought, and felt an unknown fear rise inside her.

Along with the wrought-iron bed, there was a scarred chest of drawers, and a lattice-back rocker. *Sad neglect* was the phrase that came to mind. *Where am I?*

Like a punch to the stomach, the answer hit her. "Oh, no," she cried. To stifle another cry, she jerked the pillow from under her head and covered her face with it. She was in a strange place with a strange man, and she couldn't remember who she was.

The truth, in that dark moment, was so overwhelming that she thought she'd black out from sheer hysteria. She drew several deep breaths, and the world righted itself once again.

She tossed back the sheet and eased upright, then swung her legs over the side of the bed. She wasn't about to let stiff limbs stop her from getting up. She sat still for a minute and no longer felt dizzy. Her focus was clear as ever. And she was hungry, ravenously so. Had it been the smell of bacon that awakened her? While it smelled too good to pass up, she hesitated a bit longer.

The thought of facing the surly, grim-faced man who was her reluctant host was not pleasant. On the heels of that thought came the unsettling dream she'd had last night. She had dreamt he'd folded her close against him—and remembered how protected she'd felt.

Stephanie's fingers dug into the pillow. Why was her mind playing such mean tricks on her? This man meant nothing to her, except as a means to an end. Was she losing her mind after all? No. She was merely suffering repercussions from the accident.

She had to believe she had done the right thing in coming here. She also had to believe that he'd help her find her identity. Flint was her only hope, as no one else at the hospital had time to worry about her.

She was on her feet when she saw the stack of folded clothes at the foot of the bed. She wondered where they had come from and who had put them there. *He* had been to her room. Her cheeks flamed. She felt her heart beating. Surely he hadn't touched her when he'd brought these things . . . ? No. It had been a crazy dream, and it had meant nothing. When she walked to get the clothes, she noticed her legs had the consistency of jelly.

Later, dressed in jeans, pink shirt and tennis shoes, Stephanie made her way into the kitchen.

He stood in front of the stove. Like her, he was dressed in jeans and a shirt. But where her outfit was new, his was anything but. The jeans were faded and tight fitting, calling attention to his slim hips and powerful thighs. His shirt was worn, too, and hung open, revealing a flat stomach.

Unwittingly, her eyes roamed freely over taut skin bronzed by the sun. She tried to turn away; she tried to ignore that disturbing feeling that curled inside her. She could do neither.

As if he sensed her presence, he looked up. Their gazes connected and held.

Wetting her lips, she stammered, "I...uh...good morning."

Seven

"**W**hat are you doing up this early?"

Flint's chilled, coarse voice, so unexpected, stopped her cold. A long moment passed before she could answer him.

"Actually, it's not *that* early. But even if it were, I couldn't stand the bed any longer." She strove to keep her voice casual, refusing to let his boorish attitude get to her. Dismayed, she realized she hadn't pulled it off; she sounded both breathless and defenseless.

He tried to smile, but he didn't pull that off either. The endeavor was merely a meaningless flexing of his facial muscles. "You may as well have a seat. Your breakfast is ready."

She hesitated, her eyes scanning the kitchen. Like the living room, through which she'd just passed, this one was equally cluttered. And dingy. The walls needed painting, as did the cabinets. But first, everything could use a good scrubbing—the curtains, the countertops and the floor.

Apparently she hesitated too long or he again read the censure in her eyes, for when he spoke his voice was insultingly cold.

"I hope you weren't expecting the Hilton, Ms. Marsh."

"Look...I'm—"

He cut her off. "It's too bad we *all* can't have the best of everything."

"I hardly think soap and water would fit into that category."

He raked her with unkind eyes. "I don't give a damn what you think."

"I know you don't, only—"

"And you wanna know something else? Not everyone's born with a silver spoon in their mouths."

Stephanie bristled. "And you think I was?"

"For starters, you don't dress in designer clothes nor do you own a jewelry store unless you have money."

"That's not true," she said hotly. "But in any event, I can't defend myself."

He said nothing for a while, during which Stephanie nursed a frantic need to lighten the mood, but nothing lighthearted came to mind.

Then out of the blue he mumbled, "If I'd known I was going to have company, I would've done some cleaning."

She saw the muscles along his jaw round in knots, and she knew what that must have cost him to say. "I don't want you to think I was criticizing because I wasn't." She took a breath and forced herself to go on. "I'm...just grateful for your help."

"You have a strange way of showing it."

She didn't want to aggravate an already taut situation so she swallowed another stinging retort and turned away.

After a moment he said, "So how 'bout some breakfast?"

"Thanks," she said, still a bit shaky, but glad he had decided to drop the matter. "Only don't go to any trouble for me."

A brief smile lent a fleeting warmth to his features. "No trouble. You're bound to be hungry."

"Actually I am."

"Want a cup of coffee?"

"Sounds good, or at least I think it does."

He filled a cup of the steaming liquid without responding.

"Thanks," she murmured. Instead of sitting down, she crossed to the window behind the table and looked outside. The day shaped up to be a fine one. In a distant pasture, a clump of blue wildflowers swayed in the spring breeze. A huge live oak watched over them while two feisty squirrels used it as a racetrack. Somehow, she knew she'd never noticed something so trivial as nature's pets playing chase. But her brush with death had changed all that. It had changed *her*.

"Okay, so how do you like your eggs?"

Flint's question jolted her. How *did* she like her eggs? "I . . . I don't know," she whispered, swinging around and staring at him.

"Hey, calm down," he cautioned as he took in her eyes—twin mirrors of misery. "It's no big deal. I'll fry you a couple over easy to go along with the bacon and biscuits."

Stephanie shook her head, having recovered from the shocking reality that something so simple as what she ate for breakfast could turn out to be something so important. "I have a feeling that's way too much food."

"I wouldn't think you'd have to worry about your weight."

His glance appraised her, seeming to linger a moment longer than necessary on her neck, then her breasts, which were unconfined beneath her T-shirt. The bra nestled among the panties had been too small. By the time his gaze reached her eyes again, she trembled inside.

"Every woman has to worry about her weight," she said, speaking impatiently to mask her alarm.

But she need not have worried. He no longer looked at her. He concentrated on the task of removing the bacon from the iron skillet and placing it on paper towels to drain. She watched his hands and wondered again if she'd actually felt them on her skin last night or if it had truly been a dream.

Feeling her face suffuse with color, she averted her gaze, appalled at her thoughts. More than that, she was appalled at her behavior. You would think she'd never found a man attractive. Surely that wasn't the case; nor was it the point. Her only concern should be regaining her memory. So why was she focused on this man who begrudgingly offered his hospitality?

"Eat up," Flint said.

His abrupt voice and the sound of the plate clattering against the Formica-topped table roused her into action. She moved back to the table and sat down.

They ate in silence, or rather Flint ate in silence. Stephanie took no more than two or three bites of each item, then she pushed her plate away.

He looked up, his eyebrows raised. "Something wrong?"

"No, actually it was delicious."

A smirk crossed his lips. "Yeah."

"It was, really," she said with a fixed smile. "It's just that right now I have a bit more on my mind than food."

Flint shoved his own plate aside and reached for his coffee cup. After taking a sip, he looked at her over the rim. "Nothing yet, huh?"

"Nothing." Her tone was deflated. "Isn't that obvious when I can't even remember whether I like eggs or not?"

"It won't do any good to beat up on yourself, you know."

"I know, but I can't help it. I feel so useless, so frustrated."

"I'll help you any way I can. I told you that, and I meant it. So if there's anything you remember, anything at all..."

"Not so much as a glimmer," she said in a stricken voice. "And that's what scares me, that and the fact that somewhere out there my family is most likely crazy with worry. And..." She broke off and sighed.

"And what," he pressed.

"And I don't have any money..."

"So, I can lend you some."

"I couldn't let you do that."

"Why?"

"I just couldn't."

"Suit yourself."

She squared her thin shoulders. "Besides the money, there's the clothes you...chose."

"I didn't choose them."

"Oh." He probably had one of his women friends do the honor, she thought snidely. But she didn't dare ask.

"So what's wrong?" he demanded curtly.

The question caught her off guard. "With...what?"

"The clothes," he said impatiently.

"Nothing's wrong with them...only...all of them don't fit."

"I see." Once again his eyes dipped to her breasts as if he knew exactly which item she was referring to. And once again her face tinged with color, though she tried as before to control it.

"I...I don't want you to think I'm ungrateful because...I'm not. And as soon as I can, I'll pay you back." Her voice was so husky it was barely discernible.

His eyes moved from the top of her head, over her face and throat, back to her breasts. "Whatever you say."

And quite suddenly they had nothing to say to each other. They realized that simultaneously, and that made the situation more awkward. Their glances met, then fell away as both pretended to examine the room as if searching for something. It was a most unwieldy moment for Stephanie, and in a rash attempt to shift it back into balance, she stood up and once again crossed to the window.

Casually she said, "While I'm here, I...I want to earn my keep."

He seemed taken aback by her words, and his lips tightened. "What did you have in mind?"

"That's just it, I don't know."

"The doctor's orders were for rest."

"I will, but I can't just...freeload."

"It's okay by me." His tone was mocking.

"I could clean your house."

He shot out of his chair, and in a split second he loomed over her. "Forget that."

"Are you going to snap my head off every time I say something you don't like?"

He backed away. "Hadn't planned on it."

"So, let me help," she pressed with a forced smile, determined not to let him further intimidate her, suspecting his bark was much worse than his bite. "I'm sure if I dabbled in antique jewelry, I'm bound to like antique houses."

His dry laugh sounded like cornstalks rubbing together. "Think so, huh?"

"Sure. Besides, this place has possibilities." She was warming to the subject, or was it his sudden good humor?

He held up his hand. "Whoa. I might let you tidy up a bit, but nothing else. And only after you're stronger."

That hard note was back in his voice, but she ignored it. "Have you ever thought of improving it?"

"Yeah, a million times, only I don't have the money."

That stopped her cold, and she didn't know what to say, so she didn't say anything. Finally, to relieve the heavy silence, she asked, "Have you always been a rancher?"

"No."

Deciding that getting the desired information out of him would be like pulling eye teeth, she went about it with a tenacity disguised by her casual manner. "So how did you make your living?"

"I worked for the DEA."

She didn't try to mask her shock. "But...that's the Drug Enforcement Agency."

"One and the same."

"And you don't work for them anymore?" she pressed.

"Technically, I'm on a leave."

"Did something happen?" She knew his patience was running out. In fact, she'd expected him to tell her to go to hell long before now.

"Yeah, you might say something happened. A drug bust went sour, and I got carved up like a piece of meat."

Stephanie's face lost its color.

"Satisfied?" he demanded harshly.

"I'm ... I'm sorry. I didn't mean to..."

He reached for a battered Stetson and jammed it on his head. "Forget it. I have."

She stood, and with her heart pumping as though she'd just run a marathon, she started toward the door.

"Where are you going?"

She stopped. "To ... my room."

"Good, be ready, say, in about fifteen minutes."

"For what?" she asked, startled.

"We're going into town so you can keep your appointment with Abe." He paused. "Afterward, we'll stop by the store so you can ... er ... exchange that item that was too small."

Heat surged into her cheeks, and she shifted her gaze.

"Well, what are you waiting for?"

She rushed the rest of the way to the door, only to stop and spin around. "Will you tell me the truth?"

"About what?"

She passed her tongue across her dry lips. "Last night."

"What do you want to know?"

"Did you come to my room?"

"You don't remember?"

"No."

"You had a nightmare."

She peered down at the floor then back up. "So you...you did hold me?"

"Yes, I held you." He opened and closed his mouth, as if strangling.

A second lapsed into a minute, and still neither spoke or moved.

"Thank...you," Stephanie whispered at last.

He allowed his droll humor to surface. "You're welcome."

Another few seconds dragged by.

Finally, Flint said. "Well?"

"Well what?" She took a long, slow breath to steady herself.

"Are you going to stand there all day?"

"No, no, of course not," she said, and turning, fled the room.

She couldn't be sure, but later when she thought about that incident again, Stephanie was certain his laughter had followed her.

Eight

The April wind was blustery. It stood his longish hair on end and hissed through the grass like a reptile. The sun, equally as strong, glared down on him like a petulant god.

Flint ignored both as he took his frustration out on the fence he was fixing. He didn't remember ever hammering a nail so hard into a piece of wood as he was now. He paused and wiped the sweat out of his eyes and off his forehead, but it did no good. The minute he slammed in another nail, sweat drenched him again. Still, he kept working.

Three days had passed since he'd taken Stephanie to town. First, she'd shopped. Then he'd driven her to the doctor's office and sat in on the visit.

In Abe's office, he could still see Stephanie's stricken face, hear her pleading with Abe to help her. He'd watched from his position against the wall, his arms crossed over his chest.

Stephanie had sat in front of Abe's desk, her eyes large and troubled. "I was sure by now I'd remember something."

"What I told you in the hospital still applies," Abe said patiently. "You can't rush this. So try not to worry—that merely aggravates things. Just continue to take those pills when your head pounds. And don't do anything strenuous."

Now, as Flint hammered another piece of wire onto the fence post, Abe's last warning brought to mind Stephanie's offer to clean his house. Damn! Was that a hoot, or what? Somehow he doubted she'd ever pushed a broom in her life, much less picked up a dust cloth.

Anyway, that was the last thing Stephanie needed to do, especially when she looked so fragile that a light puff of wind could blow her away. But that didn't stop her from looking sexy as hell.

She'd climbed into the truck, and that action had outlined her breasts, instantly defined their roundness—something he didn't want to acknowledge. Yet as much as he ached to deny it, electricity hummed between them and had from the first time they had met.

He'd made it a point to keep his eyes off her and on the road, but that hadn't kept him from shifting uncomfortably behind the wheel. And he still shifted uncomfortably as he reached for another nail.

It was hell to be poor, he thought, driving another nail in. By now he figured he should've been able to hire a full-time hand, but his herd hadn't progressed enough to allow him that luxury.

The only thing worse than being broke was his obsession with Stephanie Marsh. He'd tried to avoid her, had assured himself he'd acquired an immunity against her type. Only he hadn't. She was just too damned attractive.

The feel of her in his arms had reawakened an appetite that he thought had long been buried. She'd been under his roof only three days, and already he had thoughts of her writhing under him, whimpering in climax.

So why didn't he just take her? What could be wrong with feeling again? Maybe in losing himself in her, he might find himself again.

But that wasn't the answer, and he knew it. Even if she let him touch her—which was a big if—making love to her wouldn't work. Their relationship was a dead-end street. He saw no reason to start something that would go nowhere.

His only option was to find out who the hell she was, then send her packing. Flint stared at his jerking hands. He needed a drink in the worst way.

"Stop it, Carson!" he muttered, and sucked air deep into his lungs. He should take the initiative, he knew, hire someone to find out Stephanie's identity. Because of his years in law enforcement, he had connections and was not above using them. All he had to do was pick up the phone to a private-eye buddy in Lufkin.

Yet he hesitated. Why? Could it be he was reluctant for her to regain her memory because she would no longer be dependent on him? Hell! He hoped not. Surely he wouldn't stoop that low?

No, that wasn't the case. He wanted her to leave before he did something stupid, something he'd regret for the rest of his life.

His mind, his thoughts were suddenly in a jumble he couldn't untangle. So rather than try, he packed his things and mounted his horse and headed toward the house.

If it weren't for the loss of memory, she would be pleased with her recovery. Rest had made the difference. She could move now without wincing, and the terrible headaches were at least bearable. Still, she knew she had a ways to go before she could be pronounced one hundred percent fit again.

She was fortunate to be able to relax during the day while Flint worked. At night she was almost afraid to close her eyes. She feared another nightmare would attack her subconscious. She did not want a repeat performance of that first night.

Just thinking about that incident made her uneasy. But then thinking about *him* made her uneasy. In spite of the hospitality, she knew she had severely disrupted his life. Flint resented it, resented her, even though most of the time she couldn't decipher what lay behind those deep green eyes when she'd catch him looking at her.

Despite that, or maybe because of that, he intrigued her and made her want to know what made this lonely man tick.

Stephanie scoffed, however, at such nonsense, reminding herself that she was only a temporary houseguest and nothing more. Besides, she didn't want to mar this beautiful day with dark thoughts.

She finished dressing and walked out of her room, only to come to a sudden halt. She thought at first her eyes were playing tricks on her, but after she blinked she knew better. The living room, while not sparkling, was clean and straight. Flint had been busy.

A smile tugged at her lips. "Well, I'll be damned," she whispered, then wandered into the kitchen. He'd been at work there, too.

With that smile locked in place, she dashed out the kitchen door into the wind and sunlight. The instant she rounded the corner of the house, she saw him. He rode across the pasture, and again she was dumbstruck, held by the sight.

God, but he looked tall in the saddle, man and beast moving as one.

He must have seen her leaning against the fence rail in the backyard, because he immediately reined the horse in her direction.

Her heart raced, and her emotions felt scattered. She tried not to stare, permitting herself only furtive glances, but as he neared, she scrutinized him from his hat down to his scuffed boots. He was a magnificent animal, more perfect than the gelding he rode.

Stephanie tried to kill her thoughts and shift her gaze, but she couldn't, especially after Flint stopped the horse directly in front of her. He sweated profusely, she saw. His hair edging his Stetson was wet, and his shirt was plastered to his sculptured body. He breathed heavily.

She felt herself responding to the pull of that raw magnetism, so strong that it left her weak. And more lost than ever. She didn't even know who she was; she was fighting for her own identity. So how could she think about this man in sexual terms? But he was sexy—mouth-wateringly sexy.

He sat atop the horse and regarded her in silence. His eyes saw through her blouse and burned into the deepest recesses of her body, telling her as plainly as spoken words that he was aware of her thoughts.

Flint then swung out of the saddle gracefully and stood within touching distance of her.

"Hi," she said inanely, her cheeks scarlet.

His smile mocked her. "Hi, yourself."

Silence.

"Er...are you through working for the day?"

"Yeah," he drawled, "I thought I'd knock off and go see Ed."

"Oh." She tried not to show her disappointment at being left alone for the remainder of this beautiful day.

"Wanna come?"

Stephanie liked Mary Liscomb on sight, as well as her bear of a husband. Because of Flint, they welcomed her without pretense.

Anxious to show off their home, Ed and Mary took her on a tour of the gardens before going inside.

The interior was more lush than the outside, Stephanie thought. The floors in the great room and hall were oak and shone like glass. Marble covered the stairs and the entryway. Everywhere the walls were white and the scent of peach potpourri was prevalent.

Ed and Mary insisted they remain for lunch. Even though she felt Flint didn't want to, he gave in to Mary's cajoling.

Now, following a delicious meal, she and Mary were enjoying a second cup of coffee in the breakfast nook off the kitchen while the men discussed business in another room.

"I'll have to admit we were shocked and still are that he brought you home with him." Mary smiled.

Stephanie smiled back at her hostess. "That's understandable."

"Flint just doesn't do things like that," Mary added. "In fact, I've never known him to fly by the seat of his pants, if you know what I mean."

Stephanie smiled again. "I know what you mean. But when I look back, I'm not sure he had much choice." Stephanie admitted.

Mary raised delicate eyebrows. "Oh?"

"You mean Flint didn't tell you that I practically begged him not to leave me?" Even as she confessed this, she felt awkward.

Mary laughed deep in her throat. "Why, honey, talk is the one thing that he doesn't do."

"You're certainly right about that."

"You don't know the half of it. He won't let you do one thing for him unless he can return the favor, which goes to prove that underneath that tough hide is a kind man. You know he's a pilot, don't you?"

Stephanie shook her head, trying to follow Mary's change of thought. "No . . . no, I didn't."

"That doesn't matter, really. The point I was about to make is that Ed's offered him his plane a number of times, but do you think he's taken him up on the offer? Of course not. He's proud and mule-headed to a fault."

"But you wouldn't change a thing about him, would you?" Stephanie smiled, but her tone was serious.

Mary grinned sheepishly. "We love him like a second son."

"So that must mean you know him well."

"No one knows Flint. He refuses to share himself. I feel that's because he's known more than his share of pain."

"I know he was married." Stephanie was aware she was going on another fishing expedition and felt bad, especially as Mary's reluctance was obvious.

"Yes, but it didn't last." Mary's tone was troubled. "While he was in the hospital with a hole in his side, his wife slapped him with divorce papers."

Stephanie's heart gave an unexpected twist. "How awful."

"That's what we thought. Though, of course, he won't talk about it. So we don't ask or push."

"I just hope I can repay him someday for helping me."

"Oh, honey," Mary said, switching subjects again, "it must be terrible not knowing anything about yourself."

Stephanie took a sip of coffee as if it could stave off the threat of tears. She'd been doing so well keeping her feelings in check. "I feel like I've been tossed in the middle of an ocean without a life jacket."

"That must be awful." Mary reached over and squeezed her hand. "It's a miracle both you and Flint are alive."

"When I get to feeling sorry for myself, I remind myself of that."

"So what are your plans?"

Stephanie thrust a hand through her thick mane. "I don't know."

"So you plan to stay with Flint indefinitely, then?" Mary pressed in a soft voice.

"No...no, of course I don't."

Mary watched her carefully. "You're welcome to come and stay here, if you'd like. It's just Ed and me milling around in this big house by ourselves."

Stephanie should have expected the invitation, but she hadn't. And though she was touched by Mary's offer, the thought of leaving Flint filled her with panic. Crazy as that sounded, it was the truth. But she couldn't tell Mary that. "I..."

"You think about it," Mary cut in quietly.

"You ready to go home?"

Flint's unexpected and coarse voice pulled her up short. How long had he been there? Had he heard Mary's offer? She swung around and met his gaze. As usual it gave nothing away. He leaned against the doorjamb as though he hadn't a care in the world. She knew better. Averting her gaze, she stood. "I'm ready when you are."

"Surely you don't have to go yet, Flint."

"'Fraid so, Mary. I've been up since four this morning mending fences and I'm still not finished."

"Ah, hell, don't pay her no mind," Ed put in, coming to stand beside Flint in the door. "She thinks the day doesn't begin till noon."

"That's a boldfaced lie, Ed Liscomb, and you know it."

Everyone laughed, then said their goodbyes.

"They're lovely people," Stephanie commented several minutes later, watching Flint's competent hands steer the truck down the drive.

"The best."

"I had... a great time. Thanks for taking me."

He turned toward her, and his gaze made a slow search of her face. "Were you ready to go home?"

Home. "Of course," she managed to whisper.

When he turned his attention back to the road, she closed her eyes, her thoughts reeling. Home. Her mind toyed with it. She found she liked the sound of it.

Too much.

Nine

Had she been at Flint's ranch for only a week? It seemed a lifetime. The last two days had been filled with nothing but emptiness. And frustration.

Something told Stephanie she was the type who stayed busy, worked hard and consciously prided herself on her ability to cope with any situation.

But she had nothing to do or look forward to save the passage of time, and this inactivity lowered her deeper and deeper into depressed loneliness. How long had it been since she'd laughed? Even the two trips back to Ed and Mary's had failed to lift her depression, although Flint's closest friends had done their best to boost her spirits.

The last time she'd gone into town with Flint to get supplies, she'd stocked up on magazines and paperback books. But soon she tired of reading, nor was she interested in the soaps.

And then there was Flint. While he went out of his way to see that she had everything she needed, he also went out of his way to avoid her.

He rarely joined her for any meal except dinner, which she prepared. She hadn't known if she could cook, but she found, to her delight, that she could. She knew he appreciated her endeavor as he always ate heartily before excusing himself and going to the cubbyhole off his bedroom that served as his office.

Twice, though, Flint had stayed to drink a cup of coffee. But his company had its drawbacks. His close proximity, the intimidating warmth of his body, his disturbing appraisal of her never failed to shatter her composure as no spoken words of his would have done.

Still, she would have preferred his presence, as unsettling as it was, to the loneliness. Today was falling into that same pattern as the other days, only this time she wasn't going to sit idly by. Things could not go on as they were. The time had come for her to take matters into her own hands and find out who she was.

She had made it a point to get up early in hopes of cornering Flint before he left to tend to his cattle. But again she'd been too late.

As she walked outside, the sun sparked the sky into changing panoramas of color. She paused and stared, then drew the clean morning air through her lungs. One could overdose on its freshness, she thought with a whimsical smile.

Shielding her eyes, she looked toward the barn, hoping she might get lucky and catch him this time. He'd commented last night at the dinner table that he had several sacks of salt blocks he had to load onto his pickup.

"I'd like to help," she'd said before she thought.

His expression had given nothing away, but she sensed she'd shocked him.

"May I?"

The corners of his lips curled, and it wasn't an amusing smile. "You can't be serious."

"And just why not?" she snapped.

"Because the barn's hot and dirty and no place for a woman."

"You mean it's no place for me, don't you?"

His eyes traveled a reckless path down her body. "I wouldn't think slumming in the barn would appeal to you."

"You don't know what would appeal to me." She heard the pain in her voice. Dammit, why was she letting him get to her?

He stood abruptly, and when he did, his chair made a loud scraping sound on the worn floor. "You're right, I don't." With that he turned and stamped toward the door.

She'd stared after him, trembling. Then she blinked back the tears and cleared the table. Before she finished, she had broken two dishes.

She had planned to talk to him the previous evening, but after that less than amiable conversation, she'd put it off. Just as she forced that unpleasantness to the back of her mind, Flint walked out of the barn.

"Flint!" she called.

He swung around. "Yo."

"Wait, please. I want to talk to you."

He strode toward her, his stride impatient, like everything else about him. He had on dusty jeans, a blue shirt and battered Stetson, giving the term "working cowboy" new meaning.

Definitely he was a fine specimen. But the physical appearance was merely icing. His formidable presence would be felt no matter where he was or how he dressed. He simply radiated power.

By the time he reached her, her mouth was dry. Crazy or not, the attraction was there, potent and swift.

"What's up?" he asked without preamble, though his tone held none of the contempt from last evening.

"We need to talk."

He raised his eyebrows. "You're up kinda early, aren't you?"

"Boredom can do that to you."

She saw something in his eyes spark and knew her veiled sarcasm had struck a nerve. But then he grinned a mocking grin, while his eyes ran down her slender figure with blatant appreciation. "That so, huh?"

"I don't find this amusing," she said primly, feeling anger rise in her throat.

His face changed. "No, I guess you don't. But then I wouldn't know, never having been bored."

"Unfortunately I don't have that luxury," she said snidely.

"Come on, let's walk," he said without warning.

"All right." She cast him a sidelong glance, uncertain of his mood. "Can you spare the time away from work?"

"Would it make any difference?"

Her gaze clashed with his. "No."

His only response was the tightening of his jaw.

For a moment they walked in silence, each lost in their own thoughts.

When they reached a clump of pecan trees just inside a fenced pasture, he paused and leaned against one of them. "What's this all about? Mary?"

She frowned. "Mary?"

"Yeah, Mary. Didn't she ask you to stay with them?"

"Oh, you heard?"

"I heard." His tone was bleak. "So what are you going to do?"

"What...what do you want me to do?"

"For God's sake, Stephanie!"

"Does...does that mean you want me to go?"

"No, dammit. It doesn't!"

She sucked in a deep breath, and when she did, the scent of sweat, of cows, of flesh filled her lungs, drugging her. She was more aware of him than ever before.

He muttered a curse at the same time his eyes probed hers—as if he were trying to pull her inside him.

The air shook between them. Then a tiny sigh suddenly escaped through her lips and broke the spell. His eyes shuttered, and his face became blank.

"So if it's not about your leaving...?" He sounded tired now and impatient.

"In spite of what the doctor said, I feel I need to do something to try to find out who I am."

"Have you thought about a private detective?"

She tossed her head as if to clear it. "No... but then I haven't been thinking rationally, either. That sounds logical, though."

"If you decide to go that route, let me know. I have connections."

Her face fell. "Sometimes I think I'm doomed to remain in this black void forever."

"You aren't."

"You sound so sure."

"I trust Abe," he said simply.

"So do I, but—"

"Are you still having... those nightmares?"

She circled her lips with her tongue, and once again their eyes connected. The night she had cried in his arms once again rose to the forefront of her mind. His thoughts mirrored hers, she knew, for his eyes darkened and his breath quickened.

"Sometimes," she said haltingly.

They looked at each other a moment longer, then Flint cleared his throat. "Can you make heads or tails of them?"

"Yes and no. Once I dreamed about the crash...dreamed there was a fire..."

"Go on," he urged.

"That's all," she insisted, weary with the strain of trying to recall. "That's why it's so frustrating. It's almost like it's there only it's not."

"Well, I see it as a good sign."

"Maybe. But in the meantime, I need something to occupy my mind."

"I told you I had to work." There was censure behind his words.

She lowered her eyes, conscious of the heat in her cheeks. "I know...it's just..."

"For starters, I guess you could play the P.I."

Her head came up, but before she could reply, he went on, "Remember you mentioned checking with the airlines." He shrugged. "And calling the jewelry stores. They're long shots I know..."

Her eyes came back to life. "I could make some calls myself, couldn't I?" she asked eagerly.

"I suppose you could, now that you're feeling better."

"I'm positive I could get a Houston directory from the library."

Flint leaned his head sideways and was quiet for a moment. "You're excited about this, aren't you?"

"I told you I'm about to go crazy without anything to do."

"Speaking of something to do," he said, "I've gotta get back to work." He pushed away from the tree. "What about you?"

Stephanie's features clouded as she envisioned the long, empty day ahead. "I guess I'll go for a walk."

He hesitated, then said, "Maybe...er...we could take in a movie in town tonight, if you'd like, that is."

Stephanie drew back in surprise, not sure she'd heard him correctly. But when she deciphered the expression on his face, she knew she had. He looked as though he'd rather be hung from the nearest tree than do what he'd suggested.

Well, that was just too bad. This was one time he should've kept his mouth shut and didn't.

She broke into a sudden and radiant smile. "I'd like that. I'd like that a lot."

Long after he'd returned to his chores, she was still smiling.

Flint was in a bad mood. He couldn't believe he'd offered to take her to the movie. Again he cursed his careless tongue, taking his anger out on the pitchfork and bales of hay. He'd only moments before finished loading the pickup with salt blocks for distribution. Still uptight, he'd decided to stack the hay.

Shirtless, he jabbed the fork into the guts of the third bale and hoisted it atop another one. His muscles tensed and burned.

Maybe he should have encouraged her to go stay with the Liscombs. Flint didn't know how much more of this "togetherness" he could take. He'd thought Stephanie was too fragile to uproot, but now he wasn't so sure. Despite her lack of memory, she seemed more able to cope than he did.

He could see her now, in his mind's eye, standing next to him, the sunlight warming her white skin to a honey color, skin that was as smooth and flawless as a perfect diamond. He ached to touch her. It made him physically ill. And not because of his celibacy, either. He wanted *her*.

But that was not to be, and he knew it.

"Forget her, dammit! She's not worth it." The sound of his own voice seemed to calm him, and for a moment he mulled the situation over rationally, calling a spade a spade.

He had nothing to offer her, except a toss in the sack. Though she sometimes behaved with airs, and while that needled him, she deserved better than that. And so did he. She'd just mess up his head even more than it was already.

He paused and dragged air through his scorched lungs, then wiped his forehead. The sweat-drenched rag was halfway back into his pocket when he heard the scream.

Fear seized him. His blood turned to ice water and froze his limbs. Then he heard it again. Dropping his pitchfork, Flint tore out of the barn.

Stephanie had no idea how long she'd been walking or where she was. Time, though, was of no importance. She had no reason to hurry back to the house. But at least she had something to look forward to—two things actually, helping to track her past and a trip to the movies.

She smiled. While she sensed ranch life was completely foreign to her, she was adapting well, she thought. If only Flint would let her do something to help him, she'd almost be content. She shook her head, thinking how crazy that sounded.

She knew the reason behind it. Flint. Her smile widened into a grin. She still couldn't believe he'd offered to take her to the movies. She'd bet anything he was choking on those words about now. He was definitely a most unpredictable man, which made him that much more exciting. And dangerous.

Stephanie's smile disappeared and she sighed. For someone in her predicament, the last thing she needed was the complication of an affair, especially with a man who was so different, so hard. Yet she believed that underneath the cold, sarcastic face the world saw, there lurked a heart that was desperately in need of love. He would never admit it, though. No one could ever get that close. Least of all her.

But when he looked at her with those smoldering eyes...
She yanked her thoughts away from this enigma of a man and concentrated on her surroundings. She had wandered inside a pasture dotted with black cattle busy munching on grass and wildflowers.

Distant pines rose heavenward. Nearby were oaks and one lone cottonwood, though its trunk was twice the size of the oaks. Cattle grazed near a pond. Unpaintable beauty lurked everywhere. Stephanie simply stood without moving and took it all in. She bent and picked a bouquet of wildflowers while the wind gently whispered against her face.

She didn't notice the animal until she stood once again. Nestled amongst a stand of tall grass, a few yards in front of her, lay a baby calf.

"Oh, you precious baby, you," she cooed, inching forward carefully so as not to frighten it. Had she ever seen one so young? Somehow she thought not, except maybe in pictures.

Stephanie stopped within arm's length, squatted down and balanced one knee on the ground. His coat was as black as midnight, but that was all she had time to notice before the calf noticed her. Immediately, it shook and tried to stand. But its thin, lanky legs were so wobbly, it couldn't.

"I'm sorry, I didn't mean to scare you," she whispered.

Her soft tone, however, had no effect. The calf continued to tremble and stare at her through wary black eyes.

Stephanie had gotten to her feet with every intention of distancing herself from the animal when she heard an odd sound. Her head popped up and her mouth fell open. She was consumed with pure horror.

Galloping across the meadow at full speed and snorting through its nose was the biggest, blackest, ugliest looking cow that Stephanie was sure God had ever put on this earth. And the creature was heading toward her.

Stephanie couldn't think. She couldn't breathe. She couldn't *move*. Her body felt weighted down with lead, while she watched in a shocked stupor. What released her limbs from their paralysis, she never knew. She only knew that one minute she couldn't function and the next she was screaming, a blood-curdling scream. The unexpected noise seemed to incense the cow that much more. Its speed picked up.

Stephanie screamed again, but not before turning and running through the grass. "Oh, God, help me, please!" she muttered, afraid to turn around and afraid not to. But she knew she was not alone. The pounding of hooves was right behind her.

She ran as if her very life depended on it. In this instance, she knew it did.

Flint tore through the barn door and saw her. And the cow.

He took off running. He reached her the instant she rounded the huge oak. Wordlessly she flung herself into his outstretched arms. He held her shivering body close against his.

"Oh, Flint." She pulled back and gulped for so much as the tiniest breath. "Oh, thank God . . . thank . . ." Her voice failed her. But once she stopped gulping, she lifted soft and misty eyes to him.

That's when something snapped inside him. He was already shaken from the shock he had suffered when he thought she might be injured by the mother cow. But intoxicated by the feel of her against him, his fear took a new turn.

"Dammit, woman, you don't have the sense God gave a billy goat!"

Stephanie pulled her head back. The pulse at the base of her throat beat frantically. *"What?"* The word was barely audible.

"What the hell were you doing!"

The rough fury in his voice seemed to act as the catalyst that roused her from her dazed state. She shouted back, "I was looking and talking to a baby calf, that's what!"

"That's about the most asinine thing I've ever heard! You could've been killed!"

"Maybe that would have been the answer to my problems!"

"Great! That's really great."

"Will you stop yelling at me?"

"No! You should've known better."

Her breathing was as sharp as his, her temper hotter. "Well, I didn't! How was I to know that...that black *thing* would come after me?"

"Common damn sense for one thing!"

"Go to hell!"

He imprisoned her arms in his long fingers. They held that pose, their eyes engaged in battle, their breathing ragged.

"I'd watch my mouth if I were you."

"Let go of me," she rasped. Her eyes stabbed him like twin daggers.

"Not until you calm down and listen to reason."

"No!" She struggled to break his hold on her.

Anger beat through him. "Settle down, you little wildcat." But there was still no give to her.

"Let go of me!" she said again.

"Bygod will you just shut up?"

"No, I won't shut up!" she flared back. "You don't have any right to—"

He tightened his grip on her shoulders, lifted her off the ground and propelled her backward against the trunk of the tree. He anchored his arms on either side. His body became a barrier, and before she could utter so much as a whimpering sound, he lowered his head and took her lips.

Instantly his system went into shock as if he had accidentally touched a live wire.

When he pulled away for air, she said, "Flint...please..."

"Please what?" he countered hoarsely. "You've been wanting this as much as I have." He advanced his hips, deliberately letting her feel his burgeoning hardness, and after a brief pause felt her response.

"You like this, don't you?"

"Please . . . don't," she said in a voice that was softly unconvincing.

Knowing that she was his for the taking, Flint experienced a heady surge of confidence. It relieved his harsh expression and reshaped his lips into an agonizing smile while he rotated against her with a motion that was a blatant statement of intent.

"Oh . . . F-Flint," she moaned.

"I know." His voice sounded thick and shaky as he held himself rigidly against her, his need a tangible pressure building in his groin.

A moan slid past her lips at the same time he kissed her again, thrusting his tongue deeper and deeper into her mouth, wanting, needing, aching . . .

With the same urgency Flint had grabbed her, he released her. Then pulling fresh air through his scalded lungs, he turned his back and stepped away.

The hot sun beat down around them.

He hadn't allowed his iron control to slip in a long time, and the experience left him feeling vulnerable, exposed. Finally having regained a sliver of that control, Flint twisted back around and said, "Look, I—" His mouth snapped shut as he realized he was talking to himself.

Stephanie was already halfway to the house.

Ten

The buckskin gelding loped; horse and rider moved as one. Flint didn't rein to a slower pace until he reached the pond near the barn. While the gelding lapped the cool water, Flint rested an arm across the saddle horn and tried to shut off his thoughts.

The sun had long ago washed the sky a reddish gold and was now concentrated on the pine trees in the distance. He liked this time of the morning when he was alone with nature. Even after the horse stopped drinking, he still didn't move, completely absorbed in the silence.

Today he should jump another hurdle in further implementing the ideas he had picked up in Arkansas. The herd had already grown significantly. But there was still a long way to go before he could take the cattle to market and turn a profit.

He'd also made plans to start remodeling the barn. Miraculously, it hadn't come tumbling down on top of his head. Ed had volunteered to help, and Flint had taken him up on his offer. Both were anxious to get started.

All the things Flint had to do suddenly piled up in his mind until they assumed overwhelming proportions, but then he dismissed them. The tasks would get done.

He wished he could dismiss Stephanie from his mind as easily. His deep sigh shattered the silence. Lifting the reins, he nudged the animal in the side and aimed him toward the barn.

Last evening, following that scene in the pasture, he knew she had gone to great lengths to avoid him. He couldn't fault her as he would've done the same thing.

He'd doubted he could ever face her again after the stunt he'd pulled. He felt like a heel. He *was* a heel. He had taken advantage of her when she was most vulnerable, so he deserved the consequences. But in that brief, volatile moment, when he'd ground his heat against her softness and plundered her lips with his, he'd been in heaven. God, but she'd tasted so good, smelled so good, felt so good....

He'd been thinking that very thing when he'd walked into the kitchen at six o'clock this morning and had seen her sitting at the table....

Their eyes had locked instantly, and for a moment neither seemed capable of speaking.

Finally he'd cleared his throat and said, "I didn't expect you up so early."

She glanced away. "I couldn't sleep."

The dark circles under her eyes and the slight droop of her mouth proved she spoke the truth. Instead of those imperfections distracting from her beauty, however, they enhanced it, especially as the purple blouse turned her blue eyes to violet and her hair to jet black. Yet something tore at his throat. She looked so lost.

He cursed himself again before admitting, "I couldn't sleep either."

Silence surrounded them.

"Maybe I should take..."

He knew what she was going to say, and the thought made him ill. "Look, I know this doesn't excuse what I did, but it won't happen again," he said, damning himself again for his lack of control.

"I'm as much to blame as you." She spoke as if she were out of breath.

"No, you're not," he said savagely. "I was way out of line."

She hadn't argued. She had stood instead and offered to fix him some breakfast, which he'd declined. After filling his thermos with coffee, he'd hurried toward the door like the gutless coward he was. He hadn't slowed down until he'd reached the barn.

Now Flint realized nothing had been settled, merely postponed. He did not know how much longer he could go on like this. A demanding pressure built between his thighs as he thought about how much he wanted her, how much he wanted to suckle those nipples, bury his hardness inside her...

The emotions raging inside him were such that he didn't see Ed leaning against the entrance to the barn until he was almost on him. Flint pulled the gelding up short.

From under the brim of his hat, Ed stared at horse and rider and drawled, "'Bout time. I had all but given you up."

"What brings you over this early?" Flint asked, swinging out of the saddle.

Ed removed his hat, then scratched his head. "Thought we might get started on the barn."

"I'd like to, but there're a couple of cows in the south pasture that need attention. I just found them."

"Need any help?"

"Nah, but thanks for the offer."

"Anytime."

Flint shifted his gaze to the dilapidated structure and shook his head. "Maybe next week we can start tearing down the back side of this heap." He paused, lost in thought. "Think I'll ever get this place in good working order?"

"We both know what it takes. Time and money."

Using his Stetson, Flint slapped a patch of dirt off his thigh. "Time I got. Money I don't."

"You know how to remedy that."

Flint held up his hand. "Don't say it. I won't take your money, Ed. With what little I have left from Uncle Charlie and with what I've managed to save, I'll make it."

"You're about the stubbornest sonofabitch I know."

Flint grinned. "That so, huh?"

"That's so, and you know it."

Flint grinned again while he unsaddled the gelding and led it inside the barn.

Ed followed him, the cool dimness of the barn a welcome relief from the bright sunlight and April humidity.

"How're things going?" Ed asked casually.

Too casually, Flint thought, cutting his friend a hard glance. "They're fine."

"Hey, don't give me that. You got a burr up your butt about something."

Flint stiffened. "What makes you say that?"

"Don't know. Just a hunch."

"I wouldn't count on those hunches too much, if I were you."

Ed snorted, and when he did, his beer belly shook.

In spite of himself, Flint smiled. "You best lay off that stuff."

"What stuff?" Ed's face was innocent.

"You know what stuff. It's gonna kill you."

Ed rubbed his belly and smiled. "Ah, but what a way to go."

"I agree. I could use a couple of beers myself right now."

Ed's features sobered. "Sorry, I shouldn't . . ."

"No apology necessary."

"So is it your houseguest that's got you wishin' you could fall off the wagon?"

Flint's first reaction was to tell Ed to mind his own business, but he didn't. He knew that underneath that gruff talk, Ed was concerned. He'd told Ed shortly after they met about his bout with the bottle, because right off Ed had insisted he drink a beer with him.

"Okay, so she's a problem."

"Think she'll ever get her memory back?"

Flint grabbed a rag off the rickety table beside him and rubbed on the saddle. "I'm beginning to wonder."

"Damned shame." Ed's eyes twinkled. "She's sure a fine-looking woman."

Flint raised his head and glared at him.

Ed didn't flinch. "Yeah. Now, I couldn't be cooped up with her, and—"

"You've made your point." Flint's tone was testy at best.

Ed chuckled. "Yeah, I guess I have at that." He paused. "Wanna join the womenfolk for a cup of coffee?"

"You mean Mary's with you?"

"As we speak, she's inside talking to Stephanie."

"What about?" Was Mary trying to persuade Stephanie into coming to their house? He ground his teeth together.

"The dance we're having at our place."

Flint felt relief on one hand, but new suspicions were roused on the other. "I hope you're not getting at what I think you are. You know I don't want any part—"

"Well, something tells me that's about to change."

This time Flint snorted. "No way."

"We'll see." Ed chuckled knowingly. "Come on, let's go get that coffee."

Stephanie cradled her banging head in her hands and prayed for relief. None came. Besides suffering another nightmare during the night, her mind reeled from the confrontation with Flint.

Earlier, she had stumbled into the bathroom at the end of the hall, and after filling a cup with water, had swallowed two of the pills prescribed by Abe. She had gone back to bed and told herself she needed the sleep after her ordeal. In reality, she knew she was postponing facing her conscience for her part in yesterday's debacle.

Now, as she dressed, the scene paraded before her mind in living color and added to her confusion. How could she have behaved so wantonly? She might as well have let him rip her clothes off and make love to her on the spot.

What had come over her?

At first she had blamed her actions on her condition, on the fear and uncertainty that hovered over her like a dark cloud. That was part of it, sure. But that wasn't all. In his arms she had felt alive, captivated by everything that was happening to her, as if his mouth, his hands, his strong arms were guiding her.

She should be ashamed. She *was* ashamed. Yet she hadn't wanted him to stop. And that had scared her, made her run.

To make matters worse, when she saw him earlier in the kitchen, she had wanted to fling herself back into his arms. Should she leave? Go to Mary's? Logic said yes while her heart balked.

"What a mess," she moaned, before standing and hustling to the cabinet. Just as she raised the coffeepot, something bright outside caught her attention. She looked through the window; Ed's pickup filled her vision. Both doors opened, and Ed and Mary hopped out.

Stephanie moaned again. While she enjoyed Mary's company, now was not a good time. Not only did she feel terrible, she looked terrible, which was bound to bring on questions she wouldn't want to answer. But short of being rude, she had no choice but to be sociable as Mary was headed toward the house while Ed went toward the barn.

Five minutes later Mary sat at the table in front of her, sipping coffee and chattering nonstop.

"I hope you don't mind my crashing in on you this early, but Ed thought maybe Flint might like to get started on his barn."

"That's fine. I was about to get started making calls." Though she tried to keep the edge out of her voice, she couldn't.

"You're becoming more frustrated by the day, aren't you, dear?"

"I'm afraid so."

Mary reached across the table and squeezed Stephanie's hand. "Maybe you're trying too hard, not giving yourself enough time. It's only been ... what, a week, week and a half?"

"Thereabouts, but it seems like forever."

"Well, the way I see it, a party is what you need."

Stephanie wrinkled her brows. "A party."

"Uh-huh. Our dance club's monthly social is at our place, and it's going to be a big shindig."

"I'm sure."

"We'd love for you to come."

The thought of moving with Flint in time to the music ... Alarm flared in Stephanie's eyes. "Oh, no, I couldn't."

"You don't have to dance, not if you don't want to. There's tons of other stuff to do."

"Such as?"

Mary laughed. "Eat."

"Mmm, that sounds good."

"I'm glad to hear you say that. You can certainly use a few pounds."

"You sound like Flint."

Mary gave her a strange look, but whatever was on her mind, she didn't say, much to Stephanie's profound relief. She wasn't up to the third degree today, concerning her and Flint's unorthodox relationship.

"In addition to a barbecue," Mary said, "there'll be fried catfish, hush puppies and fries."

Stephanie drew back in surprise. "Jeez, how many are y'all feeding? The five thousand?"

"Actually, it's just a handful. Our club's small." Mary's smile widened. "But those who do come eat like they've been felling trees."

"Sounds like fun." Stephanie's tone was whimsical.

"So come. You and Flint."

"Oh, no, I don't think..." Though her voice failed her, her mind did not. The possible consequences of dancing with Flint, being held against his rock-hard body, moving in time to music, didn't bear thinking about.

"I was hoping you'd be receptive and talk Flint into it." Mary sounded disappointed. "As we both know, he's a hard nut to crack. Ever since he came here, we've been trying to get him to join our club so that he could meet his neighbors. But he's flatly refused, and we haven't been able to budge him yet."

"I'm not surprised."

"I'm not either, but that doesn't mean it has to stay that way. Besides, it would do you good. It just might put a little color back in your cheeks.

"Well...I'll think about it. Only I can't, *won't* speak for Flint."

"Great. In the meantime, why don't you go shopping with me? I have scads of things to buy, even though I'm having it catered. I could use the company and you the change of scenery. Right?"

Stephanie's face brightened, only to then dim. "I really should start calling—"

"Ah, come on."

Stephanie felt pulled two ways. While she felt the urgent need to try to find out who she was, she wanted to take it easy. The latter seemed to be the most pressing. "All right, you win," Stephanie said, suppressing a sigh.

"You ladies mind sharing some coffee with us?"

Both Stephanie and Mary, caught unaware, swung around and watched as Flint and Ed strode across the threshold.

Mary had eyes only for Flint. "Guess what Stephanie and I have been discussing?"

"The dance." Flint's tone was dry as parchment.

"And she's agreed to come and bring you with her."

Eleven

"Well, what d'you think? You having a good time?"

Stephanie smiled at Ed, who was busy stroking his full beard. "The party's wonderful."

"Ah, come on now. You being from the city, you must've been to lots of shindigs like this."

Stephanie winced visibly.

"Sorry," Ed said awkwardly, "I forget . . ."

"Don't apologize." She forced a bright smile. "I'm sure you're right."

Ed squeezed her shoulders. "You have a good time now, you hear. If you need anything, you just holler." He paused and aimed his gaze toward Flint. "Why don't you go ask that sour-faced fellow to dance?" He grinned, then winked. "Just might loosen him up."

Flint was propped against a tree, near the table laden with goodies.

Stephanie's lips twitched. "I think I'd rather take my chances on stepping in front of a Mack truck."

Ed threw back his head and laughed. "I'll have to hand it to you, you got his number." He paused again. "So, are you?"

"What?" she asked innocently, but she knew what he was getting at.

"You know what. Ask him to dance."

"No."

"I dare you," Ed challenged, his whiskey-edged voice deepening.

She smiled with syrupy sweetness. "The answer's still no."

"Oh, heck." He grinned and snapped his fingers. "I sure had you figured for a gambler."

Stephanie merely laughed.

"Well, since there's not gonna be any fireworks, I guess I'd better circulate. Orders from my old lady. Will you be all right?"

"I'll be fine. I was on my way to help Mary, anyway."

"See you later."

Stephanie nodded vaguely, having already turned her attention back to Flint, who continued to lounge against the tree, his Stetson hiding his eyes. As usual, he looked mouthwateringly sexy, dressed in a pair of pressed jeans, polished boots and white chambray shirt that accentuated his tan. He affected her despite her efforts not to let him.

Again the thought of dancing with him did strange things to her body. Her heart raced, and her palms sweated. But she was wasting good energy. He wasn't about to dance with her or anyone else. His boorish attitude left no doubt that he'd rather be anywhere but there.

And she found it hard to believe that he actually was. She'd have to give Mary credit; she had pulled a fast one. When Mary had announced that she, Stephanie, had consented for both of them, Flint had glowered at her....

"Did you tell her that?"

Stephanie licked her lips while wanting to strangle Mary. "Actually, I—"

Mary cut in. "Now, Flint, don't go getting—"

"Oh, what the hell," he barked. "We might as well go and get it over with."

Mary's expression turned incredulous. "Did you hear that, Ed?"

"Sure did, honey. And we'll hold him to that, even if I have to hog-tie him."

"That'll be the day," Flint countered with the beginnings of a smile on his lips.

His sudden good humor hadn't fooled Stephanie. Something told her that if their eyes were to collide again, she would see a murderous glint reflected in his.

He hadn't mentioned the party, however, until this morning when he'd told her to be ready by six.

Now, as she pulled her gaze from him, Stephanie smothered a sigh and made her way toward the side entrance to the house. The night couldn't have been lovelier, she thought as she meandered through the tables set up on the grounds.

The air smelled fresh and sweet. Stars littered the sky. Lanterns hung from trees and posts surrounding a portable dance floor in the middle of the huge yard. A band and singer crooned the latest country-western ballad while dancers, wrapped tightly in one another's arms, swayed to the music.

When she and Flint had arrived, the party had been in full swing. Mary had met them when they rounded the corner and introduced Stephanie to the other couples. She was welcomed immediately, though she couldn't help but notice that Flint was the one who garnered the most attention from several unattached females.

Mary had then insisted they take advantage of the food, which was displayed with the same skill and decorative taste as everything else. Barbecue, catfish and Mexican food— tacos, chicken and beef *fajitas*—crowded the long table.

Stephanie had chosen a little of each while Flint had chosen a lot of each.

She'd been in a festive mood as Flint had actually talked to her on the way, explaining about his cattle and the progress he'd made with them. He'd also told her about the calf he expected to be born soon.

The days preceding the party hadn't been too bad, either. He'd actually taken her riding and had let her watch him and a hired hand, Smitty, work on the barn. She'd been their gofer.

But once they had reached the party, his mood had changed. Now, however, she knew it had not changed for the better. He hadn't wanted to come, and he made sure everyone knew it.

That thought was still uppermost in Stephanie's mind when she entered the kitchen, only to suddenly stop. Instead of stepping into Mary's kitchen, another one flashed in front of her eyes, one with bright oranges and yellows. *Her kitchen?* She blinked several times until the vision cleared.

"Stephanie, honey," Mary cried, "what on earth? You look like you've just seen a ghost."

"Perhaps I have—my past."

Mary set down a bowl of potato salad and grasped one of Stephanie's hands. "Here, sit down. You're not making sense."

"Yes, I am," she said excitedly, sinking into the chair, her face no longer ashen. "When I walked in here, a picture of my kitchen swam before my eyes. I could see every detail so clearly."

Mary clapped her hands. "Why, that's wonderful news. Have you mentioned that to Flint?"

"No, not yet."

"Are you going to?"

"Yes, but right now I'm going to ask him to dance." Once the words left her mouth, Stephanie was stunned by them.

Then recovering, she said breathlessly, "Ed dared me, you know." Was it the dare that prompted such madness on her part, a madness she couldn't even put a name to?

Mary laughed. "Good luck. Better you than me."

"For heaven's sake, I won't bite."

"Are you sure?" he drawled.

Stephanie had found Flint swaggering toward the table where a huge urn of iced tea sat. Before he could refill his cup, she'd approached him.

Now, as he peered down at her with a scowl on his face, she didn't know whether to curse him or hit him.

"Jerk," she muttered under her breath.

He heard her, though, and chuckled. "I've been called worse."

Color mounted in her face, but she didn't back down. "I'm not surprised."

He simply looked at her for a long moment, then in a rough voice said, "Come on."

The platform was packed, but that didn't stop Flint from pulling her onto the floor and drawing her into his arms. Still she hadn't expected to feel the heavy crush of his hard body against hers, nor have his arms clamp around her with such force.

Tension stretched her nerves despite her attempts to relax. And the scent of his warm skin didn't help any, especially as her mouth pressed against the open vee of his shirt. She wet her lips and ached to stroke that vulnerable spot with the tip of her tongue. She blew warm air there instead.

"God, Stephanie!" he grated into her hair at the same time she felt his involuntary arousal. But Stephanie was too engrossed in her own reaction to move away, feeling as if something had burst inside her, exposing forces far too strong to contain. She felt plugged in to a new high and began to move sensuously against him in time to the music.

"What the hell do you think you're doing!" The words sounded tortured, but he didn't push her away. Instead, he tightened his hold and followed her lead.

His chin grazed her hair along with the heated draught of his breath. A slight tilt of her head and their lips would meet. The thought was not just a heady temptation, but an exciting ache as she knew he wouldn't be able to resist her.

But the memory of that other time brought her abruptly to her senses. This was not a game to Flint. He was not a man to be toyed with. With a gulp she pulled herself together and stiffened in his arms.

He thrust her to arm's length, his dark eyes expressionless. When he spoke, his voice still didn't sound like his own.

"Are you ready to go?"

"Yes."

Five minutes later they left.

"There's something I want to ask you."

They were halfway to the ranch, and this was the first time either of them had spoken. They were too shaken and too wary after what had just happened on the dance floor to say much of anything.

"All . . . right," Stephanie said.

Without warning, he swung the truck off the highway onto the grassy shoulder.

Her eyes widened. "What are you doing?"

"What does it look like I'm doing?"

"Stopping."

He didn't respond.

"But . . . why?"

"To take care of a little unfinished business."

"I . . . I don't understand."

"You will."

She had just parted her lips to say more, when he reached out and pulled her toward him. His voice against her lips came out tight and clogged. "Ever since the other night, I've been wanting this and now tonight..."

"Don't talk," she breathed. Her hands, which seconds before had been idle, crawled behind his neck and threaded through his thick hair. "Just kiss me."

She felt him hesitate as if he were having second thoughts, and her senses clamored in frustration. But then, with a groan, he found her lips with greedy accuracy.

Clinging to him, she gave in to the searing heat of his mouth, the hungry invasion of his tongue. She twisted in his arms so that her throbbing breasts were embedded in the ungiving wall of his chest. The flesh between her thighs came alive, and her stomach plummeted as if on a descending elevator. She knew this was insane, but she wanted him. How she wanted him.

As before and equally as sudden, he jerked his lips from hers, his breathing erratic.

"Flint..."

"Don't look at me like that," he said in a strangled tone.

"I...don't understand. You..." She couldn't go on, feeling sick.

"Surely you know it's stop now or not at all! And I don't think you want me to take you here in the front seat of this truck like two animals in heat."

His words assaulted her like a fist to the stomach. She drew back and tried to say something. But there was no need; her grieving eyes spoke for her.

He turned away as if he couldn't bear what he saw there. "Believe me, you'll thank me for this later."

While the inside of the truck was silent, sounds of the night throbbed around them. Crickets chirped. Katydids cried. The wind howled.

The longer they remained silent, the more the tension mounted. Stephanie was aware of him beside her with every beat of her heart. And despite his coldness, her nerves were on fire. On fire for him. Closing her eyes, she inhaled his scent. She ached to touch him. Again.

Instead she stole a glance at him. He was watching her. A muscle ticked overtime in his jaw. She had to relieve the explosive silence or scream.

"What . . . did you want to ask me?"

"I want to take you up in Ed's small plane."

She didn't know what she expected, but it hadn't been this. "No," she said flatly, fear thickening her tongue.

"You need to fly again and so do I. Besides, I thought it might help trigger your memory."

"You hate yourself for . . . wanting me, don't you?"

If the sudden change of subject stunned him, he failed to show it. His eyes didn't flicker as they made a slow search of her face. "Yes, dammit, I do."

She bit down on her lip to keep from crying. And for the longest time they listened as the silence once again hung heavy over them.

Finally Stephanie turned to him and said, "All right, you win. I'll go up with you in the plane."

He faced her again. "What made you change your mind?"

"The sooner I get my memory back, the sooner I can leave."

"And you can't wait, can you?"

All at once her voice betrayed her. It quavered. Without warning, tears trickled down her face. "Only because that's what *you* want."

He looked at her as if he were going to grab her again, longing intense on his face. It took her breath away.

But instead of touching her, he let loose a string of colorful expletives, cranked the truck and spun back onto the road.

Twelve

The sky was perfect. It reminded Stephanie of a sapphire that had been polished to its gleaming best. She could reach out and touch it; she just knew she could. But she was too frightened to try.

So she remained strapped in the seat of the noisy little plane with her heart lodged in the back of her throat. It threatened to choke her each time Flint so much as moved the yoke.

She had been positive she wouldn't be able to set one foot inside this ugly machine—and not because of the previous crash. That was still a blank in her mind. But when Flint came to assist her inside, a nameless fear deep inside her rendered her stiff-legged.

"You're having second thoughts, aren't you?"

She nodded.

Wind caught his hair and tossed it around. She watched a loose strand tickle his forehead. "It's your call," he said.

Stephanie licked her parched lips. "Let's do it."

They were airborne several minutes before he looked at her and commented, "That wasn't too bad now, was it?"

"Yes," she whispered, biting down on her lower lip to keep her teeth from chattering.

His eyes registered concern. "You aren't going to be sick, are you?"

"No...no I don't think so."

"I don't suppose you could look down. The trees and wildflowers are something to see."

She wet her lips. "I'm...I'm sure they are, but if it's all the same to you, I'd rather see them from ground level."

"Is anything coming back to you?" Flint asked after a moment.

"No," she said, and rested her eyes on him. That was when she noticed the white line around his mouth. How could she have been so insensitive? Flint had gone through the same nightmare as she had, maybe even worse because he was conscious throughout the horrifying ordeal. "What about you? Are you okay?"

"I was a bit shaky at first, but I'm fine now."

"If only something would jar loose in my memory..." She paused and tried to push back the despair playing havoc with her inside, but to no avail. She felt like crying.

"You'd best stop punishing yourself, or you're never going to remember."

Flint brought the Cessna back in for a safe landing, sensing she'd had enough. By the time her feet were on the ground, Stephanie was near tears.

"Are you sure you're all right?" Flint's gaze bored into her.

"No, I'm not sure about anything."

"When we get home, you should lie down for a while."

"What about Ed and Mary?" Out of the corner of her eye, Stephanie saw the Liscombs making their way toward the plane.

"They'll understand. You go ahead and get in the truck. I'll explain to them."

Stephanie flashed him a grateful smile.

He looked at her for a long moment, then turned toward Ed and Mary.

Her mind seemed a dark and gaping hole; too many thoughts battled for air. Was she dreaming again? She moaned, tossed the covers back, rolled from one side of the bed to the other. What was wrong? What was happening to her? She had to be dreaming ... about the crash ... about Flint ... about the plane ride ...

The moan came out a wail. She shot up in the bed, clutched the sheet to her naked breasts while her eyes jumped wildly around the room.

"Oh, my God," she whispered.

"If there's nothing else, I'll be on my way."

Flint nodded at Smitty Williams, the slender, wiry man who was thankful for the chance to work, even if it was only part-time. "That about covers it for now."

"Will you be wantin' to do some brandin' next week?" Smitty asked after he had limped to the barn door.

"Hope so," Flint said, rubbing the back of his neck. "But I can't say for sure. Ed's been on my tail to get started on this pile of crap."

"Well, just holler when you need me again."

"You take care of that leg now, you hear."

Smitty waved his hand. "Will do."

Alone, Flint mopped his brow, then gathered his tools. The front pasture gate was broken and had to be repaired before some of his herd got loose. He could have let Smitty fix it, but he wanted—*needed*—to do it himself, though Lord knows, he had more than enough to do already. Still, manual labor was his best mental therapy.

Stephanie. Forever Stephanie. That slender, black-haired witch had invaded his life and turned it upside down. Half the time he couldn't think straight, he ached for her so much.

But he wasn't about to give in and indulge himself. He'd made the mistake of touching her once too often as it was. To do so again would be inviting self-destruction. So far he'd risen to the challenge.

It'd been hard, though, especially this morning when he'd taken Stephanie up in the plane. He'd watched her face turn red, then white, then gray. He'd had to quell the urge to pull her into his arms and assure her everything was going to be all right.

Even afterward when he'd seen the fear, the uncertainty still reflected in her eyes, before she walked into her room and closed the door, he still hadn't given in to his urges.

Flint's hand suddenly stilled, as did his thoughts. A gusty breath from the edge of the woods brought him around. A doe stood poised and stared at him, defiance in every line of its young body. The animal repeated the strange sound, then bucked its head as if to show its disapproval of Flint's presence so close to its domain. Before Flint could react, it darted through the trees.

A brief smile touched his lips as he set about his task. He yanked off a rotten piece of wood, only to drop it.

"Sonofabitch," he muttered, lifting a finger to his lips, but not until he pulled out a sliver of wood with his teeth. When the bleeding stopped, he picked up his hammer and battered the remaining wood until it lay in a rubble at his feet.

"Long time no see, good buddy."

Flint whirled around, then lunged to his feet. "Why you ol' sonofagun, you! Haven't you learned yet you can get your head blown off for sneaking up on someone like that!"

Lee Holt, his friend and ex-partner at the agency, cocked his head to one side and grinned. "Not without a gun they won't," he drawled.

Flint returned the grin and extended his hand to the tall, sandy-haired man sporting wire-rim glasses across his nose. They made him look more like an English professor than a drug agent. But looks were deceiving. He was a sharp-witted, tough and highly skilled agent.

And he was the only man who Flint would trust with his life. In job-related incidents, they had been through hell and back and that made for a special friendship.

"What brings you to this neck of the woods?"

Lee shoved his glasses farther up on his nose. "Guess I wanted to see for myself that you were in one piece after that crash."

"Well, as you can see, I am."

"Anyway, didn't I warn you I'd show up on your door-step one of these days?"

"Yep, but I didn't believe you."

"My grandmother lives in Lufkin, remember?"

"Ah, that's right." Flint removed his hat and again wiped his brow. "You want some tea or Coke?" Flint paused. "You know I don't keep any beer..."

"I was hoping that was still the case," Lee said, casually stuffing his hands into the pocket of his slacks and scruti-nizing Flint closely.

Flint changed the subject. "You on vacation?"

"Sort of." Lee shifted his gaze.

"What does that mean?"

"Let's walk. You can give me the grand tour."

"Look, Lee," Flint began, his suspicions growing, "if you're really here about—"

"Hey, lighten up, will ya."

Flint scowled.

They walked only a few steps when Lee stopped. "You sure you're okay? I mean you sure that crash didn't..."

"What makes you think that?"

"Could be because you're up to your butt in alligators."

Flint's features turned cynical. "You always did have a way with words, Holt."

"I try," Lee responded with a grin. Then it faded, and his expression sobered. "I saw the way you were attacking that wood as if it was one of the thugs dealing drugs."

"Don't remind me."

"Hey, partner," he said, "seems to me like you're still nursing one helluva sore inside you. If you don't take some good medicine mighty soon, you'll up and die of blood poison."

"And you think coming back to that stink hole is the right medicine?"

"Yeah, as a matter of fact I do. Best I can tell, ranch life hasn't improved your disposition one iota or your outlook on life."

"It had up until a few days ago."

"So what happened?"

"There's someone...er...staying with me."

Lee's mouth fell open. "You have a houseguest? Now, that's a crock."

"Shut up," Flint grumbled darkly.

Lee grinned. "A woman."

"Yes."

"Well, that's been known to put some pep in ye ol' gumbo."

Again Flint scowled. "When did you get to be such a comedian?"

Lee's eyes narrowed, and the humor fled. "Lots of things have changed since you've been gone."

"If it's all the same to you, I'd rather not hear about them, either."

Lee shrugged. "Okay."

Flint wasn't fooled. He knew he wasn't going to get off the hook that easily. Lee was here for a reason, and Flint knew he wouldn't leave until he unburdened himself. Lee was just biding his time and humoring him.

"So how did you come by your houseguest?"

Flint gave him a thumbnail account of the accident and Stephanie's plight, deleting only the personal aspects of the traumatic situation.

"That's something, man," Lee said, shaking his head. "In case you don't already know it, I'm glad you're safe."

"That's comforting to know," Flint's tone dripped with sarcasm.

"I guess that's why we work so well together, huh?"

"Worked. Past tense. *Comprende?*"

Again Lee shrugged. "So tell me about her?"

"I already have."

"No, you haven't."

Flint didn't say anything.

"I thought you wanted off that ferris wheel for good, my friend."

"If you're referring to a wife, two point three children and the house in the suburbs with the white picket fence around it, you're right."

Lee scooped a lock of hair off his forehead. "Then come back to work."

"Are you outta your mind?"

"You haven't resigned yet, Flint."

"Only because I haven't had time."

Lee sank against the nearest tree. "Dammit, man, you can't. The agency needs you. *I* need you. I've had three partners since you left, and I swear none of 'em had enough brains to fill a thimble."

Flint grinned. "You don't say?"

"Aw, man, I'm serious."

"So am I." Flint looked off in the distance. "I like it here. This land is gonna heal me."

Lee sneered. "You can't be serious about this cowboy game?"

"Well, I am," Flint said flatly.

"Just say you'll think about it."

"I'll think about it, only because I owe you."

"That's all I'm asking," Lee said, slapping Flint on the back. "Come on, show me this ninth wonder of the world."

"How long you planning to hang around?" Flint asked.

Following the tour, he and Lee had wandered back to where Lee's car was parked. Lee was inside his car, and Flint's elbows were bent on the vinyl top. He peered inside.

"A couple more days."

"I guess your grandmother's glad to see you."

"Yeah." Lee grinned and rubbed his stomach. "She's been puttin' the groceries on the table."

"That's obvious," Flint said, and dropped his gaze to his friend's protruding stomach. Before Lee could make a suitable comeback, he added, "Are you planning to stop by again?"

Lee grinned. "Are you kiddin'? I wouldn't miss meeting this lady for anything."

"Who said you were going to meet her?"

"Did I ever tell you you're a real pain in the butt, Carson?"

"Every day we worked together," Flint said drolly.

"Well, I haven't changed my mind."

Flint grinned a lop-sided grin and slammed his hand against the car door. "Go on. Get outta here before I give you something to whine about."

He watched in silence as Lee cranked his car, backed up, then spun his tires. Dust rose and clogged Flint's nostrils and throat. "Hey, you bastard, I'll get you for that!"

"Flint?"

At the sound of Stephanie's voice, he whipped around. For a moment he treated himself to a slow perusal of her. He assumed she had just awakened as her jeans and shirt were rumpled, even askew. And her eyes had a slightly glazed look. Nevertheless, with the wealth of her black hair in careless disorder, she made a picture that would stay with him for a long time.

He cleared his throat and stepped closer. That was when he noticed how pale she was. "Is something wrong? You look like you've just seen a ghost."

She shook her head so that her hair brushed her cheek. "Actually, I think I've just laid them to rest."

He frowned. "Care to explain that?"

Her delicately drawn features went curiously still, and she didn't say anything.

"Stephanie," he prodded, searching her face.

Through the concealing thickness of her lashes, she looked at him and smiled tremulously. "My memory has returned."

Thirteen

The statement ripped through him like a dull blade. Yet he kept his face impassive.

"So you finally know who you are."

"I can't believe it, but it happened just like Abe said it would." Stephanie's voice held awe, and her eyes were wide, as if she couldn't believe the sudden turn of events.

"Why don't we go sit on the porch?" Flint suggested abruptly.

Stephanie perched on the edge of the swing, and Flint leaned against a post.

"So when did things fall into place?" he asked, sifting through his feelings and not liking any of them. Why was he overreacting? He should be relieved she had opened that dark chapter in her life. And he was. Only...

"Just...now, actually," she said. "I...woke up from my nap, and everything was there."

His chest swelled as he drew air deep into his lungs and braced himself. "Everything?"

"Everything." She didn't so much as flinch under his direct gaze. "Even our less than amicable conversation on the plane."

A sickly sun peered through the now overcast sky while the silence built.

"But I don't hold that against you," she added in a breathy rush. "Especially after all you've done for me."

"Forget it."

She rejected that with an impatient toss of her head. "I have no intention of forgetting it."

"So what's next?"

"Notify my family, of course."

"And who is that?"

"My mother. If she's back from Europe."

"So that accounts for why she hasn't tracked you down."

"She didn't even know I was going to Arkansas."

"What about your dad?"

"He's . . . dead, and I'm an only child." She paused and took a steadying breath. "But I have to notify Kathy Gentry, who runs my shop."

"She didn't know your travel plans either, I take it."

"No. She knew I was going to check several sources, but she didn't know I was going to Arkansas."

"If only you'd told me the name of your business, much of this mess could've been avoided."

"It's Collections by Stephanie."

His head moved in the briefest of nods. "What about the man at the airport? Who was he?"

"David Weston."

"Go on."

Her white upper teeth imprisoned her lower lip for a moment. "He's my ex-fiancé, actually."

"So what's he to you now?" he asked tersely, shocked by the things he felt.

Without hesitation, she explained in detail about his aunt's jewelry.

"Someone oughta teach that creep a lesson." There was a hard set to Flint's jaw.

"He's harmless, really. It's just that he doesn't like being told no."

"Sounds like someone I know," he said, more for his own benefit than hers.

"Are you referring to your visitor?"

His eyes settled for a moment on the gentle swell of her breasts. "Yeah," he said tightly, his eyes flickering.

"Is he a . . . friend?"

"A friend and my ex-partner."

"He's trying to get you to return, isn't he?"

"How did you know?"

She shrugged. "I didn't, I just guessed. So what are you going to do?"

"I don't know. But I don't want to talk about me right now."

She eased back in the swing and didn't say anything.

"So when are you leaving?"

"Actually, I was thinking I might stay a while longer." Her smile was fragile. "If you don't mind, that is."

Shocked silence greeted her words. Flint couldn't respond even if he'd wanted to. He was too busy grappling with his own emotions. Logic told him she would eventually regain her memory. Yet he hadn't been prepared for it.

But neither had he been prepared for the bombshell she just dropped, having convinced himself that once she reclaimed her identity, she'd be out of his house and life forever. Only now she asked to stay. Suddenly everything was more tangled than ever.

She should leave. That was the sane recourse. Every day the ache for her grew worse. It was all he could do not to touch her, while savoring what it would be like to do just that, to taste her skin, feel her nipples come to life under his tongue . . .

In the backwash of those emotions, nausea washed through him. Yet the thought of her leaving was unbearable even though she stirred feelings he didn't want to face.

"Flint?"

"Do you think that's wise?" His expression was that of a man in torment.

Her mouth etched into a weak smile. "Probably not, but if I promise not to bother you..."

"That's not the point, and you know it."

"Just for a few more days, that's all I'm asking."

"Why?"

"I...I was planning to put some distance between David and myself by visiting a friend in Austin..."

"So you figure this is as good a place as any to hide?" For a second he had thought she wanted to stay because she cared.... Fool, he diagnosed grimly, his heart twisting at the pain she never failed to arouse in him.

"Something like that."

He stared at her and then turned away, shoving back his hair with a restless hand.

"Please."

He swung around, but instead of saying anything, he stared at her while his heart pounded in his chest.

"I could help you repair the barn," she said in a voice tinged with huskiness.

A slow smile spread from his lips to his eyes, kindling small fires. "Yeah, I guess you could at that."

"Thanks for everything, Mary."

The older woman grinned. "Don't thank me, I'm the one who had a good time. It's comforting to know someone can out-shop me."

Mary had just helped her unload several armloads of packages and was now back in her car, ready to head home.

Stephanie peered down at her and laughed sheepishly. "I did go overboard, didn't I?"

"Not at all. If you've got it, why not flaunt it." Mary's eyes turned serious. "By the way, welcome back to the real world, my dear."

Sudden tears clouded Stephanie's vision. "Thanks, Mary. Believe me, it's good to be back."

Two days had passed since her memory had returned. So far, things had gone smoothly. But then, she'd seen very little of Flint. They had both been too busy—Flint with his cattle and other chores and she with reacquainting herself with her life and responsibilities.

Following a long and traumatic talk with her mother, during which Flora had insisted she leave "that godforsaken place immediately" and return to Houston, Stephanie called Kathy. That conversation had been much more pleasant. She'd learned that things on the business front were fine, though Kathy had gone into hysterics when Stephanie informed her of what she'd been through.

Having taken care of those heart-wrenching duties, Stephanie had gone into town and wired her bank for money. Then she'd visited Ed and Mary. That was when she and Mary had planned this shopping expedition.

"How much longer do you plan to stay?" Mary asked, bridging the short silence.

Stephanie's good humor waned. "A...few more days. I have to get back to work."

"We'll miss you."

"I'll miss you, too."

Mary laughed. "Well, there's no point in getting all maudlin now. You haven't gone yet."

"That's right, I haven't." She squeezed Mary's shoulder. "Thanks again. I'll talk to you later."

The minute she walked back into the house and eyed her purchases, her heart filled with excitement. She couldn't wait for Flint to come in so that she could show him what she'd bought. Glancing at her watch, she saw it was already five o'clock. If she was going to prepare a steak dinner as planned, she would have to hurry.

But instead of making her way toward the kitchen, she plopped down on the couch and opened the packages. She spread the items on the couch and two chairs.

"You did good, Stephanie Marsh," she said aloud with a broad smile. "Yes, ma'am, you did good."

Displayed in front of her were two colorful bedspreads as well as sheets, towels, glassware and pictures for the house. Spaced across the back of the couch were several shirts for Flint.

She didn't feel guilty about spending the money, either. That was the least she could do as Flint had saved her sanity, if not her life. She was aware that buying him things could in no way repay him, but nonetheless, it was something she wanted to do.

Besides, she wanted to leave something of herself behind. Abruptly, like a dark cloud dims the bright sun, the joy went out of her. When she thought about leaving, she always reacted like this. Yet she should have left two days ago.

Sure, she'd wanted a reprieve from David and his harassment, but that was only a smoke screen. She couldn't stand the thought of leaving Flint, which was ludicrous in itself. They were as different as two people could ever be. And even if they weren't, they had no future.

Flint Carson was not about to commit himself to a woman, least of all to her. And she didn't want him to, did she? Of course not. She was satisfied with her life and was eager to get on with it. But there was the unvarnished truth she could no longer deny: she was totally and completely under Flint's spell.

Thrusting these unsettling thoughts aside, she rushed into the bedroom and changed into a white jumpsuit she'd just bought. Satisfied that she looked her best, she made her way into the kitchen.

She had the steaks, baked potatoes and salad prepared with the coming of twilight. Only after she heard Flint shout his thanks to Ed for helping him in the pasture did she develop a case of the jitters.

"Cool it," she muttered, and hurried into the living room where she backed calmly against the mantel. Still, when she heard Flint rattle the front door knob, she almost jumped out of her skin.

"Stephanie?"

"In here."

He appeared in the doorway, and their eyes met. The connection between them was palpable. Her eyes dipped to his chest. His sweat-drenched shirt was unbuttoned to his navel. She felt her insides shake with wild heat.

His eyes darkened, as if he could read her thoughts, and he took one slow step toward her. Then unexpectedly, he stopped, his eyes on the couch. For the longest moment, he didn't say anything. Stephanie held her breath.

"What's all this?"

"Mary and I went shopping."

He made a growling sound in his throat. "I can see that."

She smiled tentatively. "I bought them for you and...the house."

His features could've been hacked out of stone. "Take them back!"

"What?"

"I said take them back."

"But...why?" Pain slashed her face.

"I don't want them, that's why."

"But...you need..."

"Dammit, where do you get off telling me what I need?"

The look in his eyes was frightening. Her lower lip trembled. "I didn't mean—"

"I don't care what you meant. Listen up, because I'm not going to say this again." He loomed over her now, his eyes narrowed slits. "I don't need your money or the things it can buy! Understand?"

Stephanie stumbled backward, her eyes rimmed with tears.

"Go on, get out of my sight."

Her lips quivered so hard she could barely get the words out. "I hate you, Flint Carson. I hate . . . you!"

Fourteen

Her soft sobs woke him up.

"Sonofabitch," he hissed, before gritting his teeth and flouncing onto his back.

The sobs continued.

He wouldn't tell her he was sorry because he wasn't, not for sticking up for his rights. But he shouldn't have yelled at her, he decided, staring up at the ceiling. That was childish and immature and totally unlike him to lose control. Usually he was slow to boil. But when he did, he always cut his victim's throat—verbally—with soft, cold, calculated words.

With Stephanie, however, that technique hadn't worked. She made him do crazy things. She made him say crazy things. She made him crazy period.

That was just too damn bad, because if tonight hadn't proved the difference between his life-style and Stephanie's, then nothing ever would. She was the "haves," and he was the "have nots."

The sobs didn't let up, and a coldness swept over him. He groaned, then pounded the pillow. Damn these cardboard-thin walls, he thought violently. If only she hadn't wanted to remain here...if only he hadn't let her. She hadn't fooled him; he knew what she was up to. She saw him as a challenge. That had to be it. And she wanted him. He saw that, too. Taming this misdirected cowboy was a game, and when she was done, she would cast him aside like a dress she'd worn once and no longer wanted.

So what was the solution? Send her packing. Yeah, first thing in the morning he'd do just that. Meanwhile, he couldn't stand her tears. The sound ripped his gut to shreds.

He untangled his limbs from the sheet, grabbed his jeans and slipped them on. He reached her room seconds later and eased open the door. He got no further. Surprise held him rooted to the spot. She sat in the middle of the bed, the sheet clutched against her, and stared at him through wide, tear-stained eyes.

The night suddenly seemed hot and breathless. Or was it because he couldn't get his breath? The dappled moonlight on her ivory skin was the most beautiful thing he'd ever seen.

His tongue stuck to the roof of his mouth. The realness of the situation rendered the nerves and muscles in his groin tight. But that wasn't all. Instinct told him something momentous was about to happen. He couldn't identify it or understand it, but he felt that whatever it was would change him forever.

"Flint?" Her voice came out a mere whisper.

"I...er...heard you crying."

Her eyes gleamed with fresh tears. "I'm...sorry I disturbed you."

The sheet slipped then, and his breath hung suspended. He knew she was naked. And not just her breasts either. All over. His heart sounded like a gong; he was certain she could hear it. His skin was on fire while his legs trembled as if he'd run uphill.

"Are...are you all right?" he finally managed to get out.

She sniffed. "I'm fine."

Only she wasn't, and they both knew it.

Throwing caution to the wind, he strode to the bed. But when she peered up at him, her lashes clumped together in tiny spikes, he froze again, the visible tension in his body made anything else impossible.

Seconds ticked into a minute, and still their eyes held. The silence grew thicker.

"Flint," she whispered again through slightly parted lips.

That was the break he needed, her husky voice, the quickening pulse at the base of her throat. He knew she was as aroused as he was.

Her words proved him right. "I...don't want you to leave me." Her voice came out as an unsteady thread of sound.

"Are you..."

"Yes, oh yes."

"Stephanie...I..."

As if she sensed he was about to leave, she whispered, "Don't...go. Please."

She became an unwitting conspirator then. Stifling a groan, Flint slowly lifted her to her feet.

"Oh, Flint, I was so...scared." She clutched him hard, then drew back as if unprepared for the hardness that stabbed at her stomach.

"See how much I want you."

Once he shed his jeans, he reached for her again and pulled her cheek onto his chest. His flesh seemed to melt into hers, and he groaned.

"Hold me, hold me," she begged.

Wedged together, they fell back onto the bed. With her pinned beneath him, he simply looked at her. Her hair spilled around her like a swatch of black velvet.

"You're beautiful." His rough tone held reverence.

Silence overtook them. Each wondered if this meshing of their bodies was a mirage, a figment of their imagination. There had been no preplanning, no scheming to experience the ecstasy for the taking. In one moment fear had shackled their bodies—in the next, a burgeoning ache fueled them.

Flint took her mouth, hesitantly at first. But then her warm lips parted and their tongues collided, slippery and coiling. Ignited, he raised his head and gazed at her. Her eyes were closed, her moist lips still parted. Growling deep in his throat, he sank his face in the silk of her hair; he could smell the sun there, and daffodils. He trailed kisses across her shoulders, down her arms, to her hands and felt her flesh quiver.

"You're perfect, every inch of you."

"Oh, Flint," she murmured as he touched several fingers with his tongue before he turned his attention to her breasts. They rose and fell with labored breathing while her nipples pouted and beckoned under his warm mouth.

He continued to lave her nipples, and Stephanie moaned as if goaded by unbridled desire. He shifted positions finally and stapled her flat belly with the same hot nipping kisses, only to then move lower. The instant his tongue touched her with a rhythmlike music, she squirmed and made soft murmuring sounds.

Soon she tried to move away, but he refused to relinquish his prize.

"Please," Stephanie gasped. "You're driving me crazy."

"I know."

She cried out, and he forgot everything but the need to be inside her, to fill her. He began with long and slow strokes, and elevated to quick and hot. She clawed at his back.

Blood thundered through him. "Oh, Stephanie!"

"Now!" she cried.

He wanted to pull back, to prolong the sweet pain, but he couldn't hold off the burning heat that spilled from him. She sucked at the air and cried out again.

Flint held her until their breathing returned to normal. Even at that, an hour passed before he forced out the words that had to be said, past his lips.

"Stephanie."

"Uh-huh?"

"This . . . doesn't change anything . . ."

She stiffened against him, then pulled away. "I . . . know." Her voice was low and broken. "Just please . . . don't tell me you're sorry."

"Never," he said with rough huskiness, and he reached for her again.

The following morning, after she had loaded the rental car with the packages she intended to return, Flint intercepted her in the kitchen.

As their eyes met, she couldn't find her breath for the fever his nearness aroused in her.

He averted his gaze and said, "There's something I want you to know."

"What?" she asked, her heart sinking.

"Er . . . I don't make a habit of making love without—" He broke off, while his Adam's apple convulsed as if something were lodged in his throat.

She couldn't help him out; her own throat was too full.

"Without protection," he got out. "But . . . last night, I lost control."

"I know."

"So I guess what I'm getting at is it possible . . ."

"No."

He blinked. "No. Are you sure?"

"It's the wrong time of the month."

He drooped visibly, yet his dark eyes searched her face hungrily.

Unable to stand not touching him, she said, "Look, I've got to go."

Skirting past him, she went out the door.

They acted as if they walked on glass. But that didn't lessen the tension. When they were in the same room, it crackled. One wrong look, one touch, and their emotions would skyrocket again.

She tried to stay away from him as much as she could. She nursed her own hurt and insecurities. So did he.

To relieve her anxieties, Stephanie took long walks and even jogged a few miles. One day Mary came to her rescue, took her to a huge flea market in Canton where she found several pieces of nice jewelry and sent them special delivery to Kathy. It felt good to be back doing her job, which was what she loved best.

Or rather *had* loved best. The instant Flint's mouth had burned a trail down her body, she'd known she would never get him out of her system. But her feelings for him went beyond the physical, though she had to admit she'd never been loved so thoroughly, so deliciously, or so expertly.

Certainly she'd felt nothing like that the few times David had made love to her. And never had he taken the liberties with her body she had allowed Flint. The thoughts of what his mouth and tongue had done to her never failed to bring a scalding flush to her face.

While she basked in his lovemaking, he had touched her on another plane. He had touched her heart. She was in love. For the first time in her life she had fallen in love. So she should deserve to live happily ever after, right? Wrong. Why? Because she had chosen the most pig-headed, stubborn, proud man on the face of the planet, who was not interested in a relationship—long-term or otherwise.

But one thing she knew for certain: she wasn't about to let him push her out of his life before she found the answer.

Today, as she waited for Abe to see her for the final time, that thought was uppermost in her mind.

"Well, young lady, how are you?" Abe asked, suddenly joining Stephanie in one of the small rooms.

She smiled, glad of the interruption. "Fine."

"Well, let's just take a look-see here."

They were quiet while the doctor examined her.

His eyes twinkled. "You're in tip-top shape, my dear."

"Oh, Doctor, that's wonderful news."

"You're free to get on with your life."

If only that were true, she thought with a sinking feeling in the pit of her stomach. Her life would never be the same again. Flint Carson had made sure of that.

Stephanie extended her hand. "I want to thank you for all you've done."

Abe batted the air. "I'm thankful things turned out well for you."

Stephanie smiled again. "I'm sure I'll see you again."

Abe winked. "Count on it."

Later, she was about to get into the car, when an unexpected hand on her arm stopped her. Jerking her head up, she looked into the face of her ex-fiancé.

"David!" she exclaimed. "What on earth?"

The pressure on her arm increased. "Just shut up and get in the car."

"But..." she spluttered.

"I said get in the damn car!"

Stephanie did as she was told only because she didn't want to create a scene, something she knew from experience that David was very capable of.

Inside the vehicle Stephanie faced him, and in the coldest voice she could muster said, "What's the meaning of this?"

"Don't play Miss High-and-Mighty with me, sugar. I'm not that dim-witted cowboy."

"What are you doing here, David?" This time her voice sounded tired and bored.

"You know why I'm here."

"How did you find me?" She held up her hand. "No, let me guess. Mother."

He grinned a sly grin. "She still thinks we're a match made in heaven."

"I'll see you in hell first."

He grabbed her wrist. "That may be sooner than you think if you don't give me back my aunt's jewelry."

"I told you that was a done deal," Stephanie retorted, wrenching her arm out of his grip and backing as far against the door as she could.

God, how could she have ever considered marrying him? She shuddered inwardly. Comparing him to Flint—well, there was no comparison. The thought of David touching her ever again made her skin crawl.

David ran a hand through his thinning hair. "Then get them back."

"That's impossible." Deciding to try another tactic, she spread her hands and said, "Look, you know I'm in the business to make money. Now, if I were in the habit of reneging on my sales, I wouldn't be in—"

"I don't give a tinker's damn about your reputation," he snarled. "It's my butt I'm worried about."

"What kind of trouble are you in?" she asked on a resigned sigh.

"Let's just say I owe my bookie more than I can pay."

She gave him an incredulous look. "Oh, David, how could you?"

"Save the platitudes, will you?" He pawed the air. "Those jewels are mine, Stephanie. My aunt promised them to me. And I want them back. I have a buyer who'll pay me probably three times what you sold them for."

"At the risk of sounding like a broken record, it's a done deal."

"Well, I suggest you undo it."

Her chin jutted. "Or what?"

"I'll make you sorry you ever met me."

Without warning, she yanked up the door handle. "Either you get out or I go to the authorities." Seconds ticked by. "It's your choice."

"All right. But I won't give up." He leaned over and trailed his finger down one cheek. "You think on that, sugar, you hear?" Then he got out of the car.

Stephanie managed to control her trembling hands, but it took some doing. He was bluffing, she told herself. Anyway, what could he do? She hadn't lied to him. She no longer had the jewelry. She would put the incident behind her. As long as she kept in mind that he was all talk and no action, she would be fine.

Besides, she wasn't going to let that creep ruin the rest of this beautiful day. Holding that thought, she cranked the car and sped toward the ranch.

And Flint.

Fifteen

Birds chirped busily as they flitted through the treetops. A dog barked angrily from the other side of the pond.

"There you go, big fellow," Flint crooned, and with the sun beating down on his back, he brushed the gelding's mane.

The horse nickered, then slapped Flint with his tail.

"Yeah, I know you want me to work on you some more, but no can do. I got a living to make, remember?"

The animal turned solemn eyes on him and stared.

He chuckled. "Okay, okay. One more good brushing, then it's back to the pasture you go."

Flint knew he was wasting time he didn't have. But he couldn't seem to get his gears shifted this morning. In fact, he hadn't been worth a damn since he'd spent that night in Stephanie's arms.

He would give his blood to make love to her again. The thought of that now made him hard, made him ache. Well, too bad. He'd just have to learn to live with his urges. He was still what he was, and she was still what she was.

Even assuming he was going to make a decent wage on his cattle come market time, he still had zilch to offer her. She was used to the best of everything, while he was content to scrape by on nothing.

His unruly thoughts had numbed him into immobility. The sound of a car door jerked him back into action. He turned around, expecting to see Stephanie. Instead, he saw an unfamiliar woman get out of a Lincoln Town Car and walk toward him.

Instinct told him she was Stephanie's mother. It wasn't so much the resemblance—although the same finely drawn features were obvious—that gave her away. It was the haughty tilt to her nose.

He tossed the brush aside, then pushed back his Stetson and waited. She stopped within arm's reach.

"Are you Flint Carson?" she asked in a perfectly modulated voice.

On closer observation, he noticed that her face was too thin, to the point of gauntness, as was the rest of her body. He could see now where Stephanie got her bent for thinness. But that was where the likeness ended. Stephanie was dark-headed; this woman was blond and not very tall. Even her designer suit failed to hide her bony curves. Yet, she held herself as if she wore the crown jewels fastened beneath the French twist at the nape of her neck.

"Yes ma'am," he said at last in response to her question.

If she caught the mocking edge in his tone, she gave no indication. She clutched her hands tightly in front of her. "Well, I'm Flora Marsh, Stephanie's mother."

Flint could read her mind—she wasn't about to shake his hand for fear of getting something Clorox couldn't take off. He almost laughed aloud.

"Your daughter's not here."

Her nose tilted a little higher. "And just where is she?"

"In town."

"Town?" She looked around. "You mean this godfor-saken place has a town?"

"Yes, ma'am," he drawled, a cutting smile on his lips. "And we have indoor toilets, too."

Silence followed as menacing as a jab of a lightning bolt.

Her lips shriveled like a prune. "There's no reason to be crude," she snapped.

"Whatever you say, ma'am."

She flushed, and her eyes blazed, but when she spoke, her voice was cool and composed, "I suppose I should thank you for what you did for my—"

"You don't owe me a thing, lady."

This time she flinched under his savage abruptness. "Well . . . maybe not, but—"

Again he cut her off. "If you'd like to wait for your daughter inside, go ahead. I have work to do."

He meant his rudeness as a slap in the face, and she took it as such. But dammit, if anyone needed to be brought down a notch or two, it was this dame.

"Thank . . . you," she said in her haughtiest tone yet. "I can assure you that as soon as my daughter gets back, we'll be out of your house."

His only response was to pat the gelding on the butt and watch as the animal swished his tail in response.

"Goodbye, Mr. Carson." Her features were now pale and pinched. "I can assure you that we won't trouble you again."

He tipped his hat. "Yes, ma'am."

When she was out of sight, he thought seriously of jumping in his pickup and heading for the nearest bar and getting blind, stinking drunk. He knew from past experience that wouldn't solve a thing. But manual labor would. He stalked into the barn and grabbed his tools. He discarded his shirt and climbed on the top of the barn that was still intact.

He wasn't stupid or naive enough to believe in love at first sight, Flint reminded himself as he pulverized a two-by-four with a nail and hammer. Nor could it grow and mature unless two people understood and accepted each other. True, he was a man with strong physical hungers, but he did not regard that as the cornerstone of love.

What was perhaps even harder to digest—he thought very carefully about this now—was that once he'd taken Stephanie, she seemed to regard him as more than a bed partner, someone worthy of respect. He silently basked in that newfound pride, thinking that just maybe there was a chance for them.

But with Flora Marsh's untimely arrival, what secret hopes he might have harbored were effectively crushed. The dismal truth again stared him in the face... he had nothing to offer her except himself—and that wasn't good enough.

Flint heard a second car door slam and immediately climbed down from the rafters. Stephanie had returned. She saw him, and just as her mother had, walked toward him. She didn't stop until she was within touching distance.

"What'cha doing?" she asked in her newly developed East Texas twang.

He didn't respond. Their gazes locked, the pointed tip of Stephanie's tongue circled her lips, wetting them.

"Don't," he groaned, thinking about how that hot tongue had dipped into his navel before going lower...

"Flint." Her voice sounded thin, and her color was high, as if she could read his mind.

He ground down on his back jaw. "You've got company."

"Company? Me?"

"Yes."

"Who?"

"Your mother."

Stephanie's face lost its color. "My mother... here?"

"Yep." His tone was mocking. "And she's come to rescue her baby daughter."

The hostile silence stretched while mother and daughter continued to stare at each other.

Finally Flora said, her voice taking on a cajoling, whining tone, "Surely you don't mean you're actually going to stay here?"

"For the final time, yes, I do."

Stephanie turned her back on Flora and walked to the front window. They were in Flint's living room where they had been for the past thirty minutes. Hardly a kind word had passed between them.

When Flint told her that Flora was here, she was stunned. First David, then her mother. She'd decided she had definitely done something wrong to deserve such punishment.

Flora's unexpected appearance shouldn't have been a surprise. But somehow it was. She hadn't thought her mother cared enough to see firsthand that her only child was all right. But then, Stephanie suspected that wasn't the reason Flora came, although she never got a straight answer out of her.

"Well, I simply won't leave without you, that's all," Flora said to Stephanie's back. "I just can't stand the thought of you being in these woods another minute... or with that... distasteful man."

Stephanie swung around. Her eyes flashed. "God, Mother, you're something else. You didn't even know 'that man' until a few minutes ago. So how can you judge him?"

"Oh, I can judge him all right," Flora replied haughtily, moving to the edge of the couch. "I know all about him. When you told me where you were, I had him checked out."

Stephanie gasped. "You never cease to amaze me."

"Now, darling, don't take that attitude. I did it for your own good."

"I suppose that's why you told David where I was." Stephanie's voice was rich in sarcasm.

"Exactly. You've hurt him badly, and I think you should reconsider. After all, he's our kind—"

"Spare me, Mother. I'm sure you don't know this about your sanctimonious David." Something hard crept into Stephanie's eyes. "But he's so desperate for money to pay off his bookie that he's threatening me because I won't return his aunt's jewelry to him."

Flora raised a hand to her chest. "Oh dear, how awful. Threatening you? I had no idea."

"Oh, really."

Flora colored. "Well, maybe he isn't right for you. But then neither is that—" she broke off, distaste lowering her voice "—drunken, has-been cop."

"Stop! Stop right now!" Stephanie's voice gained strength. "You have no right to say that about him!"

Flora's lips tightened. "The fact that I'm your mother gives me that right. And I know he's not for you. And I don't want you getting involved with the likes of him. It isn't only a question of different backgrounds, Steph."

Her tone grew suddenly warmer. "It goes much deeper than that. Surely you haven't turned a blind eye on how hard, how crudely he lives." A shudder shook her frame. "How you've stayed here as long as you have is beyond me."

"Are you finished now, Mother?" Stephanie demanded coldly.

"Only if you'll admit that it'll take a woman of his own kind who can make him happy."

"You can stop worrying," Stephanie said, scraping over the pain. "Even if I wanted him, he doesn't want me."

"Thank God one of you has some sense."

Stephanie swallowed around the lump in her throat. "Yeah."

"So you are coming with me?" Flora asked, her tone brighter, as if sensing she had won the battle if not the war.

"No. I'll leave in my own good time and not a minute before."

Realizing she had pushed as far as she dared, Flora stood, then crossed to Stephanie. The kiss, when it came, was as cool as her mother's lips. Stephanie forced herself not to flinch.

"I'll expect a call the second you get back to your apartment. We'll have lunch and put this unfortunate episode behind us."

"Take care, Mother," Stephanie said in a flat voice.

Once the Lincoln was nothing but a cloud of dust, Stephanie walked back to the barn. The door to the storeroom was open. Through it, she could see Flint.

"Hi," she said tentatively, standing in the doorway.

He turned slowly, and her heart stumbled. He looked as hard as a statue and just as unyielding.

"It won't work," she said quickly.

His eyes were vacant. "I don't know what you're talking about."

"Yes you do. You're trying to shut me out. Again." She ignored his smirk and went on, "I think we should talk."

"So talk."

"We...we have to come to terms with what...happened between us."

"There's nothing to come to terms with." He scowled.

"I don't believe that, and neither do you."

A vein jumped in his temple. "Where's your mother?"

"Gone."

"I expected you to go with her. She said you didn't belong here, right?"

"Yes, but it doesn't matter what she said. I'm a big girl now. My mother no longer controls my life."

"Sure."

Stephanie gave him a measured look. "I can understand why you'd think differently with her coming on like gangbusters." His smirk was more pronounced this time. "And that's what she did, right?"

"She's a hard woman."

"And one who doesn't know how to love," Stephanie whispered softly. "It's a frightening thing to realize that about your own mother, but I finally did. And when it happened, it set me free."

It was the first time she had admitted out loud the emptiness she had felt as the only child of the autocratic Flora Marsh. Flora had mastered the ability to take from others without giving anything of herself in return. At one time Stephanie had admired that trait. Now it sickened her.

"So back to us," she whispered into the silence.

"Look, just because you're no longer influenced by your mother doesn't change things."

"Yes, it does." A sense of futility filled Stephanie, but she fought against it. "Don't you see—"

"Save it," he spat. "Your mother's right. You don't belong here."

His words were like a hot poker. "Is that Flora talking or you?"

"Me."

The silence in the room suddenly turned into a wall of ice.

"I don't know if you're just too shortsighted," Stephanie said, shaking inside, "or just too pigheaded to see what's right in front of your face!"

With that she turned and flounced to the door.

"Stephanie?"

She eased around, her heart lodged in her throat, hope burning in her eyes. "Yes?"

He opened his mouth, only to close it suddenly. "Forget it."

Pain swept through her. She wrapped her arms around herself and kicked the door closed with a bang.

Sixteen

Two weeks. Such a short time for so much to have happened. A frown slipped across Stephanie's face. Before the crash, life had been relatively simple. Now everything had shifted; she had to cope with a new world. She wondered if her life would ever be the same again. No. Flint had seen to that.

How could she have known that it would be this moody, withdrawn rancher who would steal her heart? But something special had drawn them together, and she had willfully turned her back on the past to follow the overpowering promptings of her heart.

And as foolish as that was, Stephanie was determined to go for the heretofore elusive mother lode—a declaration of love from Flint and subsequent commitment.

With each day that passed, it became more difficult to hide her feelings. She ached to feel his arms around her again, ached to confess her love.

Fear kept her mute. She knew he wanted her, but lust was not the same as love. Time was running out. She couldn't remain where she wasn't wanted much longer.

While this thought weighed on her, Stephanie trudged outside to the swing on the front porch. Instead of sitting down, she walked to the edge of the house and gazed toward the far pasture. Flint and Smitty, barely visible, toiled over another rotting string of fences.

Stephanie had hoped Flint wouldn't work until dark. It looked as if she wasn't going to get her wish. She'd gone to the grocery store earlier and had plans for them to share dinner.

Since her mother's unexpected visit two days ago, she'd only had glimpses of him. He'd planned it that way, she knew. The strain of being under the same roof and not touching told on both of them.

When the two men showed no signs of quitting, she turned away, her shoulders slightly slumped. That was when she saw him. Rage flooded through her. And fear.

David Weston got out of his car, his narrowed eyes targeted on her.

"What are you doing here?" she hissed.

His gait brought him within a hair's breadth of her. "I warned you, remember?"

"You're drunk!" Disgusted, she stepped back.

He grabbed her wrist. "Oh, no, you don't."

"Take your hands off me!"

His hold on her tightened. "No way, baby. Either you give me the money, or I'm going to do something we'll both be sorry for." He slammed her against the side of the house and dug his fingernails into her skin.

At first she hadn't thought he could possibly harm her. She wasn't so sure anymore. She sensed he would derive great pleasure in taking his anger and frustrations out on her. He was demented.

"So what's it going to be?"

His foul breath sprayed her face. She tried to turn away, but he grabbed her chin and held her steady. "Flint will kill you."

"But lover boy's not here." His hands squeezed her shoulders. "It's just you and me, baby."

Lobbing her head to one side, Stephanie struggled for enough breath to try to reason with him. "Please . . . don't hurt me."

Flint blinked the sweat out of his eyes and glanced at his watch. "Let's call it a day, Smitty."

"Okay by me, boss." Sweating as profusely as Flint, Smitty mopped his handlebar mustache with a rag. "I'm bushed."

"Me too. This heat is something else."

Smitty grimaced. "Thought this was spring."

"Yeah, me, too."

They fell silent as they made ready to leave, so tired they could hardly walk. Yet Flint was reluctant to go home.

What to do about Stephanie gnawed at him constantly. He tried to close his thoughts to her.

At the memory of her naked body first touching his, he experienced again the electrifying shock that had gone through him. Then every other aspect of that night flowed hotly as well. In swelling discomfort, he swung onto the back of the gelding.

Smitty mounted his horse, and together they rode toward the house. Flint saw them before they saw him. He pulled up short, and though his face showed no emotion at all, his blood turned to ice water.

"Something wrong, boss?"

"Yeah. Follow me." Flint nudged his animal into a full gallop.

A minute later they rode into the yard. Flint saw Stephanie pinned against the house by that insensitive scumbag. Worse still, Flint knew Weston was aware that riders were approaching, but he didn't release his hold on Stephanie. It seemed as if he was so pumped up, so hellbent on his mission that nothing or no one could stop him.

Primitive rage boiled through Flint. He would have liked nothing better than to beat David Weston to within an inch of his life.

Instead he remained in the saddle and said, "Let her go, Weston."

Breathing heavily, David dropped his hands, turned and glared at Flint. Flint wasn't looking at him; his eyes were on Stephanie.

"Did he hurt you?"

Stephanie drew a deep, shuddering breath and shook her head. "No."

"Now you listen here, Carson, my quarrel isn't with you."

While slowly climbing off his horse, Flint's gaze reverted back to Weston.

"She's got something that belongs to me, and I aim to—"

"Shut up," Flint said softly.

If he had reached out and hit David, the effect could not have been more alarming. David's eyes widened, and his jaw dropped. As he tried to speak, his Adam's apple twitched convulsively in his neck.

"I'm telling you—"

"Only I'm not listening," Flint said in an unruffled voice. He walked toward David with an easy, uncoiling motion. He looked him full in the face, his eyes as cold as metal. "You go on now. Get off my property."

No one said a word. No one moved. Even the air was still.

Finally Flint turned to his ranch hand. "Ah, hell, Smitty, on second thought, call the sheriff. Tell him to come pick up this piece of garbage."

"No...please," David whimpered, and stumbled backward toward his vehicle. "I won't bother her again." His narrow shoulders bent under the burden of humiliation.

"Go on, get the hell outta my sight."

Minutes later, Flint and Stephanie were alone. Stephanie peered at him, her heart reflected in her eyes.

"Don't...don't look at me like that." His voice held torment.

"What next, Flint?" she whispered.

"I...er...just wanted to make sure you were all right."

Flint hadn't been able to stay away from her. After the confrontation with David, Stephanie had showered, then disappeared inside her room where she had remained. She'd told him she wanted to be alone.

As tired as he was, sleep should have been no problem, only it was. It eluded him. So to quiet the beast raging inside him, he'd gone to check on her, to see for himself that she was indeed all right.

She had responded to his knock with a soft "Come in." Now, standing poised in the middle of the room, she stared at him with unwavering eyes. "I'm fine." Her lower lip, however, made a liar out of her; it trembled.

Flint needed no other motivation. He closed the distance between them and swooped her up in his arms.

"Flint?"

Ignoring the husky question, he crossed the room and deposited her on the bed. Whether from exertion or from rising passion, his voice came out a growl. "A little while ago you asked what was next. This is my answer."

He straightened, and with jerky movements stripped off his clothes, then sat back down beside her. Their heads came together, and the consuming hotness of his mouth closed over hers. His hands peeled off her clothing.

They drifted back on the bed and breathlessly played with each other, touching and stroking, and kissing, his lips never far from her flesh.

He pulled his mouth away and said thickly, "Not yet."

She held onto him, a trembling shape in the darkness as he sank his lips onto her breasts with such fierce intensity that it seemed to pull at all her nerve endings.

"Please . . ." she urged, gripping his buttocks.

He raised himself over her, moved his pelvis, then entered her. A moan slipped past her lips, and she twisted her hands around the small of his back and arched against him, pushing his full length inside her until there was nowhere left to go.

"Oh, Flint," she said tremulously, kissing his neck with her open lips and darting tongue. "You . . . you just seem to consume me."

His answering whisper breathed past her ear. "Don't talk, just feel."

To Flint, feeling that soft warmth yield to his bold hardness was a miracle—an ecstasy of awareness that forever increased his pleasure even as it increased his determination to clutch at the intangible something hidden beyond the wall of her giving flesh.

He told himself that it was enough merely to be inside her, but it wasn't enough. He knew it, just as he knew that despite her participation in the act, she, too, sought something beyond the act itself.

"Oh, yes," Stephanie cried, clinging to him, while urgency changed to blind panic as their bodies danced to a climax that endured endlessly, then slowly eased. And they emerged, dazed and spent, but with each heart beating its own endless message.

Before dawn she took him, her lips sliding the length of him, defining him. She wanted desperately for this night never to end, even as he made a guttural sound and reached for her. Then she was flipped into the air so that she was atop him.

From there she rained kisses over his chest, his nipples, while he lifted her effortlessly up and she at last felt him hard inside her. She gasped, but then felt him fill her with such ease that a warmth seeped through her that was only partially sexual, a warmth that encompassed a great deal more.

Time moved unhurried, seeming to pause only at intervals, as if listening for the excited moans, the meaningless murmurs that carried them into the morning's early glow.

"I don't think I could've lasted much longer without this," he murmured when they were spent once again.

"Me neither," she said.

They were quiet for a moment, then Stephanie caressed the ugly scar on his side.

"Nasty, isn't it?"

"Does it hurt?" Stephanie asked, her gaze troubled.

"Not anymore."

"Do you think you'll ever go back?"

"I don't want to."

"Then don't."

He moved out of her arms and stacked his hands behind his head. "It's not that simple. My herd has to bring in some money."

"It will. It just has to. I can't stand the thought of you going back to that horrible job."

"If I had listened to my gut instinct, it might not have ended the way it did."

"You mean the bust."

"Yeah, the bust that went sour."

"Surely they don't blame you."

"No, but I blame myself." Flint paused and breathed deeply. "There was a snitch inside, and I didn't know it."

"Then how could you blame yourself?"

"I knew something was rotten in Denmark, but I didn't listen to instincts."

"Did they finally catch them?"

"Finally."

"It was afterward that . . . your wife left you, wasn't it?"

Although she felt him stiffen, he eventually answered her. "That's right."

"What happened?"

"We were on a collision course from the beginning, I just didn't see it." Regret, rather than pain, roughened his tone. "She wanted 'things' while I wanted kids. So we decided to compromise and wait." He paused.

"Go on," she encouraged, rubbing her hand over his hard, flat belly.

"Then I killed my first person. She couldn't take it. And I was drinking heavily. But the end came when she decided I couldn't keep her in the style to which she was accustomed, so she told me to take a hike. End of story."

Stephanie fought back the tears. "Not every woman is like her, you know?"

He didn't say anything.

"I love you, Flint." There, she'd said it. She had bared her soul to this hard man, and even if he trampled it, she couldn't have not said those words.

"Don't say that . . ." he said brokenly.

"I know you don't love me . . ."

He was so long in responding again that she feared he wasn't going to. Her heart ached.

"But I do love you," he whispered, "only—"

Untold joy swept through her, but the qualifier on the end was a threat to be reckoned with.

"I can make you happy, Flint."

He didn't answer, and she feared he was retreating to his dark thoughts, shutting her out. Determined not to let that happen, she trailed a finger down the side of his face and smiled. "I can also be happy living here."

"You say that now..."

"I'll prove it to you," she said fiercely. "You just wait and see."

Flint's eyes shone as they melted into hers. And then, in response to a signal that struck silently but unerringly, they dived back into each other's arms.

Gone was the probing into a bleak and chilling past. Nothing but their revived need of each other was of importance. He crushed her against him with a pressure born of desperation, and his mouth was over hers like an open furnace. An answering fire flamed within her.

Beyond all restraint, their bodies became one.

Seventeen

An early moon rose above the pines. Flint paused atop his horse and looked as far as the eye could see. Instead of going home, after leaving Ed's house, he'd saddled his gelding and ridden off into the sunset.

His analogy drew a smirk across his lips. John Wayne might have ridden into that proverbial sunset, all right, but he couldn't. Usually, though, an outing such as this calmed the restlessness inside him. Not today.

When he'd brought Stephanie to the ranch, he had had no name for what he sought so feverishly. And with each possession of her body that elusive "something" had returned to taunt him.

When he'd finally put a name to it, he'd been stunned. He'd wanted more than her fiery responses to his body; he'd wanted her to love him.

And now that he had her love, he didn't know what to do with it. Pain lashed through him so intensely it almost took his breath away. He couldn't ask her to marry him. That was out of the question. She didn't belong here no matter what she said. Could he let her go?

He didn't know. He honestly didn't know.

The house was empty without Flint.

Stephanie had spent the better part of the day with Mary. They had visited a friend of Mary's who wanted to sell a bracelet filled with twenty silver heart charms from the 1930s. She had leapt at the chance to buy it and was still extremely excited over her good fortune.

Even now, as she lay on the couch and waited for Flint to come home, she eyed the bracelet. She couldn't wait to call Kathy. For the moment, though, her thoughts were on Flint. Something had to give. She could not continue the emotional tug-of-war with him any longer. She ached to know what the future held for them, or if they even *had* a future.

When they had confessed their love to each other a week ago, Stephanie had hoped they could begin to work toward a future together. She'd known it wouldn't be easy, that it would be a battle, but with love the motivator, anything was possible.

There were times when he lowered that cold facade and allowed her to see another Flint, a lighthearted, talkative one. He was a different person from the surly stranger who had so coldly rebuffed her that day on the plane.

Yesterday's incident jumped to mind, and she found herself smiling. He had insisted she learn to ride a horse. Although she had protested, he'd been adamant. After several unsuccessful attempts, she had finally mastered the technique of handling the gentle mare.

She and Flint had been touring the pasture and had stopped at the pond for the horses to drink when the incident happened. Flint had already dismounted and led his gelding to the nearest tree and was watching her under the brim of his hat. "I think Henrietta has had enough to drink," he had drawled.

Stephanie had turned, flashed him a smile, then patted the mare on the side. "No, she hasn't. Can't you see how thirsty she is?"

"Doesn't matter. It's not a good idea to let 'em drink too much too fast."

"Oh, all right," Stephanie said, pulling on the reins. "But it sounds like cruel and unusual punishment to me."

He harrumphed. "It's cruel and unusual punishment if you don't—"

"Oh, my God!" Her terrified scream cut off his sentence. "What's she doing! What's happening!"

The horse had paid no attention to her hard jerk on the reins and was wading deeper into the water.

"No! Stop!" she cried, yanking even harder on the leather straps.

Stephanie's panicked cry went unheeded. Flint reached the bank just as the horse rolled over and unceremoniously dumped her in the water.

"Oh!" she wailed, feeling her tennis shoes sink into the mud. She struggled to maintain her footing.

Flint stood with his arms crossed and peered down at her. "Mmm, nice day for a swim," he said, a grin tacked on his face.

"Why...you...you...!"

"Tut, tut." His grin broadened. "Don't say it. Don't even think it."

"But...but," Stephanie spluttered, placing her hands on her hips and aching to slap that smug grin off his face.

Flint threw back his head and laughed.

"Don't you dare laugh at me, you big bully."

"If you could only see yourself."

"I don't want to see myself! I know I look a horrible mess, thanks to you and that...that horse..." She gave Henrietta a scathing glare. "Why'd she do that to me, anyway?" she asked, extending her hand to Flint so he could pull her out. "I never did anything to her."

He laughed again. "Ah, don't take offense. That's just her way of telling you how much she likes you."

"Sure." She cut another glance at the mare and muttered. "You big dummy."

Flint's warm chuckle drew her back to him. His eyes moved over her, made her conscious that her wet T-shirt clearly outlined her full breasts and distended nipples.

A scorching heat flooded through her.

He cleared his throat. "Speaking of lying down."

"Here?" Her limbs felt suddenly boneless.

"Why not?"

Stephanie looked around and noticed how secluded they were. "No. . . reason."

He grinned and reached for her. "I kinda thought you'd see it my way. . ."

While there had been other tender moments, there had also been other dark ones. The old wall would suddenly appear, and he'd shut her out. Except physically. Flint's appetite for her was insatiable, as hers was for him. The nights found them linked passionately, exploring each other anew, with only the briefest of respites.

But that wasn't enough. She wanted more. She wanted a full commitment and would not settle for less.

The sudden jangle of the phone shattered her thoughts, which was just as well, she told herself.

"Oh, hi, Kat," she said after a moment. "I was just going to call you." She eased down on the couch. "You'll never guess what I found today. . ."

She was in the middle of describing the treasure when she felt an odd sensation climb her spine. Clutching the receiver, she spun around. Flint stood in the doorway, an odd expression on his face.

"Kat, look, I'll call you back in a minute, okay?"

Once the call was terminated, she stood and gave Flint a wobbly smile. "You're home," she said inanely.

"You miss your work, don't you?"

"Of course I do, but—"

"Then maybe you ought to go back."

A sudden tension gripped her. "We're not talking about my job here, are we?

"No." The reply came in a strained growl.

"So what are you saying, Flint?" Was he telling her to go? No! She wasn't ready for that.

"Stephanie..." Flint shook his head, his thoughts taking trails she could not follow.

Helplessness threatened to destroy her composure. She had only one recourse and that was to say the only thing that had any meaning in this endless moment of pain.

"I love you, Flint," she whispered brokenly. "You know that, don't you?"

He stared gravely at her for a long moment, then let his hard-held breath out like a sigh. "Yes," he said. "I'm afraid I do."

"Don't be afraid, my darling. I'm not."

He turned away in slow degrees, as if he couldn't bear to look into her eyes.

"You... told me you loved me," she said, squeezing the words out.

He twisted back around, and she watched as that closed look wiped all expression from his face.

"What is it you want from me?" he asked.

"I have to know where I stand with you," she cried in a low voice. "I have to know what you're prepared to give."

"That's just it," he said tonelessly. "I have nothing to give."

"You have yourself."

"And you deserve better. Don't you understand, I can't give you what you're used to, what you need."

"I don't want things, I want you."

"You say that now, but what about later?"

Stephanie hardly breathed. "For God's sake, my love for you isn't some passing fancy."

"What happens if I decide ranching isn't for me? Or better yet, what if I can't make a go of this place? Then what?" His eyes flared in his weathered face. "Well, I'll tell you what. I'll have to go back to the agency, and I wouldn't ask another woman to go through that again."

"Are you . . . going back to the agency?"

"I don't know."

"Well, we'll just have to cross that bridge when we come to it."

He shoved blunt fingernails through his hair. "It's not that simple."

"I'm not like your ex-wife, Flint," she said in a soft choked voice.

"You think I don't know that?" His voice sounded warped. "Oh, hell, maybe we should discuss this tomorrow."

Stephanie turned her back on him, feeling sick. That something special between them had disappeared and had left only a room full of emptiness. She had never felt so unwanted and useless.

"There won't be a tomorrow, Flint." Her voice faded until it eased altogether. But she wouldn't cry. She wouldn't give him the satisfaction. Still, it was an effort to speak again. "You're right, there's nothing here for me."

"There never was. I tried to tell you that, only you wouldn't listen."

The silence of the room became a cold and alien thing that clamped down around them and held them helpless.

Tragedy had thrown them together. Desire had kept them together. Now harsh pride was parting them.

Stephanie put a hand to her throat. In that soundless void, her voice, when it finally came, sounded raw and loud. "Not only are you a fool, Flint Carson, but you're a coward. A damned coward!"

"Stephanie . . ." Her name came out an agonized cry.

She left without another word.

Eighteen

"**Y**ou won't believe it!"

Stephanie turned from the filing cabinet and stared at Kathy Gentry. "Won't believe what?"

They were in Stephanie's cubbyhole of an office. She had been trying to get some much-needed book work done, but as usual she found it hard to concentrate.

"Get this. Mrs. Hoffman bought that Battenbury tablecloth and matching napkins." The scattering of freckles across Kathy's nose stood out, calling attention to her pert features. "Yeah, that old tightwad finally coughed up some real cash."

Stephanie's lips twitched. "You shouldn't talk about Mrs. Hoffman like that."

"Why?" Kathy quipped with a grin. "It's the truth, and *you* know it."

A smile lit Stephanie's entire face. "Did she really pay cash?"

"As in the cold, hard kind." Kathy paused and cocked her head slightly. "You know that's the first time I've seen you really smile in two months."

Stephanie sighed. "I'm sorry I've been such a pain in the butt."

"Hey, you don't owe me an apology. I know you're going through a private hell right now. I just wish there was something I could do to help."

"You have. You've kept the store afloat, and you've been my friend." Stephanie had confided in Kathy up to a point about Flint and their relationship simply because she hadn't been able to keep it bottled inside her.

"I've loved doing both."

Stephanie took a deep breath and changed the subject. "Don't I have something I'm supposed to do this afternoon?"

"Yep. A meeting with a pawnshop dealer in Lufkin about that garnet necklace."

Stephanie snapped her fingers. "That's right. And I should be leaving shortly, too."

They discussed several other items of business, then Kathy left. Stephanie stared at her desk, thinking she ought to straighten it. But she didn't; she walked to the window and stared outside. Instead of seeing the tall buildings that lined the city streets, she saw tall trees, a pasture strewn with wildflowers and cattle. And in the midst of that, she saw a horse and rider.

In an effortless gesture, she summoned Flint before her. His face was so vivid in its nearness that she clearly saw the thick-lashed eyes, the sensual lips framing words she couldn't understand. Suddenly she was seized by an inexplicable panic.

Would she ever fill the void in her life that losing him had created? She closed her eyes and felt the ever-present sadness gnaw at her. After returning to her apartment in Houston, she had been both furious and heartbroken.

But it was the former that had given her the grit to finally say to hell with him. If he didn't want her, she didn't want him.

Too, there had been the niggling at the back of her mind that maybe there was truth in what he had said. Maybe she did belong to the city, among the bright lights, the parties, the loud and boisterous friends.

Only they were both wrong. Dead wrong. When she couldn't function after dreaming of him every night—of his hungry kisses, of his groans as he took her, sometimes tender, sometimes savage, the laughter when it came—she knew she no longer belonged here. She belonged with him. She belonged *to* him. And without him, her life was an empty shell.

Yet through all the pain and despair, she had harbored hope that he would come to his senses, see what he was throwing away with so little thought. But when the hours stretched into days and the days into months, that hope vanished.

Around her friends, which included Mary Liscomb, who had visited her twice, her customers and her mother, she put on a brave front. But she hadn't fooled anyone. Even Flora had tempered her tone and seemed genuinely worried about her.

And with good reason, because she never slowed down. Work was her panacea for coping, for getting up each morning. And though Collections by Stephanie's bank account reflected this hard work, it had taken its toll. Her bones ached. Her appetite diminished. And the loneliness was poison inside her.

Still, she'd known then, just as she knew now, that she had done the right thing. Unless he could return her love, she was better off without him. And soon he wouldn't mean any more to her than a stranger on the street.

But not today.

"Stephanie."

Startled, she spun around.

"Sorry," Kathy said, "but you told me not to let you forget your appointment."

"Thanks. I'm on my way."

A few minutes later, purse in hand, she forced her shoulders back and walked into the waning sunlight.

For two weeks Flint stayed close to the ranch, though he spent more hours brooding than he did working. He took care of his cattle because he had to, and when he could choke it down, he ate a little food.

He turned into a mere caricature of his former self. Weight fell off him. His eyes became listless, sunken caves carving his cheekbones deeper, and his skin had lost much of its tan.

Where once he'd moved with catlike agility, he now trudged heavy-footed.

"How much longer do you intend to keep this up?"

Flint didn't so much as flinch at the sound of Ed's voice, nor did he bother to look up. Instead, he swung the ax until the piece of pine looked like chop suey. "As long as it takes, I reckon."

"Care to talk?"

"Nope." Flint paused and wiped his face across his sleeve. "Just got an itch I can't scratch, that's all."

Ed rested his arms across his pot belly. "I guess that's one way of puttin' it. But we both know what that itch is, don't we?"

"Ed, I'm not in the mood for this small talk crap."

"So I won't make small talk. I'll hit you with the big stuff. You're a fool."

Flint laughed without humor. "Tell me something I don't know."

A long, heavy silence followed.

At last Ed said, "Mary's seen her twice."

Flint's jaws tightened. He went right on with his chore.

Ed watched him a moment longer, then with a disgusted shake of his head, he turned and stamped off.

"How . . . how is she?"

Ed halted, then eased back around. "She loves you just as you are, you know, only you're too damned dimwitted to see that."

Not bothering to wait for a reply, Ed turned again and ambled off, leaving Flint staring at him with his mouth gaping open.

Bone weary, Flint made his way toward the house. But when he reached the back door, he froze.

He couldn't do it. He couldn't walk across that threshold again and face the emptiness inside. He looked toward the sun quickly, seeking it's warmth for his chilled body. But on the other side of that door there was no sunlight to relieve the darkness inside his soul or blot out the loneliness that touched every nerve in his body and held him captive.

Stephanie was everywhere—her face, her smell, her laughter—on the back of his eyelids, in his cup of coffee and in every room in the house.

Turning, he stumbled down the steps and over to the nearest tree. He faced the sun once again, while tears streamed down his cheeks.

What was he going to do? How was he going to keep living without her? Had Ed leveled with him? Did she love him for what he was, not for what he should be? Dare he hope? Dare he take the chance? In that instant the decision came. He knew not how or why. He knew only he couldn't exist another day without her.

He had to try to right a terrible wrong. He had to bring her back. Then he had to prove that he wasn't the coward she thought he was, that having her beside him, if only for one day, was better than not having her at all.

But all of the above entailed work and a sacrifice of further patience. He had to fix up the house, make it worthy of her. He had to finish the barn, manicure the lawns and pastures beyond, and sell his herd . . .

A tall order, but he could do it. *He would do it.*

He secured his Stetson on his head, turned on his heels and strode toward the barn. For the first time in a long while, there was a confident swagger to Flint's step.

Flint didn't know how long he'd sat in the pickup before he mustered enough nerve to get out and walk to the front door.

Still he hesitated. It had been four months since he'd sent Stephanie away. What if he'd waited too long? What if she'd stopped loving him?

What was at stake with this visit sent the blood rushing to his head. God, but it ached, as though two boxers were slugging it out inside. Nor could he seem to get a decent breath and keep it.

When he reached the front door and touched the brass knob, he noticed his hand shook. His newfound courage began to slip. He dug deep for another breath, ignoring his heart tripping like a jackhammer, and his legs trembled as though he'd run the few yards instead of walking.

He rubbed his thigh with a sweaty palm, then knocked on the door. No response. He knocked harder and longer. Still no answer. He poised his fist to strike again when the door opened. The next instant he was face-to-face with Stephanie.

"For crying out loud . . . you don't," she began hotly, only to end in a faltering whisper, "knock . . . the door down," and stood there, her face chalk white.

The silence that enveloped them was so complete, it was deafening. Flint used the opportunity to drink in the sight of her. Though more slender than he remembered, and the bruised circles under her eyes more pronounced, she was still as lovely as ever.

At last, and into the oppressive stillness, he dropped his voice, but it seemed very far away. "Hello, Stephanie."

Her lips scarcely moved. "Good . . . evening."

The frigid formality in her tone locked his throat against further speech. Flint shifted positions, then cleared his throat, the sound harsh and raw in his ears. "Aren't you going to ask me in?"

"Why should I?"

He stood there, dying on the inside. His worst fears had come to pass and he had lost. She behaved like a statue carved out of ice. Those enormous blue eyes held no warmth. They were fixed on him with such contempt that Flint felt a corrosive acid burn his insides.

Desperate to free himself from the paralysis crippling him, he forced words around the constriction in his throat, only to discover his superhuman effort had produced only a rasping whisper.

"The reason I know is because . . ." he began, and felt his throat close completely.

"Go on."

Stephanie's voice was clear and utterly detached. She wasn't going to make it easy.

". . . I love you and want to marry you," he said in another raspy whisper.

"What?" Her lips moved stiffly.

He stepped closer, but still he didn't touch her. "Oh, God, Steph, can you forgive me for being such a fool?"

Her composure crumpled, and two big tears trickled down her face. "Oh, Flint."

Matching tears rolled down his cheeks. "I'll make it up to you, I promise."

"Will you just shut up, you big jerk." And having said that, she cried, "Oh, Flint! Please hold me. I won't believe this until you do!"

She need not have asked. He was already reaching for her.

Rain fell.

Flint dreamed of Stephanie; her flesh was moist and cool, as if it had been rained on.

He felt movement beside him suddenly, and his eyes opened. He hadn't been dreaming. The flesh-and-blood Stephanie was beside him, her long, smooth limbs tangled with his hard-muscled ones. His heart leapt, and he smiled. And remembered.

For the first time ever, he felt good inside, free of pain, whole. *Love could do that,* she had whispered a while ago when she was on top, with him rising strong and gloved in her warmth.

"Flint..."

He shifted so that he could gaze down at her. "Mmm?"

"Hi," she whispered, moving closer to him.

His flesh trembled. "Hi, yourself."

"What are you thinking?"

"About how much I love you and how close I came to losing you."

"You know that I never worried about your lack of 'things.'"

"I do now. So will you marry me?"

"When?"

He chuckled. "God, woman, you're easy."

"What can I say?" Stephanie quipped saucily. "I think it'd be nice to get married at Ed and Mary's."

"That is a good idea." His eyes turned serious. "By the way, I have a surprise for you."

"I hate surprises."

"Naw, all women love surprises."

She nipped him on the shoulder. "So tell me."

"See there, you can't stand it." Flint tweaked her on the nose before going on, "I remodeled the house and finished the barn."

She scooted up, cradled her head in her hand and peered down at him. "You did? But...how...so quickly?"

"Ed and Mary and Smitty." He grinned. "I've been such a tight ass, they were all about ready to ship me off with the next load of cattle."

She kissed his shoulder this time, and he groaned. "Missed me, huh?"

"More than you'll ever know."

"Me, too."

"What about your mother?"

Stephanie grew pensive for a moment. "I hope in time she'll come around." She broke off with a grin. "Actually I'm counting on your charm to win her over."

He made a growling noise in his throat, then answered her grin with one of his own. "I'll give it my best shot, but I'm making no promises. Your mother is something else."

"I know." She was quiet for a moment. "What... about the agency?"

"I'm not going back."

Her relief was obvious. "Have you told Lee?"

"Nope, but I'm going to when I invite him to the wedding."

"Regardless of what you decided, I would've supported you."

"Thank you for saying that." His voice was thick.

She drummed her fingers softly against his thighs.

"I can't think when you do that."

"I know," she said weakly.

Flint swallowed and forced himself to say what was in his heart. "Even though my cattle's in great demand, we won't be rich, but we won't starve, either." His eyes held a sober question mark.

"Course we won't, silly. I plan to work, too. I've been thinking about opening up a small store in Crockett."

"What about Houston?"

"Kathy thinks she can scrape together the funds to buy me out."

"Whatever it takes to make you happy, I'm all for it."

"Oh, Flint, I love you," she said with soft sweetness.

"And I love you."

"Kiss me." Her tone held sudden urgency. "Please."

Her eyes fluttered closed as his open mouth came down over hers. On fire, she moved her fingers down the rigid contours of his back while he shifted her hips back into steamy contact with his groin.

"I love you," she muttered breathlessly.

"I'll make you happy."

Their tongues flickered and met. There was an exquisite pain inside Flint as she circled her buttocks against him. "You already have, my darling," he ground out thickly.

When they were able to talk again, he whispered, "Are you ready to go home?"

Stephanie's features were suddenly wreathed in a radiant smile. "I thought you'd never ask."

* * * * *

word in action, but we won't argue, either." His eyes held
a sober question mark.

A Note from Paula Detmer Riggs

All books have a genesis, a moment when the writer
asks herself "what if." *Forgotten Dream* came from
just such a moment. "What if" a man and woman
meet, fall in love and then are parted under painful
circumstances? Nothing unusual in that, right?

But "what if" his memory of that time in his life is
suddenly erased? Does that love remain buried in his
psyche? Are there shadows in his soul that he doesn't
understand? And then, the biggest "what if" of all, does
the heart remember what the mind has forgotten? Those
were all the "what ifs" rocketing around in my head
when I sat down to write the story of Susanna and Mat.

Most authors I know do extensive research before
sitting down to write that first word, and I did more
than my share for *Forgotten Dream*. I found, for
example, that memory can be selective and
inexplicable. Momentous events can be blurred by the
more vivid remembrance of trifles. Significant
happenings can be forgotten for years, then flashed into
conscious thought by the most insignificant occurrence.
Memory can be triggered by a scent, a special touch, a
loving smile. On the other hand, memory can elude the
most passionate demand. These are just a few of the
paradoxes that confront Susanna and Mat as one
struggles to forget, while the other tries desperately to
remember.

I found *Forgotten Dream* to be a different kind of love
story, dealing with many facets of love and loss. I hope
you will, too.

Paula Detmer Riggs

FORGOTTEN DREAM

Paula Detmer Riggs

For Matthew

Prologue

He was drifting, disconnected from everything but the hot throbbing in his head. He heard someone groan. The voice was familiar. His.

He fought to clear his head. Where was he? What happened? Gray wisps of memory floated just beyond his reach, like artillery smoke. Nothing was clear; nothing made sense. The last thing he remembered was a blinding light, then vicious, twisting pain.

When was that? This morning? Yesterday? Why was he here, flat on his back in this cold place?

He tried to sit up, but he couldn't move. Panic pierced the thick fog that held him, and he cried out. He couldn't feel his arms or his legs, only the bayonet jabs stabbing his head.

Through the torment he heard a voice—soft, sweet, like soothing music. Gentle as a spring shower. He had heard...once...when...?

"Susanna?" His voice was a raspy groan pushing through his parched throat and cracked lips. He swallowed, tried to beg her to come closer, but the words wouldn't come.

Her image floated just beyond his field of vision, her slender arms outstretched, urging him to come back to her. Her smile warmed the cold places inside him. Her laughter filled him with happiness for the first time in his life. Her eyes, softly shimmering with vibrant life, pulled him into their golden depths until his soul touched hers.

For so long he had tried to forget. Years and years. But always she was there, an ache in his gut that never left him, no matter where he was or what he was doing. He was so tired of hurting. If he could just find her...

Opening his eyes a crack, he searched for her. The room was blinding white, so white it hurt his eyes. He tried to turn away from the glare, but it was all around him.

"It's okay, Sergeant Cruz. You're safe now." The voice was calm—a woman's voice. Different from the one he sought. Desperately he tried to focus on the face wavering in front of him, but the image moved in and out.

He narrowed his gaze, wet his cracked lips. "What...where...?" He couldn't seem to make the words come out right. Was this a dream? A nightmare? Why couldn't he move?

"You're in Walter Reed Hospital, Sergeant. You're going into surgery soon. Everything will be fine. Try to relax. The shot I just gave you will kick in soon."

No, he thought, fighting against the numbness that held him prisoner. He had to find her. To tell her...to explain...to beg her to forgive him.

He couldn't let her go. Not again. This time it would kill him. But even as he struggled, a suffocating cloud closed over him, carrying him into blessed oblivion.

"What did he say?" one nurse asked the other as they wheeled the unconscious soldier into the OR.

"Something about a letter. I didn't catch it all."

"Who's Susanna? I thought his wife's name was Trina."

"It was. Not that it matters, though. After the surgeon gets done fishing the bomb fragments from his brain, he'll be lucky if he remembers his own name."

Three weeks later, when Staff Sergeant Mateo Cruz woke up again, the only thing he remembered was the pain.

Chapter 1

Susanna Spencer was exhausted. She'd been awake and on her feet for almost forty hours, delivering two babies in as many days. This little one was taking his time, she thought with a weary glance toward the first rays of the sun shimmering through the dusty window. The last hour had been the worst—for both her and the weary young woman in the sagging iron bed.

Pressing her gloved hand against the ache in the small of her back, she forced life into her low husky voice. "We're almost there, Robin. Don't give up on me now, honey. Remember what you learned in class. Breathe with the pain."

A low moan answered her as seventeen-year-old Robin Clearwater struggled to bring her first child into the world. Her young husband, Romero, held her hand, his broad copper face stiff with worry. Both were residents of the Santa Ysabel Pueblo in central New Mexico, where Susanna had been the midwife for the past five years. Romero, like his father and grandfather before him, had been born in this bed, in this room.

The crude adobe dwelling had no plumbing, no electricity, no telephone. The only light came from three kerosene lanterns burning on a rickety table by the bed. The only heat came from the wood-burning stove in the corner.

Years of poor nutrition had made Robin's body unsuited for childbearing. Susanna had tried to convince the frail young mother to deliver her baby in the clinic. However, Romero had stubbornly insisted that his son be born on his ancestral land. He and Susanna had exchanged heated words several times about the danger, but she hadn't been able to change his mind.

Although the baby hadn't been due for two more weeks, Susanna had become more and more worried about Robin. Yesterday, even though she had just spent a day and a night delivering another woman's baby miles from the Clearwater ranch, on a hunch she had gone to the primitive little house. She had arrived to find Robin in hard labor, with only Romero to help.

"That's it, Mama," Susanna intoned, trying to keep her voice above a whisper. "Breathe into the pain."

Her dark brown hair, dampened by the sweat dotting her forehead, framed her pale face with waiflike ringlets, making her look nearly as young as the teenage mother-to-be, even though she would be thirty in the spring.

But unlike Robin, her body, though small, had already acquired the sensuous ripeness of motherhood. Her breasts were full and rounded, although her child had long ceased suckling. Her waist, though trim, bore a womanly curve, and her hips carried a generous fullness above the long length of her slender thighs.

"Push, Robin," she ordered, her lilting voice pitched low. "Now. That's it, push harder."

Wiping the sweat from her eyes with the sleeve of her sterile gown, she crouched between Robin's legs, nervously biting her lip. No matter how many babies she brought into the world, she still experienced a moment of panic just before the baby came into her hands.

"*Push!*"

With one final straining effort from the panting mother-to-be, the tiny infant slid into Susanna's gloved hands. "A boy!" Susanna cried. "And he's perfect!"

Her mouth curved into a tired grin behind the mask covering half of her face. The baby had sturdy shoulders and a little barrel chest, with a full head of silky black hair and a broad face that marked his Native American heritage.

His satiny skin was still wet and warm from the womb, and his tiny hands were clenched into miniature fists, as though he had come prepared to fight. Susanna quickly removed the fluid from his mouth, then gently rubbed his back, watching anxiously for the first breath to fill the round chest.

Her delighted smile disappeared abruptly. Nothing was happening. Adrenaline flooded her veins, but she forced herself to remain clam. She laid him on his back, arching his head backward to open his windpipe. Then, jerking down her mask, she placed her mouth over his and breathed. She removed her mouth, waited, her heart pounding in her throat. Still nothing.

A chill took her, even though the room was warm. She had less than four minutes before the lack of oxygen would damage the child's brain—if he lived at all.

As she bent her head to the baby's mouth again, Susanna heard Robin's frantic voice begging her to save her baby.

She had no time to reassure the frightened young couple. If the baby lived, there would be no need. If he didn't . . .

Working methodically, she breathed life into the still, little body. Over and over the small chest fluttered, then grew deathly still again.

Fighting tears and exhaustion, Susanna refused to believe she had lost him. "Breathe, baby," she pleaded hoarsely, shaking him. "Please breathe. Don't give up on me. Not now."

She started to lower her head again, but just then, as though responding to her desperate cry, the baby jerked. His minuscule lashes fluttered as he opened his mouth and sucked in. His chest expanded, filling with life-giving oxygen. His solemn-featured face wrinkled into an intense baby frown a second before he started to cry.

The blue tint faded from his coppery skin, replaced by a warm pink tinge. He waved his tiny fist in the air, and the pink deepened to an angry red. With each wail, he gained strength, until the room seemed to reverberate with his lusty squalling.

Susanna grinned, even as her soft mouth trembled in relief. "Listen to him bawl," she murmured with a laugh. "Baby has a temper."

Robin's face relaxed into a shaky smile. "Like his papa," she murmured, clinging tightly to her husband's hand.

Romero's face was flushed, but his features were composed. Like most men of the tribe, he was reluctant to show strong emotion in public.

"A son," he said in a low voice. "I have a son."

"Indeed you do," Susanna murmured, stripping off her mask and gloves and throwing them into the plastic bag she had waiting. "And by the look of that square little chin, you're going to have your hands full."

Romero's strong throat worked. "If you hadn't come when you did—" He bit off his words, a grim expression tightening his face. "I was wrong."

"Robin and the baby are fine. That's what counts."

She took a deep breath, fighting the sudden urge to lie down next to Robin and close her eyes. Forcing strength into her tired body, she bathed the baby's face, her fingers stiff from fatigue.

"You did it, Mama," she told Robin as she swaddled the now whimpering infant in a soft, sweet-smelling blanket and tidied his straight silky hair with her fingers. "I'm proud of you."

Robin tried to return the smile, but failed. "Thank you," she whispered, her voice choked with fatigue and emotion. "You brought back our son from the dead."

Romero cleared his throat. "My table will always have a place for you," he told her with formal courtesy in Tewa, the language of his people.

"Just take good care of baby. That's all the thanks I need." She raised the swaddled infant to her shoulder and closed her eyes. Just for a second or two, she promised herself. Not enough time to feel the stirring of love for another woman's child, but long enough to feel his sweet warmth. This was the only payment she needed, the only reward that mattered. A new little life, perfect and special.

The baby's whimpers subsided. He turned his head into her neck and began to suck on one wrinkled fist. She lowered her chin to rest lightly on his dewy crown. The tiny boy hiccuped, then sighed. He tried to snuggle against her. A deep sadness settled in her heart, reminding her of the still, dark emptiness that was always inside her.

"Go to Mama, sweetie," she whispered as she settled the baby into his mother's arms. Robin was so lucky, she thought. Lucky to have a new son. Lucky to have a man who loved her.

As soon as Susanna removed her hands from the baby's back, he opened his eyes and began to wail. Robin looked up helplessly. "What should I do?" she asked in a tremulous voice.

"Rub his back. He just needs to know his mama loves him." Sadness, black and limitless, touched Susanna briefly before she forced it away. This was a time for rejoicing, not bitterness.

Robin began stroking her son's back as the proud father looked on with anxious dark eyes. Gradually the shrill cries subsided into sleepy silence. Robin pressed a gentle kiss against the baby's head, then looked up.

"You should have children, Susanna," she said softly. "You love them so much."

"Maybe someday," she said with false cheer. "Right now I'm too busy taking care of other expectant mamas." She rubbed her hands over her arms, trying to force life into the tired muscles. She couldn't remember when she had eaten last. Or had eight hours of uninterrupted sleep. She fought off a yawn.

"You three need some time together before I finish up. And I need some fresh air to wake me up."

She shrugged into her warm denim jacket and left the small house, closing the door softly behind her. The early-morning air smelled of drenched sagebrush and damp earth.

Huddled against the chill, she walked slowly toward her Jeep. To the east, the sun was an orange circle in the dark dawn sky, sending lonely shadows over the pebbly sand.

Beyond the towering red wall of the mesa, the residents of Santa Ysabel were waking up. The women would be preparing fry bread and bitter coffee for breakfast, and the men would be feeding goats and sheep, or mucking out horse stalls. But out here on the edge of the pueblo, the only sounds were the whistle of the wind through the aspen leaves and the cackling of the chickens in the pen below.

Leaning wearily against the Jeep's dust-coated fender, she let the familiar sounds settle around her. She had healed in this place. Even though she had lived half her life in Albuquerque, she belonged here. The quiet mornings and simple ways of the people were a part of her soul.

Hunching the woolly collar of her jacket closer to her neck, she lifted her face to the wind coming down from the north. Tendrils of warm brown hair escaped the haphazard knot on top of her head and blew across her cheek.

She closed her eyes, savoring the pungent smells she detected in the cool breeze. Sage blossom, burning mesquite from countless fires, dying leaves.

Autumn had come early to New Mexico. Halloween was more than a month away, yet the leaves were already turning. Soon the snow would come, softening the harsh contours of the mesas.

According to long-established custom, winter on the pueblo was a time of reflection, a time for family and friends, a time to renew one's spiritual ties with the mystical forces of the universe that had guided the lives of The People for countless centuries.

She had been thirteen that first winter when her widowed father, an artist of great promise but few sales, had married Hannah Charley, a woman of the tribe with two daughters of her own.

Having grown up in the city, Susanna had been ill-prepared for the slow, often archaic life of an Indian pueblo. At first she had been appalled by the primitive living conditions and near-poverty level of existence.

For centuries the land had remained the same, awakening slowly, in rhythm with nature and its never-changing cycles.

The people were as unchanging as the land. The Spanish conquerors had given the people surnames and horses, and in a few cases a new religion. But most of the beliefs practiced within the boundaries of the reservation had their origins in antiquity. The medicine man was as important as any priest. Women were revered for their ability to bring forth new life and were accorded a special place in pueblo life. Men owned only their clothes and their saddles. Women held claim to everything else. Even the duplex Susanna lived in—and still did—had belonged to her stepmother and another woman who lived in the other half.

Her name was Lily Cruz. She had one son. Mateo.

Susanna had often seen pictures of the handsome young soldier with the laughing eyes and sexy smile, but she had never met him—until that summer when Lily died suddenly and he came home on emergency leave to attend her funeral.

Her stepsisters had talked a lot about the good-looking army corporal that summer. "None of the unmarried girls are allowed to be alone with him," ten-year-old Spring had whispered, her eyes glittering with fascination.

"Mother says he's wild, like a stallion running on the range," Summer had chimed in. "Not even the strongest woman can tame him."

But Susanna had known better. From the moment they'd met, she had been enthralled by Mat. They spent long, secret hours together, walking and talking, or simply holding hands and enjoying the beauty of the land around them.

Tough and taciturn with others, Mat listened to her in a way that made her feel as though she could trust him with her deepest secrets and most fragile hopes.

Shy herself, she had been used to the awkward fumbling of boys, but Mat was a man. He took instead of asked, but he also made her want to purr and smile and sing at the same time.

For three wonderful weeks her world had been defined by Mat and his kisses. Nothing mattered more than the time they spent together. He wanted her, and she wanted him.

When they made love for the first time, her world took on the rainbow hues of perfect happiness. To protect her reputation he had insisted upon keeping their love affair secret. With a thoughtfulness that made her love him even more, he had taken care to ensure she wouldn't get pregnant.

"Neither of us is ready for that, sweet Susie," he'd said before kissing away her fears.

When his leave had been up, he'd promised to write. When he hadn't, she'd made excuses for him. Mat loved her, she'd assured herself over and over. He wouldn't lie to her. Six weeks later Susanna discovered that the precautions had failed. Mat had gotten her pregnant.

Church-mouse poor and only nineteen, she'd been terrified. And yet, she had wanted the baby desperately. Her lively imagination began spinning out a wonderful life for the two of them. Mat would come home, and they would be married. He would take care of her and their child. They would be a family. She believed in Mat. She believed in love.

She had been a fool.

A scavenging crow screeched in the distance. Susanna shuddered and averted her face from the wind that seemed to grow sharper by the minute.

For nearly six weeks she had known this day would arrive. For six weeks she had been fighting the urge to pack her belongings into her Jeep and leave this place she loved.

After ten long years, Mateo Cruz was coming home.

"...and Aurora Olvera called about her appointment next Friday. She has to go to Gallup that day and needs to reschedule."

Stifling a yawn, Susanna scribbled Aurora's name at the bottom of the long list of calls she needed to return. It was nearly ten. As soon as she had walked through the door of her duplex, she'd called the receptionist at the clinic for her messages.

"Anything else?" she asked the woman on the other end of the line.

She heard the sound of an exaggerated sigh. "Nothing else, except that I'm in love."

So what else is new? she wondered privately. Lupe Becenti was eighteen and cute as a spring lamb. She was also man-crazy.

"I thought you were bored with Ralph Horse Herder." Susanna rested her elbow on the desk and leaned against the receiver, letting her eyes drift closed.

"Forget Ralph. I'm talking about our new Police Chief."

Susanna's eyes opened with a snap, and her head came up so fast her senses whirled. "He's here already?" The question was out before she could stop it.

"Is he ever! I saw him arrive when I was walking to work." This time Lupe's sigh sounded more like a moan. "I read all the stories in the paper, didn't you? About how he almost died when that bomb exploded under his car and all. In Colombia or Bolivia or one of those South American countries where they're having all those drug wars."

"Brazil," Susanna corrected, staring at the words on her pad. They wavered in front of her, and she closed her eyes tightly. "He was on duty at the embassy there."

"Whatever. Anyway, it was so awful, all that blood, and his poor wife being killed 'cause she was driving instead of him."

Susanna opened her eyes and raised her gaze to the ceiling. Her eyes stung. "If that's all the messages—"

"People say he was in the hospital for months and months," Lupe continued as though she hadn't heard. "You can tell, too, 'cause he walks with this sexy limp, and he has scars on his face, not bad ones exactly, only you can't help but notice them. My sister said he was the best-looking boy in her class. All the girls were crazy about him. 'Course, now, he's not what you'd call handsome, but there's something about him, like those guys in the movies who're always taking on the bad guys alone because everyone else is too scared."

Susanna felt herself stiffen. "Take my advice, Lupe. Stay away from Mat Cruz." Her voice came out fast and harsh, but she was too tired to care. "He's not your type."

There was a sudden pause. When Lupe spoke again, her voice was sharp with curiosity. "Hey, this sounds interesting, Ms. Spencer. I didn't know you knew him."

Susanna cursed the rash impulse that had made her want to protect her young friend. "Forget I said anything," she said, suppressing a sigh. "I need a nice long nap."

"Rough night, huh?"

"Two rough nights—and days." She glanced toward the bundle of soiled surgical scrubs she had dropped by the front door. Tomorrow or the next day she had to find time in her crowded schedule for a trip to the Laundromat in Chamisa.

"One more thing, Lupe. Please tell Dr. Greenleaf that Robin Clearwater will bring her baby in tomorrow for a postnatal exam. I've already signed the birth certificate."

Lupe repeated the message in the precise way Susanna had taught her. One of the first things she'd learned when she'd first started delivering babies was meticulous accuracy. A mislaid call from a client could lead to terrible consequences.

"What time will you be in?" Lupe asked when she finished.

Susanna glanced down at her khaki pants. Two days ago they had been crisply ironed, and her blouse had smelled of sunshine from the line. Now they were both wrinkled and limp. She was beginning to feel the same way.

"Late this afternoon, unless I get an emergency call. I'll see you then."

"Right. Oh, and Ms. Spencer?"

Susanna stifled a sigh. "What?" she asked as pleasantly as she could manage.

"When you see Mateo Cruz, you'll understand what I'm talking about."

Susanna mumbled something and hung up. Mateo Cruz was the last person she wanted to see.

Putting aside her pen and pad, she dropped her head and tried to rub the kinks from her neck. Like it or not, however, she had to see him one more time, if only to prove to herself that he no longer had any power over her.

What they'd had was as cold as yesterday's ashes. Nothing he could do or say would bring it to life again.

Another yawn escaped her, and she grimaced. More than anything she craved a bath and a nice long nap. And maybe, if she had the energy to prepare it, a cup of the herbal tea Grandfather Horse Herder had blended for her when she'd had the flu last month. To keep harmony in her body, he'd explained. Lord knows, she could certainly use a lot more of that right now.

"Move, Susanna, or you'll turn to stone right here." Feeling every aching muscle, she pushed herself to her feet and made her way down the hall to her bedroom.

She lived alone. Her nearest neighbors were John and Aurora Olvera, who lived on a large horse ranch three miles north. The Santa Ysabel Medical Clinic and Tribal Headquarters were four miles south. Until last week, Old Man Nez, a distant relative of Lily Cruz, had lived next door.

She was still angry about that. Couldn't they have found their precious new police chief another place to live? she grumbled to herself. Someplace closer to the center of things? Who did he think he was, anyway? Some kind of hometown hero, come back to thrill the locals?

"So he has a chest full of medals. Big deal," she muttered, as she kicked off her shoes and flopped onto her big white bed.

Well, this was her side of the duplex, leased to her because she was Hannah's stepdaughter. Mat had better learn to respect her privacy but quick.

Annoyed that her heart suddenly seemed to beat faster every time she thought of him, she let the serenity settle around her. The house was so quiet she could hear the wind rustling through the bare branches of the aspen trees outside.

She took a deep breath and held it, then slowly released the trapped air. Suddenly feeling tense, she stood and walked to the window. The day was crystal-bright, and the dry brown vista wavered in front of her eyes like a shimmering mirage.

A gust of wind blew against the pane. Even though the bedroom was warm, she shivered. She had been gazing out this same window on a hot July dawn when she'd seen Mat for the first time. He had been standing next to the crumbling wall that marked the boundary of the leasehold, watching the sunrise.

He'd had the look of a man who had just gotten out of bed. His glossy black hair had been tossed into careless disarray, as though by his pillow. His hard-hewn jaw had been covered by a dark stubble. Above the strong bridge of his nose, his brows had been drawn in a thunderous frown, as though he were angry at the awakening day.

He was naked to the waist, and barefoot. His snug jeans rode low on his hips, the top two buttons carelessly left undone.

His chest was wide, his waist lean and hard, his shoulders capped with the thick muscles of an extremely strong man. His skin, the color of hand-rubbed copper, was smooth and glistening in the sunlight.

Susanna must have moved. Or perhaps her thoughts had somehow intruded into his. Before she could duck out of sight, he had turned to impale her with dangerous black eyes that made her pulse flutter like a butterfly caught in a net.

A slow, audacious grin creased the hard planes of his face as, with what seemed to be deliberate slowness, he dropped his gaze to the rounded contours of her small breasts outlined against her thin cotton nightgown.

Something powerful and reckless flashed in his midnight pupils. One lean hip cocked higher, as though beckoning her to him.

She went hot all over. And then a strangely pleasurable feeling began in the pit of her stomach, spreading quickly to fill her with unaccustomed excitement.

Run, she had told herself at that instant, but already it had been too late. She had fallen in love with him.

"I never had a chance," she whispered, disgust turning her hazel eyes to a dull, lifeless gold.

Susanna jerked her gaze away from the barren yard. She seemed a stranger now, that lonely, naive girl standing mesmerized at the window. "Maiden with shining eyes," her stepmother had called her that summer.

When Mat had finished with her, she had no longer been a maiden, and the shine in her eyes had been caused by tears.

Susanna glanced toward the old cedar chest at the foot of her bed. *Don't!* screamed a part of her. *Leave the past alone.*

But that wasn't possible now. Mat Cruz was back in the pueblo, living in the house where he had been born. For better or worse, they would be living only the width of a wall apart.

Sooner or later, he was sure to bring up that summer when they had been lovers. Why not? As far as he was concerned, everything had turned out fine. He'd had his summer fling and walked away without a backward glance.

Muscles aching, she knelt on the cold tile and opened the chest. Her winter sweaters were stored here, along with her mother's wedding veil and an old album of family pictures. Tucked into the pages of the album was a letter.

Her fingers felt clumsy as she opened it. The black ink was tear-splotched and faded, but the words were still there, written in spiked, heavy letters, as though the pen had stabbed at the paper.

Susanna knew them by heart, but she made herself read them again.

Susanna,
I'm not much at writing letters so I'll make this short. You might be pregnant, but the baby isn't mine. I made damn sure of that. And even if it were, I'm married now. My wife is expecting a baby. Find someone else

and marry him. Give your baby a name. Forget about
me, just as I plan to forget about you.

It was signed "M.C."

Susanna went cold inside, just as she had done on that
long-ago morning. At first she hadn't believed him. It had
taken some doing, but she'd tracked down his phone number and called Mat in San Francisco.

A woman had answered. "Trina Cruz," she'd said in a
voice filled with pride. Mat hadn't lied. He'd been married.
Maybe he'd been married all along.

Susanna heard the brittle crackle of paper and looked
down. Her fist was clenched around the letter, her knuckles
white, the veins in her slender wrist distended.

Forget? How could she forget the moment when she
stopped trusting? When she stopped believing in happy
endings and started hurting? How could she forget the child
she had lost—the child he had denied?

Oh no, she thought with a deep bitterness. She would
never forget.

Relaxing her hand, she carefully smoothed out the crumpled letter, then refolded it. She returned the letter to the
album. Then, quickly, before she could change her mind,
she lifted the album aside. Nestled in the bottom of the
chest, wrapped in tissue paper, was a rag doll, her own
handmade version of Raggedy Andy.

Shaggy black yarn framed a round face sporting black
button eyes. Tiny gold freckles marched across pink cheeks.
The bright red grin was mischievous and just a bit crooked.

Her hands shook as she lifted the doll from the chest and
smoothed her palm over the miniature denim overalls. The
hair was matted where sticky hands had clutched. The
stubby foot was ragged where a small mouth had chewed.
A spot of strained plums stained Andy's cheek.

She pressed the soft toy to her lips, inhaling the faint scent of baby powder. ''Bobby,'' she whispered, choking on the pain. ''Mama misses you so much, so very much.''

A choking sob convulsed her throat, and she bit her lip to keep it from escaping. She wouldn't cry. Not again. Crying only made her weak. And it couldn't bring back her son. Nothing in this world could do that.

Carefully, as though it were made of the most precious materials, she replaced the doll in its cocoon of tissue paper. Then, head bowed, she reaffirmed the vow she had made years ago. She would never forgive Mateo Cruz.

Chapter 2

Mat Cruz braced his strong right hand against the wall and stared through the window at the dusty plaza. Outside, the air was crisp and the wind was brisk. The cottonwoods hugging the banks of Wildcat Creek had already lost their leaves. The gnarled branches seemed weary and vulnerable, like a formation of infantrymen struggling home after a bloody battle.

Like me, he thought, rubbing his aching temple.

"Don't overdo, Sergeant," the doctor had warned when he'd given in to Mat's demand and discharged him three weeks early. "You're still weak."

Weak, hell, Mat thought in savage frustration. He felt as shaky as a raw recruit after his first day on the obstacle course. But that would change, now that he was out of that damn hospital and away from the nervous Nellies who kept nagging at him to take it slow. He'd taken it slow for months, and what good had it done?

He needed to push himself to the limit, find out what he could do and what he couldn't. And then he would work on the things he couldn't do.

Talk about instant humility, he thought with sardonic self-mockery. One night he'd gone to bed thinking he'd had it all wired—a clear shot at the top of the heap, a job he loved, the respect of his men.

Three weeks later he'd opened his eyes in an army hospital, helpless as a newborn, great gaps in his memory, unable even to say his name. His wife was dead, his kids shipped off to San Francisco to stay with his sister-in-law, his career blasted apart by the same shrapnel that had ripped into his left side.

The doctors had all but written him off. He would be lucky if he regained ten percent mobility, they'd told him with brutal man-to-man honesty. But the army took care of its own, they assured him. He would always have a home in one of the VA hospitals.

The hell he would, he'd shouted at them, struggling so hard to move they'd had to sedate him. He'd gotten mad then. Killing mad. The smug bastards with their degrees might have given up, but he hadn't. A man was only defeated it he stopped trying. Mat Cruz could handle anything but defeat.

Jaw tight at the memory of those nightmare months, Mat turned his wrist so that he could see his watch. 1200 hours, he thought, and then frowned. No, it was noon. He was a civilian now. He'd better get used to thinking like one. After all, this was his first day on his new job. Chief of Tribal Police.

He tightened his hand into a fist and studied the place that was to be his home. The tall adobe buildings reminded him of the Presidio in San Francisco, where he'd been stationed when he'd married Trina. Only those buildings had been red brick, and these were mud. Most of the structures were also years older than the nineteenth-century fort, perhaps hundreds of years older. Exactly when they'd been constructed no one knew for sure.

Unlike the bustling hospital that had been his home for the past nine months, no one seemed in a hurry in Santa Ysabel. A knot of local men, some wearing traditional garb and black reservation hats, others in jeans and flannel shirts, stood in front of the Tribal Headquarters, smoking and talking.

A few tourists wearing expressions of curiosity on their Anglo faces wandered here and there, their designer finery and expensive cameras looking distinctly out of place.

Overhead, the sky was the pale blue of early fall, without clouds to soften its monochrome monotony. Against this flat background the sun shone with a chilly brilliance, casting a shadow over the sturdy footbridge where his nine-year-old daughter, Melissa, sat reading a story to her baby brother, Cody.

Three or four picture books lay scattered on the sun-bleached planks like bright patches of life in a dead landscape. Cody, not yet two, bounced up and down on his fat little rump, his attention divided between the book in Missy's lap and two half-grown yellow dogs wrestling in the dust a few feet away.

"I need candles for Cody's birthday cake," Trina had said that last morning. "I'll drive you to work so I can have the car."

The moment she'd turned the key, the bomb had exploded. Because he'd been in the passenger seat, he'd been thrown clear, his left side a bloody, unrecognizable mess. Trina never had a chance. The assassins hired by the drug cartel to thwart the war on drugs in South America had claimed another innocent victim.

No matter how many times or in how many different ways the shrinks told him it wasn't his fault, he would always feel responsible.

When the war on drugs turned hot, he had asked for assignment to the American Embassy in Brazil, where the international task force was headquartered. They had needed an experienced noncom, a man used to working as a military policeman, to head up an elite twenty-man security detail.

He'd been the perfect man for the job. Hell, he'd even called in a few favors to get the billet. He had wanted to be where the action was. And why not?

Mat Cruz had been a man with a goal. Six stripes by the time he was forty. Master Sergeant, the best of the noncoms. A soldier's soldier, respected by privates and generals alike.

He clenched his left hand. A hot splinter of pain shot through his wrist, followed by an icy numbness in his long blunt fingers. When he had finally emerged from the drug-induced fog they'd kept him in for weeks, to discover his left side completely paralyzed, they'd told him he was lucky, that he still had the use of his right hand. The bastards hadn't even considered the fact that he might just be left-handed. The only thing his right hand could do as well as his left was caress a woman's body.

At the moment, however, a woman could be a walking centerfold and he wouldn't be interested. Not that he didn't miss sex. He did. But he'd been without it a long time, so long he no longer counted the months. He had stopped sleeping with Trina after she'd told him about her affair with his CO, the one designed to cadge him a plum job in the Pentagon. When he'd refused to accept the new assignment, she'd been coldly furious. One by one, sparing him none of the details, she had recounted the other affairs she'd had over the years.

That night he'd left the house in a rage, determined to find a woman who would welcome him home with an eager smile and a loving hug instead of bitter complaints and accusations. To his chagrin, he'd discovered he wasn't a man who could cheat on his wife, even though she'd been unfaithful. Instead, he'd gotten blind drunk every night for a week. After that, he no longer cared what she did, as long as she was discreet.

Sensation returned to his fingers, sharp stinging needles running up his wrist. It sometimes went on for hours like that. It had been a long road back, nine endless months of grueling hard work learning to walk and talk and live again.

No matter what else he did now, no matter how many hours of therapy he put in, his once-powerful body would no longer be perfect. Partially disabled, the army doctors had termed it when they'd retired him on a disability pension. A damn cripple, was what they meant. At age thirty-six, after eighteen years in army khaki, he'd been out of a job, scrapped like an obsolete weapon.

It hurt like hell.

"Feel at home yet?"

Mat half turned toward the deep voice. John Olvera, Chairman of the Santa Ysabel Tribal Council, stood in the doorway. "Not yet," Mat said with a twisted grin. "But I'm working on it."

Olvera dropped his dusty Stetson onto the desk and joined Mat at the window. The Tribal Chief was a rancher by choice, a diplomat by education. He was past forty, and looked it, but the lines in his face and the experience in his eyes gave him a quiet strength that Mat respected. He'd seen the same look on countless combat veterans, the ones who'd fought the hardest and talked the least.

"If you need more time to settle in, take it," Olvera said. "We've done without a Chief of Police for a few hundred years. We can survive without one for a few more days."

Mat managed a smile. His face was still stiff from the repairs made by the plastic surgeon. The doctors had done the best they could. At least his face no longer looked like hamburger, but he had a feeling it would be a long time before he was comfortable with the stranger in the mirror.

"Thanks, but it's time I got off my duff and made myself useful again."

"It's your call. The Council intends to help all we can."

"You've done plenty already," Mat told the man who was technically his boss. "Getting the house in shape and the office ready, putting the Bronco at my disposal. Hell, John, I'm used to army snafus and red tape. This is 4.0 treatment."

He glanced at the newly constructed cell in the corner of the office. Considered a sovereign nation by the United States government, Santa Ysabel had the right to make its own laws and enforce them, so long as they didn't conflict with federal statutes.

Olvera ran his finger along a strip of peeling beige paint on the wall. "Sorry we didn't get the office painted. I ran out of money." A rare smile softened the stern lines of his face. "That happens a lot around here."

Tribal Headquarters was almost sixty years old. The thick adobe walls had been patched and repatched. Metal tubing snaked up one wall and across the ceiling to the overhead light fixture that had been installed less than ten years ago. A month ago this space had been a storeroom. It still smelled musty.

Mat lifted his shoulders in a shrug. "Painted walls are the last thing on the list. First we need to hire two deputies, and then we need to get them trained and out on regular patrols. Driving here this morning, I nearly got clipped by some cowboy in a rusted-out Chevy. Must have been going eighty at least. Thank God no one got in his way."

John grimaced. "Tell me about it. With the clinic open to outsiders and the pottery studio selling to tourists on a regular basis now, we've created a nightmare. A day doesn't go by without a complaint, tourists looking in the window, kids tramping over the graves in the burying ground. Even my wife is mad as a little hornet because someone broke into the studio a few nights ago and wiped out the petty cash drawer."

Mat inhaled slowly. It had been a long time since he'd felt like a cop. "Tell her I'll be by today or tomorrow to take her statement."

John laughed. "She'll like that. But be prepared. She'll take you on a grand tour. That studio is her pride and joy."

Mat nodded politely. "Should I know her?" Already this morning he'd run into two people who had clearly remembered him very well. To him, however, they had been total strangers. He still wasn't sure they had believed him when he'd explained about the amnesia.

John shook his head. "She grew up in Texas. I met her when she came to the pueblo as part of a team of archaeologists from SMU. She was their pottery expert."

"How long you been married?"

There was a slight hesitation before the other man answered. "Almost a year this time. We were divorced for five years before I talked her into taking me back. It was a hell of struggle, though. The woman is stubborn."

Mat had the feeling there was more to it than that, but something in John's tone warned him not to push it. Instead, he crossed his arms and leaned his good shoulder against the sagging window frame.

"I looked over the applications for deputy you left on my desk. Three or four look promising."

John raised a black eyebrow. "Which ones?"

Mat hesitated. His short-term memory was still good, but he sometimes stumbled over unfamiliar names. Slowly, he listed the applicants he had decided to interview.

"Sounds good," Olvera said when Mat finished.

"What can you tell me about them?"

Mat listened intently as John gave him a concise rundown on the backgrounds of the applicants. As he listened, he also studied the other man.

John Olvera was someone else he didn't remember, though he should have. Santa Ysabel was a big place in square miles, but very small in population—just over two thousand. Over the years most of the families had become intertwined, so that nearly everyone was related one way or another. John belonged to the Fire Clan on his mother's side, as did Mat. According to pueblo beliefs, they were cousins.

Two months ago Mat had just finished another frustrating therapy session and had been lying sweat-drenched and shaking on his bed in the ward when John had walked in, a job offer in his briefcase.

"The pueblo needs a police force," the man with the intelligent eyes and blunt manner had told him straight out. "Two deputies and a chief. That's you, if you want the job. Interested?"

Hell, yes, he'd been interested. Santa Ysabel needed him, even if the army didn't. He'd been given a new start, and he intended to make it work. It had to. He didn't have a second option.

"Any one of them will work damn hard for you," John said when he finished describing the candidates.

"You have any favorites?" Mat's voice was carefully devoid of expression. In the army, the man at the top generally wanted a favor for a favor. Mat had hated it, but he'd learned to live with it.

John looked at him sharply. "If you mean, is there anyone in particular I want you to hire, no." His eyes narrowed at the sun-weathered corners. "This is your department. You run it. You have a problem. You handle it."

Mat felt some of the knots in his belly loosen. "Fair enough." He glanced toward the stack of applications on the desk. It felt good to have decisions to make again.

"Those your kids on the bridge?"

Olvera's question sent a rush of chagrin flooding through him. He'd forgotten all about Missy and Cody. Damn, he thought, calling himself a few choice names, he was off to a great start.

"Yeah, they're mine, though right now I'm not so sure they're crazy about that idea. Missy looks at me like I'm some kind of sideshow freak, and Cody doesn't even remember me."

"Give it time."

Mat glanced toward the bridge. Cody had climbed into his sister's lap, his thumb now firmly poked into his mouth. His son had changed from a baby to a toddler while he'd been at Walter Reed. Those months were gone, lost to him forever. He forced back a sigh. Regret was a useless emotion. It solved nothing and made a man hurt inside.

"Soon as I get settled, I need to enroll Missy in school here. She's having nightmares again, and she's way too quiet. Having kids around her again might help her adjust."

"Hell of a thing, losing her mother that way."

Mat acknowledged the unspoken sympathy with a stiff nod. He hated to think about things that were out of his control. He'd done enough of that when he'd been flat on his back with nothing to look at but the ceiling for hours at a time.

Facing himself, accepting the guilt for the misery his ambition had caused Trina and his kids, had hurt more than the most excruciating physical pain.

He'd made mistakes—lots of them. He'd been selfish and arrogant, taking what he'd wanted from life without a thought to the consequences. But that was in the past. He couldn't change the things he'd done. He could only change the man.

"How about you?" he asked Olvera. "You have kids?"

A look of deep sorrow passed over Olvera's lean face. "We had a daughter. She died at birth. That's one of the reasons we have a midwife here now, and a clinic with a full-time doctor." His expression turned grim, as though he were remembering something painful. Whatever he was thinking, though, he kept to himself.

Mat understood. A man kept his worst pain private where it couldn't be used by his enemies to make him vulnerable.

A door slammed down the hall, the sharp crack boring into Mat's head. His left hand went to his hip, but the .38 Special that had been such a part of him was still locked in his suitcase. He wasn't yet on duty.

Just as well, he thought, opening his hand. The fingers still stung.

John glanced at his watch. "I'm late," he muttered. "Guy from Albuquerque wants to buy one of my mares. He's probably already at the ranch." He pulled a key ring from his pocket and removed two keys.

"Here's the key to the office and the one to your duplex. Yours is the one on the right, same place you lived in before. Soon as I knew you were coming for sure, I had it fixed up for you."

He held out the keys. Mat started to extend his left hand before he remembered and quickly switched hands. If John noticed his awkwardness, he didn't let it show.

"Susanna Spencer lives next door. If you need anything, I'm sure you can borrow it from her. She's been back for five years now."

"Who?" Mat pocketed the keys.

"Susanna Spencer. Robert Spencer's daughter? He married Hannah Charley when Susanna was a teenager. She lived here until she was eighteen, nineteen, something like that, before she went off to nursing school in Albuquerque."

Mat rubbed his forehead. He searched his mind, but the name meant nothing. "Tell you the truth, John, I don't even remember the house, let alone who lived next door." He hesitated, fighting the feeling of savage rage that came over him whenever he had to face one more thing he couldn't do. Or remember. "The first twenty-six years of my life are gone. Lost. The doctors think I'll probably never remember."

"Come to think of it, you were probably gone by the time she came here to live, anyway." He grinned suddenly, taking years from his face. "You'll like her. She reminds me of a little dynamo, always going someplace in a hurry, usually with a smile on her face. Anyway, she's the midwife I was talking about."

"I didn't realize there were still such things as midwives these days."

"There aren't many around. I found that out when I went to hire one. That's why I was so damn glad to find Susanna. She's not Indian, but she knows the customs and the language, so I broke tribal policy and hired her. It was probably the best chance I've ever taken. The infant mortality rate is way down and still falling, thanks to her." A grin broke over his weathered face. "Watch out, though. When she's riled, she's a real pistol. Doesn't take any guff from anyone, not even me."

Mat felt a shiver rip through him, though he wasn't sure why.

"Thanks for the warning, and for...everything. A few months ago—" He broke off, suddenly embarrassed by the rush of gratitude he felt for the Tribal Chairman.

Their eyes met, Mat's bleak, John's dark with understanding. "A few months ago I found us one hell of a police chief," John said in a low, strong voice, extending his right hand. After a split second's hesitation, Mat did the same.

John strode to the desk and grabbed his hat. "*Adios,* Chief. Call me if you need anything." He left, the sound of his boot heels gradually fading into the heavy silence of the old building.

Mat pushed both hands into the pockets of his new jeans and shifted his gaze to the bridge. Cody was crying. Again.

At least his son was too young to remember the violence, he consoled himself. But Missy wasn't as lucky. Before anyone had thought to shield her, she had seen pictures of her father's torn face and bloody body on TV and heard the commentator describe her mother's death.

Once she had giggled at the silliest things; now she scarcely laughed at all. Her big brown eyes, once alive with joy, were filled with the kind of sadness most adults never had to face.

I'm sorry, baby, Mat told her silently, regret biting deep. If I could have died to save Mama, I would have. The bastards just didn't give me the choice.

A feeling of helplessness twisted in Mat's gut. He had served two tours in Vietnam without thinking much about dying. He could whip a platoon of hardened veterans into shape without raising a sweat. But being both mother and father to his kids terrified him.

He swore a vicious oath that would have impressed even the crudest gunnery sergeant. It didn't help.

The coffee tasted like battery acid and smelled worse. Mat slugged down the last inch in the cup and waited for the caffeine to kick in.

It was late afternoon, and he and the children had just moved into the small two-bedroom apartment that was to be their home. The kids were in the other room, sorting through the things they'd brought with them from California, their voices shrill and grating on his ragged nerves.

Their first day on the pueblo had turned out to be a disaster. Cody had thrown up all over himself at lunch, Missy had pulled a fit when she'd discovered she was to share a bedroom with her brother, and Mat had gotten lost on the bone-jarring drive out to the house where he'd spent the first seventeen years of his life.

By the time he'd reread Olvera's directions and figured out where he'd taken a wrong turn, he would have killed for a cigarette, a quart of rye and eight hours of solitude without any more problems and frustrations.

He put the cup on the small table next to the cheap couch and rested his head on the lumpy cushion. Eyes slitted, he studied the living room, trying to find something, anything, to jog the memory tapes that had somehow gotten erased by the surgeon's scalpel.

Built low to the ground, with thick walls and small windows to blunt the glaring rays of the summer sun, the house was dimly lit and smelled of old timber and wood smoke. The floor tiles in the living room were pitted with age, and the ceiling showed signs of a leak. A large fireplace took up one wall, its blackened stones suggesting heavy use.

The place reminded him of army housing. Ugly as sin, but built to withstand a direct attack—like one Mateo Cruz, ex-army NCO.

Shifting his gaze to the vista beyond the window, he studied the empty land, praying for some spark, some stirring of remembrance in his mind. But nothing seemed familiar—not the squat red mesa, nor the barren, windswept land surrounding it.

He had studied the unemotional facts in his service jacket until they had been etched into his mind. He knew he had been born in this house, in the very room where he had stowed his few personal possessions. He knew that he had gone to school in Chamisa, joined the service when he graduated, finished first in his class on the army's toughest obstacle course during boot camp. He knew his mother's name, but not his father's, and that he was illegitimate, a half-breed, caught between two worlds. He knew when he had been married, Trina's maiden name, the date his daughter had been born—six months after her parents had wed.

But the details, the feelings, the living, breathing memories of those things, were gone. He knew his mother's name, but not her face or her voice. He knew his ancestry, but not the boy who had grown up Indian. He knew why he had married Trina, but had no memory of ever loving her.

It was driving him crazy.

"Welcome home, Cruz," he muttered, closing his eyes. In a minute he would drag his tired body into the bedroom and unpack. The house was clean. He would give it that. And someone had stocked the cupboards and refrigerator with staples. Now, if he only knew how to cook, they would be in great shape.

At least his sister-in-law had potty-trained Cody while the kids had lived with her. That was one less thing he had to learn how to do.

Suddenly a scream cut through the silence. "Stop it, Cody," Missy shouted from the bedroom. "That's my stuff."

"No, no. Mine." Cody's outrage matched his sister's—in volume, anyway.

What now? Mat thought, closing his eyes. He'd always thought he was as good a father as the next man. Now he was beginning to discover just how ignorant he was when it came to the day to day hassles of raising two independent, strong-willed kids. In that, at least, Trina had been exemplary.

"Let go, or I'll tell."

"No, mine."

Mat sighed. Another battle to mediate. He ran the palm of his hand down his face. It'll be better tomorrow, he told himself, sitting up.

"Daddy!"

The sharp sound of breaking glass accompanied Missy's anguished cry.

"Look what you did!" she shouted. "You broke my perfume."

Cody began to scream.

As he shot to his feet, Mat's heart kicked into a gallop. Raw fear shuddered through him for a split second before the icy calm that had saved his life under fire more than once took over. Whatever it was, he would handle it.

When he reached the bedroom, the cloying scent of strong perfume nearly made him gag. "What the hell?"

Cody sat on the floor, surrounded by bits of frosted glass, his chubby foot clutched in his hand. As soon as he saw his father, his screams grew louder.

"Ow-ee," Cody wailed, letting go of his foot and holding up both hands.

Mat scooped Cody into his arms, patting his back awkwardly. "It's okay, scout. Daddy's got you." He glanced around the sparsely furnished room, then sat down on one of the beds.

Cody cried louder, peeking at his father through long wet lashes. Quickly, Mat examined the damage. The cut was small. A Band-Aid and antiseptic should take care of it.

Some of the fear eased from him. He hugged Cody tighter. "It's just a scratch. Don't even need the medics for this one."

It was then that he noticed Missy. She stood a few feet away, her face whiter than the walls. Her eyes were huge pools of terror.

"Cody hurt," the little boy said, twisting like a pretzel until he could see his foot.

Mat dropped a reassuring kiss on Cody's silky black head. "Yes, I know. Daddy will wash it off and put some ointment on it in just a little bit. First I need to talk to your sister."

He redirected his attention to his daughter. "Your brother's still a baby," he told her with the awkward gentleness of a man who was more at home barking out orders to men almost as tough as he was. "He didn't mean to drop your perfume bottle."

Missy stared at the drop of bright red blood on the tile, both hands pressed over her ears. "It's not my fault, it's not my fault," she said over and over.

"Missy, I didn't say it was. I heard you tell him to put it down."

"I tried to take it away from him, Daddy," she cried, her shrill little voice quivering. "I told him it was mine." Her fawn brown eyes filled with tears. "Aunt Patty gave it to me so...so I could...remember...Mommy." The tears turned to sobs.

Mat swore silently. He could back down the meanest drunk with just a look, but one crying little girl made him go weak inside.

"Sweetheart, calm down. Don't cry, okay?" He hesitated, then reached out his hand, and she came to him, folding into the circle of his arm like a terrified kitten seeking shelter.

"It's okay, baby," he said into her tangled curls. "We'll get through this, you'll see. You and me and Cody, we'll be a family again."

He felt Missy shake her head against his shoulder. "We can't be a family without M-Mommy."

Mat dropped his forehead to Missy's little girl shoulder, then raised it quickly before she could feel the weight. As gently as he could manage, he lifted her small chin until she was looking at him again. "Yes, we can, baby," he said quietly but firmly. "If we help each other, take care of each other—"

"Aunt Patty said you can't even take care of yourself," Missy blurted out in a rush, as though she'd been holding the words in too long. "I heard her tell Uncle Mark that you shouldn't even be out of the hospital yet. She said me 'n' Cody would just make it harder on you to...to adjust."

Fury twisted in him like a barbed hook. Trina's sister had been barely civil to him the few times she'd brought the children to see him in the hospital. It hadn't taken much to figure out that she held him responsible for Trina's death.

"Aunt Patty is wrong," he said, his voice barely in control. "I need you and Cody to help me remember how to be a daddy again." His hand trembled as he wiped the tears from her cheeks.

"Okay now?" he asked.

Missy sucked her lower lip between her teeth and nodded. She didn't look okay, but at least she'd stopped crying.

Mat tightened his left arm around Cody's chunky body, then stood up. "There's a first-aid kit in the duffel bag in my room," he told Missy in a calm voice. "Get it for me, will you please?"

Without another word she walked across the hall to the other bedroom.

Mat carried Cody into the kitchen and sat him on the counter, his feet in the sink. He washed the blood from the fat little heel, then lifted Cody's foot to the light streaming through the window over the chipped bowl.

The cut continued to ooze slowly as he wiped the sticky blood away with his fingers. Cody cried out, and tried to pull away. "Hurt Cody," he said with wide-eyed indignation.

"Sorry, scout," Mat muttered. "The sliver is still in there."

"Daddy?" Missy stood at his elbow, her mouth trembling, the first-aid kit clutched tightly in her hands.

"Thanks," he said, taking the small metal box from her. Missy's gaze jerked from his face to the blood on his hand. Her face paled even more.

"Missy?" Mat asked urgently. "What's wrong?"

"I feel sick," she choked. Before he could say another word, she spun away from him and ran from the room. A second later he heard the bathroom door slam shut.

What next? Mat thought, rubbing his stiff jaw.

Next you bandage up your son, he thought grimly. Then you try to find a way to make things right for your daughter without screwing up any worse than you already have.

He found a clean towel in the second drawer he tried, then set about removing the splinter of glass. But it was embedded too deeply to remove without tweezers. Which he didn't have. And even if he did, his left hand couldn't begin to manage the precise movement needed. His right had the strength, but not the dexterity.

He would have to take Cody to the clinic near the center of the plaza.

"Saddle up, soldier," he said as he lifted the boy into the crook of his left arm. "We're going to take a trip back into town."

Cody brightened. "I' cream?" he asked eagerly.

Mat laughed. "I guess I can stand another trip to the Prickly Pear Café if you can," he said, carrying the boy into the living room. Missy would have to go with them. He couldn't leave her alone.

He started toward the hall. A flash of red caught his eye, and he walked to the window, staring thoughtfully at the Jeep parked in the ramshackle carport. His memory stirred. Hadn't Olvera said something about the woman next door going to nursing school?

What was her name? Susanna something?

"What the hell, it's worth a try." He ruffled his son's hair. "Right?" Without waiting for an answer, he shouted to Missy that he was going next door for a minute, then headed out the front door, Cody still in his arms.

A sharp gust of wind hit him head-on. The air had turned from crisp to cold. When he reached his neighbor's front door, he turned his back to the wind, trying to protect the boy from the chill.

He knocked on the bright pink panel, then waited. Another gust of wind, more biting than the first, blew his hair over his forehead and kicked bits of gravel over his boots. Cody ducked his head into the curve of his father's neck.

Mat knocked again, harder. His hand went numb. He bit off an obscene curse. "C'mon," he muttered. "I know you're there."

Just as he raised his fist to beat on the door one more time, it opened. The woman who stood there was tiny, barely tall enough to reach his shoulder. She had obviously been sleeping. Her cheeks were flushed, her mouth soft, her exotic gold eyes half-open and blinking drowsily, reminding him of a small barn owl. A large white T-shirt reached to midthigh, covering her body like a soft drape, delineating every generous curve.

Mat sucked in. Something moved in his head like a shadow passing over a darker background. He frowned. Had he known this woman? he wondered.

"Susanna?" he asked politely.

The moment he spoke the sleepy-owl look fled from her eyes. Her soft mouth compressed, her chin came up, her face hardened.

"Hello, Mat," she said, her voice cold and unfriendly. "Welcome home."

Chapter 3

The rest of the cold words Susanna had rehearsed stuck in her throat. Mat had a child in his arms, a solemn, black-haired little boy peeking at her through lashes as dense and blunt as his father's. His small cheek was pressed to Mat's leaner one. His square chin had the same stubborn line, his miniature black brows bore an identical slant. But unlike the man's world-weary black eyes, the boy's were an innocent brown. Like Bobby's.

She forgot to breathe. A longing to hold his sturdy, healthy little body against hers grew inside her until she had to press her hands to her stomach to keep from reaching for him.

"Hi," the toddler said shyly, his mouth opening in a toothy grin. "Cody wants i' cream."

He was dressed in blue corduroy rompers with extra padding on the knees and a blue-and-white striped T-shirt. The one little brown foot she could see was bare, the chubby little toes curling in.

Making herself smile brightly, she reached out to tweak those tiny toes. But even as she smiled at Mat's son, she was coldly furious at the man himself.

How dare he bring his son to see her like this when he had denied the child the two of them had created? she seethed silently.

Then she remembered. Mateo Cruz would dare anything. Integrity was only a word to him. Rules meant nothing. He thought only of what *he* wanted, what *he* needed, what *he* could take.

"Hello, Cody," she murmured to the little boy, ignoring the man who held him. "I'm afraid I don't have any ice cream. Would a lollipop do?"

The little boy shook his head. "I' cream," he said in a stubborn voice.

Mat drew a slow breath, seeking to ease the tension that had gripped him the moment his new neighbor had looked up at him, her eyes only half-open, her mouth full and soft from sleep. He felt as though he'd taken a nine-millimeter slug in the gut, but for the life of him he didn't know why. Maybe because, for the first time in months, his body had quickened at the sight of a pretty woman.

"This is a hell of a way to say hello, I know," he said as politely as he could manage, "but I need your help."

Her eyes narrowed, and he found he liked the way they confronted him through the thick gold-tipped lashes. He appreciated directness in a woman.

"Cody stepped on a piece of glass. It's still in his foot. I can't get it out." He lifted Cody's leg so that she could see.

Susanna inspected the small wound with critical, experienced eyes. The cut seemed superficial; it had already begun to clot. No sutures would be necessary, just a Band-Aid and a generous measure of TLC.

Relief traveled through her. Ten minutes and the child would be walking on that foot again. A tiny smile grew in her mind. Running is more like it, she thought, holding his sturdy little foot in her palm.

"Ow-ee," Cody said, wrinkling his brow as though trying to decide what he was supposed to do next.

"Yes, darling, I see," she said softly, all too conscious of the man watching her so intently.

"Where do you want him?"

Reminding herself that Mat had never held her son in his arms, never kissed him or hugged him or contributed a penny to his support, she stepped back and opened the door wide. "Take him into the kitchen. The light's best in there."

Mat stepped over the threshold, then waited while she closed the door against the afternoon chill. The wind caught her before the door was fully closed, plastering her shirt against her like a body stocking. Shivering, she shoved the door the final inch until the latch clicked.

He'd been right, he thought with an unexpected rush of masculine interest. She was small, but her body was surprisingly ripe, the kind that raised a man's blood pressure to dangerous levels.

"Maybe you should change into something . . . warmer," he suggested, his frank gaze shifting to her breasts for a heartbeat before returning, unrepentant, to her face.

He let his gaze rest on her mouth long enough to imagine what it would feel like against his, but not so long that it appeared obvious.

Blood surged to her cheeks. How dare he look at her that way? she raged, somehow keeping her temper in check because of the child between them. Did he think he could waltz back into her life and pretend nothing had happened? Was that how he saw her—a convenient lay right next door? Sweet, stupid Susanna, an easy target?

Not this time, she vowed silently. This time she knew better than to mistake sexual need for love. The next time she took a man to her bed, she would know that he loved her for herself and not what she could give him.

"I'll get my medical bag." Leaving him standing there staring after her, she retreated to her bedroom and closed the door.

She rummaged through the drawers of her bureau for clean clothes, then stripped off her shirt. Cool air from the open window hit her naked body, and her nipples hardened, as though possessive hands had brushed over them. Deep inside her body a whisper-soft tension spread to the most intimate part of her.

Dropping the shirt in a heap at her bare feet, she quickly pulled on a bra and panties, her most disreputable pair of jeans, an old sloppy sweatshirt. She didn't bother with shoes. Nor did she comb the sleep tangles from the unruly brown hair waving past her shoulders.

Why should she care if Mat Cruz found her desirable or not? She shouldn't, she answered firmly, punctuating the thought with a determined nod of her head. He wasn't worthy of another thought, another ounce of energy. If it hadn't been for the little boy, she would have slammed the door in his face.

Her voluminous medical bag, stocked with emergency supplies, sat in its usual spot by the door. She reached for it, then paused to take a few bracing breaths.

Involuntarily, her gaze went to the pristine white wall opposite. The master bedroom in the other apartment was separated from hers by ten inches of adobe. In the quiet of a summer night with the windows open he would be only a whisper away.

"So I'll sleep with the windows closed," she told herself with a grimace.

Squaring her shoulders, she opened the door and left the safety of her white bedroom. It was a short distance—a few steps down the hall, to the living room and then into the kitchen.

As soon as she entered, Mat looked up. The man must have terrific peripheral vision, she thought sourly, glancing down at her bare feet. As far as she knew, she hadn't made a sound.

He stood by the sink, holding his son with one strong forearm under the boy's chubby bottom. His shoulders were still massive, wider than most, and slanted toward his strong corded neck in heavily muscled lines that suggested sinewy strength. Beneath the crisp cotton of his pale blue shirt, his torso was hard sinew and lean muscle tapering slightly to the low-riding line of his belt. If his massive injuries had restricted him in any way, it didn't show.

Turning away, she switched on the overhead light, then placed her bag on the kitchen table and snapped it open. Busying herself laying out her supplies, she studied him without seeming to.

His face had a hawklike leanness and a stillness that suggested enormous restraint. His jaw was hard, inclined to be square, and his mouth, too ruthless to be sensual, marked him as a man used to being in command.

Those things were the same, but there were differences, too.

Deep lines now bracketed lips that looked stiff, as though he had forgotten how to smile. On the left side of his face, faint white scars angled away from the corner of his eye to disappear into the glossy thickness of hair now threaded with a generous measure of silver. Another thatch of scars scored his rigid jaw, reminding her of a wind-scoured granite cliff.

He still stood tall, nearly six feet, but he clearly favored his left side. His feet, shod in boots that looked new, were planted wide; his lean hips still angled in that same raw male aggressiveness she'd seen before, but the cocksure arrogance that had once been such a part of him was missing. Had Mat learned humility? she wondered, and then dismissed the thought out of hand. Nothing could humble this man.

"This where you want him?" he asked in the faintly accented voice she remembered.

"That's fine. Put his foot in the sink."

"Can I help?" Mat asked, his deep voice sounding incongruous in the room that had heard only female voices since she had moved in.

"I'll manage," she said in the curt professional tone she'd developed as a student nurse to ward off unwelcome advances from overly aggressive male patients.

Surprise flickered in eyes that still reminded her of sun-warmed ebony, but instead of the devilish laughter she remembered, she saw shadows there, the kind that came from hours of haunting agony.

Something twisted inside Susanna, but she refused to give the emotion a name. If it had no name, it didn't exist.

"Here you go, scout," he told his son, hefting him onto the edge of the white porcelain sink. "Sit still for a minute, okay?" He dropped a quick kiss on his son's head, then stood back to give her room.

Susanna, in the act of turning around, didn't see him move until it was too late. She slammed into him, the breath escaping her lungs with a soft gasp. Hands full, she was thrown off balance. His reflexes were quicker than hers. One arm looped around her waist, holding her steady until she found secure footing. She had an impression of musky warmth and coiled strength before she pushed away.

"You okay?" he asked, his hand still outstretched to catch her if she fell.

"No problem," she managed to get out. For all the changes she had noted, there was one she hadn't explored, but the momentary pressure of his body against her told her that, in one very elemental way, Mat had not changed at all. He was still powerfully male.

Susanna cleared a sudden flurry of nervousness from her throat. "So, Cody," she said as she washed her hands and dried them on a clean towel. "Let's see if we can get rid of that nasty old piece of glass, okay?"

The little boy bobbed his head. " 'Kay," he said, popping his thumb contentedly into his mouth. He seemed fascinated by the whimsical clay rabbit with floppy ears that sat on the counter.

"This is Skippy," she said, rubbing the bunny's ear. "He's a tickle bunny."

Cody removed his thumb long enough to ask quite seriously, "What's that?"

"Here, I'll show you." She picked up the small figure and poked it gently into his stomach, tickling him until he curled his tiny body over her hand. He giggled helplessly, his sturdy legs kicking in excitement, the cut in his heel temporarily forgotten.

Mat felt an odd sensation in his gut, a kind of softening that took him by surprise. They looked so right together, the shy little boy and the spirited woman with sunshine in her smile. She was good, a natural with kids. Cody was obviously smitten.

His left leg, the one that had been in a cast for months, began to stiffen up on him, and he shifted position, waiting for the painful knot to ease.

"Get out of my light." Her voice was cold.

Mat obeyed, then caught himself. He was the one who usually gave the orders. He wasn't used to taking them, especially not from a pint-size pixie who couldn't weigh more than a hundred pounds. I'll give you that one, lady, he told her silently. Just don't push it.

Aloud, he said in what he thought was a friendly tone, "He's shy with strangers."

Susanna spared Mat a cool look. "He doesn't look shy to me." She glanced pointedly at Cody, who was busy playing with a drip from the faucet, his head pillowed trustingly against her breast.

"Hey, scout," Mat said in a plaintive voice. "You just made your old man look like a jerk in front of this lady, you know that? You and me, we're supposed to be pals."

Susanna refused to smile. When he'd been in a playful mood, Mat had been irresistible. In fact, that was one of the things she'd loved most about him—his ability to make her laugh. Thank God she was no longer susceptible, she told herself firmly.

She put the miniature bunny into Cody's hands, then skillfully, talking nonsense to distract the squirming toddler, set to work.

Mat stood behind her, careful to stay out of her light. As he watched her work, he noticed how small and capable her hands were. They would be strong, he thought, and gentle against a man's face.

Like a hawk swooping toward prey, his imagination carried him into the bedroom. Into bed. With this woman next to him, her hands exploring his body. Caressing. Stroking.

His belly rippled involuntarily, then hardened. Below his belt, his body reacted. God help him, it had been a long time since a woman had touched him intimately. He hadn't realized until now just how much he'd missed that.

In the hospital he had been surrounded by women—nurses, therapists, even a fair number of doctors. If he had wanted sex, it had been available.

He simply hadn't been interested. But he was now.

He shifted his weight, trying to ignore the sudden stirring in his loins. The woman had a serenity about her, an air of ladylike dignity, that fascinated him.

In the sunlight her hair seemed to change color with each slight movement of her bent head. Sometimes it was a deep rich brown with a hint of red, suggesting a hidden temper. Sometimes it was threaded with gold, like a priceless tapestry he'd seen once in a museum in London, and so soft looking it begged to be stroked.

Beneath her tumbled bangs, her face had a classical fragility of line and a daintiness of structure that made a man want to slay dragons and fight duels in order to win one of her smiles.

Her eyebrows were the richest shade of brown he'd ever seen, her lashes equally dark and lush, casting little shadows on her cheeks.

And then there was her mouth. Full, naturally red, with soft corners and a surprisingly sensuous curve to the bottom lip. He'd never seen a mouth more suited for kissing.

Mat reached for a cigarette in his breast pocket, then remembered that he had quit in the hospital. Damn, he needed a smoke.

"There. All done." Susanna kissed the plump little foot in her hand, then smoothed her finger over the Band-Aid she'd just applied.

"Aw done," Cody echoed, a smug look of satisfaction crossing his face.

Susanna hesitated, then lifted him into her arms. His short little arms twined trustingly around her neck. "Cody aw done," he said again, snuggling against her, his breath warming her neck. One hand still clutched the tickle bunny.

"You were such a brave boy," she murmured into his ear. "I'm so proud of you." She began to rub his solid little back.

"My son likes you," Mat said quietly, leaning back and resting his elbows on the counter.

"He's a darling. How...how old is he?"

"Almost two. His birthday's in January, the same as my daughter, Melissa. She'll be ten."

January, Susanna thought numbly. Bobby had been born in March. Mat hadn't lied in the letter. Another woman *had* been carrying his child when he'd made love to her that first time.

Abruptly she turned her back on him and walked to the table, Cody still cradled in her arms. With one hand she rummaged in her bag and came up with a red lollipop.

"This is for being such a good boy," she told the wide-eyed toddler with a grin.

"Lolly," he said joyfully. Somehow he managed to get the cellophane off and the lollipop into his mouth before Susanna could settle herself in a chair.

Leaning back, she shifted him in her lap so that he was cradled in the curve of her arm. I'll only hold him until he finishes the candy, she told herself firmly, resting her cheek on his head. Just a few more minutes, until he feels safe again.

Mat hesitated, then pulled out the chair opposite and sat down. As he stretched out his legs, Susanna noticed that the left one didn't quite straighten all the way. It was thinner, too. Not much, but enough to be noticeable, especially when he was wearing tight jeans.

Her gaze jerked back to his face. The deepened lines around his mouth and the hard look of frustration in his eyes told her that he had guessed her thoughts.

"I had some trouble a few months back," he said with a definite edge to his voice.

"I know," she said, a chill creeping across her face. "I read about the bombing in the newspaper. I'm . . . I'm very sorry about your wife."

"So am I," he said in a weary voice. "I keep slowing things down in my mind, trying to change the way things happened. But no matter how I replay it, I can't put myself in her place." His hand slowly formed a fist. His jaw, flushed with dusky color, was equally tight. Something told her that he hadn't spoken of these things to anyone before.

A part of her wanted to believe he deserved the pain he was feeling. Another part wanted to hold him in her arms and comfort him.

She inhaled sharply. Had she lost all sense? she thought disgustedly. Hadn't she learned anything in ten years?

Yes, she had learned to protect herself from men like this who preyed on a woman's natural instinct to feel compassion for the suffering of others.

The sympathy that had started to bud inside her withered and died.

"At least you're still alive," she said more harshly than she'd intended.

"Yeah, that's what I told myself about a thousand times in the beginning," he said sardonically. "It finally got through my thick head to be grateful."

Cody mumbled something she didn't catch. She looked down to find his little face lifted toward hers inquisitively. His cheek was red where it had rested against her sweatshirt, and he looked rumpled and sleepy.

"All done?" she asked. He nodded, and she pulled the soggy sucker stick from his mouth. She kissed his sunburned nose, then pressed his head to her breast.

Mat leaned forward to touch the little boy's shoulder. "Cody, say thank you to Ms...." He gave Susanna an apologetic look. "Sorry, I forgot your last name."

Forgot?

Susanna nearly choked. This was too much. Mat knew her as intimately as he must have known Cody's mother. He had been her first lover, her only lover. She had loved him, trusted him, believed in him. He had given her a son as darling and sweet as this one. How dare he treat her as though she were a stranger?

Susanna met his questioning gaze with ice. "I know I've changed, but not all that much," she said, turning down the chill in her voice another few degrees. "Surely your memory isn't that bad?"

Something savage and hard ripped across his face. "As a matter of fact, it is," he said with steel in his voice. "I can't remember anything that happened to me before Melissa was born.''

Susanna gaped at him, her breath ruffling Cody's hair.

''Are...are you saying you're suffering from partial amnesia?''

''That's what they tell me.'' One side of his mouth moved upward, giving his scarred face a saturnine hardness. ''Fancy term for a damn nuisance.''

A nuisance, she repeated in stunned silence, her pulse drumming in her head. He didn't remember. He truly didn't remember making love to her—while she remembered everything. The nights under the stars when he groaned out her name on a wave of hot throbbing release, the stolen hours in his arms spent dreaming of the life they would share, the desperate aching sadness when he kissed her goodbye with such fierce longing. ''Think about me,'' he had said before he'd climbed onto the bus in Gallup.

And she had. His rare slow smile, his devilish eyes, his sexy laugh, had been with her every day, every hour, every moment. She'd seen him in the face of his son. She had loved him in her dreams, even as she told herself she hated him. While she had been praying to forget, his memories of her had been wiped away in one blinding second.

''Maybe your memory will come back,'' she said, letting her gaze slide from his face.

''Maybe it will,'' he agreed.

But did she want it to? Did she really want him to remember the foolish, adoring girl who'd all but begged him to marry her?

No, she thought. This way she was safe. This way *she* had the advantage.

''Maybe you could help me fill in the blanks,'' he asked when she looked at him again. ''When did we meet?''

She knew that her cheeks were burning and that her mouth was tight with the need to choose her words carefully, but she forced herself to speak in a matter-of-fact tone. "When you came home for your mother's funeral. You had a special leave."

Mat nodded. She would have been a kid ten years ago. Fifteen, sixteen, something like that. No doubt she'd had every buck on the pueblo chasing after her. Hell, she probably still had her pick of men.

"Were we friends?" he asked, his voice dipping into the seductive huskiness she had once loved.

Pain tore through her, almost as fresh as it had been ten years ago. It isn't fair, she wanted to shout. She wanted to tell him the truth, to rail at him, to recite his own words back to him, the cold cutting words that had shattered her dreams.

But she didn't dare. It was better to keep the past buried.

"No, we weren't friends," she told him, her tone putting a period to her words.

And we're not going to be, Mat finished for her. The message was as clear as if she'd shouted it in his face. What the hell had he done to make this woman dislike him? He quickly thought back over the time he'd been with her.

Sure, he'd given her a few admiring glances. So what? Most women who were as good-looking as this one were used to masculine admiration.

He inventoried his vocabulary. Surprisingly enough, he'd kept things clean, and he'd been polite. He'd even let her boss him around. So why the cold shoulder?

"Is there something I should know?" he asked, in the deadly still tone the men in his command had come to fear. "Something that's got you putting up a No Trespassing sign before you even know me?"

Susanna didn't know how she'd lost the upper hand. She only knew that she had. She gritted her teeth and angled her chin.

"I like my privacy," she said stiffly. "Most people do around here."

He digested that, his features edged with a dangerous hardness. And then he grinned. The hardness changed instantly to an even more dangerous charm that made her catch her breath. At the small sound, his grin widened.

"I'd better get my tired little soldier home," he said, his gaze dipping lower. "Looks like he's worn out."

Susanna realized that Cody had indeed fallen asleep, his small face pillowed on her breast. Awkwardly, trying not to wake him, Susanna lifted the little boy away from her.

There was a damp circle on her breast where his mouth had rested. She pretended not to notice. So did Mat. But she knew that he had.

As he took his son into his arms, Mat was tempted to brush against her soft breasts. Nine out of ten guys wouldn't think twice, but that wasn't his style. At least, it wasn't now. He didn't know what he'd been like before he married and settled down.

"Thanks for the help, Susanna." He stopped, then grinned. "I still don't know your last name."

Her silence ended in a terse "Spencer."

Mat filed that away, along with the picture of her small chin rubbing the back of Cody's head and the image of her suntanned thighs peeking out from under the T-shirt she'd worn earlier.

He extended his hand. "I'm glad we met. Again."

She hesitated, then accepted his touch. His hand was so much larger and callused to a hard smoothness on the edges. "I owe you one," he said quietly, his fingers exerting a warm pressure.

"Forget it," she said, tugging her hand free. She didn't like the way her skin burned where he had touched her, or the familiar tightening in her stomach as her hand slid into his.

Casually, as if it were the most natural thing in the world, he reached over and fingered a strand of her hair where it curled against her neck. His knuckles brushed her skin, and she stiffened. Beneath the sweatshirt her heart pounded so hard she was sure he could see each thundering beat. Her face felt frozen. It took all the control she could muster to keep from jerking away from him.

"Goodbye, Mr. Cruz," she said coolly.

Mat fingered the soft strand of hair. "Like Thai silk," he said, as though talking to himself. "Beautiful." As casually as he'd taken it, he dropped the long strand.

"Goodbye, Ms. Spencer. You may not know it yet, but we *are* going to be friends."

Without another word, he turned and walked out of her kitchen.

Susanna stared at the shadows stretching across the ceiling. It was late. She should be asleep, but bits and pieces of her conversation with Mat swirled like a maelstrom in her mind.

No doubt he was sleeping soundly on the other side of the wall, the things they'd said to each other already forgotten. And why not?

He didn't remember the feel of her hand on his body the way she remembered his. He couldn't hear the low moans of passion that she had whispered into his shoulder the way she still heard his fierce groans.

She stirred restlessly, trying to find a comfortable spot. Her mouth was dry, and her body felt oddly heavy. Even her breasts felt unnaturally full, and the nipples hurt every time she moved.

Sighing in exasperation, she kicked at the covers that were suddenly too constricting. Sensations she had forgotten ran up her spine, spreading heat and longing into every inch of her. She had known only one man's body. Mat's.

Timid at first, she had soon grown eager to explore every corded muscle. Her mouth had tasted his mouth, his flat nipples, his salty skin. Her hand had burrowed through the soft hair below his navel, exciting tiny ripples of reaction under her fingertips. His skin had been smooth and hot, as though his blood ran faster than hers. And his chest had been wide and solid as granite, but wonderfully comfortable as a pillow for her head after they'd made love.

Arching her back, she stretched her legs toward the foot of the bed, trying to drive the tension from her muscles and the ache from her bones.

Her skin felt tight, and her lips tingled. She turned onto her stomach and rubbed against the mattress, trying to ease the strangely pleasurable tightness between her thighs. But it only grew worse, provoking powerful stirrings inside her.

She had felt this way before, right after Mat had returned to San Francisco. Then she had welcomed the intimate trembling tormenting her. Each time her breasts had ached in this special way, she'd remembered his mouth closing around the throbbing tips. Each time the familiar yearning had settled between her legs, she'd remembered his potent body thrusting into hers as though staking his claim.

Her soft mouth compressed, she pushed herself upright and stared through the window at the thin sliver of moon rising over the mesa.

A lovers' moon.

No! she told herself in desperation. Think of something else. Anything.

Frantically she searched her mind.

Tomorrow. Think about the things you have to do tomorrow.

Tomasa Delgado was due for her monthly checkup at nine. Then Dr. Greenleaf had a hysterectomy to perform at ten, and she was scheduled to assist.

Susanna sighed. She still had to get out to the Clearwater spread to check on Robin again. Sometime in the afternoon would be best. If it was a nice day, she would pack a lunch and eat on the way. Out by the ruins maybe, or in the Canyon of the Chosen.

She would take a blanket, get some sun, maybe hike into the shadowy canyon spot known as the Meeting Place of the Gods.

The first time she'd gone there, Mat had been with her. She could still see him, his worn boots planted firmly on the uneven boulders, his bare chest as unyielding as the copper brown wall of rock behind them.

He'd worn threadbare jeans and boots that had been in the back of his bedroom closet for years. One square hand had rested on the red shirt he'd rolled into a makeshift belt and tied around his lean waist. His hat, an old one with a braided leather band, had shaded his eyes.

Susanna tried to blink away the vision. Tried and failed.

This time she knew very well the signals that her body was sending. From the moment she'd emerged from the haze of sleep and seen him standing on her doorstep, she had been aware of him, not as a man she had tried to forget, but simply as a man, a rugged, hard-edged man with eyes that didn't smile and a look of loneliness about him. She had seen that look before.

On the day of his mother's funeral.

Groaning, she turned her head on the pillow and closed her eyes, determined to blank out the painful memories. No, she thought suddenly. It was better to remember. The pain would act as a barrier to the attraction that still lay heavy inside her.

Susanna shifted restlessly, sinking slowly into the past.

It had been late afternoon, but the sun was still warm. Shadows filled the sacred place, making her move closer to Mat's strong body.

"You ever been here before?" he asked almost absently, breaking off a piece of sage to sniff its pungent scent.

"No," she said in a hushed voice. "Have you?"

"Lots of times." His jaw clenched, then relaxed. "First time I came I was a year old, the time when a father takes his son to the medicine man to ask for a special blessing. For the fierceness of an eagle or the bravery of a mountain cat or the strength of a grizzly, mostly, though I've heard about men who ask for the sharp eye of a hawk or the wisdom of an owl."

Susanna sat on a smooth rock still warm from the sun and studied him from beneath the rolled brim of her floppy hat. Lily Cruz had never mentioned Mat's father.

"What did your father ask for?" she asked, trying to imagine an older version of Mat.

This time his jaw remained tight. "He wasn't there. My mother brought me. The elders refused to allow her to speak." His mouth twisted. "They told her the gods would be angry to hear from a woman without honor."

Susanna cast her mind over the various customs Hannah had described for her. She had no memory of this one, but she knew the ceremonial rituals were often kept secret from outsiders, especially those that were held most sacred.

"Where... where was your father?"

He shrugged. "I don't know," he said, his voice taking on a chill. "My mother never talked about him except to say that he was a white boy she met while she was attending the Indian boarding school near Gallup. A *rich* white boy whose parents wouldn't let him marry a dirty heathen."

A soft gasp escaped Susanna's lips. "Don't talk like that. I like the beliefs of your people, especially their feeling for nature and its... its loveliness. Sometimes I wish I'd been born Indian."

Mat tugged his hat from his head and rested it on one crooked knee. Sunlight caught in his short-cropped hair, giving him a dark halo.

The farther they'd gotten into the canyon, the more he'd seemed to change. It was as though he were becoming a different man in a different time, shedding step by step the patina of civilization until he seemed as primitive and as potentially volatile as the dormant volcanoes to the west.

"When my mother was your age she was one of the prettiest girls in Santa Ysabel, but none of the young men would offer for her because she had given birth to a white man's child."

His brows met together over his blade straight nose. She saw the flash of pain in his eyes, and the rigid control around his mouth.

"She told me once that my father loved her. That he would have married her if it hadn't been for his father's money. She never stopped loving him, for all the good it did her. For all the good love does anyone." He made it sound like a curse, bringing a soft protest from Susanna that he ignored.

Susanna didn't consider the prudence of her actions. She only knew that Mat was alone and desperately unhappy. Rising from her place on the rock, she went to him and wrapped her arms around him, resting her cheek against his thundering heart.

After a startled instant, his powerful arms closed around her small body so tightly she couldn't move. He smelled wonderfully male, and his skin was hot, like the sun-washed rocks surrounding her.

A deep satisfaction spread through her. This very strong, very dangerous man needed her. She'd read somewhere that the greatest gift a man can give a woman is to need her, and now she understood what the author had meant.

Suddenly the torturing pressure on her arms relaxed. The agony bled from his eyes. His mouth lost its hard tortured edge as it brushed hers.

Instantly, small shivers shot through her.

He stared at her, an arrested expression on his face. "Don't tell me that's the first time you've ever been kissed by a man?" He sounded shocked and just a bit nonplussed.

Still shaking, she could only nod.

"Did you let me kiss you because you feel sorry for me?" he asked with silky softness.

Susanna saw pride flare in his eyes, along with a bleak look she couldn't identify. "No," she whispered. "I wanted you to kiss me. I've wanted that since I saw you that first morning."

"Why?" He sounded as though he didn't quite believe her.

She shook her head. "I just know I want it inside. My father told me to always do what feels right, deep down."

His mouth jerked in a small movement that might have grown into a smile if his face hadn't been so tense. "Does this feel right?"

This time his mouth moved lazily over hers, exciting a rush of sensation flooding through her—like the heady feeling she always got when she stood at the edge of a steep cliff and looked down.

"Yes," she whispered when the brief kiss ended. "It feels right, like . . . like I've been waiting all my life for you."

His touch was gentle, even deferential. His hands moved down her arms to capture her hands. He lifted them to his shoulders, then angled his head and kissed her again.

This time the sensations coursing through her were laced with a heady exhilaration, unlike anything she'd ever felt before. Is this what it's like when a woman wants a man? she thought, her eyes springing open in wonder. The sensation localized, centering in a place deep inside.

"I want to make love to you," he said without pretense. "Here. Now."

Yes, she thought, oh yes. "Why?" she asked, suddenly afraid.

His hands circled her waist, pulling her against him. "Feel that? That's why." He began rubbing against her, his pelvis moving in a tantalizing circle. She knew the rudiments of male physiology, but she'd never before felt the power of a man's sexual arousal.

"You make a man crazy, Susanna. Your body is so ripe I'd kill to know what it feels like to be inside you. But your eyes keep asking me questions I can't answer." He groaned, his jaw clenching. "I've never met a woman like you before."

Heady feelings of instinctual feminine power shot through her. He wanted her. Shy, awkward Susanna Spencer. Mat thought she was special.

She swallowed the fear rising to her throat. "Make love to me, Mat," she whispered. "Please."

Instantly, as though waiting for a signal, Mat released her. A dark flush colored his high cheekbones, and his eyes glittered in a way she'd never seen.

"I'm not like my father, Sweet Sue," he said. "I won't make promises I can't keep. And I won't make you pregnant."

Susanna realized she was crying. Impatiently she dashed away the tears, her heart pounding, her mouth trembling. He had done both, and she had paid the price.

Close by the house, a coyote howled suddenly, sending a shiver down her spine. An answering cry came, not as close. And then another.

The pack was hunting, prowling for prey, the more vulnerable the better.

Some of The People believed it was bad luck to hear a coyote howl on the night a child was born. In the old times, if such a catastrophe occurred during a birthing, the father would send for the medicine man, who would do a sing to ward off the evil spirits.

Bobby had been born in Albuquerque, in the hospital where she'd been taking her training. She had been alone. If a coyote had howled that night, she hadn't heard it. But she *had* called Mat's name, over and over, until she'd had no more voice.

In the distance the marauding pack began yipping shrilly. They'd made a kill.

Susanna felt a sudden chill. Body clenched, she slid lower into the white nest of covers and huddled there, alone in the middle of the bed that had never seemed so large before.

Remember the day you lost your son, Susanna. Remember the days and nights you cried. Remember the empty feeling that's always with you. Remember that you no longer love Mat Cruz.

Susanna turned over and pressed her hot face into the pillow. It didn't help.

Chapter 4

Susanna turned off the ignition and breathed a sigh of relief. The black Bronco with the Santa Ysabel Tribe emblem on its side was gone.

Mat wasn't home. For two days she'd avoided him. For two days she'd tried not to think about him. For two days she'd tried not to worry about the little boy with the sweet smile and mischievous eyes. She hadn't succeeded.

Dropping her keys into the oversize bag that served as a briefcase as well as a purse, she opened the door of the Jeep and stepped out into the brisk afternoon wind.

Something pink flashed past the corner of her eye, and she let out a startled gasp. A child, a small brown-haired little girl looking dejected and forlorn, sat cross-legged under the aspen next to the carport. She was dressed in a hot pink Snoopy sweatshirt that was several sizes too big and purple jeans.

So that was Mat's daughter, she thought. The child another woman had been carrying while he had been making love to her.

Sad brown eyes watched her warily as she approached, her sneakers crunching the leaves covering the hard dirt.

"Hi, my name is Susanna," she said with a friendly smile. "You must be Melissa."

"Missy," the girl corrected gravely. Intelligent brown eyes studied Susanna with open curiosity. "Daddy says I have to call you Ms. Spencer."

Susanna was careful to keep her anger at Mat from showing on her face. "But then I would have to call you Ms. Cruz, and that gets very complicated, doesn't it?"

The little girl giggled. "I guess so." Her stiff shoulders relaxed, and her mouth lost its melancholy droop.

"What're you reading?"

The child glanced down at the well-used book in her lap. "*Huckleberry Finn.* It's my favorite."

"Mine, too." Susanna grinned. "Looks like you've read it a few times." Her own copy was almost as tattered.

Missy frowned. "Most of my books 'n' things are still in some big warehouse where we used to live in Brazil. This is Daddy's, but he said I could have it until all our stuff comes on the boat. Some people gave it to him in the hospital when he was learning to read."

Susanna stared at the child. "Learning to read?" she asked, certain that she had misunderstood. Mat had been one of the brightest people she'd ever known.

Missy stood up and carefully brushed the leaves from her jeans. She was thin, all arms and legs. "Daddy was in a...a coma for three weeks. They wouldn't let me 'n' Cody see him or talk to him 'cause he was so sick. When he woke up, he couldn't talk or read or... or anything. Aunt Patty said the nurses had to feed him and give him a bath and help him go to the bathroom." She clutched the book tightly. "I asked him if he felt funny going back to school again, 'n' he said it was a humbling experience, whatever that means."

Susanna forced a smile. "I imagine it means he didn't like it much."

In her imagination she saw Mat as he must have been then, lying as still as death, his strong body mangled almost beyond repair, his mind groping to relearn things most people took for granted.

It must have been a living hell for such a restless, virile man, trapped by the damage in his brain to lie immobile for hours on end, wondering if that was how he would spend the rest of his days.

Before she'd left nursing to become a midwife, she had treated patients like him in the trauma ward. Every day she had shared their despair and their pain. Every night she'd gone home and cried.

"Did I say something wrong?"

Susanna looked up to find Missy staring at her uncertainly. How long had she stood frozen, thinking of this girl's father? she wondered. A minute? Two? More?

She swallowed. "No, of course not. I...hadn't realized that your dad had been so badly injured, that's all."

Missy's frown smoothed away. "He doesn't talk about it much. But sometimes, at night, he can't sleep very well."

Susanna refused to let herself care. She knew herself all too well. Once she opened the door a crack, the compassion she invariably felt for those who had suffered would come flooding out. She couldn't afford to feel sympathy for Mat Cruz. She couldn't afford to feel *anything* for him.

Just being near him had sparked feelings in her body that threatened the cold anger she'd used as a knife to cut away the love she'd had for him. But now that she knew she was still far too vulnerable to him, she would make sure she stayed as far away from him as possible.

"Hey, I have a book you might like," she said, changing the subject.

The child brightened instantly. "Great. I'm tired of reading Daddy's books," she said with a lilt in her thin voice. "What's it called?"

Susanna shifted her heavy bag to the other shoulder. *"Island of the Blue Dolphins.* Have you read it?"

"No. Is it about dolphins?"

Susanna nodded. "And a little girl a lot like you." She held out her hand. "C'mon. I'll show you."

She was touched at the eager way Mat's daughter slipped a small hand into hers. Her thoughts flew backward to the black days after she'd lost her own mother. For months she'd been lost—a shy little shadow haunting the shabby old house that suddenly seemed too empty and too quiet.

At the door, she hesitated, struck by a sudden thought. "Where's your brother?"

Missy scowled. "Grandmother Ettaway is giving him a bath. He dumped a whole bag of flour all over himself. Daddy's really going to be mad when he sees the mess in the kitchen."

Susanna opened the door. "Grandmother Ettaway? Is she your baby-sitter?" She gestured for Missy to enter ahead of her.

"Sort of, I guess. Daddy says her grandchildren moved away, and she needs a couple of kids like us to take care of so she won't be lonely." Missy couldn't quite stifle a sigh. "Mostly I like her, but sometimes her tongue gets all twisted and the words come out funny."

Susanna knew what Missy was trying to say. The old woman had grown up speaking her own language, learning English only when her children had insisted.

"I couldn't understand her, either, when I first came here," she told Missy sympathetically. "But it wasn't long before I picked up enough of the language to get by." Now she was fluent enough to understand all but the most obscure words.

Susanna dropped her bag onto the floor and closed the door. Grandmother Ettaway had been the first woman to welcome her to the pueblo when she'd returned. Because the motherly old woman had lost her youngest daughter in childbirth, she'd convinced many of the younger women to break tribal custom and allow Susanna, a stranger not of the blood, to attend their deliveries. After the first few times, the resistance had melted away. Now virtually all the mothers-to-be consulted her.

Susanna was very fond of the old woman. But Grandmother had to be in her late seventies. Surely Mat didn't expect her to keep up with an active toddler.

A frown tugged at her eyebrows. She told herself not to interfere, but she couldn't help worrying. Children were so terribly vulnerable.

"Do you live here by yourself?" Missy asked, avid interest sparkling in eyes shaped like Mat's but holding nothing of her father's glittering hardness.

"Yes, all alone." She dropped her arm gently over Missy's thin shoulders. Together they walked down the hall and into the spare bedroom she'd converted into an office. She kept duplicate records in the battered old filing cabinet in the corner, along with every textbook on midwifery and obstetrics she'd been able to find.

Missy stopped short, her features taking on an enchanting expression of pure delight. "Gosh, you must have more books than the library," she exclaimed in an awestruck tone.

Susanna laughed. "It sure feels that way when I have to dust them, that's for sure."

As though seeing the room through Missy's eyes, she ran her gaze over the bookshelves that covered three walls floor-to-ceiling. They'd been custom-built for her by the husband of one of her first patients.

"I wish I had these many books," Missy said in a wispy voice. "'Cept Cody would probably ruin 'em. He's always messin' with my stuff, even when Daddy yells at him not to."

Susanna came to stand next to her. "Sounds like it's hard being the big sister."

Missy shrugged. "It's okay, I guess. 'Cept he snores."

Susanna nodded sympathetically. "How about your friends? Do they have little brothers that bug them, too?"

"I don't have any friends here." A sad little note crept into her voice, and her shoulders slumped again.

Susanna's heart went out to her. Moving closer, she gave the child a gentle hug. "You'll have friends here, soon, kiddo."

Missy didn't respond. Susanna knew exactly how strange Santa Ysabel could be for someone who had never lived within its vast boundaries. But there wasn't anything she could do to take away the strangeness. She couldn't afford to become involved.

She dropped her arm and assumed an air of concentration. "Let's see, where is that book?" she muttered, trailing her hand over the rows of books.

Sun streamed through the west window and puddled on the huge, recycled school teacher's desk in the middle of the room. The air smelled musty, like the library stacks at UNM.

"Aha, here it is!" she exclaimed. She tugged the small volume free, then ran a caressing hand over the worn cover. A soft reminiscent smile lit her face. "I can't tell you how many times I've read this. I know it by heart, and I still love it."

Missy breathed a soft sigh of anticipation. "I'll take very good care of it," she said in an eager voice. "I promise."

Susanna hesitated, then strode to the desk and took a pen from the drawer. Turning to the front page, she wrote a neat inscription: "For my friend Missy. Happy reading."

To her surprise, tears welled in her eyes. For this lonely little girl whose best friends were books. For her adorable, motherless brother. For...

No, she thought. Not for Mat. Never for Mat.

She spun around and held out the beloved book. "This is for your collection."

Missy's mouth dropped open. "You mean it? For keeps?" She tucked the worn copy of *Huckleberry Finn* under her arm before taking the book from Susanna's hand.

Susanna nodded. "I told you, I know it by heart. Besides, if I want to read it again, I'll just borrow it from you."

Missy started to grin, then seemed to think better of it. "Susanna?"

"What, honey?"

"Can I come visit sometimes? When you're not busy, I mean? Daddy said not to make a pest of myself, but..."

Susanna saw the hopeful look in Missy's eyes and went soft inside. What could it hurt, really? It might be nice to have company now and then. "Sure, you can visit. Anytime at all."

"Maybe I can bring Cody some—"

The sound of hard knuckles on harder wood, demanding and insistent, reverberated through the quiet. Susanna realized she was grateful for the interruption.

"Someone sounds pretty darn impatient," she muttered, then grinned. "Sometimes babies come early. Might be an anxious father-to-be who doesn't have a phone."

She left the room, followed by Missy, who looked intrigued. "Are you a doctor, like the one Mommy went to when Cody was born?"

"No, I'm a midwife. Sort of like a doctor, but not really, because I mostly help mommies have their babies at home."

Still smiling at Missy, she swung open the door.

Mat stood two feet away, half turned away from the door, the uncompromising angles of his profile distinctly outlined against the sky. He wore a new brown Stetson, pulled low against the sun. Aviator sunglasses with gold rims hid his eyes.

He was dressed in khaki, and for an instant past and present merged before she realized it was a different kind of uniform, with the tribal insignia emblazoned on a patch below his shoulder. A large black, businesslike revolver snapped into a worn leather holster rode low on his left hip.

At the click of the latch he turned. One lean hand swept off the Stetson, while the other smoothed his thick unruly hair into rough order. His jaw was shadowed, giving him the rumpled look of a man who'd put in a long day at hard labor.

"Hello, Ms. Spencer," he said. "We meet again." One eyebrow slanted mockingly, as though saluting the sudden frown on her face.

Susanna recognized the low throb of masculine interest in his greeting and stiffened inside. She didn't want to respond when this man spoke to her. She didn't want to notice the tautness around his mouth or the lines of strain in his face.

"So we do," she replied coolly. What she really wanted to do was slam the door in his face, literally and figuratively until he got the message. *Do Not Disturb. Ever.* But, with her conversation with Missy fresh in her mind, she had to be careful to display no overt hostility. She could care less about Mat Cruz, but she would rather suffer his presence than hurt Missy.

He hesitated, as though he intended to say more, then shifted his gaze a fraction to the child at her elbow. "Missy, Grandmother Ettaway was worried about you. She didn't know where you were, so she called me at the office. Next time you go visiting, tell her where you're going."

"Yes, Daddy," she said meekly, hanging her head.

Susanna wanted to belt him. Couldn't he see how lonely Missy was? she thought indignantly. Couldn't he see the sad little droop to her mouth? Or the hurt in her face when he barked at her like that?

She gathered herself up to her full height, which unfortunately brought her mouth on a line with his strong throat. She had to arch her neck in order to look him squarely in the eye.

"It's my fault," she told him quickly. "We got talking. You know how it is." For Missy's sake, she fashioned a winning smile.

His face didn't change, but Susanna felt a prickle of uneasiness move down her spine. Something dangerous and dark was bottled up behind his rough-hewn features.

"Missy knows the rules." He raised one eyebrow and looked at his daughter. "Don't you?"

She bit her lip and nodded. "I'm sorry, Daddy," she said in a low voice.

His mouth relaxed into a brief smile. "Don't do it again, okay?"

"I won't."

"Go apologize to Grandmother."

Susanna ached for the little girl, who seemed so miserable all of a sudden. Slipping behind Mat and his daughter, she gave Missy a hug.

"Come back soon," she said with her best chin-up smile. "Any time you want to borrow a book or just . . . talk."

Some of the hurt left Missy's face. "Bye, Susanna."

"Melissa!" Mat rebuked her sternly. "What did I tell you? It's Ms. Spencer."

"It's okay, Mat," Susanna interjected quickly with a smile for the upset little girl. "I told her she could call me Susanna."

The corner of Mat's mouth moved, not much, but enough to tell her that she had intruded on dangerous territory. "I know what's best for my daughter, Susanna. Try to remember that, and we'll all get along fine."

Missy burst into tears. Before Susanna could comfort her, she was running toward her own front door.

As soon as Missy was safely out of hearing, Susanna rounded on the man standing so silently next to her. "Did you have to order her around like a damn drill sergeant?" she demanded, hands on hips. "She's just a little girl, not some . . . some recruit."

"Better she gets her feelings hurt some than die out there on the mesa because she doesn't listen to orders," he said, the steel in his voice sharpened to a razor edge.

Susanna's gaze followed the jerk of his head. Just last year a tourist from Vermont had ignored the council directive against camping within pueblo boundaries and gone wandering among the rugged foothills to the north. He'd fallen, broken his leg, and died. Alone.

She repressed a shudder. "You're right," she admitted grudgingly. "But you could have been more understanding. She's still...adjusting. She needs love, not harsh words."

"What the hell is that supposed to mean?" he asked in a deceptively soft voice. "I love her. She knows that."

"Oh yeah? Well, you sure could have fooled me."

For an instant his face went white before dusky color flooded his cheeks. "What are you, the resident expert on child psychology?"

"It doesn't take an expert to see how unhappy she is. She's been through a hard time, losing her mother, nearly...nearly losing her father. Tell her you love her more often. Show a little patience and understanding."

"Patience and understanding," he repeated meditatively, his voice silky. "Like you've shown me, right?"

His words were slipped under her guard with the deftness of a sniper hitting a target in the dead of night in a high wind. It took her a second to realize she'd been bloodied.

"Goodbye, Cruz." She stepped backward, but before she could slam the door, he flattened his palm against it.

Susanna leaned against the door and shoved, one hundred and ten pounds of determination against nearly two hundred pounds of muscle and grit.

"Take your hand off my door," she said through tight lips.

Deliberately ignoring her chilly order, Mat dropped his head and stared at his dusty boots. These days, he was never sure he was making sense when he spoke, especially when he was tired. Or like now, when he'd been taken by surprise.

Surprise? He'd damn near been bowled over by this pint-size tigress. Hell of a thing, hearing this woman with a stranger's face defending his daughter against him.

Thankful that his dark glasses hid the frustration seething in his eyes, he raised his head and took a deep breath. He was bone-tired, discouraged and hungry as a grizzly after a winter sleep. All he wanted was a bath hot enough to steam out the knots in his muscles and a few hours of peace.

"Look," he began slowly, watching an angry flush creep into the faint hollows below her cheekbones. "It's not that I don't appreciate your interest in Missy. Believe me, I do. It's just that I've had a ballbuster of a day and—" He broke off.

"Sorry about that," he muttered, slapping his hat against his thigh. "Bad habit. I'm working on it."

Suddenly he grinned, a devilish, intensely sexy grin that nearly rocked her back on her heels. She stiffened her spine.

"I was a nurse for two years before I became a midwife," she said tartly. "I'm not bothered by vulgar language."

"But you *are* bothered by me." He moved closer, sliding his shoulder along the door's hard panel until his wide chest was only inches from her breasts. He smelled of leather and sweat and dry New Mexico dust.

Her heart began to beat too quickly. "I hardly know you. Why should I be bothered by you?"

He shrugged, a controlled movement of muscles and tendons that hinted at the power hidden under the plain uniform. "You tell me."

"I just did."

Mat found that he was watching her mouth rather than listening to her words. Her lips looked enticingly soft, even when they were stretched into an angry scowl. He had half a mind to kiss that furious little mouth into a sweet sigh of pleasure.

The thought gave way to an instant reaction in his groin, faint at first, then more insistent. Whipped as he was, he was still susceptible to one Susanna Spencer. Physically, at least. Emotionally, he was walled off from everyone but his kids. And that was the way he wanted it.

He dropped his hand and shoved it into his back pocket. "Let's stop the sniping, shall we? I don't need to have a brick fall on me to figure out we have some history between us. Right?"

Susanna stood mute, refusing to reply. Her hand curled around the knob until the knuckles stretched the skin to the point of pain. Hidden behind her flannel shirt, her stomach was doing flip-flops.

She didn't want him to know the truth, not ever. She didn't want him to remember her lying naked and eager under him. She didn't want him to remember how she'd moaned helplessly when he made love to her. It would give him power over her, and that would be unthinkable.

"Right," Mat continued, answering his own question. "Since you're obviously not interested in filling in the blanks for me, I'll have to do it myself."

Panic gripped her like a strangling hand before she forced it down. There's no way, she reassured herself grimly. No one knew. Not her people or his. They'd met secretly, mostly at twilight, when she'd been accustomed to taking long walks after dinner. No one had seen them alone together. Mat had wanted it that way. He'd *insisted*.

A small smile of irony escaped her rigid control. Caught in his own trap, she thought with bitter pleasure. "Don't waste your time. There are no blanks to fill in."

Slowly, making every move count, he reached up to remove his dark glasses, then pinned her with a look that had invariably sent the recipient diving for cover. "Then why do your feathers ruffle like an angry little owl's every time we're together?"

Susanna knew she had only seconds before the shaking in her knees became too noticeable to ignore. Not that she was afraid, far from it. She was furious—with herself, for letting him push her into a corner like this.

She braced her feet and took a tighter grip on the doorknob. "This half of the house is mine. Tribal Law says a person's house is sacred territory, not to be entered except by invitation. In case you haven't noticed, I haven't issued one."

He reached out to straighten the open collar of her shirt. As he slowly withdrew his hand, his knuckles brushed the thin skin between her throat and her breasts, instantly releasing a heat that quickly spread to her face.

"I'm the police, remember?" he said in a voice as rough as a winter thistle against the skin. "How're you going to enforce that law if I refuse to cooperate?"

Susanna didn't hesitate. "With a 16-gauge shotgun." Fiery eyes the color of expensive whiskey challenged him to push it.

Mat fought down a grin. Damned if she'd didn't have the guts of a horse thief, this one.

"Okay, you win," he said, the steel in his voice now tempered with quiet patience. "This time."

He was a practical man, without false modesty. Years as a noncommissioned officer had taught him how to control men as well as lead them. There wasn't a man in ten who would even think of challenging him the way Susanna Spencer had done more than once. But one skirmish didn't make a battle.

He threw her a lazy salute, grinned and walked away. Susanna didn't even have the satisfaction of slamming the door in his face.

* * *

"Daddy, Daddy."

Mat jerked awake, his heart slamming in his chest. The sheets were wound around his body like a shroud. The bedroom was as dark as a tomb.

It took him a few seconds to realize that the night-light he'd left burning in the children's bedroom had gone out.

The shrill cry came again, sounding like a sob. Mat struggled to escape the constricting covers, then snatched up his discarded jeans and hitched them over his legs, buttoning them as he left the room.

The tile was cold on his bare feet. In his haste, he banged into the doorjamb, bruising his shoulder. He bit off a curse, trying to rub away the pain.

The hall was a lighter shade of black, illuminated by the faint glow of a thin crescent moon shining through the bathroom window.

"Daddy, where are you? Daddy." It was Missy. "Daddy, it's *dark*." The last was a wail of pure terror.

He moved faster than he'd thought he could, reaching her side before the keening sound of her voice died away.

"I'm here, baby," he said, angling his hip onto the bed and pulling her into his arms. "It's okay, Missy. Daddy's here." He leaned toward the bedside lamp and switched it on. The glare stung his eyes.

Missy relaxed slightly, but her pupils were still dilated, and her mouth trembled uncontrollably.

In the other twin bed, Cody frowned and muttered something indistinct; then, eyes still closed, he turned away from the light.

Missy pressed her small body against Mat's bare chest, sobbing. Tears wet his shoulder, and her elbow dug into his ribs. Small, surprisingly strong fingers clutched his arm with a desperation born of a terror only she could see.

"Shh, baby, shh. Daddy won't let anything happen to you." He rubbed her back, trying to reassure her. Her spine was bony, her small body as fragile as a leaf in the wind.

Her sobs lessened, then stopped. She clung to him, her legs drawn tight against his side. Wisps of brown hair framed her hot face. She shivered.

For the first time he noticed the chill in the air. He kissed her forehead, then pulled the blanket over her legs. She'd insisted on wearing a frilly little girl nightie that was much too light for the cold desert nights. He'd been too preoccupied to argue.

"Better now?" he asked in a low voice.

She nodded, her tousled hair brushing his chin. "I woke up and it was so d-dark. I couldn't breathe," she cried, her voice shaking. Mat smiled slightly. He knew all about suffocating black nights. He'd had his share, especially in the bad months before the doctors were able to tell him that he would walk again.

He tightened his arms, trying to let his little girl know he understood. "Tomorrow I'll go into Chamisa and buy another night-light, sort of a backup."

"Aunt Patty said I should try to be brave and sleep without a light." Her small fingers dug into his arms, and her thin body shook.

"Damn Aunt Patty," he said in a rough tone before he remembered he had vowed to clean up his language around his children.

Mat ignored the band of pain beginning to pull tight around his head. "It's okay to be scared, baby," he told Missy in a low voice thick with the frustration he couldn't quite hide.

"You're not."

He reached for the right words, but they weren't there. They never were when strong feeling gripped him. Emotions were powerful things, the doctors had told him. Nec-

essary, even desired. He would only get himself in trouble
if he tried to ignore them.

He had understood that. Rage had impelled him to brave
a sniper's bullet in order to save a shavetail lieutenant who'd
gotten himself in a hell of a mess outside a VC stronghold
in Quang Tin Province.

Terror of being a cripple the rest of his life had gotten him
through the gut-busting torture of rehab. Icy control had
kept him from falling apart when they'd told him his wife
had paid the price for his selfish ambition.

Except that control wasn't an emotion. Or so the damn
shrink had told him over and over.

"I'm scared of the dark sometimes, just like you are," he
said slowly. "And I'm scared people will feel sorry for me
because my face isn't very pretty anymore. Most of all I'm
scared I won't be a good daddy to you and Cody."

"Really, Daddy? You really get scared sometimes?"

"Yes, I really do. But you know what helps?"

She shook her head. "What?"

"I think about all the good things in my life. Like you and
Cody and my new job and the feeling I have when I walk
outside and the sun is shining and the sky is blue. I think
about all the people, our people, who have lived in this special place, and I'm glad I have a home."

"I don't like this place, Daddy. Everything's brown and
ugly. And everyone looks at me funny."

"Be patient, baby," he said, forcing a reassuring smile he
didn't feel. "Things will work out fine, you'll see."

"Why couldn't we stay with Aunt Patty?"

"You know why, Missy. Daddy has a job here."

Missy huddled against him, looking small and miserable. She sniffled. Mat looked around for a tissue, then remembered the box was in the bathroom. He used the edge
of the sheet to wipe away the tears. She trembled against
him.

"I'm sorry, Daddy. I didn't mean to make you mad this afternoon."

Mat felt something rip inside. Susanna Spencer's accusing voice came back to him, harsh and pain-filled. Paradoxically, this time he remembered every word.

"I'm not mad, Missy." He swallowed. "Sometimes I get tired, and sometimes I forget things I should know. I didn't mean to take out my troubles on you."

Mat closed his eyes, listening to the child's quiet breathing. The first time he'd held her in his arms he'd been terrified he was squeezing her too hard. When she'd opened her eyes and looked up at him, he'd felt a dozen feet tall and so proud he thought he would burst. Nothing had ever meant more to him than his new baby daughter. Not even his stripes. Somewhere along the way he had forgotten that.

Regret burned in his stomach. He had forgotten too many things he needed to remember.

"Missy, it's all right with me if you want to call Susanna by her first name."

Her face lit up. "Really, Daddy?"

"Really."

"She's nice. I like her a lot."

Mat realized that he did, too. He wasn't exactly sure why. Maybe because she fought so hard to defend his daughter. Whatever the reason, however, he figured he wasn't all that high on her list of people she liked. But maybe he could change that. For Missy's sake.

He dropped a kiss onto Missy's head. "Think you can get back to sleep now?"

Missy nodded.

"Can your beat-up old dad have a kiss?" he asked, surprised at how husky his voice sounded. In the days before the bombing he had taken kisses from his children as his due. Now he no longer took anything for granted.

Missy raised her chin and kissed his cheek, then, to his surprise, pressed her face to his neck and threw her arms around his chest.

His eyes stung. *Tell her you love her more often.*

He took a deep breath. "I love you, baby," he managed to choke out.

"I love you, too, Daddy," she whispered in a muffled voice. Only he knew how precious those words were to him.

He tucked her in, promising to leave the light burning, then returned to his room. After shucking off his jeans, he climbed into the lumpy bed and turned onto his side, trying to relax.

The silence pushed in around him, constricting, heavy. From the other room came the sound of the children's breathing. Tension traveled down his spine and settled in his legs. He felt every lump and sag in the old mattress. Nothing felt right, not even his skin.

He thought about the room next door, the twin to this one. No doubt Susanna had been asleep for hours, her body as relaxed as his was tense.

His body stirred. From the first moment he'd seen her, he'd been aware of an intense sensuality hidden beneath her cool facade, like a hot ember waiting to be fanned into life.

Knowing he shouldn't, he let himself imagine what it would be like to make love to Susanna. He would take a very long time, using his mouth and his hands to sensitize every inch of her sleek body. He would kiss her breasts and her belly. He would stroke the inside of her thighs slowly and thoroughly, letting his fingers trail higher and higher with each stroke until she was ready for him.

Anger pushed through him, making his muscles tight. What the hell was he doing, tormenting himself over a woman who barely gave him the time of day?

With a groan he turned onto his belly and buried his face in the pillow, trying to escape the need torturing his body and shattering his hard-won peace of mind. But he kept seeing the smile leave her eyes when she spoke to him.

He was a man who liked things clean and simple. No surprises, no hidden agendas. Subtlety escaped him. Evasion made him nervous. When he liked a woman, he made that fact perfectly clear. When he wanted her, he made that clear, too.

But there was something about Susanna that didn't quite feel right. It was as though something was driving her, something that had put her back up against him. But what?

Tomorrow, first thing, he intended to do some scouting around, talk to some people who knew him when, ask a few discreet questions.

The next time she took him on with her chin raised and her eyes smoldering with dislike, he would be ready.

Chapter 5

Mat unlocked the door that now bore his name painted in black on the window. The air inside was hot and smelled musty. Dust motes zigzagged through the afternoon light. His boot heels made a hollow sound on the bare wood floor.

Leaving the door open, he tossed his hat onto the corner of his desk, angled his hip onto the edge and ran both palms down his cheeks. He and his deputies had just put in two intense hours of target practice out on the mesa. His skin still stung from the raw wind slicing down from the north.

He flexed his injured hand. The exercises prescribed by his therapist were helping. He still couldn't shave with a blade, but he could draw his gun now without dropping it.

It had felt damn good, firing his weapon again. The cold weight of hard blue steel against his palm and the acrid smell of the exploding powder brought back a lot of good memories.

Mat stretched the tired muscles of his shoulders, then sat down and propped his feet on the desk. The old swivel chair screeched, bringing a wry grin to his face. Everything in the office had been recycled or patched. Even him.

He let his shoulders slump. His side felt leaden, numb. His leg ached with the steady dull pain that sometimes lessened, but never really went away.

All in all, though, things were going pretty well. In the three weeks since he'd hired his two deputies, Sonny Spruce and Mary Two Skies, he'd spent most of his time training them in the basics of police work, military-style. So far they'd worked out fine.

Burly and tough, Sonny had been employed in Gallup as a security guard, coming home weekends to his wife and four sons. Mat could still see the joy in the young man's face when he'd gotten the job. His words of thanks had been formal and polite, in the way of The People, but outside, where he'd thought Mat couldn't see him, the kid had thrown his hat up in the air and whooped like a warrior on the warpath.

The other deputy, Two Skies, was another story. Lured back to the pueblo by the new life John Olvera and his allies on the Council had breathed into the community, she had an edge on her that Mat didn't like.

But the woman could handle a rifle better than anyone he'd ever seen. She also had a steady look in her eye that suggested the kind of calm temperament a cop needed, especially when faced with a belligerent drunk or an irate wife looking for her straying husband. Santa Ysabel had its share of both.

Mat moved restlessly in the hard chair. His hand was beginning to throb. Jerking open the desk drawer, he took out the bottle of aspirin he kept there and shook out three tablets. He tossed them down without water, grimacing at the bitter taste, then recapped the bottle and returned it to the drawer.

Down the hall, a phone shrilled. Two rings, three, then silence. He glanced at his watch. He had a couple of hours before he had to stop by the pueblo school to pick up Missy. Most of the children walked home, some going miles, but she was city born and bred. He worried about her when she was away from him, probably more than he should.

Poor baby, he thought, resting his head against the wall behind his chair. She still missed her mother. He had a feeling that was why she spent so much time with Susanna Spencer.

"She's nice, Daddy," Missy hold told him when he'd asked her about her new friend. "She knows all about makeup and clothes, and even knows my favorite songs. She makes great cookies, too."

Mat opened his eyes and stared at the ceiling. In the polite roundabout way of his people, he must have asked a dozen people about her. Just as John had mentioned, everyone seemed to like her a lot. He had heard story after story of her dedication to her patients and her valiant efforts to improve the chances of survival for their babies. In the way of his people, some had nicknamed her Woman Who Saves Babies. Others knew her as Woman With Sunshine in her Eyes. The more he found out about her, the more he respected her.

But no one knew any more about her history than Olvera had told him that first day. Not even Grandmother Ettaway, who knew everything that happened within the boundaries of the pueblo almost as soon as it happened, had told him anything that could explain her antipathy toward him.

Mat dropped his feet to the floor and sat up. Forget it, Cruz. You have a job you like more every day, two great kids, a fresh start. The last thing you need is trouble with a woman who can't be bothered to give you the time of day.

The sound of boots tramping down the hall outside caught his ear. A second later John Olvera appeared in the doorway. "How's it goin'?" he asked, crossing to the desk and pulling up the extra chair.

Mat waited until Olvera sat. "Can't complain. How about you?"

John shrugged. "Sometimes I wonder why I asked for this job," he said, his voice laced with dry humor. "If it's not the Bureau of Indian Affairs on my back, it's the Council. One thing about our people, they like to talk things half to death before making a decision."

John yawned, then slumped back in his chair. "Speaking of talking, I stopped by to ask you to come to the Council meeting next Wednesday night. I like your idea of a Tribal Court that combines the old ways of tribal justice with military court-martial procedures. I think it might just work. But I'd like you to explain it to the Council and answer their questions."

"I'll do my best."

John nodded. "That's all any of us can do." He leaned forward, prepared to stand, then frowned. "Oh, before I forget, I ran into your neighbor on the way here. She has a problem you should know about."

Tension sliced down Mat's spine and settled in his belly. "What kind of a problem?"

"Someone broke into her Jeep and took her medical supplies."

Mat spat out an obscenity. "When?"

"Yesterday afternoon."

"Where?"

"Out by Red Horse Rock, near the Delgado place."

Mat nodded slowly, his emotions pulled in tight, the way he kept them when his temper threatened to explode. For three weeks he had worked day and night to prove that he could still cut it as a cop. All it took was one suggestion of weakness, one whispered comment that someone as respected as Susanna Spencer questioned his ability, and he would be in trouble. No one trusted a cop who wasn't tough enough to handle his job.

"You just see her?" he asked, glancing toward the window.

"Twenty minutes ago." John gave him a measuring look. "In case you're interested, she said she was on her way to the clinic."

"I'm interested." He grabbed his hat and headed for the door. "Lock up when you leave," he tossed over his shoulder. "This might take a while."

John's laugh followed him into the hall. "Good luck," he called after him. "I have a feeling you're going to need it."

Susanna leaned heavily against the desk in the clinic's reception area, staring at the indecipherable words scribbled on the message pad. She had two women ready to deliver. The message could concern one of them.

"Sorry, Susanna," the harried receptionist whispered, darting a quick look over her shoulder. "I took a coffee break, and Dr. Greenleaf covered the phones for me. You know how awful his writing is when he's in a hurry."

Susanna shot Lupe an exasperated glance. She was exhausted, her nerves worn to a frazzle during an especially difficult early-morning delivery, but she had a full calendar of afternoon appointments and a house call to make before she could call it a day.

She rotated her head, trying to ease the painful tightness between her shoulder blades. "Is the doctor in his office now?"

Lupe nodded. "I just put through a long-distance call."

"Okay, when he hangs up, let me know. I'll be in the lounge."

"Yes, ma'am." Lupe started to add something more, but the phone rang, and she broke off to answer it.

Just as well, Susanna thought, as she walked slowly down the hall to the first door to the left. The last thing she needed was a recitation of Mat Cruz's impressive masculine charms.

The staff lounge was tiny, hardly larger than a good-size closet. It contained a lumpy cot, an even lumpier sofa and a huge coffee maker that was never turned off.

Eyes drooping with fatigue, she drew a full cup and took several sips, waiting for the hot brew to cool before drinking deeply.

Voices came from the children's ward at the end of the hall. Someone giggled; another voice joined in. Her stomach clenched. One of those sweet little voices had reminded her of Cody Cruz. In spite of the exhaustion pushing at her, she smiled at the memory of his silky head resting on her breast.

She'd seen him three times since then—twice with his sister, playing in the yard, and once with his father. In spite of her good intentions to stay well away from the father, she was becoming more and more entranced with the children.

Susanna sighed and tried not to think about the fine line she was walking. It didn't take much insight to figure out that Missy was looking for someone to replace the mother she had lost. With every ounce of maternal instinct she possessed, Susanna longed to be that someone. But she didn't dare become too involved with the lonely little girl.

Missy wasn't her child, and she never would be. Nor was Cody. That place was reserved for Bobby. She could never love another child as she had loved him.

Too groggy to risk sitting, she wandered over to the window at the far end of the empty waiting room. Setting her cup on the wide sill, she stared at the afternoon gloom. There was a storm building near the Canyon of the Chosen. Angry thunderheads stretched like an impervious black wall up to the heavens, blocking out the sun. Long jagged shards of lightning slashed at the land, power in the raw.

She ground her teeth. The house call on today's list was in that area. "Naturally," she muttered, crossing her arms over her chest. Twice in the last three weeks she'd gotten mired in the mud after a sudden squall took her unawares.

She'd been too preoccupied with thoughts of Mat to notice the clouds piling up overhead.

Nothing had gone right since Mat Cruz moved in next door. A week ago she'd run out of firewood because she'd forgotten to order a cord when she'd run low, then spent a miserable night shivering under a pile of blankets, trying not to think of the man sleeping only a few feet away.

"Sleep," she muttered. "I just need some sleep."

"Me, I need answers."

Adrenaline shot through Susanna like an explosion, overriding the exhaustion. Before she could stop herself, she spun around to face the man she'd been trying so hard to drive from her thoughts.

He stood less than two feet away, booted feet spread, thighs hard with tension, hands loosely clenched at his sides—like a gunfighter watching for the flicker of fear in his opponent's eyes.

He knows, she thought with wild dread, her hand going to her throat. Somehow he's found out. About their lovemaking. About Bobby. About everything. Her stomach clenched, and her breathing grew shaky. Her heart thundered in her ears like the wildly fluttering wings of a trapped dove.

But who could have told him? She had told everyone that Bobby's father was a fellow student at the university, a Navajo. Not even her family knew about Mat.

"Don't you know better than to sneak up on someone like that?" she challenged, her racing heart giving her words a breathless quality.

Watching her through narrowed lids, he removed his hat and smoothed his hair with strong impatient fingers. He hesitated, looked around quickly like a man used to taking charge, then tossed his hat on the bunk.

"Game's over, Susanna." His mouth slanted into a hard smile that took none of the rawness from his scarred jaw.

She drew her brows together. "What game?" she asked, searching those lightning-kissed black eyes for a hint of emotion, some betraying sign to tell her what he was thinking. But his feelings were buried deep.

He ignored her question. "John tells me you have a theft to report."

She nearly collapsed with relief. *He didn't know.* Pressing her hands together to stop their trembling, she made her voice calm. "Yes. I gave him the details."

His eyes narrowed, not much, but enough to shiver the fine hairs on the back of her neck. "Wrong person. I'm the law here. Or my deputies."

"John is head of the Council," she hedged, sending a sidelong look toward the door, gauging the distance. "I knew he would handle it."

"Are you saying I wouldn't?"

She resisted the urge to swallow. "No, I'm saying I preferred to discuss it with John."

"That's bull—"

"It's not!" she cried in exasperation, her nerves beginning to unravel. "I saw John, I mentioned it, that's all there was to it."

He digested that with a stoic calm she knew was deceptive. Instinct told her that he would be a formidable opponent at chess—or poker. He would play silently, steadily, showing nothing, taking his losses without excuse, until, ultimately, he would risk everything on one final pot. And he would win.

"You got some reason for thinking I can't handle my job?"

"No, of course not."

"Then this is personal."

Her pulse rate accelerated. Her mouth went dry. "How...how could it be personal?"

His eyes took on a cold glitter. "Since I can't remember, I don't have any way of answering that." He moved closer until only inches separated them. She noticed that one side of his mouth didn't move as easily as the other, especially when he smiled without humor, the way he was doing now.

"I saw you watching me." This time the look in his dark eyes was all too recognizable. In fact, that same look, potent and demanding, still haunted her dreams.

Susanna felt disoriented at the sudden change of subject. "What?"

Mat watched her thick curly lashes flutter against her creamy skin. For one crazy moment he wanted to pull her down on the cot, making his frustrated imagining real. But Susanna was a woman who deserved gentle handling, for all her inner steel. Not because she was weak, but because she was strong. Force her, and she would fight to the death. Woo her, and she would surrender. For the right man.

"When I was playing with Cody the night before last, you were at the window, watching. I felt your eyes on me."

In spite of the chilly weather, he'd been wearing shorts and a skintight khaki T-shirt with his name stenciled across his broad back. Every time he'd lifted the laughing little boy over his head, his biceps had bulged with an oiled power that sent small tugs of awareness darting through her tense muscles. When he'd leaned down to return the little boy to safe footing, his shorts had pulled taut over his hard masculine buttocks. He might as well have been naked.

She made her voice strong. "I was watching Cody, not you. To see if he was limping."

He saw her mouth tremble at the corners and knew she was lying. He liked the idea that she was fighting the same battle he was. "Won't wash, Susanna. The cut's been healed for over two weeks."

Susanna shot another glance toward the door. "I don't have time to argue with you now. I have a patient waiting."

"Let her wait," Mat muttered as he pulled her into his arms. Her body jerked, and her hands sought to push him away.

"I want you, Susanna. I've wanted you from the moment you opened the door in that damn skimpy shirt and blinked up at me like a sleepy little owl. And you want me. I see it in your eyes whenever you look at me."

"No." Her voice was too husky to be called a whisper.

"Yes. I may have been out of circulation for a while, but I know when a woman wants to make love, and you, my sweet Susanna, want that very much."

Before she could tell him that he was wrong, his mouth found hers. She sought to struggle again, but a part of her wanted to give in, to yield to the wild sweet force buffeting her.

His kiss was just as she remembered, intoxicating, overpowering, taking and giving with an arrogant demand that couldn't be denied.

Through the material of his shirt, she felt his heart pounding. Her own thundered in a strident cacophony in her ears. His breathing, so deadly quiet a moment before, rasped between them, warming the skin of her face.

Susanna fought the lethargy turning her muscles to warm velvet. In her mind she saw herself pushing him away. In her mind she saw herself walking away without a backward look. Still, she couldn't seem to move.

Feelings built inside her, overriding her resolve. Another kiss, a touch, a demand, and she would be lost. He would ask, and she would give.

From someplace distant she heard a child's cry. Faint at first, it grew until it seemed to pound through her head. It came from the nursery at the end of the hall.

"No," she cried, struggling wildly to push herself out of his arms. She wouldn't let this man into her life again. Not ever again.

"What the hell—" His words came out in a gasp. Somehow she found the strength to escape his hold. In a panic she whirled, aiming for the door.

He caught her before she got away. His hand closed over her wrist, and he jerked her around to face him. A savage look of frustration slashed like a whiplash across his dark features.

"Is it all men you hate, or just me?"

Susanna went cold inside. "I don't hate you." A betraying pulse throbbed in the tender place under her ear. Slowly he raised his fingers to feel the frantic pounding. She jerked away, but his body blocked her passage.

"Susanna, there's something you should know," he told her with a mocking half smile. "I was an army cop for half my life. I've met more than my share of liars, and you, my sweet Ms. Spencer, are a damn poor one."

Her control finally snapped. Maybe it was the truth of his words that made her reckless. Or, more likely, exhaustion.

"You want the blanks filled in," she said in a cold clear voice. "I'll fill them in for you. I lied to you, Mat. We were friends ten years ago, or so I thought."

Mat stared at her, his brows a dangerous black line. "Go on."

"I was only nineteen, an easy mark. It took you exactly three days to seduce me. When I found out I was pregnant, I wrote to you."

His body jerked, as though he had taken a bullet in the gut. "No!" he cried in a violent explosion of sound.

"I was so happy," she went on, as though he hadn't spoken. "I knew you'd be happy, too. After all, you had told me you wanted to marry me after I got out of school."

She lifted her face and looked deeply into his eyes. She wanted to see his face when she forced him to confront the man he'd been, the man he had so conveniently forgotten.

"You were very prompt with your answer. It was short and sweet. The baby wasn't yours, you said. Besides, even if it was, it didn't matter. You were already married, and your wife was pregnant. You were very helpful, however.

You advised me to find another man to give my child a name."

Mat inhaled sharply, the air hitting his lungs like artillery fire. She was lying. She had to be lying. A man who would do what she claimed deserved to die a slow and painful death.

Fury knotted his fists at his sides. "I don't believe you."

He watched her face go white. Her small face looked utterly defenseless all of a sudden, and her eyes seemed rimmed with a terrible sadness. "I had your child."

A sharp twisting pain ran up his spine. Oh my God, he thought. She's telling the truth.

He had to clear his voice twice before he could speak. "Tell me about the baby."

Her mouth trembled, but she made herself say the words. "He was adorable, so bright-eyed and alert, with the longest eyelashes I've ever seen on a baby. I named him Robert for my father. Bobby. He...he was a good baby. Sweet. He used to suck on his toes and talk nonsense to himself in the morning before I went in to change him." Her throat stung, but she made herself continue.

"Not that he was an angel. He . . . he had a temper, too. I remember one time when he was learning to crawl. He'd get going so fast he'd get his arms and legs tangled up and fall flat on his little nose. He'd be furious with himself, but he wouldn't give up." Her hands began to shake, and she pressed her trembling fingers to her belly.

He took a step forward, then stopped, his hands clenching at his side as though to keep him from reaching for her.

"What...what happened to him?"

Susanna managed a slow trembling breath. The tears she'd suppressed for so long escaped her control and began streaming down her cheeks. "He...he died when he was nine months and two days old."

"Susanna," he began, then stopped to clear the sudden huskiness from his throat. "I don't know what to say."

He lifted a hand toward her, then let it drop. He was suffering, but she couldn't afford to care. He deserved this pain, she insisted to herself. He deserved to pay for what he had done, just as she was paying.

"Don't give it another thought," she said with a bitter smile. "Ten years ago you told me to forget you, and that's exactly what I intend to do."

Slowly, feeling each beat of her heart pulsing furiously through her rigid body, she turned and walked out of the room.

Chapter 6

Aurora Olvera, Susanna's two o'clock appointment, was waiting in her office when she arrived.

"Sorry I'm late," Susanna said with a too-bright smile as she closed the door behind her. "My father called and left a message with Brad who, of course, scribbled two lines of unintelligible gibberish. I had to wait until the darling doctor got off the phone to have him translate."

"Sounds like John. When he's in a hurry, his handwriting looks exactly like hieroglyphics." Aurora was tiny and vivacious, with laughing gray eyes and a mischievous smile.

Six years ago, during a visit to her mother-in-law in Santa Ysabel, she had gone into labor and had lost the child she had been carrying because there had been no medical facilities on the pueblo. Her marriage to John Olvera had broken up after that.

Susanna didn't know all the details, but she did know that he had been in South America at the time instead of with Aurora, as he had promised, and that Aurora had held him partly to blame for the baby's death.

The women of the tribe loved to talk about the campaign
John had waged to change the things about himself that had
driven Aurora away. The younger women thought it was
wonderfully romantic the way he had lured Aurora back to
the pueblo to begin the Artists' Cooperative, then convinced her to marry him again.

Susanna had met Aurora during that time and had liked
her immediately. The two had become good friends and,
sometimes, confidantes. Susanna had never known Aurora
to break a confidence.

Keeping her expression carefully controlled, Susanna
slipped into the immaculate white coat hanging on the back
of the door, then dropped into the padded chair behind her
desk.

In the ladies' room, where she had gone to compose herself, she had told herself over and over that she had done the
right thing.

Now that Mat knew why she didn't want anything to do
with him, he would leave her alone. There were plenty of
available women on the pueblo. It wouldn't take him long
to find one willing to satisfy his needs.

Reaching for Aurora's file on the low cabinet behind her,
she said over her shoulder, "You look particularly perky this
afternoon. I like your hair longer. Reminds me of Kathar-
ine Hepburn in the forties."

Aurora fluffed the thick curly page boy that gleamed with
coppery fire. Since she and John had remarried, her face
had taken on a glow of happiness that Susanna envied.

"John and I made a deal," Aurora said with a grin.
"He's promised to take at least one afternoon a week off,
and I promised to let my hair grow."

"Is that why I saw you two riding out by the ruins last
Sunday afternoon?"

Aurora colored. "We had a picnic, in the place where we
made love for the first time."

For an instant Susanna remembered a man as tough as rawhide kissing her, holding her, every powerful muscle in his body taut with restraint. Something softened inside her until she remembered that she and Mat hadn't made love. They'd simply had sex.

Dismissing him from her mind the way she'd disciplined herself to do years ago, she picked up the thick file in front of her and quickly skimmed her notes.

Aurora settled back in her chair and crossed her legs. "So, how's it going with you two?"

Susanna's hand jerked, spilling papers onto the desk. She lowered the file to the desk and awkwardly gathered the papers into a ragged pile. "You two who?" she asked warily.

Aurora looked confused. "You and Brad Greenleaf, who else?"

Relief made a fast trip through Susanna's tense body. Now she was getting paranoid, for Pete's sake. "We see each other now and then. For dinner or a movie. He's a nice man. I like him."

"But no fireworks, huh?"

Susanna shook her head. "Not really, no."

"Well, there's always our new police chief. I'll bet he could generate plenty of heat."

Susanna's fingers pressed so hard on the manila folder that it creased between them. Did every woman in the pueblo want to talk about Mat Cruz? First Lupe, then the women in her prenatal class, and now Aurora.

"For some women, I suppose," she muttered, replacing the papers in the folder.

"John likes Mat a lot. He said that there are some men born with a warrior's spirit, men who never compromise, who never surrender no matter how much punishment they take."

Susanna took a deep breath, then picked up her pen. "So—how're you feeling?"

Aurora's smooth brow creased in a puzzled frown. "Why do I think you don't want to talk about Mat Cruz?"

"I'd rather talk about you, that's all," Susanna managed smoothly.

Aurora gave her a penetrating look. "In other words, mind your own business, Aurora."

Susanna heard a faint note of hurt in her friend's voice and dropped her pen. "I'm sorry, Aurora. I didn't mean to sound snippy." She slumped back in her chair and rubbed her burning eyes.

"Don't ask me to explain it, but whenever the moon is full, I can always count on at least one middle-of-the-night delivery. This week I've had two. I think I'm terminally tired."

The other woman regarded her in silence for a long moment, her eyebrows pulled together in a thoughtful look. "I had that same condition once, right after John came back into my life. I couldn't seem to get enough sleep. Then, when I did sleep, I kept dreaming about *him*."

Susanna gave a humorless laugh. "Tell me about it." She sighed again. Weariness was making her ears ring and her vision blur. "Life is so blasted complicated sometimes. Just when you think everything is going along just fine, something...happens."

"Meaning Mat Cruz?" Aurora questioned softly.

Susanna sighed. "Yes, meaning Mat Cruz. I...met him once, when he came home for his mother's funeral." That much, at least, she could admit. Sooner or later, when the women got together to discuss the return of the prodigal son, she would be asked the usual questions. Did she remember him? Didn't she think it was a shame about his face? Did she have a crush on him like all the other young maidens?

Aurora nodded. "I wondered. I mean, since your families lived in the same place. You must have been young then."

So young and so foolish. Susanna sighed. "Nineteen. I thought he was the most gorgeous man I'd ever seen." Her laugh was bitter. "But you don't want to know all that. It'll only depress you."

"Sounds like you're the one who's depressed." Aurora hesitated, then added softly, "I've never seen you look so upset. If it would help to talk, I'm willing to listen. God knows, you've listened to me go on for hours about trying to have another baby."

Susanna was tempted. The incident in the lounge had shown her just how volatile her emotions could be around Mat Cruz. She had lost control and that made her intensely vulnerable, something that couldn't happen again.

Telling Aurora might vent the explosive power still waiting to take her unawares. Just saying the words might act as a safety valve of sorts, maybe even a catharsis.

Tell her, a small voice urged. She'll understand.

Susanna took a deep breath. "We were lovers. We were careful, but . . . I got pregnant anyway."

Aurora gasped softly, her face losing its radiant glow. "My God. You and Mat . . . a baby?"

"No one knows that I once had a child except my family, and I never told them the father's name." She picked up the pen she'd just discarded and began stabbing the blotter with the point. In a wooden voice she told Aurora what had happened ten years ago, ending with a description of the scene in the lounge.

The color drained from Aurora's face. Her eyes widened in horror, and she swallowed hard. "He really doesn't remember?"

"No. If you'd seen his face . . ." She sighed. "If I didn't know better, I'd think he really cared. But then, he's always been a great actor."

"Dear God, what a mess!" Aurora commiserated. "No wonder you didn't welcome him home with open arms."

The two women looked at each other in silence, each thinking about the revelations Susanna had just made.

Susanna was surprised to discover how much better she felt after unburdening herself to her friend. Aurora was one of the strongest women she knew, and one of the most compassionate.

"What happened to the baby?"

Susanna stared at the slashes she'd made in the blotter. It was as though she'd made those same jagged rips in her heart.

"I loved Bobby so much, Aurora. I tried so hard to make a home for him. I worked a double shift. I even took in ironing at night, but what with day care and all the things a baby has to have, I couldn't seem to make enough money to stay ahead of the bills. And then I got sick. Pneumonia. I thought it was a bad cold, that I would be fine. One morning my landlady found me unconscious." She bit her lip, breathing in strength to continue. "While I was in the hospital, they put Bobby in a foster home. They . . . they said I wasn't capable of taking care of him."

"Oh no, Susanna. They didn't take him away from you?"

"No, but there was a hearing. My baby-sitter and my neighbors and even Bobby's pediatrician testified that he was healthy and happy. My landlady told them what a good housekeeper I was, and that Bobby was always laughing and clean when she saw him."

She managed a small smile. "After I recovered, things were better for a while. But then, gradually, I fell behind on my rent. My landlady was sympathetic, but she couldn't carry me forever. Finally, after four months, she sent me an eviction notice. I looked and looked, but I couldn't find a cheaper place that would take a child."

"What about your family?"

"At the time my father was supporting a family of four on the little money he could make selling his paintings at art fairs in Gallup and Albuquerque. He offered to take us in, but you've seen my place. Can you imagine six of us in there?"

Aurora shook her head. "No, I can't. Your place is scarcely big enough for two."

"When things got desperate, I swallowed my pride and applied for state aid. The welfare people said I had to quit my jobs to qualify. But I made more money working than they could give me, so I was caught in a Catch-22."

"What did you do?" Aurora asked quietly.

Susanna took a deep breath. "When Bobby was nine months old, I gave him up for adoption."

"Oh, Sue," Aurora whispered, her eyes filling with tears. "I'm so sorry."

Susanna had trouble speaking. "So am I. I'll be sorry all of my life, but I couldn't stand to see Bobby deprived any longer. I thought about the children I saw in the welfare office, with their shabby clothes and lifeless little faces. They were all so...pale, like wispy little ghosts." She fought off a sob. "I couldn't make him live that way, Aurora. I just...couldn't. Not my precious baby."

It had taken weeks, months, before she stopped searching for Bobby's sturdy little body in a crowd. Even now, the sight of a dark-haired baby boy in his mother's arms tied her in knots for days afterward.

"I tell myself he's happy now. I *know* he's happy. The agency assured me that the couple who...who adopted him were wonderful people."

Aurora wiped the tears from her cheeks with her fingers. Silently Susanna plucked a tissue from the box in the drawer and handed it over.

"Thanks." Aurora blotted her eyes. "What did Mat say when you told him about the adoption?"

Guilt shivered through Susanna. "I didn't tell him. I lied and told him Bobby was dead."

"Why?" Aurora asked in a puzzled tone.

"I can barely stand to think about those terrible times. I don't want him asking me questions, saying things that would hurt. I don't even want to...to remember."

She stirred restlessly in the chair, trying to ease the tightness in her muscles. "I hadn't even intended to tell him about the baby, but it just...came out. Maybe I wanted to hurt him. I don't know. I've thought about it often enough—the words I'd say and how I'd say them." Her mouth twisted, and her voice hardened. "I'm only human, Aurora. I told myself that hating him would only hurt me, but sometimes—" She broke off with a shrug.

"Sometimes you need the hate as a crutch to help you stand the pain," Aurora finished for her in a soft voice filled with understanding.

"Yes, that's it, exactly." She stood up and walked to the window. The day had grown even darker. Like her mood. Slowly she turned, resting her spine against the cold pane.

"Have you ever felt so guilty you wanted to hide in a dark room and scream?" she asked in a dead voice. "Have you ever felt such shame you wanted to shrivel up and die?"

Aurora shook her head. "No, thank God."

"I have. When that social worker looked me in the eye and told me my son would grow up poor and illegitimate because I had too much pride to do the 'right thing' for him."

Aurora gasped. "What a dreadful thing to say!" she cried softly. "And so unfair."

"But true," Susanna said in a sad tone. She felt her face crumple, but she forced down the tears. Crying wouldn't bring Bobby back, or make the truth any less scalding.

"I know I had no choice, Aurora. I know I did the best I could, but sometimes—" her voice wobbled "—sometimes I wonder what might have happened if I'd held on just a little longer. Maybe I could have found a cheaper place or a better job or...or written to Mat again." She bit her lip until the pain grew too sharp to bear. "Maybe that awful woman was right, Aurora. Maybe I had too much pride."

"Sue, don't *do* this to yourself," Aurora exclaimed earnestly. "It won't help. I know. I second-guessed myself for years after Dawn died. If I just hadn't come to the pueblo that weekend, I thought. Or if I had brought my mother with me to drive me to the hospital when labor started." She sighed. "I nearly made myself sick, but nothing changed. Finally, with John's help, I made peace with it."

Susanna glanced down at her scuffed running shoes. Appropriate, she thought. Running was exactly what she wanted to do at the moment.

"There's something else..." Her voice faded away.

"What?"

"Did John tell you that Mat has two children?" she asked, returning to her chair.

"Yes, he told me."

"The little boy is so much like Bobby I can hardly stand to be around him. And yet I can't seem to make myself stay away. When...whenever I'm home during the day I slip next door and play with him. It's...it's almost like having Bobby in my life again."

"Is there any chance at all for you and Mat?" Aurora's voice was quiet.

"Chance at what? An affair?" She skimmed her palm over the arm of her chair. "That's what Mat wants, Aurora. He told me so. And if I know him—and I *do*—that's all he wants."

Aurora gnawed on the corner of her lip. "I understand what you're saying, but I'm wondering..." She fell silent.

"Wondering what?" Susanna prompted.

"Well, I felt the same way about John once. He even admitted he hadn't loved me when we were married the first time, but he changed, Sue. He fought for me. He made me believe in him again. Now...now I've never felt more loved. Or been happier."

Susanna remembered the expression on Mat's face when she'd told him. She'd seen guilt there, and remorse. And for an instant, before belief had settled like lifeless stones in the black depths of his eyes, fury. What she hadn't seen was love.

"Mat isn't going to fight for me," she said flatly, ignoring the bleak, cold feeling settling in the pit of her stomach.

Her fingers trembled slightly as she opened the folder. "Let's talk about something more pleasant, like a baby for the Olveras. You're here to find out if your... picnic was successful."

Aurora drew a nervous breath. "If it wasn't," Aurora said lightly, falling in with Susanna's determined mood shift, "there's always the hayloft."

Susanna smiled. "No hayloft for you, Mrs. Olvera," she said, her voice wobbling. "By my calculations, *and* the results of the tests, you're already eight weeks pregnant."

Aurora stared at her, both hands pressed against her cheeks. "I... Oh, Sue. I was afraid to hope." She began to cry, laughing even as the tears splashed onto her cheeks. "John will be so happy."

Susanna nodded, too choked up to speak. She was so happy for her friends. And so terribly sad for herself.

Thunder cracked overhead, reverberating over the empty mesa like a sharp cry of pain. Head lowered against the driving wind, Mat ran along the edge of a dry wash gouged like an open wound into the hard earth.

He moved with a ragged stride, each step clawing at the scar tissue of his legs until he felt as though his skin were ripped open and bleeding. Each rasping breath he took scorched his lungs. Sweat beaded his forehead, and his sweatshirt was plastered to his skin by the wind.

Ahead was the Canyon of the Chosen, its red limestone walls rising like a ghostly city against the stormy dark sky.

Behind him trailed a tortuous line of miles covered stride by stride, more miles than he'd thought he could run again.

Exhaustion gripped every part of his body, but his mind refused to shut down. With every punishing yard he traveled came an echo of Susanna's voice. *I had your child.*

A son who would have been Missy's age now—if he'd lived.

A knifelike pain shot through his side, driving the breath from his burning lungs and bending him double. Hand pressed to his side, he half ran, half stumbled, to the shelter of a jagged outcropping of rock at the mouth of the canyon.

Struggling for air, he slumped against the wind-scored boulder, head hanging, eyes closed, waiting for the cramp to release him.

How long had he run? An hour? Two? More? He no longer had a sense of time.

He was alone in this place, with only the ghosts of his ancestors to witness his agony. The burning pain eased enough to allow him to rest against the cold hard boulder that kept him from sagging to the ground.

Slitting his eyes against the driving wind, he surveyed the stark vista surrounding him. Nothing looked familiar, and yet he knew this place. In legend, if not in fact.

The supernatural beings who caused the wind to blow and the rain to fall resided here, along with the spirits of the Chosen Ones. The great leader, Cadiz, was rumored to have been buried in the same spot where he'd once planned his victorious battle against the white invaders.

Mat licked his parched lips and tried to swallow past the choking dryness in his throat. Somehow he knew he had always wanted to be a warrior, too. To be as brave and as honorable as Cadiz.

The army had pinned row after row of medals on his chest. His superiors had promoted him for his skill at leading men and praised him for his courage under fire. A hero, they'd called him. A coward was more like it, and a lousy excuse for a man.

God help him, he didn't want to be the man Susanna had described, the man she so clearly despised. Deep in the dark place in his soul, however, he knew he could have been. Maybe he still was, even though he told himself he'd changed.

Lightning split the sky overhead, followed almost immediately by the sharp crack of thunder. The air smelled of sulfur and rain. Mat's chest heaved, but he couldn't seem to draw in enough air.

He'd done his damnedest to find an excuse, some justification, for his actions. For the past week, alone at night, his children asleep across the hall, he had struggled to remember the lost years, desperate to prove her wrong about him. But the effort only brought on one of his savage headaches.

The baby wasn't yours, you said.

Bitter self-hatred shivered through him, cutting into his gut like the killing thrust of a bayonet. It hurt like hell to know he'd lost a son. It hurt even worse to think he'd denied that son.

Raising his left hand, he stared at the spiderweb of scars. He'd been dead inside when he'd come back to the pueblo. And then he'd met Susanna.

She'd made him feel like a man again. When she smiled, he felt warm inside for the first time in nine cold and lonely months. When she spoke, he had to fight the urge to catch the words with his mouth. When she had pressed a kiss to Cody's dark head, his own body had surged into life. The more she pushed him away, the more he had wanted to get to know the woman behind the reserve.

The hell of it was, he already knew her. At least, he knew the innocent young girl she'd been ten years ago—if only he could remember.

She sure as hell knew him, however.

She also hadn't forgiven him. He had a gut-deep feeling she never would. Why should she?

Mat pressed the heels of his hands to his eyes, trying to blot out the look of unbearable grief on her face when she'd told him.

How had she stood it?

He dropped his hands and raised his stinging gaze to the black thunderheads. Had she been at the hospital when she'd lost the baby? Or home alone, desperately calling for help? For him?

He had known pain, the physical kind that tore at a man until there was nothing left but blinding agony. He had known terror that he would spend the rest of his life a quadriplegic. He had known the sorrow of losing the mother of his children. He had survived those things because he'd had no choice.

But he wasn't sure he could have survived the loss of his child.

His chest heaved. Remorse twisted in his belly like a barbed hook. He'd made a mistake—a bad one. And then tried to shirk his responsibility, like the selfish bastard he'd been then. Susanna had paid the price for his selfishness.

He muttered a curse into the wind. Rain began pelting him with cold stinging drops. He cursed again and pushed himself away from the wall. Taking a shuddering breath, he started jogging toward the home he shared with Susanna, pain searing through his thighs with each excruciating step.

When he'd left the hospital, he'd thought the worst was behind him. But he'd been wrong.

Every day he had to face her. Every day he had to find a way to live with the grief he'd caused her. Every day he would wonder what would have happened between them if he had been a better man.

Mat lifted his face to the driving rain, his vision blurred by the stinging drops that tasted salty, like tears. He had endured months of physical pain that tore at him in blinding agony without crying.

He wasn't crying now. Mat Cruz never cried.

Or did he?

Chapter 7

Mat stood in the middle of the kiva, garbed only in a soft deerskin loincloth. The men seated on the benches lining the perimeter of the large subterranean room watched him with expressionless eyes. John Olvera sat directly in front of him, along with most of the Council members. As a distant cousin and the man Mat respected most in Santa Ysabel, John was there as a representative of the Fire Clan. The others were witnesses chosen by the medicine man, Grandfather Horse Herder, to guard the secrecy of the ancient ritual.

No one spoke. No one made any sign of recognition. Only if he disgraced himself in their eyes would they speak. And then their words would be carefully chosen to heap shame on him.

An inky sky studded with cold stars was clearly outlined in the large square entrance in the roof. Light from the fire crackling in the pit to his right illuminated the large sand painting at his feet.

Mat stood stiffly, glancing now and then at the crude ladder that was the only exit from the sacred place. Was he making a mistake, standing vulnerable and nearly naked in front of the very men whose respect he craved?

Years of living in the white man's world, following his rules and seeking his approval, had taken him far from the simple beliefs of his people. Could he put aside the doubts that flowed in his veins along with his mixed blood and open his heart to the ministrations of a pagan shaman?

He kept himself very still, counting the heavy beats of his heart, each slow beat reminding him of the shame that was always inside him. He prayed that Susanna might someday forgive him. He had no confidence that he would ever be able to forgive himself, even with the help of the Healing Way. Without it, he had no hope at all.

Grandfather drizzled the last of the red sand onto the sacred figure portrayed in the dirt. The kachina was large, with the face of an eagle and talons for hands. He was garbed in turquoise robes and held a coiled whip in his beak. His very name made Mat shudder. Giver of Terrible Pain and Forgiveness.

The painting finished, the medicine man began to chant, his reedy voice suddenly taking on a deeper tone as the ancient words rolled from his barrel chest.

Mat bowed his head in humility and supplication as he had been told to do, trying his best to follow the convoluted song, but the words were unfamiliar, buried along with the memories of his childhood in the black void.

The plea was a simple one. That the man prostrate before Warrior Father be allowed to atone for the dishonor he had brought on himself and his clan. That he be freed from the bonds of his shame so that he might walk in the path of honor again. That he be restored to harmony in his spirit.

Suddenly a man clothed only in a turquoise breechcloth slid down the ladder into the kiva so quickly he seemed a blur.

A mask with the same fearsome features of the kachina hid his face. His body was painted in black, but his hands were coated in yellow. A braided rawhide whip trailed from one large fist.

At a word from the medicine man, Mat dropped to his knees and then to his belly, spreading his arms as the arms of the figure in the dirt were spread.

He closed his eyes and made himself relax. "Whatever you do, don't stiffen," John had warned him. "Otherwise, the lash will cut deeper, and you might cry out."

To cry out was to give in to the shame sickness, and the Healing would be a failure.

Grandfather knelt beside him, chanting steadily. With the tip of an eagle feather and paint made from clay and pollen, he drew three lines across Mat's shoulder blades. The old man's voice droned monotonously, adding to the dread building in Mat.

Get on with it, he wanted to shout, but haste was the white man's way. The Guiding Spirits were deliberate and slow, each word, each action, each movement, precise and meaningful. Nothing could be hurried. Nothing could be omitted. Even the ancient ceremonial vessel sat in the same spot near the figure's outstretched hand where it had been placed throughout the centuries.

In the way of The People, he tried to free his mind of impatience, filling it instead with the shimmering image of Susanna's face. Her smile. Her golden eyes.

The first lash came without warning, snaking across his shoulder like the hot slice of a razor-sharp blade. To purge his body of dishonor.

He bit through his lower lip, somehow keeping his agony inside. Sweat broke out on his brow, and his fingers dug into the dirt, seeking handholds to keep him anchored. His every instinct urged him to run, to escape, but the memory of Susanna's pale sad face kept him motionless. He deserved this humiliation, this pain, and more, for what he had done to her and to his son.

This time he heard the hiss of the rawhide as it cut the air. To purify his mind.

His flesh split in a red line, and he nearly strangled on the sickness springing to his throat. One more, he told himself as he clung to the image of Susanna's golden eyes. Slowly he opened his eyes, half believing that she would be there.

Dimly, as through a haze, he was aware of the fire, the jangle of small bells tied to the ankle of the kachina, the stinging wetness of the sweat dripping into his eyes. He heard the rasping of his labored breathing, smelled the musky scent of the dirt beneath his cheek, felt the fear choke his throat.

The last blow came quickly and, surprisingly, without pain. To cleanse his soul.

His body sagged in relief.

He had done it. He hadn't disgraced himself.

Cool water from the fragile bowl bathed his shoulders, dripping into the dirt. Grandfather scooped up handfuls of the red clay and patted them onto his torn skin, making a soothing balm. With each healing touch Grandfather intoned softly,

"In honor may I walk,
In honor may I walk,
In courage it is finished.
In courage may I be healed."

Chapter 8

Susanna threw down the tire iron and tossed the last lug nut next to the others in a little pile in the dirt next to her flat tire.

"What a way to end my day off," she muttered, staring glumly at the skirt of her best dress. Her sheer nylons, snagged on a mesquite branch as she was getting the jack from the rear of the Jeep, were already ruined. The filmy silk dress didn't stand a chance.

She inhaled slowly, summoning the strength to complete the task. In the distance a bird called to its mate, a mournful two-note song that wasn't answered. The evening breeze ruffled her hair and chilled the skin above the dress's plain round collar. Shivering, she pulled the lapels of her thin jacket closer to her neck.

"You can do this," she said, trying to buoy her spirits. "Piece of cake."

She moved to the rear bumper, where she had already attached the jack, and began levering the heavy Jeep higher.

Her face grew hot, and her breathing puffed into the chill twilight quiet like a laboring engine.

It was Sunday, the day she tried valiantly to keep free from appointments. Technically, she had weekends off. Sometimes she managed an entire day away from the pueblo. Once in a great while she managed two.

Today she had driven to Gallup to celebrate her father's birthday, returning later than usual. Fifteen minutes from home her Jeep had blown a tire.

"I...hate...this," she gasped, almost out of breath. The flat tire came off the ground, turning a slow circle on the axle. Sighing with relief, she flexed her cramped shoulder muscles, then tugged the wheel free and propped it against the fender. Dirt streaked her skirt, and she grimaced.

"So much for chic," she muttered, opening the tailgate. To get to the spare tire she needed to remove nearly all of the supplies crammed into every nook and cranny of the rear compartment.

Just as she stuck her head into the back, a hawk screeched overhead. Looking up quickly, she scanned the surrounding emptiness, an uneasy feeling stealing over her. She was alone in the vastness—a bright spot of lilac silk in a brown landscape.

The sunset shimmer had faded into cinnamon. In another half hour or so the twilight shadows would disappear into the black emptiness of night. Until moonrise it would be too dark to see what she was doing.

The hawk screamed again, then streaked toward the ruins starkly outlined against the western sky.

Working as fast as she could, she removed the boxes one by one, stacking them haphazardly at her feet. Suddenly she heard a distant rumble of thunder. Slanting a worried glance toward the sky, she was surprised to see stars twinkling down at her, faint but clearly visible. That's funny, she thought. No clouds. So how could it storm?

It couldn't, she realized an instant later, her uneasiness growing. Holding her breath, she listened. The noise swelled, then grew more distinct. Hoofbeats, coming toward her fast. Her heart tripped, and her throat constricted.

Just last week two women students from Tucson had been assaulted and robbed near the ruins. By an Indian riding a brown horse, they had told Mary Two Skies who had been on patrol that night.

Shaken and close to collapse, neither woman had been able to provide a useful description. Just that the man had reeked of liquor and had spoken filthy obscenities in unaccented English.

"Calm down," she muttered, struggling to swallow her fear. No doubt it was John Olvera. His ranch was due east about six or seven miles. Aurora had often mentioned the solitary rides he took when his emotions piled up on him.

But John rode on a dun-colored stallion. The horse plunging toward her was dark—black, maybe, or brown. She narrowed her gaze, but the bareheaded rider sat forward in the saddle, his features blurred by the speed at which he rode.

Glancing around frantically, she spied the tire iron. Hand shaking, she retrieved it from the ground and hid it behind her back.

The horse grew larger, the rider's face now distinguishable. Susanna inhaled sharply. It was Mat.

He reined to a stop, gravel flying from the horse's hooves, dust rising in a shadowy cloud. He wore chaps over his jeans and a fleece-lined vest over a soft-looking flannel shirt open at the throat. His clothing and even his wind-tossed hair carried a light powdering of dust.

"Problems?" he asked, resting his gloved hands one on top of the other on the saddle horn. He slouched easily in the saddle, making Susanna immensely aware of her own rigid posture.

"Nothing I can't handle."

If her curt tone bothered him, he didn't show it. "You ever changed a tire before?"

"Yes, lots of times."

Why didn't he just leave? she thought irritably. Surely he didn't want to have anything more to do with a woman who made her dislike so obvious.

The mare sidestepped nervously, her iron shoes clattering against the gravel. Mat calmed her easily with the pressure of knees, his gaze never leaving Susanna's face.

"Want some help?"

"No, thank you." She flicked a glance at the sky. In a few minutes she would have to change the tire by touch. She managed to repress a shudder.

Mat saw the fleeting look of anxiety cross her face and muttered a curse under his breath. Most women would have been reduced to tears by a flat tire out in the middle of nowhere. But Susanna wasn't like most women. She had an obstinate determination that rivaled his own and the resiliency of a willow reed, easily bent but rarely broken.

Still, she *was* a woman, dressed more for candlelight and champagne than hard manual labor. He kicked his feet out of the stirrups and glanced toward the sky.

"If you have a flashlight, get it," he ordered as he swung down from the saddle and ground-tied the mare. Like it or not, Susanna would have to put up with him. No matter how much she detested him, he wasn't about to leave her here alone.

Susanna felt a frown cross her face. The man might be used to spitting out commands, but she wasn't used to obeying them.

"I don't need a flashlight," she stated in a flat tone. "And I don't need help."

"In other words, you don't have a flashlight."

Susanna ground her teeth at the note of masculine disapproval in his voice. "I have one," she admitted grudgingly. "But the batteries are run-down. I intended to replace them, but..."

Mat swore succinctly. "Tomorrow, first thing, you get yourself to a hardware store and buy batteries."

Susanna bristled. "I'm perfectly capable of taking care of myself, thank you."

Mat spared her an impatient glance. "Maybe you haven't heard, Susanna. Two coeds from Arizona were attacked not too far from here the other night. They thought they could take care of themselves, too."

Susanna hesitated, then threw the tire iron to the ground and tilted her head at a defiant angle. "I heard," she said, trying not to notice the smile that played at the corners of his mouth.

Mat chuckled. "You've got guts, I'll say that for you, even if your common sense leaves a lot to be desired."

Even in the gathering dark, she could see the tiredness etched into his lean cheeks. When he moved, his limp was more pronounced than usual, as though he'd been riding for too many hours.

In the shadowed light he seemed larger than life and determined to have his way. Arguing would simply be a waste of time.

She gestured toward the open tailgate. "The spare's under the floorboard. You'll have to move the boxes." She knew she was behaving ungraciously, but she couldn't afford to let down her guard.

He nodded. Then, taking his time, he pulled off his gloves, tucking them into the narrow belt cinching the well-worn chaps. Unbuttoning his cuffs, he rolled one sleeve to the elbow, then did the same with the other, revealing thick wrists and powerful forearms corded with sinew and roped with prominent blue veins.

Two strides took him to the back of the dusty vehicle. "Looks like a twister struck in here," he said, angling a glance toward her stony face.

"I have my own system," she said in an affronted tone. "It works for me."

His mouth softened into the half-reckless, half-boyish grin she remembered. Suddenly she realized that this was the first time she had seen him grin that way since his return. "How do you know what's missing?"

She blinked, still caught up in the sensuous promise of that slanted white smile. "What?"

"The robbery. I still need the details." He began removing boxes, stacking them neatly in front of the haphazard pile she'd already started.

"I filed a report," she declared in a stubborn tone. She thrust her hands into the pockets of her jacket and walked to the front of the Jeep.

"Not with me."

As he worked, Mat watched her in the way of all cops, showing little, seeing everything. In her dress and heels she looked different. Softer, more approachable. Delicately feminine, like the purple wildflowers that could only bloom after the last thaw of winter.

He found himself wondering what it would be like to run his hand over the soft curves barely hidden by the simple design of her dress. Something shifted inside him, elusive and secret, like a sigh in the dark.

Without exercising his usual care, he grasped a heavy canvas bag with his left hand. He couldn't hold it, and it crashed to the ground. There was a tinkle of breaking glass, followed instantly by the cloying scent of strong antiseptic. Something wet spread rapidly over the tan canvas.

Mat fought down a vicious need to smash his half-useless hand into the Jeep's frame. "Sonofabitch," he grated, his jaw stiff, his frustration obvious.

Compassion softened the hard edges of Susanna's resolve, but she made herself ignore the insistent little voice that urged her to forgive this man.

She, more than most people, knew the terrible frustrations he faced every day as he struggled to compensate for the damage done to his brain and body.

But she had suffered damage, too, she reminded herself grimly. Giving up her son had left scars as angry and painful as those marking his face and scoring his body.

"Whatever it is, I'll replace it." His voice was tight, and his mouth was bitter with an inward-turning anger that hadn't been there before.

"Don't worry about it. It's only disinfectant," she said, stooping down to open the bag. "There must be cases and cases of it at the clinic."

"I'll clean up my own mess." His left hand clamped over hers, sending a quick spurt of adrenaline into her already overloaded system. Slowly he tugged on her arm, forcing her to stand.

"Will you give me a chance to clean things up, Susanna?" His voice was low, stiff, the voice of a man not used to asking for what he wanted. "Will you let me make it up to you for hurting you?"

Exerting only enough pressure to enforce his will, but not enough to bruise her delicate skin, he pulled her closer until her thighs brushed the smooth leather of his chaps. His chest was an immovable pillar of muscle and sinew, his breath warm on her face. His eyes, so intensely aware, so deeply masculine, held her immobile. Suddenly it was so quiet, she heard only the sound of their mingled breathing.

"Bury the past, Susanna. Concentrate on the future. Let me be your friend."

His fingers tightened only slightly, but enough to warn her of his superior strength. She felt the warmth of his touch spread up her arm. Because her pulse reacted immediately, she knew she had to be very careful with this man.

"You're not my friend, Mat. I'm not yours," she said, trying to pull away. "I'm not sure we were ever really friends."

His thumb moved against the pulse leaping in her wrist. "That doesn't mean we couldn't be."

"It's too late for that." She pulled her hand from his. Her skin still felt alive where his fingers had pressed.

"Only if you want it to be." He glanced toward the setting sun, his face as shadowed as the deepening night. Susanna had a sudden sensation of terrible loneliness. Were they his feelings she sensed? she wondered sadly. Or her own?

When his gaze returned to her face, it carried a new expression, one that made her catch her breath. Here was the man who had come back from the dead inch by tortuous inch. Here was a man who never gave up, no matter how terrible the odds against him.

"All I want is a second chance. I'll do all the work."

It was a mistake to look into those eyes. There were questions there she didn't want to answer, promises she didn't dare trust. "I don't believe in second chances."

His mouth moved, an ironic smile raising his scarred cheek. "But I do. And I promise I'll never hurt you."

I promise I'll never hurt you.

Her answering smile was tinged with bitterness. "You have a way of breaking your promises, Mat. I learned that the hard way."

"A lot of things have changed in ten years, Susanna," he told her in a husky tone. "Me, most of all. A man learns a lot about himself when he's flat on his back with nothing to do but think about things that hurt, things that make him ashamed. I was a lousy father and a worse husband. From what you tell me, I was a damn poor excuse for a man."

His voice roughened, and his face tightened until the bones seemed about to poke through the dark skin. "But that's history. I can't change that. All I can do is show you that *I've* changed, that I would rather die than hurt you again."

He stopped then, as though he'd said all that had to be said, all that was necessary. Perhaps for him that was true. But what about her? What did she want? It shook her to realize she didn't know.

Mat fingered a strand of hair as he had done that afternoon in her kitchen. He had declared unequivocally that they would be friends. But lovers was what he had meant. A small shiver passed through her, and he drew back his hand as though he had resolved to be patient with her.

"Have dinner with me tonight. You pick the place."

His mouth moved closer, sending her heart thundering like the hoofbeats that had brought him to her.

"I'm busy." Even as she said the words, she knew that she wanted his mouth pressed against hers, that she wanted to feel his body against hers. Involuntarily her lips parted, bringing quicksilver fire to his eyes. His head dipped another inch.

"Tomorrow night, then."

"No, Mat. Not tonight or tomorrow or any time." Desperation gave her voice a hurried quality. "I'm not interested in an affair with you."

The undamaged corner of his mouth slanted into a bone-shivering half smile. "My memory's pretty shaky, I admit, but for the life of me, I can't remember saying anything about an affair. Just dinner." The half smile became a grin that sent shock waves to her toes.

"However, it is an interesting suggestion," he added in a husky voice. "One I'll give some thought."

She already had. Too many times for her peace of mind. That realization added fuel to the always smoldering sexual awareness between them until it was like a hot flame inside her. She had to flee or be badly burned.

Bunching her fists, she said slowly and distinctly, "Stay out of my life. Don't try to be charming. Don't try to be nice. Don't even talk to me."

"Susanna—"

"I mean it, Mat." Once started, she couldn't seem to stop. Maybe she had held the words in too long, or maybe she needed them to prop up the defenses that he seemed determined to shove aside. "Whatever feelings I had for you died when...when I lost Bobby. As far as I'm concerned, you're just a man I wish I'd never met."

His eyes went still. His face seemed to change, and yet not a muscle moved. Whatever he was feeling, it was locked up tight behind that hard facade. Susanna wished she had that kind of control.

He nodded slowly, his eyes dangerously still. The lines in his face, etched there by hard experience, somehow seemed to deepen. "Whatever you want from me, you can have. Just be damn sure it's what you really want."

Was it? she asked herself hurriedly. Did she want this man to treat her as a stranger? To stop looking at her with those fierce obsidian eyes as though trying to see into her soul? To stop kissing her and holding her and flirting with her?

Maybe it wasn't what she wanted, but that was what she had to have in order to keep herself safe.

She drew breath. "Yes, that's what I really want."

Mat set his jaw. Surrender wasn't a word he counted in his vocabulary. A man never gave up, no matter what punishment he had to take in order to win. Retreated, yes. Rested if he had to, regrouped, rearmed, changed strategy if necessary, but he always fought until he won—or died.

A man also paid his debts, and he owed Susanna a big one, one that he knew now he would be paying for a long time.

"It's getting dark," he said in clipped tone. "I'd better get that tire changed." Without giving her a chance to answer, he turned away, his wide back straight and proud.

Susanna bent to retrieve the lug nuts scattered at her feet. She had gotten exactly what she wanted, so why did she feel so alone?

* * *

The ringing of the phone gradually penetrated Susanna's troubled sleep, jerking her from yet another dream of Mat. Feeling disoriented, she pressed her face into the pillow and groaned. He had been making love to her.

Her heart pounded, and her skin tingled. The dream had been so real. Too real. Her breasts were heavy and hot, and her lower body was tight with tension.

The phone shrilled again. "Okay, okay," she muttered, her voice thick. Eyes still tightly closed, she groped for the receiver by the bed, praying it wasn't another emergency.

Because Brad Greenleaf's surgical assistant was down with the flu and because Susanna was still qualified as a surgical nurse, she had helped him perform an emergency appendectomy during the early hours of the morning, returning home just as the sun was coming up over the mesa.

A quick look at the clock told her it was nearly five in the afternoon. She had slept nine hours. Thank goodness it was Sunday.

"'Lo."

"Susanna, it's Aurora. Did I wake you from a nap?"

Susanna fluttered her eyes, trying to clear her foggy brain. "No, I'm not awake yet," she said on a yawn.

She heard Aurora chuckle. "Want me to call back?"

"No, give me a minute." Susanna pressed the phone to her ear with her shoulder and used her hands to push herself upright. Her nightshirt slid sensuously over her skin, sending ripples deep into her sensitized body. She bit off a moan and tried to find a more comfortable position.

After years of living in the quiet, she had suddenly become hypersensitive to noise. She couldn't seem to breathe properly when Mat was next door. Sometimes, in the dead of night, she woke up to discover she was holding her breath, listening. Or was it waiting? She was never sure.

"Everything ready for the party?" Susanna said into the receiver when she was feeling coherent again. Tonight the

Santa Ysabel Artists Cooperative was celebrating its first birthday with a party. As executive director, Aurora was acting as hostess.

"It better be. I had Grandfather do a blessing for us yesterday, and today my students have spent all day decorating and fixing the food. If something goes wrong, I'll blame it on the clay spirits."

Susanna smiled into the receiver. Afternoon sun streamed through the window to pattern the floor tiles, and the scent of wood smoke from the fire she'd built in the fireplace two nights ago still lingered in the air.

"Are you going to autograph copies of your book?"

"No, but maybe I should. I'll be lucky if it sells a dozen copies."

A former professor at the School of Fine Arts at SMU, Aurora had just published a textbook on pre-Columbian ceremonial vessels in which she showcased the rare and, until now, never publicly glimpsed Santa Ysabel polychrome bowls, both of which were considered virtually priceless by art appraisers worldwide.

Susanna stifled another yawn. "Hey, I bought one. It's wonderful. I love the way you make history seem so real. I can almost see those ancient potters you talk about."

"Don't laugh. I think they're still living in my house somewhere, haunting me."

Susanna heard a shout in the backyard, followed by a peal of little-boy laughter. Her gaze flew to the window. Cody and Mat were playing ball.

From the things Missy had told her during their almost daily chats, she knew that Mat worked ten-hour shifts during the week and every other weekend. When he wasn't working, he tried to spend time with his children. But all too frequently, it seemed, he came home so tired he fell asleep in his chair, with Cody in his lap and a storybook on his knee.

"Susanna? Are you there?"

"Sorry. I . . . What did you say?" She tried to drag her gaze away from the window, but she couldn't seem to stop watching the laughing little boy. And his father.

"I asked if you would do me a favor."

"Of course."

"Actually, the favor is for John." Aurora sounded apologetic. "He's been trying to reach Mat for over an hour about some kind of security problem for tonight, but his phone is always busy. It might be off the hook."

Outside the window Mat tossed the ball to Cody, his movements unusually awkward, as though his back were giving him trouble.

Cody missed the ball, and it bounced off his wide little chest. With an excited squeal, he toddled across the yard after it, his short legs pumping furiously.

Bobby would have been like that energetic little boy. She closed her eyes in an effort to block out the pain. It didn't help.

"What do you want me to tell him?" Sudden tension made her voice unusually husky.

Silence hummed over the wire. "Sue, if you'd rather not . . ."

"No problem," she said heartily, faking a laugh. "Mat and I aren't enemies, you know."

"How's it going? With the two of you, I mean." Aurora's tone was sympathetic.

Susanna tightened her grip on the phone. "It isn't. We nod politely when we meet. He goes his way, I go mine. It works just fine."

"He thinks you're pretty terrific."

Eyes opening wide, Susanna nearly dropped the phone. "What did you say?"

"He's been out here a lot, riding, mostly, or sometimes helping John for the exercise. He talks about you a lot, mostly about how good you are for his daughter." Susanna heard Aurora take a deep breath. "I've seen him ride. He reminds me of John before we got back together. I think he's in a lot of pain because of what he did."

Susanna shifted her gaze to the window again. She knew the feeling. "He'll get over it."

She heard a sigh. "You're really determined to punish him, aren't you?"

Susanna gasped. "That's not fair, Aurora. I thought you, of all people, would understand."

"I do. That's why I don't want you to make a bad mistake."

Susanna closed her eyes. "You sound like you're on his side."

There was a pause. "I nearly lost John because I couldn't let go of my pain. I don't want you to make the same mistake."

How could she lose what she'd never had? She took a tighter grip on the receiver. "I see Mat outside. I'll tell him to call John."

A sigh came over the line. "Lord, you're stubborn."

A smile tugged at Susanna's lips. "I'll see you tonight."

"Come early, before seven."

They exchanged goodbyes, and Susanna hung up, then returned her gaze to the scene beyond the dusty pane. This time Cody trapped the ball in his arms, his small mouth pursed in concentration.

Every time she saw Mat's son she thought about Bobby. Every time she saw Missy she wondered about the boy he had become. Was he tall, with his father's wide shoulders? Had he learned to handle his fierce temper? Did he still hate peas? Did he know he was adopted? If so, did he hate the woman who had given him up?

She took a ragged breath, pressing her hand to her lips to keep them from trembling. Oh, Bobby. I didn't want to do it. I *didn't*.

Ten minutes later, her composure still shaky but her eyes dry, she stepped off the small stoop into the backyard and walked resolutely toward the man and boy a few yards away.

She had exchanged her nightshirt for a thick warm sweater and pulled on a pair of soft corduroy slacks. Her hair was piled into a loose knot on top of her head. Her face was still scrubbed clean.

Mat saw her before she had taken more than a few steps. "Afternoon," he said with a nod as curt as the tone of his voice. Surprise filtered through her for a moment before she realized he was keeping his promise to give her exactly what she wanted. So why did she feel so hurt all of a sudden?

"I have a message for you," she said, letting him know by the tone in her voice that she had sought him out for no other reason. He remained silent, watching her with eyes narrowed against the setting sun. Before she could continue, Cody caught sight of her.

"Zana," he shouted, his round face breaking into a toothy grin. "Come play ba'." He began to run toward her, his chubby arms outstretched, his scuffed sneakers raising puffs of dust with each step.

Unable to resist when he called her by the name only he used, she caught him under the arms and swung him around. He shouted in glee, his brown eyes shining with excitement.

Mat kicked a clod of dirt across the yard and settled his shoulders, trying to ease the tightness in his neck. Didn't the woman own clothes that fit? he thought irritably, stabbing the toe of his boot into the hard ground.

He'd never thought a sweater that was three sizes too big could be sexy, but damn it, this one was. Maybe because the soft folds outlined just enough of her breasts to send a man's imagination into overdrive. Or because the stretched-out ribbing drew the eye to the most sensuous part of her thigh.

Tired as he was, his body began to stir, making him grit his teeth. He jammed his fingers into the back pockets of his jeans and told himself he was a fool in words that would have impressed the devil himself.

"Up, up," Cody cried as Susanna lowered him to the cradle of her arms. She bent her head to blow a kiss into his tiny ear. He giggled, ducking his head against her shoulder to escape her teasing mouth.

Without seeming to, Mat watched them laughing together, their eyes lit with a sparkling happiness that made him ache in some private, rarely visited place deep inside himself. He had never felt that kind of uninhibited joy, not in the span of time he recalled, anyway. In his gut he had a feeling he had never experienced it.

Jealousy stabbed him hard enough to bring a scowl to his face. What kind of man was jealous of his two-year-old son, for God's sake? he thought, running his hand across his suddenly knotted belly. One who was frustrated, that was what kind.

Sensing Mat's impatience, Susanna set Cody on his feet, then gave him a little pat on his bottom. "Go find your ball, sweetheart."

Mat stopped his son with a firm hand on his chubby shoulder. "It's time to go in, now, scout. Grandmother will give you a cookie."

"Cookie," Cody repeated agreeably, toddling across the yard, arms akimbo, sneakers raising another cloud of dust. At the door he turned and waved bye-bye before banging his chubby fist on the door. It opened instantly to reveal the matronly form of Grandmother Ettaway.

"You said you had a message for me?"

"Yes, call John at the ranch," she said stiffly when Cody was safely inside. Was this the way it was going to be from now on? she wondered. The two of them exchanging stilted conversation when they happened to meet? Not quite looking at each other when they passed? "He's been trying to reach you, but your phone has been busy."

Mat muttered a few choice words. "Cody likes to talk to the dial tone. I've punished him, talked to him, bought him a toy phone of his own. I've even put the phone up where he can't reach it, but it looks like he found a way." His face softened as though he were going to smile, then closed up again, shutting her out. "Thanks for the message. I'll take care of it."

Susanna, fighting a smile of her own at his description of his son's exasperating naughtiness, felt as though he'd slapped her.

"You're welcome," she said stiffly as she started to walk past him, but he caught her hand, spinning her around to face him. Every time he thought about that damn letter he'd written, he wanted to punch a hole in the wall she'd put between them. Every time he remembered holding her in his arms and kissing her, his body tightened with the kind of raw need that drove a man with a hard lash. Two weeks of cold showers had put a rough edge on his temper.

"Is this the way you really want things to be between us?" he grated. *"Is it?"*

She heard the raw note in his voice, and the sound was like a knife piercing her heart. Her instinct for people told her that she had finally hurt him. Was Aurora right about her? Was she trying to cause him as much pain as he'd caused her?

She was suddenly ashamed of herself. "No," she admitted with a sigh. "Sooner or later the tension between us is going to hurt the children and I would ... hate that very much."

He glanced toward the sky, his lean face more gaunt than usual, as though he'd lost weight. He jammed his hands into his back pockets and dropped his gaze to the ground between them for a beat before slowly raising it to her face.

"I was dead wrong, Susanna. Shamefully wrong, and that's something I'll have to live with for the rest of my life." It was a statement—unequivocal, steely, uttered in the flat cadence of a man who didn't make excuses or spare himself in any way.

Susanna stared at him, trying to reconcile this man with the image of the one who had used her, then discarded her like so much soiled laundry. She couldn't make the two merge. Like crude ore forged to tempered steel by the fiery heat of pain and suffering, Mat *had* changed, in his heart and in his soul.

If things were different, if they still had Bobby, maybe...

Mat moved closer. His skin exuded a musky heat that spiraled into her senses like potent wine.

"Start over with me," he urged in a low deep voice. "Let me take care of you this time." His scarred hand found the curve of her neck. His fingers rubbed the knotted muscles at the nape until they were as fluid as warmed honey.

The land around them had gone unnaturally still, as though the earth were holding its breath. She raised both hands and pushed against his shoulders. It was like trying to move one of the river oaks deeply rooted into the banks of the Wildcat.

"Is that what you really want, Susanna? For us to be strangers, two people who just happen to share a house?"

"Yes." Her voice caressed the word, giving it the opposite meaning.

With a husky groan Mat lowered his head and fitted his mouth to hers. He tasted her lips slowly, thoroughly, his hands cupping her shoulders as gently as he could manage.

She shivered, and he pulled her closer, his arms and his body offering protection from the wind. His body heat began seeping into her pores, warming her with a familiar excitement that made her feel good all over.

She slid her arms around his neck, burrowing her fingers into the thick shaggy hair covering his nape. He stiffened, and a hard shudder rippled across his shoulders.

He drew back, wiping his kiss from her mouth with the pad of his thumb. She fluttered her eyes open and looked up at him, her mouth still soft and full from his kiss. It took all of his control to keep from giving in to the hunger prowling inside him.

"See how good it can be between us," he whispered, fighting the need to kiss her again.

Clasped in his loose embrace, Susanna was intensely aware of him. In the hushed serenity of the afternoon, he seemed even more restless than ever. His sexuality was almost as powerful as his corded arms and well-muscled thighs. When she was in his arms, nothing mattered but the way he made her feel inside. When he kissed her, she wanted to beg him to take her higher and higher until she was lost in a dizzying whirl of sensation.

But what would happen when her needs were sated? Would he expect her to be his mistress? Would the women come to whisper about her the way they whispered about Lupe? Would she ultimately become an object of pity when Mat tired of her?

"It's late," she murmured, her voice unnaturally low. "I have to get ready for the party."

His grin was a slanted line of regret. "Yeah, and I'd better call John before he has second thoughts about the new Chief of Police." Mat raked a hand through his hair, leaving it even more untidy. "You mix up a man's priorities, Susanna Spencer."

"But I have mine in order, Mat," she said firmly, struggling to ignore the melting heat that still smoldered inside her. Her face tingled where his afternoon beard had rubbed. Her mouth, sensitized by his kiss, felt swollen. "A romance with you isn't on my list."

If she hadn't been watching his eyes, she would have missed the flash of emotion in his eyes, so quickly did he erase it.

"Why did you let me kiss you?"

"I shouldn't have." It wasn't the answer he wanted, but it was the only answer that was safe.

He let out a long ragged breath. "You wanted me. You still want me. I see it in your eyes."

Her innate honesty wouldn't allow her to lie. Besides, what good would it do? He was right. His kisses had burned all the way to the soft warm part of her. But there was more to life than drugging kisses and stolen nights of sexual fulfillment. Mat wasn't offering his love, only his body.

"Sex is easy, Mat. We proved that ten years ago. But it doesn't last, not like love."

His mouth jerked. "What's love? My wife swore she loved me, but that didn't keep her from cheating on me with damn near every guy who looked her way. If that's love, I don't need it."

Susanna was suddenly very weary. There it was, the gut-deep essence of the man spelled out in seven short words. It was simple, straightforward, even honest.

She took a deep slow breath, fighting the need for him that still raced through her veins. "But I do."

She turned and walked away.

Chapter 9

Mat flipped up his collar and began tying the plain black tie. What once required a quick three or four seconds now took much longer.

He scowled at his reflection in the cracked mirror over the bathroom sink. Twenty minutes in a cold shower had cooled his ardor but done little to improve his mood.

He needed a drink. Hell, he needed a bottle, he amended savagely. And a woman. Any woman, as long as she was willing. He'd make sure she had a good time, wouldn't he? Damn straight he would. Mat Cruz knew how to take care of a woman.

Didn't he?

A muscle jumped at the edge of his hard jaw. Who the hell was he kidding? He didn't want just any woman, no matter how beautiful or willing or sexy. He wanted Susanna.

Impatiently he tugged the knot snug against his collar, then flipped down the starched collar points. One quick glance told him he was presentable enough.

Not that it mattered much, he thought, gripping the smooth sides of the sink and dropping his head. He would be working tonight, not making love.

He closed his eyes, summoning the image of her face just before his mouth took hers. He had been awestruck by the soft sheen of her eyes as she gazed up at him, her lips trembling slightly, her breath catching in her throat. Not even the threat of a slow painful death could have kept him from kissing her. He had intended to be patient with her, to prove that he wanted more from her than he had taken ten years ago. But when her mouth had softened under his, he hadn't been able to pull away.

He still felt her hands clinging to his neck, pulling him closer. His body still ached from the hot rush of blood her kiss had stirred in him.

Damn the woman, he thought, and then was ashamed of himself. She was right in everything she'd said. He didn't love her, and he wasn't about to pretend he did. According to her, that was exactly what he'd done ten years ago.

The hell of it was that he also couldn't pretend he didn't want her. Just being around her made him hurt in ways he hadn't known existed. Not just physically, but in some protected, half-forgotten part of his soul, where he longed to believe he deserved to be loved.

A familiar tightness ran up his spine to the muscles between his shoulders. His hand went to the back of his neck, working on the knot that always seemed to be there these days.

He'd come so close to putting a crack in that icy wall she had built around herself. He might be out of practice, but he wasn't dead. He knew when a woman was responding.

Yeah, she had wanted him sexually, all right. It was the rest of him she didn't want—unless he could prove that he loved her. Which was the one thing he *couldn't* do.

His mouth slanted into a cynical smile. God sure as hell knew how to make a man pay for his sins, he thought. Give him a glimpse of heaven and then tell him he can't have it—except in his dreams.

Admit it, Cruz, he demanded silently. God had nothing to do with this particular punishment. You put yourself in this purgatory. It would almost be funny—if it didn't hurt so damn much.

"Daddy?"

He glanced over his shoulder. Missy was hovering just inside the door, a worried look pinching her small face.

"What's wrong, baby? You don't look very happy."

She shuffled her pink bunny slippers nervously. "Are you gonna spank Cody 'cause he knocked over the phone so Mr. Olvera couldn't call us?"

Mat bit off a sigh. When he'd found the phone off the hook, he'd blown up. At the time Susanna's words were ringing in his ears and his body was still taut and aching. But that had been no reason to take it out on his kids.

"No, baby, I'm not. Cody didn't mean to be naughty. I know that now."

She fiddled with the sash of her robe. "You yelled at him," she said in a small voice. "Why did you yell at him if you weren't mad?"

Mat took a slow breath. How did a man explain to his nine-year-old daughter the violent need to lash out that had gripped him when he realized he didn't have a chance in hell of making things up to Susanna?

"Let's have a talk, you and me."

He took her hand and led her into his bedroom. He sat on the edge of the bed, then pulled her onto his knee. She sat stiffly, her hands pressed together between her legs, her eyes full of confusion.

"Daddy made a mistake, Missy," he said, smoothing her hair. "It's not the first one I've ever made, and it won't be the last. I shouldn't have yelled at Cody, and I shouldn't have blamed you for letting him play with the phone. But that doesn't mean I don't love you, because I do. And I need you very much." He dropped a kiss on her head. "Okay?"

She nodded, then circled his waist with her thin arms and rested her head against his chest.

"I wish you were staying home so we could play Chinese checkers."

The forlorn note in her voice made him flinch. He'd taught her to play because the doctors told him the movements necessary to manipulate the tiny marbles would be good therapy for his partially paralyzed hand.

For the past three nights he'd promised to play a game with her after dinner. One night he'd been called out to help Two Skies handle a domestic squabble that had threatened to escalate into a brawl. The other two nights he'd been so tired he'd nearly fallen asleep at the dinner table. He'd gone to his bed as soon as he'd tucked the children into theirs.

"I have all day off tomorrow," he told her gently. "We'll play as many games as you want." He rubbed her back, feeling the sharp little bones of her spine through the soft robe.

She sat up, her eyes bright again. "Promise?"

"Cross my heart." He touched the tiny cleft in her chin with his thumb. Her small features were a feminine version of his, with the exception of her chocolate-brown eyes. Those were her own.

"I have to warn you, though," he said with a grin. "This time I intend to win."

Missy's mouth took on a mischievous pout. "Uh-uh. I'm the champion of the world, remember? You even said so."

He chuckled. "Yeah, but I'm catching up."

She shook her head. "I'm the bestest."

"That you are, the bestest daughter a daddy can have." Mat kissed her, then slid her from his lap. "Baby, do me a favor and ask Grandmother Ettaway if she's going to spend the night or if I'm supposed to take her home when I get back. She told me at dinner, but I forgot."

"Okay. Be right back." Missy skipped out, her good humor restored. Mat envied her. A few soothing words, a few warm hugs, a kiss or two, and her world was in order again, he thought as he transferred his keys and wallet from the dresser to his pockets.

Missy returned, munching on a cookie. "Grandmother said she'll stay if it's real late when you get back. Otherwise, she needs a ride."

Mat pinned his badge to his shirt, then turned to face her.

"I doubt I'll be late, unless the parties here are wilder than I think they are."

He hated the nights he had to drag the children from their beds to accompany him while he drove the housekeeper across the pueblo to her apartment. But it couldn't be helped. He wouldn't leave them alone, not even with Susanna next door.

If things had been different, maybe, but . . .

Forget it, Cruz, he told himself with a biting anger. The woman is not about to let you into her life.

His teeth ground together. What was so damn great about love, anyway? Half the guys in his outfit had sworn they'd loved their wives, but that hadn't stopped most of them from fooling around when they got the chance.

Missy climbed onto his bed and sat cross-legged in the middle, watching him unlock the olive drab footlocker where he kept his weapon when it wasn't on his hip.

"Daddy, is Susanna going to be our new mommy?"

He nearly dropped the Colt. "What makes you ask that?" he asked as he strapped on the gun.

"You and her were kissing. I seen you when I was helping Cody wash his hands for supper."

Mat saw the hope in her eyes and felt sick inside. He didn't want to make her sad, but he couldn't let her go on hoping.

"Once, a long time ago, before you were born, Susanna and I met each other right here in this house. It was when your Grandmother Cruz died. Remember I told you I grew up here?''

Missy nodded solemnly, her eyes watching him intently.

''Well, I did something really bad to Susanna, something that made her feel sad inside. Because of that, she doesn't want to be my friend.''

Her jaw took on a stubborn slant that reminded him of Susanna. ''You could say you're sorry. And then she'd like you again.''

He pulled Missy close and rested his chin on her head. If only it were that easy.

''That's just it, Missy. I said I was sorry, but it didn't make any difference. Sometimes, when you hurt someone very badly, saying you're sorry isn't enough.''

He framed her small face with his hands and kissed her forehead. ''Walk me to the car. Daddy needs a little tender loving care tonight.''

Susanna's Jeep wouldn't start. She had forgotten to turn off her headlights when she'd returned at dawn, and the battery was dead.

She was already half an hour late for the party, and the studio was a good twenty minutes' drive from her house.

Calling herself a few choice names, she dropped her forehead to the steering wheel and closed her eyes. ''This isn't happening,'' she mumbled. ''Please tell me I'm still asleep.''

''Having trouble?''

Susanna raised her head to find Mat standing between her Jeep and his Bronco. Missy was with him, dressed for bed in her robe and slippers.

''You might say that, yes,'' she told him with a disgusted look at her beloved Jeep. Why now? she wanted to mutter.

She had planned to be gone before he left his house. Now it seemed he was her only hope of getting to the party at all.

The thought made her grit her teeth. She opened the door and stepped out, just as Missy ran up to give her a hug.

Mat approached more slowly, his gaunt face wiped clean of expression. She had time to notice that he looked crisp and professional in his uniform—and dangerously sexy—before she returned Missy's hug.

"You look pretty," the little girl said when Susanna released her.

She managed a smile for the little girl. "Thank you, sweetie."

"Daddy's going to a party tonight, at the place where they make pots and things, but I can't go because he's working." Missy slanted a curious look toward Susanna's intricate silver earrings. "Are you going to the party, too?"

Susanna glanced toward the Jeep. "I was, until my car wouldn't start."

"Is it broken?" Missy asked.

"Not exactly." Conscious that Mat stood watching her from a few feet away, she forced a smile to her face. "I need one of those cars with a computer that talks. You know, like, 'Susanna, you've left your lights on again, dummy.'"

Missy giggled. "Cody has a teddy bear that talks. It's his favorite. Daddy says it's going to self-destruct some night."

Susanna thought about the rag doll in the cedar chest. It hadn't talked, but Bobby had loved it. The agency hadn't let him keep anything from his former life, not even his tattered blanket. Susanna would never forgive them for that.

She took a ragged breath. "How's school?" she asked, smoothing Missy's hair.

"Okay," Missy said with a noticeable lack of enthusiasm. "We have a new teacher. Miss Knifechief. She said she went to school with Daddy, but he can't remember her." She cast a quick glance toward her father. "Can you, Daddy?"

"No."

Mat shoved his hand into his pocket and watched Susanna without seeming to. Her blouse was the color of a

cactus rose, and cut like a man's shirt, with full sleeves and
tiny cuffs. Made of some soft material, it just begged to be
touched. But not by him. The expression on her face told
him as much.

He leaned against the Bronco and dropped his gaze to his
dusty boots, listening absently to Missy's chatter. Was this
the way he was going to feel every time he ran into Susanna—like a man locked out of the one place he wanted to
be?

"I could use a push," Susanna told Mat when Missy ran
out of things to tell her. Sometime during the past two hours
she had decided that she would be friendly but distant when
they met again. It was the only way the two of them could
coexist in such a small place.

He glanced toward the lonely road leading to town. The
light was almost gone. In another few minutes it would be
dark.

"Your battery might be ruined, in which case your lights
will go out on you before you get halfway to the studio. Be
better if you rode with me."

Impatience was stamped on his face, along with another
emotion she couldn't read.

"The battery's only a few months old. By the time I get
to the studio it'll be charged again," she countered, trying
not to notice the way his tailored trousers fit snugly over his
lean hips and strong thighs.

"What if it isn't?" Arms folded, he leaned against the
Bronco and crossed one ankle over the other. In spite of the
relaxed pose, his lean body radiated a tightly coiled energy
that sent darts of warning down her spine.

"Then I'll deal with it."

"Right." He dropped his gaze to her red huaraches.
"How far do you think you'll get in those?"

Instead of answering, she turned her attention to the little girl at her side. Missy had enough problems without
having her precariously balanced world upset by something

she couldn't understand. "It's getting pretty chilly out here, sweetie. Maybe you should go on in now."

Missy's gaze shifted to her father, but unlike the last time the three of them had been together, she seemed much more comfortable with him. Susanna wondered if he had taken her advice to reassure the timid little girl. And then she knew that he had. Sadness settled like a hard lump in her stomach. Mat would have been a good father to Bobby.

"Susanna's right, baby," Mat said quietly. "Run on in now."

He moved away from the Bronco and bent to wrap his arms around Missy's small body for a good-night hug. Susanna moved away, but not before she remembered how safe she had once felt in those strong arms.

"Will you check on me when you get home?" Missy asked, clinging to his strong neck.

"First thing I do," he said, kissing her cheek.

"Bye, Daddy." She turned toward Susanna, suddenly looking shy. "Bye, Susanna."

She gave Melissa a hug. "Sleep well," she said, her heart tearing. All that she was cried out to love this darling child and her adorable brother. But she couldn't allow that to happen. Mat was bound to get married again. And the woman he chose would become the mother of his children. She wouldn't want Susanna interfering. Susanna understood that. The maternal instinct was fierce. In spite of all the years, she still considered herself Bobby's mother. The woman who was raising him was simply a surrogate.

Missy ran toward the house, then turned to wave before she opened the door. "Have a good time," she shouted before disappearing inside.

Now that she and Mat were alone, Susanna was even more aware of the tension between them.

"Will you give me a push? *Please?*" She had trouble keeping her vow to be polite. The man had a way of looking at her that made her forget a lot of things, things she needed to remember in order to keep from ending up in his bed.

"You hate having to ask me for anything, don't you?"

Was it a trick of the light that gave his face such a vulnerable expression? she wondered as he moved toward her. Or was it her own thoughts coloring her perception? "Does it matter?"

"No," he said in a tone she'd never heard before. "It doesn't matter."

He nodded toward her Jeep, his eyes opaque, as though he'd mastered the thoughts that had put shadows there. "Hop in, and I'll give you a push."

"Thanks."

She slid into the driver's seat and started to close the door. Mat stopped her with a hand on the frame. "I'll follow you. If this thing stops again, you're getting in with me. No arguments."

She opened her mouth to protest, but the rigid way he held his jaw stopped her. Mat was not a man a rational person deliberately crossed. He had given in this time, not because of anything she'd done or said, but because it suited him. If she pushed him too far, she just might find herself walking to town. She closed her mouth with a snap, sealing her words inside.

"Wise move, Susanna," he said, turning away. She thought she heard him chuckle.

The open house was winding down. Most of the families with small children had come and gone. Those that remained were in a festive mood, filling up on goodies from the two long tables covered with food and drink, talking buoyantly in a familiar mixture of Tewa and English. Susanna had done her share of both eating and talking, but after nearly three hours her feet hurt and her throat was dry.

She slipped through the crush to the drinks table, where she drew a cup of coffee from the large urn. Behind her, she heard a burst of laughter coming from the corner where John Olvera and the other members of the Council were entertaining guests from other pueblos throughout the state.

Mat stood alone a few feet from the group, his eyes moving restlessly over the throng. He rarely spoke to anyone, and when he did, it was only briefly. It was very clear that he was there to keep order, not to socialize.

The trip to town had been uneventful. The Bronco had stayed behind her the entire way, and Mat had been waiting for her when she'd climbed out of her Jeep in the makeshift parking lot. Without exchanging a word, they had walked into the party together. The People were too polite to stare, but they had been noticed nevertheless. For some reason, knowing that they were not really together made her terribly sad.

When she'd known him before, she hadn't really liked him, not in the way a woman should like the man she loves. Craved his lovemaking, loved him dearly, yes, but the arrogance he'd worn on his shoulders had put a wall between them. Now that the arrogance was gone, so was the wall.

If they had been meeting now, for the first time, she had a feeling she would like this man very much. She hated to admit it, but she was becoming more and more ambivalent about her feelings for him. And that was dangerous.

As though feeling her gaze on his face, Mat turned his head slightly, bringing his eyes in line with hers. The room was full of copper-skinned men with black eyes and dark hair. But his eyes had a dangerous glitter in them instead of humor, and his face was lean where most were broad.

It was a virile face, sculpted by a bold hand, without a hint of softness. Except when he smiled. And then the brutal lines eased and his mouth took on a vulnerable slant.

Her mouth started to relax, and then she realized he wasn't smiling. If anything, he looked as though he resented her glance.

A wave of embarrassment climbed up her neck. She jerked her gaze away so quickly that her hair tumbled over her forehead. Her hand smoothed it into order again. From the corner of her eyes, she watched him move into the crowd.

As he passed a group of teenage girls, they stopped chattering to direct veiled glances toward Santa Ysabel's new Police Chief. For many of the guests this was the first time they'd seen him. Had he heard the whispers of the women lamenting his lost good looks, or the subtle speculation about the ability of such a badly injured man to father more children?

Susanna bit her lip. He was probably the bravest man she had ever known, and maybe the strongest, not only physically, but inside, where it counted most. Not too many men had the grit to start over the way he'd had to do.

"I'm not sure which of you looks worse. Mat, I suppose, although he hides it better." Lost in thought, Susanna hadn't noticed Aurora arrive at her side.

Susanna poked a dent into the top of the white foam coffee cup with her fingernail. "Sometimes I think I should accept that offer from the women's clinic in Santa Fe. I'm a nervous wreck. I've overdosed on peanut butter cups so often lately I've gained seven pounds, and I keep misplacing things, like my stethoscope and other minor pieces of equipment like that."

Aurora gave her a sympathetic look. Even though she was only a little more than two months pregnant, her figure was fuller and her complexion glowed. Susanna envied her.

Two Council members, bedecked in silver and deep in conversation, approached, excusing themselves as they reached past Susanna for cups.

The women moved out of the way, finding a quiet spot near an open window. Susanna tugged the soft lapels of her shirt away from her throat, letting the fresh air cool her heated skin.

"It's got to be ninety in here."

"More like a hundred."

Susanna took a sip of coffee. "Yuck," she muttered, staring into the muddy liquid. It tasted as bitter as her mood. "Either John made this coffee or there's something dangerous growing in that pot."

Aurora laughed. "Poor John. His coffee has become infamous." Her expression softened. "He thinks it'll cure just about anything."

Susanna took another sip, then winced. "And I thought hospital coffee was bad." She sent a pointed glance toward the paper cup filled with orange juice in her friend's hand. "Why didn't you warn me?"

"Because you looked like you needed something strong to perk you up."

"That's true enough," she admitted with a sigh. "I can't seem to catch up on my sleep." Not when she lay awake night after night thinking about Mat.

She let her gaze drift toward the other side of the room, but instead of Mat, another man caught her eye. Stocky, with a bull neck, he had unusually short hair and mean-looking eyes.

His beefy shoulder was angled against the wall as he stood chatting with one of the young potters, a wispy-looking woman named Alice Comacho.

"Oh, my God," she said in a shocked whisper. "That looks like Buck Ruiz."

The brother of the former Tribal Chairman, Ruiz had been twice convicted of assault and battery. The last she'd heard, the man had been in prison in Santa Fe.

"It is Buck," Aurora answered in a disgusted voice. "He's out on parole. Again."

"What's John going to do about it?"

Aurora finished her orange juice, then crushed the cup in her strong potter's hand. "Nothing. As long as Buck doesn't break Tribal Law, he's entitled to live here." She hesitated, then added softly, "Actually, Buck is Mat's problem now. That's why John was trying to reach him, to tell him about Buck."

"I thought you said it was a security problem."

"It is. John wanted to make sure Mat knew about him before the party started. He was afraid Buck would show up drunk and cause trouble."

"He doesn't look drunk, but he certainly looks like trouble," Susanna muttered, noting Alice's flustered expression. Susanna didn't like the man. She never had. He seemed to swagger, even when he was standing still, but she had to admit he had a certain outlaw appeal. Maybe that was why Alice looked so smitten.

"I hope Alice knows what she's doing," Aurora said in a tight voice. "As I told John, it wouldn't surprise me to find out Buck was the one who accosted those two coeds."

Susanna went cold inside. "What did John say?"

"Not much. You know how he is. He never says anything until he's thought it through. But I had a feeling the same thing had occurred to him. I also think that's one of the things he wanted to talk with Mat about."

As the two women watched, Buck held out a hand and Alice took it. Together they started for the door.

Across the room, Mat watched Susanna shake her head at something Aurora Olvera said. The two women were the only non-Indians in the room. Both were striking women, but Susanna was the one who riled his blood.

He'd been a fool to walk away from a woman like her. So why had he? After a dozen operations and more painful procedures than he wanted to count, he'd sworn he would never let a doctor touch him again, but now he realized he would do anything to regain his memories of his time with Susanna, even let the damn surgeons slice open his head again.

But there was nothing more to be done. No more surgery, no more hypnosis sessions to dredge up buried images, nothing. The blackness in his head would always be with him, not as noticeable as the scars on his face, but just as difficult to accept.

Mat took a quick survey of the room. The party was still going strong. Everyone else seemed to be having a great time. Especially Susanna.

She hadn't been alone all evening. Damn near every eligible man in the room had talked to her at one time or another, especially that good-looking kid who ran the clinic. What was his name? Greenleaf?

Mat ran a hand down his left cheek, then glanced at the scars disappearing under the cuff of his shirt. Slowly his hand closed into a fist.

Every time she smiled at another man, he wanted to kill the guy. Every time she threw back her head and boomed out that wonderfully infectious laugh of hers, he felt a sharp prodding inside. It galled him to realize he was jealous.

Just the sight of her provocative thighs in those white jeans made him want to drag her off to his bed and make love to her until she forgot the past. But life didn't work that way.

Frustration knifed through him. Before the bombing he would have gone a few rounds with the barracks champ to ease the tension knotting his belly. Or ridden his vintage Harley to the limit of its power. Now he could only grit his teeth and wait it out.

"Chief?" Deputy Spruce stood at his elbow, a worried look on his pockmarked face.

"Problems?" Mat asked in low tone.

"No, sir. Well, not exactly. It's past eleven. Should I put in overtime tonight?"

Mat glanced at his watch, then shook his head. "Take off. Two Skies and I will handle things 'til the party breaks up."

"Thanks, Chief. I wouldn't ask, but my wife's been sick, and now my oldest boy's gone and caught what she had."

Forgotten Dream

He and Mat exchanged a few more words, then Spruce left.

Mat shifted his gaze to the corner. Aurora was now talking to someone else. Susanna was gone.

It took him less than a second to determine that she was no longer in the studio.

He bit off a furious oath. She had promised to let him know when she left so that he could make sure her battery had recharged.

A scowl tightened his face as he hurried to the exit. Good thing he'd learned patience during his convalescence. Otherwise Susanna would find out what happened to a woman who pushed a man beyond his limit.

Chapter 10

"Please, Buck. Don't do that!"

Recognizing Alice's voice, Susanna stopped fumbling in her purse for her keys and sent an anxious glance in the direction of the shrill cry. The moon was nearly full, but the far end of the deserted parking lot where she stood was deeply shadowed. She saw nothing but pickup trucks and Jeeps.

Suddenly, from the same direction, to her left, she heard the harsh rasp of a man's laugh. "You know you want it, bitch. You been givin' me the eye all night."

"No! Don't, Buck. Please don't." The frightened voice stopped abruptly, muffled into silence.

Fear pounding in her head, Susanna half ran, half walked toward the sounds of scuffling feet, searching the shadowed spaces between vehicles. The studio was too far away for anyone to have heard. She was alone.

Heart pounding, Susanna pulled up short, her breath stopping. She heard the sound of a scuffle between two parked vehicles. Buck Ruiz had Alice pushed up against the door of a battered Chevy half-ton, his knee insinuated between her thighs. One hand was busy inside her blouse.

"Let her go, Buck," Susanna ordered, stepping forward until she was so close she could smell the rank odor of sweat and cheap whiskey coming from him.

His head snapped up, then swiveled toward her. A sense of danger ran down her spine, but she stood her ground. Over his shoulder, Alice's eyes sought hers beseechingly.

"This ain't your affair, lady," he growled. "Turn on around and git the hell outta here before you git hurt bad." In the shadowed light, his smile was an ugly slash in his dark face.

She took another step, and her foot kicked something hard, sending it flying. It landed with a clink against the front wheel of another truck to her left. A hasty glance told her it was a whiskey bottle. No doubt empty now.

"You heard Alice. She doesn't want you to kiss her," she told him quietly. Without seeming to, she gauged the distance to the bottle. It wasn't much of a weapon, but it was all she had.

"Help me, Susanna," Alice beseeched, her voice rising to the point of hysteria. "He's drunk and—" So quickly his hand seemed to come from nowhere, Ruiz backhanded her. Alice's head snapped back, and blood trickled down her chin. Cringing, she tried to wrench away.

Susanna ran toward the bottle, but before she reached it, Ruiz grabbed a handful of her long hair and jerked her backward. She fell heavily, sending a jolt of pain up her spinal column.

"Stay the hell out of my business," he warned, his voice a menacing growl. "Or the next time you'll get hurt worse'n that."

He opened the door to the truck. "Get in," he growled to Alice, his hand closing over her arm to force her to do as he ordered.

Susanna managed to drag air into her lungs, enough to bring life back into her frozen muscles. She lunged for Buck's legs, but he kicked her hand away. Her wrist began to throb where the toe of his boot had caught her.

"Hold it right there, Ruiz. You're under arrest."

Susanna exhaled in relief. Mat stood two feet away, his legs spread, his hand close to his gun. Thank God, she thought. Now that it was over, she began to shake.

Ruiz froze, then spat out a crude curse. He released Alice with a jerk of his hand, then drew himself up slowly, his smelly body exuding menace.

"You okay?" Mat asked Alice, who nodded, her hand pressed against her swelling cheek.

"He's drunk," she managed to gasp out in a strangled voice.

"Move away from her, Ruiz," he ordered in a tight cold voice. "Now."

"What'll you do if I don't, cop?"

"Don't try me." Mat's voice was glacial.

Susanna was afraid to move. From the corner of her eye she saw Alice huddled against the fender of the pickup, looking equally frozen.

Seconds ticked by. Neither man moved, each measuring the other. Finally Ruiz shrugged, his mouth twisting in derision. "Hell, no woman is worth a bullet," he muttered, glaring at Alice. "'Sides, she's too damn bony for my taste."

Mat watched him in silence for several counts, then his gaze flashed toward Susanna. "Are you hurt?"

"Just my dignity," she said with a shaky laugh.

She thought he smiled, but the light was too poor to be certain. "That'll heal."

"I heard her screaming, so I tried to stop him," she explained, her voice still slightly breathless. "I didn't know what else to do."

"Next time, come get me or one of my deputies."

"Don't worry, I will." She inhaled slowly, still slightly dazed. Her backside felt bruised, and her scalp ached, but two aspirin and a hot bath would take care of that.

She started to get up, but a muscle in her back crimped into a painful knot, and she cried out. Mat shot her a quick glance. At the same moment, Ruiz lunged forward.

Before Mat could react, the other man's knuckles caught him in the face, breaking his nose. Pain exploded in his head, temporarily stunning him. Blood spurted in a hot sticky rush, covering his cheeks and dripping onto his shirt.

Shaking his head to clear his vision, he fought back instinctively, landing a quick blow to Buck's gut. His hand stung, then went dead. He connected with his right to the jaw, sending a jarring pain through his wrist.

Buck's head snapped back, his lip split. He roared out an obscenity; then, with a maddened bellow, he attacked with an alcohol-fueled frenzy, his shoulder catching Mat in the groin. Pain exploded in a blinding flash in Mat's gut. Doubled over in agony, he slowly sank to his knees, his head swimming. He fought to remain conscious, refusing to give in to the blessed oblivion that waited.

"Ain't no cripple gonna arrest me," Ruiz spat out, his voice twisted with scorn. "Remember that next time you think about spoilin' a man's fun, *Chief*."

The toe of his boot caught Mat in the side. This time the pain set off skyrockets in his head. Through a bloody haze Mat was dimly aware of the slam of a truck door, followed by the roar of an unmuffled engine and the spinning of tires. Gravel sprayed over him, and exhaust fumes fouled the air.

"Mat! Oh my God, Mat." Susanna was shaking so hard she had trouble scrambling to her feet. Everything had happened so quickly, and yet she still had seen every blow Mat had absorbed.

With that kind of battering, he had to be badly hurt. She had to get him to the clinic.

Hands trembling uncontrollably, she fumbled in her purse for a tissue, then used it to wipe away the worst of the blood streaming down his face. A gash like a jagged comma split the corner of his mouth. One eye was already starting to swell shut. The other was slit in pain.

Mat opened his eyes to see the worry twisting Susanna's face. He was supposed to be taking care of her, not the other way around. Fury at his helplessness roared through him as he shook off her hands and staggered to his feet.

With stinging eyes, Susanna watched him fight to keep on his feet. The blood on his shirt looked black in the moonlight, and his face was drawn and shadowed. Praying that her shaky knees would support them both, she slipped an arm around his waist and said urgently, "Mat, put your arm around my shoulder. Your ribs may be broken. We have to get you to the clinic."

He heard the urgency in Susanna's voice, and something more. Pity. His gut twisted until the pain was worse than the agony in his side. "Leave me alone," he muttered. "Don't need your help."

Digging deep into the last of his strength, he shook her off. He wasn't going to another damn hospital. Not ever. He'd had enough of needles and bedpans and cloying sympathy.

"Alice, go get John Olvera," Susanna ordered in a low voice. "Tell him to hurry."

"No," Mat managed to rasp out, each word an effort. "No one...don't need an audience." Blood from his fractured nose ran down to the back of his throat, and he began to cough, each wracking movement sending the pain deeper.

Alice looked at Susanna, her eyes wide with horror. "What should I do?" she asked in a broken voice.

Susanna glanced at the stiff line of Mat's shoulders. His breathing didn't sound as painful, and he seemed to be gathering strength. Intuition told her that he would feel unbearably humiliated if the entire community knew of this incident. She couldn't let that happen.

"Don't do anything, yet," Susanna told Alice. "And for heaven's sake, don't tell anyone what happened."

Mat's strength returned in stages. The red tide receded from his head. The hot iron stopped stabbing his side, leaving a throbbing ache that was bearable. His stomach stopped churning, and some of the numbness left his legs.

Susanna watched him with stony eyes. The man was impossible, she thought angrily. Stubborn, intractable, reckless, bullheaded—she piled up the adjectives, telling herself she was glad she was smart enough not to fall for him all over again.

He took one step, then another. Somehow he made it to his Bronco without passing out. His left hand closed around the handle. Icy cold, it kept slipping away from him. He had to try twice before he could get the door open.

Susanna watched helplessly as he climbed in, closed the door and started the engine. "Lord save me from macho men," she muttered, feeling helpless and frustrated. All her protective instincts told her that Mat needed her, but he would rather injure himself more severely than admit it.

"I feel awful, Susanna," Alice whispered next to her. "Like . . . like it's all my fault, him getting beat up and all. My sister's always telling me I'll get myself into trouble, flirtin' the way I do and all." Her voice broke. "She's gonna throw me out of her place when she finds out, I just know she will."

Susanna tried to comfort the distraught girl as best she could, but her attention was on Mat. The Bronco was moving slowly, but in the right direction. The road's deep ruts had to be torture for his bruised body.

What if he passed out at the wheel? Or started to bleed internally? She glanced at her Jeep.

"Do me a favor, Alice. Find John Olvera and talk to him privately—and I mean *privately*. Tell him exactly what happened, and be sure to tell him that Buck has taken off somewhere, and Mat's in no shape to go after him. Ask him to call me in an hour or so, okay?"

The girl nodded, her expression bleak. Her hand clutched the torn remnants of her blouse together at the neck. "And don't tell anyone else but your family," Susanna warned in a low tone. "It won't help Chief Cruz if this gets around, and it won't help you, either."

At the moment Buck was John's problem. Whatever he did about it, she only prayed he wouldn't embarrass Mat.

As soon as Alice was on her way, Susanna hurried to her Jeep.

Thirty minutes later she pulled into the carport and shut off the motor. Mat had pulled the Bronco into the circle of light near his front door.

Susanna snapped off her headlights, then hurried to him. As she approached the driver's door, she slowed her steps, expecting him to emerge, but the door remained closed. Through the window she saw that he had slumped over the steering wheel, apparently unconscious.

She took a deep breath, then opened the door on the driver's side. His cheek rested on the hand that still gripped the wheel, his face turned toward her. Sweat glistened on her skin. His hair was plastered to his forehead and the back of his neck. His eyes were closed.

A gust of chill wind caught her in the face, and she shivered. He couldn't remain here, she realized. Somehow she had to get him inside.

Hand shaking, she touched his cheek. His skin was clammy. "Mat, wake up. You made it. You're home."

He groaned, then stirred. The eye that wasn't swollen opened slowly, closed, then opened again as he gathered strength.

"Enjoying the view?" he muttered, his voice thick with sarcasm.

Susanna reminded herself that he was a proud man who wouldn't take well to defeat and managed to hang onto her temper. "Not particularly. It's cold out here, and I'm tired."

"So go on inside."

"That *is* the plan. Now, if you'll just let me help you—"

Mat's control snapped. He couldn't take much more of her pity. "Stop mothering me," he ground out. "That's the last thing I want from you."

"I'm not mothering you. I'm a nurse, remember?"

"Fine. Go nurse someone else."

At the hoarse note of frustration in his voice, Susanna drew back, the hand she'd stretched toward him knotting into a fist. "Have it your way," she threw at him stiffly. "Pass out in the dirt. Let Missy or Grandmother Ettaway find you in the morning."

She stepped backward two paces and crossed her arms over her chest. Go ahead, kill yourself, her attitude seemed to say.

Mat glared at her, his pride and his battered body in direct conflict. A man protected his woman. He was the strong one, the one she depended on to do the hard jobs, the tough, dirty jobs, the one she turned to to keep her safe from bullying bastards like Ruiz.

At the moment, however, he wasn't sure he could stand on his own two feet, let alone help anyone else.

Holding his breath against the burning in his ribs, he climbed out of the Bronco and slammed the door behind him. Hand clutched to his side, he walked stiffly toward the door to his half of the duplex.

"Mat, wait," Susanna called, hurrying to his side and grabbing his forearm. "You can't go in there. Not like this. What if Missy wakes up and sees you? She would be terrified."

Mat glanced down at his ruined uniform, then dragged a hand down his stinging face. It came away bloody. One glimpse of him like this and Missy would start screaming. He couldn't let that happen.

"You're right. She can't see me like this," he muttered, each word taxing his strength. He turned his back to the side of the house and slumped against the rough adobe. He was about at the end of his string. Another few minutes and he would be out cold.

Rousing himself, he gave Susanna as much of a smile as he could manage. "Give me time to get out of sight, then go get her and take her to your place for the rest of the night. Ask Grandmother to stay with Cody."

Susanna shook her head. "It makes more sense for *you* to stay at my place tonight. In the morning I'll explain to Missy that you've been in an accident but you're fine. If she wants to see you, I'll tell her you're sleeping." A ghost of a smile flitted across her face. "By the time she gets back from school you'll be your old self again."

He wanted to argue, but he knew Susanna's plan made sense. Much as he hated to let her see how bad off he really was, he couldn't risk hurting Missy.

The wind whistling over the mesa stung his cheek, and he shuddered, feeling cold to his bones. He shuddered again.

"Come on," Susanna said in a low voice. "I'll make us some hot coffee, and then I'll slip next door and tell Grandmother that you won't be home tonight."

"Sounds promising," he managed with a lopsided grin that hurt his mouth. "What do you have in mind?"

"Forget it, Cruz," she said around the lump in her throat. The man was half dead, and yet he was flirting with her. She should be outraged that he refused to take no for an answer. Instead, she was unbearably touched by his grit in the face of defeat.

Defeat? No, she thought instantly. Mat might have been beaten, but he wasn't defeated. Mat would always fight back, no matter how slim his chance of winning. He would find Buck Ruiz and arrest him.

Things she didn't dare feel threatened her composure. She didn't want to admire his courage. She didn't want to love him.

Her breath stopped. Something twisted inside, then tore lose, releasing an emotion that stunned her.

It couldn't be. She couldn't have fallen in love with him again.

But... but that was exactly what she had done.

The thought stunned her, until she grew as still as Mat. If he reached for her, if he let himself need her, she would be lost. All she'd ever wanted was to be needed, to be the one person in the world who mattered to someone, mattered more than anything else.

Please hold me, she told him silently. Show me I matter to you more than your stubborn macho pride. Show me nothing else is as important to you as I am. Show me you love me.

She held her breath, watching as Mat opened his eyes and pushed himself away from the wall, then groaned as his bruised gut protested the movement.

He swayed toward her, and she felt herself reaching out to help him, but at the last moment he jerked away from her as though her touch pained him more than his wounds.

The disappointment went deep, so deep Susanna had to bite her lip to keep from crying out. In silence, her heart bruised and sore, she led the way inside, watching him without seeming to. "Can you make it to the kitchen? The—"

"The light's better there," he finished for her, reminding them both of the day he'd brought Cody to her for first aid.

"Yes," she said woodenly, leading the way. She pulled out a chair and indicated that he should sit.

Too tired to argue, Mat did as he was told, feeling like a damn fool. Five years ago—hell, a year ago—he could have taken a pounding like this and still licked the bastard with enough energy left to haul Susanna off to the bedroom to celebrate. Now he could barely make a fist, and the chances of seeing her bedroom were somewhere between none and none.

Sighing, he let his weight rest against the chair back. The rungs hurt him where the marks from the lash were still tender.

"I'll get my kit," she said without looking at him.

Mat watched her walk toward the hall, then disappear into the room that was no doubt her bedroom. His mind followed her there, tried to picture the place she slept, the *way* she slept. More than anything he wanted her to be sleeping in his arms, her head pillowed trustingly on his shoulder. More than anything he wanted to be the man she loved.

He folded his arms on the table, cradling his aching head, and gave in to the bottomless weariness clawing at him.

Two minutes later, when Susanna returned, she found him out cold.

A heavy silence blanketed the house, broken only by the click of the bathroom door as Mat walked into the hall. He moved cautiously, carrying his boots, his bare feet making no sound on the tile.

It was early—a few minutes past six. He'd wakened at first light, his body stiff and sore, his face a mass of painful bruises. He'd been disoriented and surprised to find himself in a strange bed, until recollections of the night before had come crashing back. He'd been coldcocked by Buck Ruiz, and Susanna had taken him in so that Missy wouldn't be upset.

His ego had taken a beating, too, especially when she'd had to help him out of his bloody clothes. There he'd been, in her bed at last, stripped nearly to the buff, and there hadn't been a damn thing he could do about it.

The last thing he remembered was the soothing sound of her voice as she urged him to take a couple of aspirin. When he woke up, he'd been alone—and depressed as hell.

A hot shower had helped. The clean clothes Susanna had fetched for him last night had made him feel presentable again, but there was nothing he could do about the marks Ruiz's fist had left on his face.

What're a few more scars? he thought. Once he had taken his good looks for granted, even traded on them. Men had envied him. Women had looked at him with smiles instead of that half-fascinated, half-pitying look he'd come to dread.

His mouth tightened. Susanna had been the only woman who hadn't looked at him that way. He almost wished she had.

He paused at the entrance to the small living room, his gaze going unerringly to the woman lying on the couch. Sometime during the night the heavy woolen blanket had slipped to the floor, leaving her small body vulnerable to the chilly night air.

She slept on her back, her face turned toward him, a small frown between her sleek brows, as though her dreams troubled her. She was breathing deeply, her mouth slightly parted, her cheeks faintly pink. One hand rested just below the swell of her breasts; the other curled into an open fist near her cheek. She was wearing a faded blue football jersey that had somehow become bunched above her hips, revealing silky bikini panties almost the same color as her skin.

His heart rate kicked into high, and his body began to swell. Battered as he was, he still wanted her.

But it was more than a physical ache tormenting him. He wanted to be her friend. To be there when she needed him. To offer advice when she asked for it, unspoken support when she was too proud to ask.

Slowly he crossed the room, trying to ignore the need that grew more insistent with each step. Putting down his boots, he used both hands to pull the blanket over her.

Holding his breath against the pain, he bent to brush her mouth with his.

She stirred, her gold-edged lashes fluttering. She muttered something he didn't catch against his mouth, then sighed his name. Her lashes settled on her cheeks again, casting sensuous shadows against her creamy skin. With the sunlight in her hair and gentleness in her eyes, she was irresistible.

Mat drew back, knowing he should leave, yet unable to make himself move. The house surrounded them with a soft silence, and the morning sun bathed the room in glistening amber light. He had a sense of serenity, of peace, as though time had stopped.

The craving to touch her, to share himself with her one more time, was overpowering, beyond his ability to resist. He dropped carefully to one knee, then the other. His hand slid beneath the blanket to flatten gently against the swell of her thigh, his fingers resting on the lacy edge of her panties.

Her skin was smooth, heating his palm. A few inches to the right and he would find the hot, moist essence of her. Higher and he would discover the sleek rounded contours of her breasts. The need prowling his gut sharpened, dug in deep, sending hot flames of desire racing along his veins.

Still trapped in a dream of Mat, Susanna felt her breathing quicken and her heart rate tumble into a more rapid rhythm. Sensations ran up her leg, into her belly, rising to her warm full breasts. She stirred restlessly against the hard cushions beneath her, feeling small tugs of desire surrounding her nipples. Was she asleep? Or was Mat really there, his warm palm resting on her hip?

Sighing through parted lips that still felt the pressure of his, she opened her eyes to find him watching her with expressionless eyes.

A helpless pleasure shot through her. He was there—the man she loved.

"It's early," he murmured. Beneath his slanted eyebrows a V had formed and was deepening. "Go back to sleep."

His fingers tugged her nightshirt lower, covering her thigh. Small flutters of pleasure followed the whisper-soft pressure of his hand.

"All you all right?" she asked, her drowsy gaze skimming the bruises staining his jaw.

"I'll survive."

She'd checked on him at two and again at four. He'd been restless, but sleeping deeply, his rangy body stretched across her bed, clad only in his shorts.

Heat spread along her cheekbones as she remembered the feel of his corded legs as she slid his trousers from his powerful legs. He'd been furious when he'd been forced to accept her help. He'd been even more furious when he had become noticeably aroused at her touch.

Slowly her hand came up to touch the swollen gash by his mouth. Mat flinched, not from pain, but because her touch was unexpected.

Susanna frowned. "I didn't mean to hurt you."

"You didn't."

He cupped her hand in his, turning the palm inward and drawing it to his mouth. His breath rasped against her skin, hot and moist.

Susanna inhaled swiftly, feeling the insistent heat of desire kindle inside her. She lay perfectly still, afraid he would leave, more afraid that he would stay.

Using his finger, he traced the fullness of her mouth so softly he scarcely felt it himself. Her lips trembled into a smile.

Mat wanted to kiss her so badly that he had trouble thinking about anything else. "Did you know that Hopis consider a smile to be sacred?" he asked, his voice rasping deep.

She blinked up at him, her eyes going wider. "No, but I think I agree with them."

"Your smile is sacred to me, Susanna. Someday I want you to smile for me and really mean it."

He wanted to tell her that he forgot the things he could no longer manage when he was with her, that he felt like a whole man when she was in his arms. He wanted to tell her that her smile blunted the hard edges of the guilt and pain that were always with him, that he needed her the way he'd never needed anyone in his life.

But she didn't want to hear those things from him. She only wanted to hear that he loved her. But love was something he would never feel again.

"The morning suits you," he said instead. He loosened her hair, combing the long thick strands with his fingers until they cascaded over her pillow in glossy fragrant waves. "Did we ever make love at dawn?"

She shook her head. "You were afraid someone would notice that I was gone."

The breath he drew in slowly was ragged. "I wish I could remember, Susanna. I've tried, but that time is like a black hole in my head."

Slowly, knowing she shouldn't, but impelled by the need to take away some of the raw pain she felt radiating from his tense body, she raised her arms to his strong neck and drew him down to her.

"Kiss me," she whispered against the hard firm contours of his mouth.

His groan shuddered against her parted lips. His kiss wasn't gentle, but Mat wasn't a gentle man. His world had been the world of hard men and even harder duties to perform. She didn't expect tenderness from him. She didn't expect anything from him but pleasure, the kind that was softening her muscles to sweet, warm silk.

Driven beyond his control by weeks of denial, Mat slid the blanket from her body, replacing it with his hands. Susanna arched toward him, eager to feel his callused hands on her skin again.

With an absorption that consumed him, his blunt fingers explored, touched, grew warm with the need to know more of her skin. He felt her strain toward him, her small body taut with the same need, taxing his control.

His hand trembled as it sought her breast. She filled his palm, firm and round. He felt her warmth through the smooth knit of her shirt, and he wanted more of her. All of her.

Susanna pressed against the large hand cupping her breast. She didn't want to love him, had tried not to love him, but she did. And loving him as she did, she also wanted him desperately. Nothing mattered but the demanding touch of his hand and the soft pressure of his mouth against her throat.

His hand skimmed down her side, found the hem of her shirt, moved beneath the soft material to the even softer skin it covered. Her belly quivered under his touch, and she whimpered deep in her throat.

A rush greater than any drug shot through him, sizzling through his veins. He couldn't get enough of her. His fingers moved lower, slipping inside the thin scrap of silk. His fingers rubbed the downy hair beneath, sending ever-deepening sensations along her skin.

His fingers followed the sensations, dipping into the waiting heat. He felt her body contract, heard the ragged intake of her breath. He slid his mouth to her earlobe, nipping gently, savoring the helpless trembling of the hand clutching his shoulder.

Her breath warmed his neck as she gave small eager sighs of pleasure. He wanted to bathe himself in her warmth, to drown in the pleasure he felt touching her and kissing her and tasting her.

His mouth moved lower, to the small pointed nipple beneath the thin cloth. His tongue touched the hard tip, wetting the material in a ragged circle.

Susanna arched toward him, rubbing her breast against his hard mouth. She felt a shudder travel the length of him, heard a harsh moan escape his corded throat.

Mat lifted his head, his breathing taking on a tortured edge. His swollen body throbbed against the straining buttons of his fly. Another minute, a few more seconds, and he would be beyond the point of stopping.

It wouldn't take much more to have her clinging to him helplessly, as desperate for him as he was for her. But this time things had to be honest between them. Clean. He wouldn't dishonor her again.

"I want you, Susanna," he whispered hoarsely when her lashes fluttered and her drowsy gaze sought his face. "But I need to know you want me as I am, without promises, without the words of love that neither of us means."

No words of love.

Susanna heard the warning in his voice. Mat was offering to make love to her, but not to love her.

Sliding her arms from his neck, she angled her body into the corner of the couch and drew her knees to her chest. He hadn't lied this time. At least that much had changed.

"You'd better go," she said with as much dignity as she could manage, her body still burning from the touch of his hard fingers. Somehow she made herself ignore the small ripples of need that continued to run like a slow-moving current down her thighs.

Mat saw the glow of desire fade from her eyes, leaving him feeling as cold as drenched ashes inside. He brought her hand to his mouth and kissed the place on her wrist where her pulse jerked in small angry beats.

Desire clawed at him, urging him to pull her into his arms, to use his mouth and his hands to convince her that she was wrong, that she didn't need love.

But she seemed so small and fragile in the gentle morning light, like a dew-washed bud. And so easily trampled.

He would rather ache forever than hurt her again.

"I'll always be sorry I couldn't give you what you wanted," he said as he let her hand slip from his.

He grabbed his boots and walked away from her—while he still had the strength to go.

Chapter 11

The door to John Olvera's office was half open. Mat rapped once with his knuckles, then pushed it wide and walked in without waiting for an invitation.

John looked up from his desk, his eyebrows arching in surprise. "You look like a man spoiling for a fight, but not with me, I hope."

"No, not with you." Mat tossed an envelope onto the desk, then realized he was standing at attention and made himself relax. During the weeks since they'd begun working together, John had become more friend than superior.

John picked up the letter but didn't open it. "What's this?"

"My resignation."

John tore the envelope in half. "Not accepted," he said, dropping the two halves into the trash basket by the cluttered rolltop desk. "Anything else you need?"

Mat ran a hand over his jaw. His bruised skin was raw where the electric razor had scraped off his whiskers. "Maybe you don't know what happened last night."

"I know. Alice told me. She said Buck took off like Spirit Stealer was chasing him."

"You go after him?"

John smiled. "No way, Chief. I'm just a rancher, remember? I figured I'd only mess things up if I tried to do your job."

Mat knew exactly how much he owed this man. First, a chance to start over, and now, his self-respect. If John had roused the other men last night, Mat Cruz would always be considered no better than a woman in their eyes.

He balled his fist and beat it softly against the desk. "You need to know, John. I blew it. I'm rusty as hell. I should have read that guy better. That doesn't say much for me as an example for Spruce and Two Skies."

John laced his fingers behind his head and leaned back until the old swivel chair creaked. "That's a crock, and you know it."

Mat's head snapped up and he started to interrupt, but John held up a hand.

"There's no defense against a sucker punch," he said in a matter-of-fact tone. "I ought to know. Ruiz came at me with a knife once, a year or so ago. I would be dead now if Aurora hadn't warned me."

Mat felt some of the tension ease from his bruised gut. Among the young men of the tribe, John's courage was legendary. It meant a lot to know that John still believed in him.

"Looks like you might be right about Ruiz being the number one suspect in that incident with the college girls." Mat shoved his hat to the back of his head and lowered himself into a vacant chair. His muscles were sore and stiff, and his broken ribs made it difficult to breathe properly.

"Looks like. He was sent up for half killing a hooker in Gallup."

"Any idea where he might have gone?"

John rocked back and forth, his thoughts focused inward. "His brother Diego has the spread next to mine. Buck stays there, mostly."

"Do you know when he got out of prison?"

John shook his head.

Mat took off his hat and ran his hand through his hair. "I'll make some calls, talk to his parole officer. If he was free when the assault took place, I'll send for a mug shot and show it to the victims, along with others. If we get a match, I'll swear out a local warrant and ask for help from other local jurisdictions."

"Then what?"

Mat managed a stiff smile. "I've done some research on our ancestors. Seems Wind Warrior advised Cadiz to dig a deep pit and bury the lawbreaker up to his neck, then spread honey on the man's head and wait for scavengers to mete out justice. According to Grandfather Horse Herder, it was most effective at keeping the crime rate down."

John threw back his head and laughed. "It is tempting, isn't it?"

Mat ran two fingers over the swollen bump that used to be the bridge of his nose. "Very tempting. I have a feeling we wouldn't lack volunteers to dig the pit."

John agreed. "I might even be first in line."

Mat remembered the humiliation he'd felt when Buck's boot had crashed into his side. "I'll flip you for it," he muttered.

John grinned. "Sounds good to me." His grin faded suddenly. "All joking aside, if you hadn't shown up when you did, Alice and Susanna could have been hurt badly."

Mat didn't want to think about that. His defeat at the hands of a worthless man like Ruiz still felt raw.

"Actually, Susanna was putting up a damn good battle. When I arrived, she was trying to pull him down by his legs." He thought about the fiery look of determination on her face when she'd been fighting Ruiz. Her feelings went deep, probably deeper than he could imagine. If she loved a man . . .

"She still has a hook into you, doesn't she?"

"You might say that, yeah. For all the good it does me."

Mat realized he'd fallen silent, and that John had been watching him in that thoughtful way of his. Before he'd asked John to be his sponsor for the Healing Way, he had told him the whole story. As much as he knew, anyway.

He stood abruptly, then sucked in against the pain. "Since I'm still drawing a paycheck, I'd better get busy and earn it."

John slanted him a meditative look. "You're going after Buck, aren't you?"

"With everything I've got."

The Bronco bounced from side to side. Dust billowed behind like a long red wake. The steering wheel jerked violently under Mat's hands, requiring all of his strength to keep it steady.

He cursed steadily over the whine of the engine, praying at the same time that the vehicle wouldn't snap an axle. The trip from his office to this remote part of the pueblo normally took sixty minutes under the best of conditions. He'd done it in a little over forty, fighting a brisk headwind all the way.

But he didn't dare slow down. Susanna needed him. Her message had said it was urgent.

"Come as soon as you can," she'd said into the machine in his office. Because he'd been following up a lead on Buck Ruiz in another part of the pueblo, he had gotten her message several hours after she'd left it.

"Hell of a police force without radios in their patrol vehicles," he muttered, downshifting a split second before making the sharp turn to the Comacho leasehold.

Susanna's Jeep was parked in front of the largest of the sagging adobe buildings. He pulled in next to the dusty Jeep, twisted the ignition, and was out of the truck before the engine stopped turning over.

Favoring his still tender ribs, he ran as fast as he could toward the pale blue door. It opened before he reached the sagging stoop, and Susanna stepped into the stinging wind.

Dust swirled around them, and the air smelled of rain. Susanna squinted against the gusts, her face stark white, making the purple shadows under her eyes even more noticeable.

"What's wrong?" he asked without preamble. She looked so exhausted that he wanted to sweep her into his arms and hold her until she regained her strength. But that would only make it harder when he had to let her go.

In the two weeks since they had almost made love he had done his best to avoid her. Or maybe she had been the one doing the avoiding. Either way, he hadn't seen much of her.

Her mouth began to tremble, but she managed to compose herself. "Buck Ruiz came looking for Alice early this morning, just after the men went out to tend the sheep. When ... when he didn't find her, he beat up her sister, Rebecca, trying to make her tell him where Alice was."

Mat swore steadily and viciously, then asked in a low voice, "How is she?"

"She's badly hurt, but she'll survive." Her voice choked, and her teeth gnawed at her lower lip. "The... the baby she was carrying wasn't so lucky. The attack brought on premature labor. I ... I tried everything, but I couldn't save him."

Her voice broke, but she held on to her control. She had to. If she started crying, she might never be able to stop.

She glanced around, feeling as lonely as the empty land surrounding them. For the first time in years she felt terribly helpless—and alone.

"This is the second child she's lost," she murmured in a sad voice. "The first was right before I came here. When she got pregnant, I promised her everything would be all right."

The wind caught her words, drawing them out like the lonely notes of a bugle playing taps. Mat curled his hands into fists to keep from reaching for her.

"Sometimes things happen that are beyond your control. All you can do is fight it through the best way you can, the way you did when you took on Buck Ruiz with nothing but grit as a weapon."

His voice was surprisingly gentle, so gentle she wouldn't let herself trust the feelings the husky sound evoked in her.

Her shoulders slumped, and she huddled into her heavy sweater. She was so tired. "I'd better get back to Becca," she said, gathering herself together.

She started to turn away, but he stopped her with a brief touch on her arm. "I'll find him for you, Susanna," he vowed in a hard cold voice that she knew came from an even colder anger. "I'll make sure he never hurts anyone else again."

He bent his head and brushed her lips with his. This time there was no passion in his kiss, no hard-driven demand, only a healing tenderness. "I won't ever let anyone hurt you again," he murmured, flattening his hand against her cheek. "Not even me."

He turned and walked away. Without looking back, he climbed into the Bronco, backed around expertly and sped away. Frozen in place, her own hands replacing his on her cheeks, Susanna watched him until he was only a black speck in the distance.

Then she burst into tears.

Susanna pulled into the carport and killed the engine. The clock on the dash said 12:20. Her aching back told her that she should have been in bed hours ago.

She'd been in the operating room since nine, helping Brad deliver twins by cesarean section. Before that, she'd been with the mother-to-be while she had tried to deliver her baby naturally. Complications beyond her control had made that impossible, and she'd called Brad to do the surgery.

Yawning, she fumbled in the seat next to her for her bag. The moon was past full, its glow dimmed to a faint silver shadow against the black sky, but the light she routinely kept burning over her door shone like a welcoming beacon.

Leaving her keys in the ignition, she shoved open the door and started to step out. Lights, reminded a weary voice inside her head.

Grimacing, she snapped off the headlights and rolled up the window before getting out. Mindful of the dark windows in the other half of the duplex, she closed the door with a soft thunk instead of her customary slam, then made her way with dragging steps to her front door.

She reached for the knob, then froze. Someone had opened the door next door. Her spine shivered, and her breath quickened. Mat was up late.

She had seen only glimpses of him in the past week since their conversation at the Comacho leasehold. From Aurora, she'd learned that he'd put out a warrant for Buck's arrest and that he'd contacted the authorities in the surrounding area, but Buck appeared to have gone to ground somewhere. Like a rattler in high summer, she thought, veering toward his door. Maybe Mat had some information for her.

But it was Melissa who stood there, blinking like a frightened little rabbit.

"Missy, darling, you should be in bed," she chided gently, brushing back the child's sleep-tumbled hair.

Melissa huddled against the door frame, looking far younger than her years. "I've been waiting and waiting for you to come home," she said in a small scared voice.

"I'm here, honey. What's wrong?" Susanna dropped her bag by the door and looped an arm over Missy's trembling shoulders.

"Daddy's awful sick, Susanna. I'm scared he's going to d-die." Her thin voice ended in a sob.

"Where is he?" Susanna stared through the inky living room to the dim light spilling into the hall from the smaller of the two bedrooms.

"He's in bed." Missy began to cry, her thin body shaking with frightened sobs that wrenched at Susanna's heart. "Oh, Susanna, I don't want anything to happen to my daddy."

Comforting the child as best she could without knowing what was wrong, Susanna hurried to the master bedroom. There was enough light from the hall to throw the room into a silvery grayness.

Mat lay on his back, his body stretched diagonally across the double bed. Bathed in shadows, his face looked more gaunt than usual. His eyes were closed, his teeth bared against a terrible pain. His hands were wrapped around two rungs of the brass headboard, which he had bent out of shape in his agony. The covers were twisted around his waist, as though he'd been thrashing for hours.

Susanna approached the bed, quickly scanning his face and bare chest for signs of injury. None were apparent, only a network of jagged intersecting scars that had only half-faded. "Mat, can you hear me? Are you awake?"

He groaned, then tossed his head from side to side, his breath coming in rasps. His hair was wet, plastered to his head. The pillow beneath him was soaked with the sweat that poured from his body.

"My God," she whispered. "What is it?" She shot a quick glance at the child hovering in the doorway. "Missy? Do you know what happened?"

The terrified little girl hung back, her lower lip clamped between her teeth to stop the sobs.

"He gets headaches, sometimes," she choked out. "I don't know what to do, Susanna. Sometimes he says things I can't understand."

Susanna heard the edge of hysteria in the child's voice. "I'm a nurse, Missy," she reminded her in a calm voice. "I won't let anything happen to your daddy."

Missy wrung her hands. "He said not to bother you. He said he could handle it all by himself."

Susanna glanced over her shoulder. Mat groaned again, then began to mumble incoherently. The muscles of his arms bulged, raising ropes of straining sinew against his coppery skin. The bed shook with his struggles.

"Missy, try to remember. Does your daddy have medication for his headaches? Pills, maybe?"

"Yes, big yellow pills."

Susanna snapped on the light, wincing at the sudden glare. Fighting the fear that constricted her throat, she searched the table by the bed. She saw a clock, a paperback book, Mat's watch, but no pill bottle.

"Missy, help me, okay?" she asked, turning back to the little girl. Missy nodded, her eyes trained on her father.

"Check the medicine chest in the bathroom and see if you can find the yellow pills."

Without a word Melissa turned and ran from the room. A second later, Susanna heard the medicine chest open.

"No, no, God, no," Mat mumbled indistinctly, then groaned. With a sudden violent movement he rolled over to his stomach and buried his face in the pillow. His big hands clutched the damp foam rubber, the long powerful muscles of his back bunching from the strain.

Susanna sat on the edge of the bed and used the sheet to wipe the beaded sweat from his thickly muscled shoulders. More scars lined his back, different from the others.

"This is all I could find, Susanna," Missy stood by the bed, a small plastic vial clutched in one hand, a glass of water in the other.

Susanna took the bottle and scanned the label. Percodan. Relief poured through her, and she allowed herself to relax slightly.

"That's it, honey, thanks." She took the glass from Missy and placed it on the nightstand next to the lamp. Opening the vial, she shook out two tablets, which she placed within reach.

She hesitated, then took Missy's cold hands into hers. "You go on back to bed before you catch a chill," she whispered, brushing the tears from the little girl's white face. "I'll take care of Daddy."

"Promise?" Missy asked tremulously, her brown eyes beseeching. She looked so small and fragile that Susanna wanted to wrap her in love and tell her nothing would ever hurt her again. But that was a promise no one could make. Not even someone who wanted to love her as much as Susanna did.

"Promise," Susanna said solemnly, crossing her heart with two fingers the way she used to do when she was Missy's age.

Missy hesitated, then threw her arms around Susanna's neck. "Tuck me in, please, Susanna," she begged in a small voice.

Susanna hesitated, then realized that Missy needed her as much as Mat did. "Okay." Susanna took her hand and led her across the hall. The bedroom was lit by a small lamp, in the shape of a gingerbread house, that sat on the dresser.

Two beds sat side by side. Cody lay curled in the center of his, his thumb in his mouth, his breathing slow and even, a ratty teddy bear with a chewed ear clutched under one chubby arm.

A sad little smile formed in Susanna's mind. He looked so much like Bobby it hurt to look at him. And then she remembered that Bobby would be almost ten now, with features so changed that she might not even recognize him if they chanced to meet on a crowded street somewhere.

Somehow tearing her gaze away from the peacefully slumbering little boy, she bit her lip to keep from moaning at the pain that tore at her.

Missy climbed into her bed and slid down against the pillow. Her face seemed very small and lonely against the colorful pillowcase. Wishing desperately that she could do this every night, Susanna carefully tucked the sheet and blanket around her, then bent to kiss her forehead.

"Night-night, honey," she whispered in an unsteady voice. "Try not to worry about your daddy."

"I won't. Not if you're here."

Susanna felt tears well in her eyes. Missy was so special to her, and yet she dared not think of her as anything but a friend.

Swallowing her anguish, she hesitated, then turned toward the other bed. Smoothing the woolly blue cover closer to Cody's stubborn little chin, she kissed him gently, then hurried to the door, closing it behind her.

In the master bedroom, Mat groaned again, turning his face away from the sound of her footsteps. The first thing she had to do was get the pills down his throat, she told herself with a calm that threatened to shatter any moment.

Touching him gently on the shoulder, she bent low to say in a soothing voice, "I need you to turn over, Mat. Now."

She pushed against his hard shoulder, trying to ease him onto his back. His muscles flinched at her touch. She made herself tighten her grip. If she could get his shoulder over, the rest of him would follow, but his body was too heavy.

Through a haze of pain, Mat heard a voice, felt a touch. Gentle hands, he thought. Warm. Nice. She smelled nice, too. Like flowers. A shadow of thought, not even solid enough to be considered a memory, passed over his mind, then sank into the black void.

"Mat, listen to me," Susanna urged, keeping her voice low in order not to hurt his head. "You have to turn over so I can help you. Please, Mat." He bit off a groan, but allowed her to shove him to his back.

"Help me, Mat. Sit up." He opened his eyes and looked at her. Pain dulled his black eyes and furrowed his brow. He struggled to focus, his face contorted into harsh lines.

"Susanna?" His voice was hoarse.

Susanna saw the unfocused look in his eyes and realized he was only semiconscious. She had seen men in the throes of pain like this try to smash their heads against the nearest wall in order to find relief.

She bent lower so that he could hear her. "Yes, it's Susanna," she said, letting her hand linger against his damp jaw. "I want you to swallow these pills."

He blinked up at her, his dark eyes slitted against the light. Murmuring encouragement, she slipped her hand under his neck, raising him enough so that he could swallow the potent painkiller.

His eyes closed. "Damn head," he muttered when she eased him back onto the pillow. His breathing was labored and his skin clammy. He rubbed his cheek against the damp pillowcase. A shiver ran through him, and he muttered a curse before turning on to his stomach again.

It was cold in the room. She had to keep him warm. Taking care not to jostle him, she untangled the sheet wrapping his lower body, uncovering lean, sinewy legs covered with soft-looking black hair and tight, muscular buttocks.

Susanna felt desire begin to flow through her like flame-warmed brandy. As a blushing nineteen-year-old, she had mapped that body with her hands and her mouth, touching and tasting, filled with the giddy power she'd held over him whenever she touched him.

God, Susanna. No one has ever loved me the way you can. Don't stop. Don't ever stop.

Gritting her teeth, she pulled the sheet over his restless body, then added the blanket she'd found bunched against the brass footboard.

She hesitated, then slipped the sodden pillow from beneath his beard-shadowed cheek. Casting a quick glance around the room, she found its mate on the floor, as though flung there. Retrieving it quickly, she settled him against it.

When, inadvertently, her hand squeezed his shoulder, he flinched, flinging out his arm and dragging her against him. For an instant she lay there stunned, her cheek pressed against his thundering heart.

"So sorry," he mumbled, moving restlessly beneath her. His hand slid down her back to her bottom, holding her firmly in place. Instinct told her there was nothing erotic in his actions. He was simply seeking human comfort the way people in excruciating pain often did.

"Don't leave me," he muttered. "Susanna? Where are you?"

"Here, Mat. I'm here."

His arms relaxed, and she edged away. He muttered a few words that she couldn't understand, then sighed heavily, his big hand groping for hers. His fingers curled around hers, imprisoning her hand completely. His eyes fluttered closed.

The clock ticked off the minutes until ten had passed. Susanna's shoulder began to cramp.

Uncurling from her uncomfortable position on the edge of the hard mattress, she tried to pull her hand from his warm, possessive grasp.

He stirred, his brows sliding into a fierce frown. His fingers tightened until she nearly cried out from the pain. Gritting her teeth, she huddled into a ball, her knees pulled to her chest. The narcotic would hit him soon, and then she would slip away to her own bed.

Closing her eyes, she tried to ignore the feel of Mat's callused hand against hers. "I love you," she whispered into the silence. So very much, she added silently. And I can never tell you.

Heartsick and weary, she closed her eyes and drifted into a doze, taking with her the memory of Mat's tormented, almost-handsome face.

Chapter 12

Mat woke at first light, his mouth as dry as Deadman's Arroyo, his head full of cobwebs. Running his tongue over his bottom lip, he tasted the salty tang of sweat. His muscles ached, and his face felt battered, as though he'd just gone three falls with the heavyweight champion—and lost.

He groaned and closed his eyes, letting the room settle around him. His hand had gone numb again, and some sadistic sonofabitch was pounding a chisel through his temple. Without moving his head, he passed his hand over his morning stubble. He needed a shower and a shave before he would begin to feel human again.

Sighing heavily, he tried to sort through his vague memories of the previous night. He'd been thinking about Susanna, hadn't he? But then, he'd done that a lot lately.

Driven by the unslaked desire that was always in him, he had tried to remember, to know what it had been like to feel her soft, welcoming body beneath his, but all he'd managed was another headache, the kind that invariably had him praying for unconsciousness.

He started to stretch out the kinks in his legs, then realized the numbness in his hand was caused by a warm weight pressing against his forearm. A frown pushed through the lethargy holding him.

He opened his eyes and turned his head. Shock took the blood from his face. Susanna was lying against his chest, her head pillowed on his shoulder. Her hair was a tumble of brown and gold against her cheek, a thick luxuriant mane that invited him to bury his face in its softness and breathe in the fresh soapy scent of her.

Shock turned to disbelief as he realized she was holding his hand, her small hand curled around his palm, as warm and trusting as a child's.

His throat felt raw, and the throbbing in his head increased. No one had held his hand in the hospital. Instead they'd simply tied him down to keep him from hurting himself.

He rubbed hard fingers across his brow. Lord, he must really have been out of it. Sometimes it got that way when he couldn't get to his pills in time. When that happened, he went a little wild, trying to escape the pain.

Damn it! Missy must have been terrified, he thought with a worried glance in the direction of the children's room. The door to his bedroom was shut. No doubt Susanna had closed it to keep the kids from hearing his groans.

Had Missy gone for Susanna, turning instinctively to the one person she knew wouldn't let her down?

He knew without having to think about it that Susanna had been there for his daughter, just as, it seemed, she'd been there for him.

But why was she still here?

She stirred, and a sigh parted her lips. Her lashes fluttered, then settled against her tanned cheeks, tempting him to trace the feathery tips with his mouth.

She was sleeping heavily, her chest rising and falling in a slow even rhythm. Each breath outlined the curve of her breasts against the soft material of her sweatshirt.

The vague feeling of longing inside him sharpened to raw male need. He clenched his thighs against the hot spur digging deep into his groin. Somehow he kept his hand relaxed against hers.

Slowly he raised his head to bunch the pillow under his neck, gritting his teeth against the hollow feeling in the pit of his stomach.

He let his gaze linger on her soft mouth, his own mouth drawn into a hard line. He should wake her. But he couldn't make himself do it.

Not yet.

He'd been alone for so long. He needed her warmth and her trust just a little longer.

As though sensing his thoughts, Susanna mumbled something in her sleep before nuzzling her cheek against the sensitive scar tissue stretched over his shoulder. But instead of pain, he felt a heightening of the need tearing at him. His pulse rocketed, and his body threatened to explode. Compressing his jaw, he made himself lie perfectly still, every muscle straining to keep from reaching for her.

Slowly, like a kitten waking from a nap in the sun, she stretched languidly, her bare feet sliding down his shin with maddening slowness. The inner part of her thigh was like slow moving heat across the top of his, and her breasts slid against his side. This time he couldn't stifle the groan that shook him.

Susanna knew before she opened her eyes that she was in Mat's bed. She felt the length of his heavily muscled legs pressed against hers. She heard the ragged sound of his breathing and felt the strength of his fingers holding hers.

His heart beat against her cheek where it lay pressed against the hard musculature of his chest, as though in the unconsciousness of sleep she had tried to get as close to him as she could.

Her pulse rate doubled. How could she have let herself fall asleep? she raged silently. She had intended to wait until he slid into a drugged sleep, then leave.

Chagrin spread through her, as hot as the blood racing up her neck and into her face. My God, she thought, squeezing her brows together in a frown, what would Missy think if she walked in on them now? What would Mat think if he woke to find her sprawled all over him? That she wanted him to make love to her, that was what. And that was exactly what she *did* want, what she would want for the rest of her life.

Taking a careful breath, she opened her eyes and began to ease away from him. Even though she was fully clothed and the sheet covered him to the waist, she could feel his thigh muscle contract into a hard knot beneath her.

Holding her breath, Susanna slowly lifted her gaze to his face. He was watching her through narrowed lids, a half-amused, half-pained look on his face. Her mouth suddenly filled with cotton wool.

"Good morning." His deep voice was rusty from sleep, and oddly tense. The tangle of black hair falling over his forehead and the dark shadow on his chin gave him a rumpled look that softened some of the hard edges of his damaged face.

"Good...good morning."

Feeling as though she were moving in slow motion, she tugged her hand from his and sat up. Her sweatshirt twisted around her torso, baring several inches of creamy skin.

As her hands fumbled to make herself tidy, she felt his gaze. Trying not to shiver in the chilly air, she crossed her arms over her breasts and hunched her shoulders. Her eyelids were still heavy from sleep, and her back was stiff from lying in one place for too long.

"How's the head?" she asked, trying without much success to crawl behind the impersonal facade of a professional. She was too aware of his body only inches from hers, and even more aware of the liquid desire slowly warming just below her skin.

"I'm okay." He glanced at the pill bottle on the nightstand. "Did you take care of me?"

"I got the pills down your throat. They did the rest."

His gaze dropped to the small hand curled into a half fist against her stomach. "Do you always hold hands with your patients?"

"Not always, no." She tried to ignore the reddened place on his heavily muscled shoulder where her head had rested. She had never woken up next to a man before, not even Mat. It gave her a funny feeling to know that she had been completely vulnerable to Mat while she slept.

"Why didn't you just walk away and let me fight through it alone?"

She dismissed his pointed question with a shrug. "Missy was terrified. I had to keep you quiet so she wouldn't panic."

He eased himself higher on the pillow, trying not to flinch at the dull throbbing in his groin. The sheet slipped to his waist, drawing her gaze. He raised his knee in an attempt to hide the powerfully swollen evidence of his need, but he wasn't quick enough.

She jerked her gaze toward the door. "I'd better go—"

Mat's hand caught her wrist. "Not yet. I haven't thanked you yet."

Pain shot up her forearm, making her wince.

He frowned. "What—?" Her skin was discolored and sore where his fingers had clutched hers during the night.

His jaw whitened. "Damn, I'm sorry." His mouth twisted with inner pain. His grip eased until her hand was balanced on his wide square palm. "I swore I'd never hurt you, and that's all I seem to do."

She felt him tremble, and something tore inside. "This wasn't your fault, Mat. I'm glad I could be here for you." With each word, her voice grew huskier.

Mat's expression changed, something that might be hope replacing the regret in his eyes. "Why are you glad, Susanna?" he asked slowly, his voice as rough as his morning beard.

"Because I don't want you to hurt anymore."

Emotion ripped his face. "When you're with me, nothing hurts anymore, not even the pity in the faces of people who meet me for the first time. When I have you in my arms..."

He gave up trying to speak and pulled her toward him. Burying his face against her hair, he held her in his arms.

"Oh, Mat," she whispered against his neck, her voice shivering because she had moved him so.

From someplace outside she heard the cheerful sound of bird song. Sunlight coming through the window warmed her cheeks.

Closing her eyes, she tried to think, but the rational part of her mind seemed somehow short-circuited. Or perhaps she was simply too tired to make sense of all the things that were happening. Whatever the reason, she had somehow allowed Mat to get much closer than she had thought possible. Now she couldn't make herself push him away.

Was that because he was determined to make amends, or because she was tired of fighting the ghosts of the past?

She relaxed against him, allowing the heat of his body to soothe away her doubts. Whatever he offered, it was more than she'd had these last ten years without him. Whatever happened later, she would have this moment, this brief time of warmth and safety. For these moments he would be hers and she would be his, the way it had been in her dreams.

He whispered her name, or maybe she only heard the husky sound in her imagination. He drew her closer, his big hand gentle but insistent on her back. Lifting his head, he searched her face.

"Smile for me, Susanna," he ordered in a raspy voice. "Make me believe you've forgiven me." His thumb touched the corner of her mouth.

Susanna thought about the things he'd told her about the Hopis. Did he, too, believe that a smile was sacred?

For the first time since she'd seen him again, she allowed her feelings to show in her eyes. In her smile.

His breath caught. "Sweetheart," he whispered. He couldn't say more. It seemed incredible to him that she was really there, that she was accepting him as he was, without the promises he couldn't yet make, without the words he might never be able to say.

Tenderness shuddered through him, filling him with a need to give her all that he had inside him. He kissed her, silently sealing his promise never to hurt her.

As his mouth reluctantly left hers, a slow shiver climbed her spine, and her mouth went dry. It couldn't be love she saw in those dark depths, she reminded herself urgently.

"Indians aren't supposed to have heavy beards," she murmured, touching his scratchy face.

"I'm only half-Indian," he reminded her, an unfamiliar look of indulgent humor softening his smile. "Or so it said in my records."

He drew his finger down her nose. His touch was teasing, even affectionate, and she felt warm all over. She had never seen him so relaxed, and it gave her a quiet feeling of satisfaction to know she had done this for him.

Sighing in contentment, she rubbed her cheek against his, and his arms tightened. "Susanna?" His breath was warm on her face.

"Hmm?"

"Did I tell you anything about my father? Who he was or what he was like?"

Susanna thought about the hurt on his face in the canyon when he'd told her about his mother and her suffering at the hands of the man who had ruined her life. The man who had taught Mat not to believe in love.

Fury at that nameless, faceless man rose in her, but she kept her features composed. "All you told me is what you already know, that he was white."

He sighed. "It's like a big chunk of me is missing."

Susanna smiled into his eyes. "You know the important things. Who you are now, who your kids are."

Mat heard the quiet reassurance in her voice and could almost feel the calluses over his heart crack open, exposing him to thoughts and feelings he'd never had before, things like a real marriage and love.

He lifted his head and looked at her face. Her eyes were soft, her long lashes tipped with gold from the morning sun, her lips still parted and rosy from the pressure of his mouth.

His senses began a slow spiral that penetrated deep, exciting him almost beyond his control. He had to kiss her again, to feel her lips part for him, to taste her sweetness against his tongue. Maybe love didn't always smother a man. Maybe, with Susanna, he could learn what it was like to be a part of another person instead of lonely and separate.

"You're so warm," he whispered in a husky voice. "I've been cold so long."

"Me, too. I just didn't know it."

Mat groaned, his mouth fitting over hers with warm demand.

Her body responded as though it had a will of its own, her thighs softening and straining against the corded hardness of his, her breasts full and aching where they pressed against the impenetrable wall of his chest.

She ran her hands over his ropy muscles, surprised at the tiny tremors she felt under her palms. The same tremors began inside her.

Mat knew he was close to losing control. But he had promised himself to go slowly. Wrapping her in his arms, he rolled until she was lying beneath him.

She gave a low moan, but it wasn't protest he heard in the throaty sound. It was desire. For him.

"Easy, sweetheart, let me make this good for you." Holding both her hands above her head with one of his, he lowered his head and began exploring the satin smoothness of her neck. His hands stroked her softness; his tongue traced the trembling curve of her mouth. With the tip of his tongue he parted her lips, leaving them wet and soft; then, with shivering slowness, he filled her mouth. She tasted warm and intoxicating, like mulled wine.

His tongue explored, tasted, caressed the tender recesses. When he had satisfied his craving there, he withdrew to taste her lips again.

Her soft moan was warm against his mouth, and he began to shake with a need to feel more of her. He drew back far enough to allow his hands to push the sweatshirt higher. His fingertip traced the pale blue wisp of lace covering her smooth white breasts.

His heart tripped to find evidence of the deeply feminine sensuality she kept so carefully guarded. As eager as a nineteen-year-old, he fumbled with the tiny hook. Somehow he managed to work it free.

He moved to his knees, then lifted her toward him. Awkwardly, long-denied hunger for her making him clumsy, he rid her of her sweatshirt and bra.

"I can't believe I forgot," he whispered, easing her to the pillow again. He kissed the satiny roundness of each perfect breast, then followed the line marking her tan with his tongue.

His hands skimmed her waist until they found the elastic waistband of her sweatpants. "Help me, sweetheart," he whispered, slipping his hands beneath her to lift her hips.

Obediently, she arched upward, allowing him to slip the pants from her.

His knee parted hers, then slid upward to rub against the V between her thighs. Ripples of hot sensation spread outward, downward, filling her. Her moan whispered between them, sending an insistent demand deep into him.

He found her breast again, his mouth leaving an exquisite brand on her skin, his hands moving beneath her to lift her toward him so that he could suck one nipple, then the other, deep into his mouth.

Susanna tumbled helplessly on a wave of desperate desire. She writhed under his hands, needing to ease the sweet tension driving her.

Ignoring his own needs, he took his time with her, using his mouth with a thoroughness that spoke of a desire to please her. With each touch of his hard hands, each kiss from his sensuous mouth, her body came more alive until she felt only Mat and the love she had for him.

She whispered his name, sending a shudder through his powerful body.

"Sweetheart, I don't want to make you pregnant again," he whispered in a strident voice that spoke of his terrible restraint. "Is it safe?"

At first, almost drowning in need, Susanna didn't understand his words.

"Are you on the Pill?" he asked, when he saw the confusion settle over her flushed face.

This time Susanna understood. She wished she hadn't. "No," she cried hoarsely, burying her face in his neck, nearly sobbing in disappointment.

Mat groaned silently, cursing his own stupidity. He had nothing in the house. In all of his fantasies he had never once thought about protecting her.

"I'll take care of you, I promise," he said in a hoarse voice. In this way, at least, he would show her that he'd changed.

Desperately she clung to him, moving her thighs over the rumpled sheet, trying to find relief from the swirling sensation of heat between her legs.

"Do you want me, honey?"

A moan whispered past her lips. "Yes, oh, yes. Now, Mat. Please, now."

Mat's hand shook as he made her ready for him. She was hot and wet and so very sweet. He eased into her, exercising every ounce of control to keep from plunging deep.

He clamped his lower lip between his teeth to keep from groaning, and the cords on his neck stood out from the effort he was expending. She tossed her head from side to side, her hands clutching his forearms. Her eyes were closed, her lips parted, her face flushed.

He thrust slowly, feeling her body expand to take him fully inside her. His breath was coming in gasps, and his blood pounded through his veins.

The tiny spasms of her body pulled him deeper. Each thrust took her closer to climax. Each movement strained his control. He fought to contain the raw hunger tearing at him. He had been without a woman too long. His body screamed for release.

Susanna felt herself rising, rising, her body moving in rhythm with his. Her muscles strained; her blood pounded.

Mat heard her soft whimpers and gritted his teeth. His gaze fixed on her face, he thrust deep, straining to the point of pain.

Exquisite tension ripped through her, exciting her, driving her. She arched toward him, desperate to ease the delicious torment.

Susanna felt the explosion start deep inside her, spreading upward and outward until she was awash in feeling. Joy pulsed through her, followed by a pleasure so profound that she lost all sense of thought, becoming the sensations filling her.

Mat felt the hot tremors surround him, and he groaned, driven to the brink by his desperate hunger. His body throbbed, still hot and engorged with blood.

Digging his fingers into the blanket, he rocked back and forth, easing her down from the peak. His muscles strained; his breathing became tortured from the savage effort he was making to hold back.

Gradually her breathing slowed, became easy. She muttered a gentle, contented sound that made him smile.

Slowly, unwilling to leave her, he bent to kiss her softly parted mouth. Her lips curved against his, and he felt a rush of satisfaction. He buried his face in the warm hollow of her neck, tasting the salty sheen moistening her skin.

He relaxed against the warm, silky body beneath him, careful to keep most of his weight on his forearms. Love me again, he wanted to beg her. Teach me how you want me to love you.

But he was afraid to say anything, afraid to break the almost mystical feeling between them, afraid to send her diving into the past again.

Adrift on a warm, wonderful ocean, Susanna stroked his back with slow lazy movements. She was floating, her body filled with a delightful lassitude. For the first time in weeks, months even, her mind was at rest. She felt nothing but sweet sensations of safety and security. She couldn't have moved if she'd wanted to.

Mat caressed her arm, feeling little tremors run under his hand. The sun from the window was warm and pleasurable on his bare back, but her skin was even warmer. He liked the touch of her and the delicate fragrance that rose from her skin.

He enjoyed sex, making sure he gave as much pleasure as he received. Not once in his memory had he made love without finding his own release.

In spite of the sharp ache in his loins, he hadn't felt this good in years. Hell, maybe he'd never felt this good. Or maybe he'd just forgotten. He sighed contentedly, savoring the exquisite feeling that being joined with her gave him.

"Was this the way it always was between us?" he asked, slipping his hand under hers to entwine their fingers. His other hand rested heavily against her breast.

Susanna's eyes fluttered open. Awareness came slowly, in stages. She was aware that she was in Mat's bedroom, in his bed. She realized that her fingers were threaded into his thick damp hair, and that he was lying on top of her, their bodies still joined. She had never felt so well loved.

"This was better," she managed to get out, her voice low and still filled with passion. Her face tingled where his morning beard had rubbed. Her mouth, sensitized by his kiss, felt swollen.

He sighed against her breast, then raised his head and kissed her. The clock said 6:15. His children would be waking soon.

He took a deep breath, trying to ignore the tension stringing him out as badly as an addict craving a fix. He had promised to take care of her, and he would keep his promise.

"I don't want to let you go, but it's getting late," he said in a voice deepened by the need that was still strong in him. "My kids get up early."

Susanna stopped breathing, straining to hear a sound from the children's room. But the silence was broken only by Mat's ragged breathing.

Clutching the blanket to her, she sat up. The light in the room had grown far brighter. Beyond the window the sky was a deep morning blue. The night was over.

She cleared her throat. "You're right. I'd better leave. The last thing we need are . . . awkward explanations."

"Stay," he said in a husky voice. "Have breakfast with us."

He began caressing her breast. Even muted by the blanket, his touch had the power to shake her to the core. Tiny pulses of excitement began building again, and her body quickened, eager to feel him inside her once more.

Susanna shook her head. "I have appointments."

The morning light touched her gently, streaking her hair with gold. She seemed young and delicate, and so lovely he didn't know how he could let her go.

"Dinner, then," he proposed. "Here with the kids. Missy's crazy about you, and you care for her. I've seen your face when you're with her. She's special to you." He traced the veins in her hand with his finger. Her hand curled into a fist.

His gaze lifted to her face. "You do care for my kids, don't you, Susanna?"

She sighed. "Of course I do. They're wonderful children, bright and affectionate, especially little Cody. He's such a little snuggle bunny."

Like Bobby, she wanted to add. But what would be the point? Talking about him only sharpened the sense of loss.

"So spend time with them. If you want, you can cuddle Cody all evening long."

For an instant the temptation was nearly overpowering, but common sense intervened before she could accept. "I don't think that's a good idea." She tried not to remember the feel of Cody's sturdy little body nestled against hers. She tried not to think about his gurgling little laugh when she teased him, or the wonderful sweetness of his hand patting her cheek.

Mat watched the yearning darken her eyes, and his throat burned. Susanna loved Cody and Missy. And she had loved their son.

Did she want another child? His child?

He could search forever and not find a better mother for his children. She claimed to have loved him once. Maybe, when she had come to love his children, she could come to care for him again.

Once he had her in his life and in his bed, he would convince her that love didn't matter. Not when they had everything else.

"Everyone likes to be cuddled now and then," he said persuasively, running his hand over her silken thigh. Her skin was still warmer than usual. From his lovemaking.

"Even you?" she asked softly.

His eyes kindled into a fierce glow. "Especially me. Come back tonight and I'll show you just how much."

His finger traced the hollow between her breasts. Instantly, her body began to respond. He only had to touch her and she came alive.

Sometimes she thought he knew her body better than she did. And that gave him power over her, power that could maim and scar.

Once he had used her as a substitute for the woman he really loved. Was he making love to her now to acquire a surrogate mother for his children? Or had he come to care for her? Could she really trust the soft look she saw in his eyes when he looked at her now?

This time she had to be sure.

"I won't sleep with you again, Mat. If...if I accept your invitation, that has to be understood."

His face closed up. "Why not, if it's what we both want?"

He sat up, and the sheet slipped down to his waist, drawing her attention to the bulge of his arousal stretching the material. Heat climbed her neck and tinged her cheek, growing hotter and hotter. So that was how he had protected her, by denying himself release.

A shiver of doubt passed through her. He'd kept his word. Didn't that mean he wanted more than sex from her?

He took her hand, the left one, and touched the bare ring finger. "I want you. I can't very well hide that. But I promise I won't do anything you don't want me to do. Okay?"

Susanna shifted her gaze to the window. The thought of being a mother again, even a surrogate one, was more than she could resist.

A mother.

No, she could never be their mother. She had to keep that firmly in her mind. But she could be their friend.

But could she be Mat's? Without expectations, without promises? Without love?

Chewing on her lower lip, she shifted her gaze to his face. The bruises had faded. His nose had healed, leaving him with yet another scar across the bridge.

He was no longer that brash young soldier who had seduced her with such fire and charm. He had aged, inside, where only he knew how much. Any man who'd had his life blasted apart the way he had couldn't help but change.

"Okay?" he repeated, his hand sliding up her arm. Tiny shivers followed his touch, and she fought the need to press against him.

"Okay."

For an instant she saw a raw flame flicker in his eyes and knew that he was going to kiss her. Her pulse leaped and her lips parted. His head moved closer. Her lashes drooped, and she held her breath.

His kiss was gentle. "Six o'clock," he said in a husky whisper against her mouth. "You bring the dessert."

Chapter 13

"Wait, Daddy, I forgot my book bag." Missy turned and sprinted toward her bedroom, reminding Mat of a small pink dust devil. Ever since she'd heard that Susanna was coming to dinner she'd been a bundle of energy, smiling and laughing and chattering all through breakfast. Mat wanted to warn her not to get her hopes up, but he didn't have the heart. Besides, he felt pretty hopeful himself.

He pushed his chair back from the table, then stood and bent over to kiss Cody on his forehead, the only place on his son's face not covered with oatmeal. "Be good for Grandmother, okay?" he admonished gently.

Cody gave him a toothy grin. "'Kay. Play ba'"

Grandmother Ettaway looked up from the potatoes she was peeling. She was a short woman, less than five feet tall, with a squat body and long gray braids. Kindness was written in every weathered line of her face, and wisdom shone in her eyes.

As soon as she'd arrived at seven, Mat had asked her to fix his favorite mutton stew for dinner. When the old lady had found out the reason, she'd beamed with pleasure and her black eyes had sparkled. They were still sparkling.

"No ball, Cody," she said firmly. "Grandmother's feet hurt today. I will tell you a new story instead, about the Wind Walker and his adventures in the Great Sky."

Cody's lower lip drooped into a pout, but Grandmother went on calmly. "After lunch, my daughter will take us into town so that we may wash the clothes. If you are good, Grandmother will buy you ice cream."

"I' cream," Cody repeated, filling up his spoon, then turning it over so the oatmeal plopped back into the bowl.

Mat crossed his arms and watched the old woman handle his stubborn son. She had her own way—far more subtle and much more effective than his do-it-or-else parenting. He had a feeling Susanna's way was a great deal like Grandmother's. For a time he hadn't been sure he would ever find out. But tonight, if all went well, he would start winning her over.

She didn't know it yet, but the lady was in for the fight of her life, one he intended to win. It didn't matter how long it took or how hard he had to work. One of these days Susanna Spencer was going to welcome him back into her life—and her bed.

"Ready, Daddy." Missy came bounding into the room, her ponytail swinging against her neck. She wore the new sweater he'd bought her last week, and the soft golden color reminded him of Susanna's eyes right after he'd made love to her.

"Okay, let's move out," he told Missy with a grin. He said goodbye to Grandmother, then ruffled Cody's hair. "Remember, Zana's coming to dinner tonight. Grandmother needs your help to make everything nice."

"Zana nice," Cody agreed with a messy grin.

Mat couldn't have agreed more.

Grandmother stopped what she was doing and followed him to the door. "You sure you don't want me to wash and iron the yellow shirt instead?'' she asked in a wheedling voice. "My bones tell me Woman Who Delivers Babies would like that one better."

"No, the blue one. It's newer."

He didn't have many clothes—only the things he'd bought when he got out of the hospital and a few shirts he'd picked up in Gallup. His civvies were packed away in the boxes that were due to arrive any day now. Or so the army had promised him when he'd made a few calls, trying to speed things up.

A part of him, however, hoped they never came. When they did, he would be faced with a tough decision. Packed away with his personal papers were the journals he had kept for so many years. In their pages he was sure to find a record of his time with Susanna. The answers he'd sought, his feelings for her then, his reason for denying their son, those things would be written there.

As he and Missy hurried through the cold morning toward the Bronco, Mat glanced at the curtained windows in the front of Susanna's apartment.

What if he found he was a worse bastard than Susanna thought? What then? Would he tell her? Or would he try to bury it in the black void with his other memories?

The sun glinted off the windows, sparkling bright. And the air smelled fresh. He had a new start here, a priceless chance at a new life where he could feel useful and needed again.

He wanted a place to belong, where he was respected for his integrity and strength and ability. He wanted to feel invincible again. But most of all he wanted Susanna. With her in his life, he would find the courage to fight for those things. Without her...

He jerked open the door of the Bronco and slid behind the wheel. He would do whatever was necessary to win this battle. He had to. His survival depended on it.

* * *

"That's bull and you know it," Mat told Diego Ruiz in a low growl. "Two witnesses have already told me they saw your brother heading this way after he beat up the Comacho woman."

"They's lying," Ruiz said around the toothpick clamped between his yellow teeth. "Buck ain't been around since he put you in the dirt."

Mat saw the gleam of derision in the other man's eyes and fought down an urge to wipe it away with his fist. He'd taken a few such verbal hits since the night outside the studio. Two Skies had told him of other remarks, most of them expressing polite concern in the way of The People about his ability to protect them from a violent man like Buck.

He understood their concerns. But he still went cold at the thought of failing them again. Of failing Susanna.

"You tell your brother I put in a call to his parole officer in Gallup."

"So what? Buck ain't done nothin' wrong."

Mat rested his boot on the sagging board that served as a front stoop and studied the look in Diego's flat eyes. The man was lying. He was also stubbornly loyal to his brother.

"Last I heard, assault was against the law, Diego. Funny thing, the P.O. thinks so, too. So Buck has a choice. He can have his parole revoked and go back to state prison to finish his sentence, or he can surrender to me and take his chances with the Tribal Court."

Diego grunted an obscenity. "Ain't no way Buck'll surrender to anyone, let alone a wimp like you, Cruz."

Rage didn't quite describe the feeling that went through Mat at that moment. In fact, he wasn't sure he could give it a name. Maybe it was better that he didn't.

"Give him the message," he repeated in a curt tone that brought a look of hatred to Diego's small eyes. "Oh, and Ruiz, if I find out you've been hiding him, I'll throw you in that cell with him."

Mat turned and walked toward the Bronco. He was shaking, and his mouth was dry. This wasn't the first time he'd been humiliated because of his physical condition. His experiences in the hospital had been humbling, to say the least. But he'd been the only one hurt then.

This time there was more at stake than his pride. If Buck Ruiz thought he had the upper hand, he might try to hurt someone else. Alice, maybe, or Susanna.

As he climbed into the truck, Mat's jaw set into a hard dangerous line. He had promised Susanna to make Ruiz pay. And that was exactly what he intended to do. One way or another.

Susanna was in the bathtub when she heard the muffled sound of Mat's boot heels on the floor next door, followed almost immediately by the gush of water running through the pipes.

Mat was taking a shower, his naked body just beyond their common wall.

Her senses quickening, she scooped bubbles into her palm and inhaled the delicate scent. Slowly they evaporated, until only a thin layer remained on her skin.

In her mind she saw these same filmy suds sliding sensuously down Mat's chest, moving in slow motion over the hard contours, wetting his skin until it was slick and warm, becoming a thin rivulet as they approached his navel.

Susanna moved restlessly, causing the water to splash against her breasts. She moved lower until her nipples were covered by the soapy water. The warm silkiness felt wonderfully erotic against her skin, like the touch of Mat's hand. Instantly, her breasts began to grow hotter and hotter until her skin felt tight and tingly.

Flattening her palms, she thought about the feel of his chest against her fingers. His skin had been resilient, warm. A fascinating mixture of rough and smooth. Her fingertips tingled, eager to explore the intimate, supremely masculine parts of him, to feel that same hardness against her hand that she'd felt sliding into her.

Her breathing grew shallow, more rapid, louder. The tub seemed too small all of a sudden, the water too cool. Her skin was hot.

Suddenly the sound of running water ceased. She held her breath, hearing only silence next door. And then suddenly she heard the squeal of Cody's voice, followed by laughter.

Daddy's home, she thought. All's right with the world. She smiled, and for a moment allowed herself to imagine what it would be like to be a part of Mat's family.

Because he loved his children, he had tried hard to make himself into a good father. But what kind of a husband would he make? In bed, he was all a woman could want.

But the passion would fade after a time. What happened then? Would they end up like those people in restaurants, staring past each other without talking, never sharing their hopes or their dreams or their fears? Never sharing themselves?

She sank lower into the fragrant bubbles and closed her eyes. Mat would never be an easy man to know. He kept too much of himself inside. Nor would he be an easy man to love, especially when he didn't want her love.

But she had no choice. Like the dawn, her day started with thoughts of Mat and ended with them when she closed her eyes to sleep. Loving him was as much a part of her as her smile and her laugh.

Sighing, she lifted her hand to drizzle water on her belly. Mat had been careful this morning. Most likely she wasn't pregnant, but as a nurse, she knew that nothing but complete abstinence was one hundred percent foolproof. She might even now be carrying his child.

Susanna's mouth curved into a tender smile. A baby, she breathed silently, rubbing her belly as though to caress the small life there. Mat's baby. Maybe a son like Bobby...

"No!" Her voice echoed loudly in the tile-lined room.

She sat up so quickly that water sloshed over onto the floor. Her skin was suddenly ice-cold, in spite of the steamy heat in the bathroom.

Crossing her arms over her chest, she stared at the vapor that had collected on the mirror over the sink, trying to summon the beloved image of her son's small dear face. But instead of Bobby she saw Cody. Instead of Bobby's voice she heard Missy's.

Alarm shuddered through her. What was wrong with her? How could she forget the fact of her son, the sound of his voice? How could she even think about replacing him in her heart, as though he had never existed?

Guilt stole through her, leaving her chilled inside. No matter how much she cared for Mat's children, she could never allow them to replace Bobby in her heart. It would be like losing him all over again.

"I mean it, Cody. No more fooling around. Finish your applesauce so I can get you into the tub before Susanna gets here."

Cody gave his father an impish grin. "Zana," he said loudly, banging his spoon on the tray of his high chair.

Mat's patience began to thin. He should have asked Grandmother to stay until Susanna arrived, but the old woman had looked almost as hassled as he was.

Gritting his teeth, he pried Cody's spoon from his chubby fingers and scraped the last of the applesauce from the plate. "Open your mouth," he ordered in a deceptively calm voice. "One last bite for Daddy."

Cody eyed him solemnly. "No, no," he shouted, knocking the spoon from Mat's hand. Applesauce splattered the front of Mat's crisply pressed shirt and plopped onto the neatly set table.

"That does it," Mat muttered in a furious voice. He stood, jerked his son from his chair and carried him kicking and laughing to the bathroom.

"Sit," he ordered, depositing the grinning toddler on the closed lid of the commode. He glanced at his watch. Eighteen minutes before Susanna was to arrive.

According to his carefully thought-out battle plan, Cody should be scrubbed and combed and looking adorable in his teddy bear pajamas. Missy should be in her best dress, her hair brushed, her face shining with anticipation. As for him...

He ran his hand through the thick hair he'd had trimmed in Chamisa on his lunch hour. It was still damp from his shower and impossible to tame. The nurses who used to cut it claimed he had sexy hair. Right now, however, it felt about as sexy as the rain-slicked coat of a very angry grizzly.

Mat groaned and glanced down at his soiled shirt. It was the only one Grandmother had had time to iron. He groaned again, then turned off the water and hurriedly began to strip his son. Haste made him clumsy, and he muttered a few well-chosen words that made his son giggle.

"Stop wiggling, Cody," he ordered. "Your old dad has had a bitch of a day. Help him out, okay?"

"'Kay," Cody said solemnly. But as soon as Mat tried to untie his little sneakers, he began kicking. Five precious minutes passed while Mat captured his bicycling legs, then struggled with a stubborn knot in one of the shoelaces. He finally broke the damn thing.

By the time he had bathed Cody and washed the applesauce from the little boy's hair, he was nearly as wet as his son. He would have to change before Susanna arrived.

"There. Don't get dirty," he told Cody as he set him on his feet and gave him a hug.

The little boy clutched his bear to his chest, plopped his thumb in his mouth and ambled toward the living room, his tiger slippers making little scuffing noises on the tile.

Now he gets sleepy, Mat thought, hurrying into the bathroom to mop up the wet floor with the nearest towel. He hesitated, then tossed the sopping cloth into the tub.

A quick glance at his watch told him that he had five minutes. He could still make it if he hurried. He stripped off the wet shirt and threw it on top of the towel. Frowning, he glanced down at the damp spots over his crotch where he had leaned against the tub. His only pair of tailored trousers were a sodden mess. His hand went to his belt just as Missy came to the door, a furious scowl on her face.

"Daddy, Cody took my new red banana clip, and he won't tell me where it is," she wailed.

"What's a banana clip?" He hesitated, then dragged the shower curtain closed and headed toward his room, Missy following.

"You know, the thing I use for my hair." She tugged at the floppy sleeve of her sweater. "It's this exact color."

Mat frowned. "Did you look in your room?"

She gave him a pained look. "It's not there. I know Cody's been messing with it, just like he messes with all my things."

Mat bit off a sigh. He didn't have time to be exasperated. "You look through his toy chest. I'll look in his hiding places in the living room."

"Make Cody leave my things alone," she said in a grumpy voice before she returned to her room.

As soon as Mat walked into the hall he could smell smoke. Biting off an oath, he hurried to the kitchen. Grandmother had told him twice to take the casserole out at five-thirty, but he'd been so preoccupied with Cody that he'd forgotten.

Calling himself a rude name, he jerked open the oven door. Smoke immediately engulfed him, bringing tears to his eyes. "Damn it to hell. What else can go wrong?"

Without thinking, he grabbed the casserole, then let out a roar of pain. The earthenware pot crashed to the floor, shattering on impact. The scorched stew coated his boots and spread in a grayish river across the worn pine flooring. Mat sucked his singed fingers, too angry for obscenities.

"Daddy, you ruined our dinner."

That did it, he thought, his patience gone. "Me!" he bellowed indignantly, turning toward the sound of his daughter's reproachful voice. "The hell I did!"

He stopped, his heart giving an extra kick against his ribs. Susanna stood next to Missy, her eyes wide, her hand pressed to her mouth. She had on the same dress she'd been wearing that night when he'd changed her tire. Silk, he thought. Soft looking. Sexy.

"You're here," he said, and then cringed. Great start, Cruz, he thought. Witty, intelligent, charming. She's sure to be impressed.

"Missy let me in," she said, setting the pie she'd brought on the counter. "I hope you don't mind." She wasn't sure if she wanted to laugh or commiserate. Probably both.

Mat heard the odd note in her voice and knew that she was trying not to laugh. More than ever, he was acutely aware of his bare chest and drenched trousers. Feeling too damn much like a character in a slapstick movie, he glared down at the gooey gravy rapidly eating through the spit shine he'd just put on his best boots. So much for dinner, he thought with a scowl. Now what was he supposed to do?

He shifted his gaze to her face, his eyes narrowing in warning. "This is not funny," he ground out in his best command voice.

It didn't phase her.

"Of course not," she said in that same odd tone. She kept her gaze fixed resolutely on his scowling face, but in her mind she saw the distinctive outline of his sex beneath the charcoal wool of his trousers.

"Accidents happen."

"Absolutely."

His brows drew together over ebony eyes that glittered dangerously. He looked rumpled, frustrated, and so sexy her breath caught in her throat.

"Cody wouldn't eat his applesauce and Missy lost her banana peel—"

"Oh, Daddy, it's a banana *clip*." Missy sounded affronted.

"Clip," he repeated in a deceptively calm tone. "And the oven started smoking—"

"Burnt offerings," Susanna offered solemnly, waving her hand in front of her face. Her cheeks had turned from pink to red, and her bottom lip was clamped between her teeth.

Mat threw up his hands. It was either that or haul her into his arms and kiss her. "Go ahead and laugh, but that was your dinner I just splattered all over the floor."

"So I see." She began to laugh, great booming peals of unrestrained mirth. It was an infectious sound, one he found hard to resist.

"Enough, woman," he said with mock menace, coming toward her. "Or I'll make you clean this up."

"Oh no, I'm the guest, remember? You're the cook."

"The hell I am. I'm the host."

She made a point of looking him up and down. Only he knew what he was doing to her equilibrium.

"Hmm, is that the latest attire for elegant dinner parties?" she asked with a pointed look at his bare chest. Almost of its own volition, her gaze traced the path her imagination had assigned to a cluster of tiny sensuous bubbles. When she reached his open belt buckle, she stopped, jerking her gaze upward to his face.

A rueful grin slashed white against dark skin. "No, this is what a harried father looks like after his son decides to play Moby Dick in the bathtub."

"I . . . Next time wear an apron," she said, loving him so much at the moment that she wanted to melt into his arms and stay there forever.

"I'll remember that."

An awkward silence fell between them. Mat began to feel like a damn fool, standing there half-naked with a beautiful woman trying not to stare at his drenched fly. He glanced toward the door. "If you'll excuse me, I'll—"

"Zana!"

Susanna whirled at the shrill cry, just in time to catch Cody as he threw himself at her. "Hi there, Scout!" she exclaimed, unconsciously adopting Mat's pet name for his son. Did that mean she had accepted everything else? Mat wondered. Him included?

"Up, up," the little boy shouted, flapping his chubby arms. Laughing, Susanna lifted him into her arms and twirled around, her skirt flaring to reveal a glimpse of slender thighs sheathed in sheerest nylon.

Mat sucked in against the sudden throbbing of his unruly sex. Had it been only that morning that he'd stroked her smooth tanned skin? Had it been only a few hours ago that he'd thrust into her soft welcoming body?

Mindful of his daughter's sharp eyes, he kept his gaze on the unadorned neckline of Susanna's dress. But even as he watched the tiny pulse flickering in the hollow of her throat, he was remembering the feel of her silken thighs sheathing him.

A silent groan shuddered through him. How in the name of all the spirits was he going to get through the evening without making love to her?

"Looks like you're in good hands," he said when she finished whirling Cody around and around.

Dizzy all of a sudden, she swayed toward him, the room moving around her. Mat reached out to steady her, his forearm sliding around her slim waist, silk against skin.

"Whoa, there," he said, his laugh almost as unrestrained as his son's. "We don't need another disaster."

For several seconds they looked at each other over Cody's silky head, her generous mouth parted in an exuberant smile, laughter still in her eyes. Emotion stirred in him, the kind that made a man lose his reason.

Was this what had happened ten years ago? Had he felt this same desperate need to make love to her? Had he wanted her so much that he'd ignored everything but the burning need in his gut?

He withdrew his arm so quickly that she staggered, but she somehow managed to keep her balance. "Uh, I'll just go see if I can find a clean shirt." He glanced at Missy. "Maybe Susanna can help you find your banana peel."

Missy giggled. "Oh, *Daddy*," she protested indignantly. "You're being silly."

"Yeah, I know," he said as he turned away. "And it feels damn good."

"Black, one sugar," Mat said as he set the cup of coffee on the low table in front of the couch where she sat curled into one corner.

"Thanks. It smells good."

"It's strong, anyway," he said with a grin as he settled himself into the other corner.

While she had helped Missy find her barrette, he had changed into a plaid cotton shirt that was clean, but needed ironing. His sleeves were rolled, his collar open. His jeans were snug, the newness worn to a faded softness by his hours in the saddle.

Susanna's glance slid past him toward the fire crackling in the grate. Light from the flames danced across the walls, giving the dimly lit room a cozy feel.

"Missy all tucked in?" she asked, angling her chin to let the fire warm her face. It was nearly ten. Mat's daughter had been allowed to stay up an extra hour, in honor of Susanna's visit.

"Yes, tucked in and probably asleep by the time I walked out of the room."

After the rocky beginning, dinner had turned out to be fun. While Mat cleaned up the mess, she and Missy had made chorizo omelets and fry bread. Cody had sat on her lap during most of the meal, licking the honey from the bread.

After dinner, Mat had asked her if she wanted to put the sleepy little boy to bed, but she had declined. The memories of another little boy, another silky black head on the pillow, would have been more than she could bear.

When it had been time for his daughter to go to bed, Mat, with a sensitivity that touched Susanna deeply, hadn't repeated his invitation. She had been grateful, but oddly disappointed that Missy hadn't asked for her.

"I'm glad you could come tonight. I was afraid you might change your mind." Mat took a sip of coffee, then stretched and rested his cup on his belt buckle. He sat in the way she had come to expect, his shoulders relaxed but straight, his knees apart and bent, his injured leg stretched out a few inches more than the other to ease the pressure on his knee.

Susanna dropped her gaze to her cup. "I nearly did."

Half a dozen times she had picked up the phone in her office to cancel this date that wasn't really a date. And then she would remember the peace she had felt in his arms and change her mind.

"What made you decide to come?" he asked.

"I knew Missy would be disappointed."

Mat angled his shoulders against the lumpy cushions and stretched his long torso, much too aware of the slender legs outlined under the silk skirt. For an instant he thought about those perfect legs entwined with his, and the tightness returned to his loins.

"What about Missy's old man? Didn't you care that he'd be disappointed, too?" His voice was low, intimate. The firelight etched shadows into his lean face, giving him the rugged look of a man used to hard times.

She slid her fingers around the smooth hard handle of her mug and brought it to her lips. The coffee was potent and hot.

"Yes, I cared. That's why I didn't call."

Did she know how irresistible she was at that moment? Mat wondered, watching the fire turn her hair to sable. Did

she know how he ached to pull her into his arms and beg her
to take him just as he was, without demanding any more
atonement for his mistakes, without needing the words of
love he wasn't sure he could give any woman?

He shifted his weight, trying to find a comfortable spot on
the hard cushion. "Tonight was difficult for you, wasn't
it?" he said quietly, surprising her. "Holding Cody, feeding him, I mean."

"A little, yes. He's very much like Bobby."

He reached for her hand and placed it on his thigh, his
hard fingers curling around hers. In comfort? she wondered. Or understanding? She didn't try to pull her hand
away, but she didn't turn her hand to accept his, either.

Mat took a deep breath, then asked in a gruff voice, "Tell
me about my son, Susanna. About...Bobby."

Stunned by his quiet request, she dropped her gaze to the
strong masculine hand covering hers. Bobby's hands had
been square, like his daddy's. "I don't want to talk about
him. It hurts."

"Please. I'd like to know."

She wanted to refuse, but she couldn't. In spite of the
problems between the two of them, he was still Bobby's father. He deserved to know something of his son.

"He was a lot like Cody," she told him in a still voice.
"Sturdy as a little tree, and so curious I knew he had to be
a scientist someday."

Mat smiled. "He didn't get that from me. According to
my school records, I barely made it through twelfth grade."

She pulled her hand free and concentrated on the flames
devouring the logs in the grate. "He got his smile from you,
and his personality. I never knew which was worse, his
temper or his stubborn need to master every new skill he
tackled in one day."

Her soft tone nearly undid him. He wanted to hold her,
to tell her how grateful he was that she had loved his son
enough to give him life, even if for a short time. But the

nervous way she played with the sash of her dress told him she was ready to bolt.

"Did he talk?"

She nodded. "The first word he learned was 'no.' He used it a lot." Her voice softened, and a gentle smile played over her lips. "And then he would look up at me and grin, like he was daring me to make him change his mind."

His spontaneous laugh touched her. "What else did he say?"

She inhaled slowly. "Mama and bye-bye and bankie." Her fingers tightened convulsively on the silk. "He was very smart and . . . and I loved him so much."

"Was he sick long?" His voice was stiff, as though asking hurt him.

It was a mistake to look into his eyes. She saw terrible grief there, and questions. Too many questions.

Tell him, urged a little voice. Don't let him go on suffering because he believes Bobby is dead.

"It's late," she mumbled, getting to her feet. "I should go."

She turned blindly toward the door, only to be pulled against a hard warm chest. His arms were protective and strong, his body sheltering. His aftershave reminded her of sagebrush and wind.

"Thank you," he said, his breath warm against her temple.

Confusion made her blink. "For what?" She tried to resist the warmth of his body, tried to keep herself stiff and distant, but the gentle stroke of his hand against her spine was so soothing.

"For having my son. For loving him. For all the things you did to make him safe and happy before he died."

Susanna heard a note of admiration in his deep voice, and she couldn't breathe. She didn't deserve to be admired, not for what she'd done.

"Please, I . . ."

Mat said softly, his hand brushing her cheek. "I understand. It hurts. But some things you just have to accept."

How? she wanted to shout. Tell me what to do and I'll do it. Willingly, gladly. She choked, and her shoulders jerked under the weight of a pain that had never completely left her.

Mat drew her into a loose embrace. "I told you the other day that I didn't need love. But I was wrong. Dead wrong. I need your love, Susanna, more than I've ever needed anything. And I intend to work harder for it than I've ever worked."

He framed her face with his hands. "Can you love me again, Susanna?"

I already do, she wanted to tell him, but she couldn't. Because if she told him that, she would have to tell him everything. About the adoption, about the contract she'd signed, promising never to try to find the little boy who was legally no longer hers, about her terrible failure as a mother.

If he blamed her, if he hated her, she would start hating herself all over again. She wasn't sure she would survive if that happened.

"You're thinking about the past, aren't you?" he asked in a low husky tone. "You're wondering if you can trust me."

"I have to be sure," she whispered truthfully.

"Then I'll just have to convince you." Mat pulled her into his arms. She closed her eyes and let herself luxuriate in his strong, warm embrace. His big scarred hand was gentle on her back, making her feel safe and cherished. Her arms stole around his lean hard waist, and he smiled against her temple, as though that small gesture pleased him.

They stood that way for a long time without speaking, without moving, warmed by the flickering fire and lulled by its muted crackle. Susanna felt a slow, heavy lethargy enter her body. She wanted to stay there forever. But that was impossible. Nothing was forever. Except the pain of giving up her son.

"Stay here tonight," he said quietly. "I need you, Susanna. I'm tired of waking up alone."

She sighed, then raised her gaze to his face. She found him watching her, his face still.

"I can't, Mat. It's too soon."

Or, she wondered as he walked her to her door and gently kissed her good-night, was it really too late? For both of them.

Chapter 14

Susanna sat in a rocking chair that had been shipped from Brazil, Cody's warm body curled in her lap. A fire burned in the grate, providing a crackling accompaniment to the story she was reading to the sleepy toddler.

It was Saturday, the last day of November. Mat had spent the afternoon unpacking the boxes that had arrived on Friday. Because she'd had to work, she had arrived late, just in time to fix *carne asada* and sopapillas for dinner, while Mat drove Missy to a friend's house for a birthday slumber party.

Now, dressed in jeans and a faded army sweatshirt that had been packed in one of the boxes, he lay on the couch, his feet propped on the arm, a book open on his flat belly. His eyes were closed, his features relaxed and vulnerable, his mouth gentle. Just looking at him made her senses tumble and whirl as though she were on a giddy carnival ride.

Tonight, she told herself. After Cody was in bed, she would tell him about his son. About Bobby. And then she would tell him that she loved him.

"One more, peeze," Cody murmured when Susanna closed the book. His long lashes drooped over sleepy brown eyes, but he refused to give up.

"How about it, Daddy?" Susanna asked, her gaze lingering on Mat's face.

His eyes opened slowly, his expression matching his son's. His grin was lazy. "You're spoiling him," he protested, but his tone was indulgent, even affectionate.

"Do you mind?"

"Nope, not a bit." The muscles of his torso rippled, then tightened as he sat up and swung his legs to the ground. "I just wish you'd spoil me just a little, too."

Susanna's heartbeat accelerated. "What about the cookies I made for you last week?"

His sooty eyebrows arched in gentle reproach. "You made me share."

"Hmm, that's true." She pretended to think. "I fixed your favorite for dinner tonight."

His sigh was exaggerated, lifting his broad shoulders in a way that emphasized the incredible strength hidden under the soft olive drab material. "Yeah, but last week you made me eat liver."

"It's good for you," she protested softly, a smile hovering over her lips. Each day she spent with Mat she fell more inexorably in love with him. She couldn't help admiring the way he disciplined himself to endure a daily hour of grueling exercises, even after the most exhausting day, or the way he worried about Missy's continuing fear of losing him, or the way he tried every day to show Susanna how much he valued her presence in his life.

He seemed to know exactly when to tease her, when to brush a tender kiss across her cheek, when to remain silent. It was a seduction of her spirit, of her soul, instead of her body, and far more difficult to resist.

But, true to his promise, he hadn't pushed her to sleep with him. Kissed her, yes. Petted her until she was a quivering collection of nerve endings, absolutely. Every night when he left her at her door, she felt the powerful arousal he made no effort to hide.

But maybe tonight, maybe after all the barriers between them had been torn down...

"Zana. One more." Cody began bouncing up and down in her lap, drawing an amused smile from his father.

Mat glanced at his watch. "It's already half an hour past his bedtime. Five more minutes and he'll be too wired to sleep. I'd better tuck him in."

Susanna heard the sigh in his voice and knew that he was achingly tired. Every day for the past week he and his deputies had borrowed horses from John Olvera and scoured the remote canyons, searching for Buck Ruiz. So far they'd found traces of a camp fire and a butchered sheep, but nothing to prove that Ruiz had been the one who'd left the signs behind.

Mat stood and stretched, then came to take his son from her arms. His hand brushed hers, and their eyes met. Hers soft and vulnerable, his glinting with a promise and a hunger that thrilled her.

"Shall we give Susanna a night-night kiss?" Mat asked his son, his gaze dropping to her mouth.

"Kiss," Cody agreed amiably around his thumb.

"Daddy first," Mat declared, bringing his head closer.

"It's not your bedtime," Susanna murmured, her heart fluttering.

"Say the word and it will be," he said, his tone as serious as hers had been teasing.

His mouth brushed hers, warm and seeking. One hand cupped her jaw, his fingers stiff with restraint. Heat burst into flame, traveling through her in a rush.

"Don't go away," he murmured against lips that wanted to cling to his. "Give me five minutes." Susanna heard the sensuous promise throbbing in his deep voice, and her fluttering heart faltered.

Five minutes, she thought. And then she would keep her promise to tell him the truth. After that ... after that ...

He'll understand, she told herself firmly, letting her gaze slide to Cody's small dark face. He won't hate me. She took a deep breath, her stomach suddenly filled with nervous jitters she could no longer repress.

"Night-night, sweetie," she said, kissing Cody's silky head. "Don't let the bedbugs bite."

Cody gave her a sloppy kiss on the mouth, his fat hand patting her cheek contentedly. "Night-night, mama."

Mama.

From a distance she heard another voice, saw another pair of chubby arms. Bobby hadn't understood why another woman was holding him, why his mama was leaving him. He had struggled to get down, to get to her. Over and over he had cried out for her.

Mama, Mama.

The soft smile froze on her lips. Her eyes widened until she saw only a blur. Her body seemed to shut down. Dimly she heard a voice calling her name. It was a deep voice, strong, resonant, yet agonized, like the pain slicing into the place where her heart should be.

"No," she whispered. "Don't take my baby." She crossed her arms over her midriff and tried to hold the pain inside.

"What is it, sweetheart? What's wrong? Are you talking about Bobby?"

She felt a hand on her cold face, its steady strength forcing her head up until she saw only the man she loved. The sorrow in his eyes nearly undid her. "There's something you should know," she said in trembling voice. "Something I have to tell you."

Mat kissed her gently, then shifted Cody to the other arm. "I'll put him down, and we'll talk," he commanded, his brows drawn. "Promise me you won't leave."

She shook her head. Where would she go?

Mat tightened his left arm around his son and walked down the hall. Cody stirred in his arm, muttering something Mat didn't catch. His ear still hadn't become completely attuned to his son's toddler jargon.

"Good night, son," he whispered, lowering Cody to the bed nearest the wall. "Daddy loves you." He hesitated, then added in a voice made rough by the emotion churning in him, "Susanna loves you, too, even though she won't let herself admit it."

The little boy frowned, then curled into a little ball and tucked his teddy bear under his arm. Mat pressed a kiss to his forehead, then turned on the night-light and left the door slightly ajar before returning to the living room.

Susanna stood in front of the fire, her features drawn and white. For a long silent moment Mat looked at the shadows darkening her golden eyes.

His gut pulled taut. Somehow he had to find a way to replace the hurt with so much happiness that she would gradually forget the bad times.

The hell of it was, he didn't know how. Nothing he tried seemed to reach past the walls she kept putting up as fast as he could tear them down.

Seeing the questions in his eyes, Susanna made herself smile. "I'm sorry," she whispered, trying to gather her courage to say the words. "I guess I'm not ready for... for another family."

Exhaustion made her voice paper-thin. Her body seemed disconnected, heavy. The air in the room was thick and smelled cloyingly of piñon smoke.

She raised her hand, then noticed that she seemed to be moving in slow motion. Her fingers touched his face, lingered on the harsh remnants of his own private nightmare, caressed.

"I'm sorry," she repeated numbly. Sorry he had suffered, sorry she hadn't been able to keep their son safe, sorry they might never have a chance to make things right.

She heard a voice, the low mutter of a curse. She dragged air into her lungs. She had to tell him.

"Mat, about . . . about Bobby—"

Strong hands lifted her; even stronger arms cradled her against a warm chest. "Shh, sweetheart," Mat ordered in a gruff rumble close to her ear. "Don't talk. You're dead on your feet. You need sleep. Whatever it is, it'll keep until morning."

Susanna let her head fall to his shoulder. His skin smelled of soap and sunshine. His arms were protective and hard. She closed her eyes and tried to blot out the pain tearing at her. But she kept hearing Bobby's voice, full of hurt and confusion, calling out to her as she walked out of his life forever. She shuddered, her defenses ripped away, her body numb. When Mat carried her into his bedroom, she didn't protest.

Matt kicked the door closed, then crossed to the bed. With one hand, he stripped back the covers, pushed the pillows against the brass headboard, then lowered himself until he sat with his back against the pillows. He pulled her into his arms.

Her small body was limp, hardly any weight in his arms, nearly as fragile as his daughter's. But Susanna wasn't a child. She was a woman in every sense, and stronger than most men he'd met. Right now, however, she had reached her own personal limit, the place where her strength was finally gone, her grief over Bobby's death alive and twisting.

Mat knew all about death and the pain it left behind. He'd seen his best friend cut in two by machine-gun rounds. He'd lost his wife in the worst way he could imagine, but he'd never felt this kind of crippling pain. He buried his face in her hair, his own pain an ache deep in his gut.

"Go ahead and cry, sweetheart," he whispered hoarsely. "Let it out."

Susanna clutched his shirt between trembling fingers and swallowed the sobs that wanted to escape. "I can't, I . . . I . . ."

"Yes, you can. Sometimes it's the only thing that helps."

"You don't cry."

Mat thought about that day in the canyon. "I've cried," he said. "When I found out I had a son I would never see."

The last of the scar tissue tore deep inside her, leaving her defenseless against the grief that had always been there, waiting.

"I want my baby," she whispered. Tears collected in her eyes and spilled over onto her cheeks. A sob escaped. Then another.

Harsh, wracking sobs shook her. She pressed her face to his shoulder and let them come. Years ago she hadn't allowed herself to grieve. The pain had gone too deep. Allowing it expression would have killed her. Now it only ripped her heart and soul with razor claws.

Mat felt the shudders shaking her, heard the muffled cries that seemed torn from her lungs. Hot tears born of a fiery agony bathed the still-tender scars on his neck.

Trapped in her grief, Susanna heard the deep rumble of a man's voice murmuring her name with a rough tenderness that soothed instead of threatened.

Beneath her cheek his heart throbbed with a hard tumbling rhythm that pounded through her until it felt like her own heartbeat.

She was dimly aware that his hand, the one bearing the terrible scars of his own agony, was stroking her hair so lightly that she felt no fear, only a wonderful feeling of safety. The tremors that shook her grew less violent. The sobs that threatened to choke off her gasping breath lessened, grew less savage.

Mat held her close, letting his body offer the comfort he couldn't put into words. Gradually she relaxed against him, her strong, slender arms wrapped tightly around his waist. Her breathing gentled. The trembling stopped.

Mat felt some of the tension leave her body, but her face was buried in the curve of his neck, and her hands still clung. His leg began to cramp, but he was afraid to move, afraid to disturb the fragile peace she seemed to have forged with the demons driving her. Gritting his teeth against the searing knot of pain in his thigh, he made himself wait it out. Sweat broke out on his brow, and his stomach roiled.

Finally, just when he knew he had to move, she stirred, like a drowsy child awakening from a long, deadening sleep. Her soft, damp cheek rubbed against his collarbone, and her breasts pressed his cheek.

Mat felt an instant response in his belly. It spread to his loins in a hot stabbing rush. He groaned silently. In another minute his body was going to send a message to hers that would shatter the frail peace between them. Now was no time to let Susanna know how much he wanted her.

"Sweetheart," he began, then stopped to clear the sudden huskiness from his throat. "Stay with me tonight. Let me take care of you."

Still trapped in her own thoughts, she looked up at him with wide, uncomprehending eyes. Teardrops glistened on her lashes, and a small V stretched between her gently arching brows.

"I don't want to be alone," she whispered, her lashes rising and falling in small fluttering jerks. "Not . . . not yet." Just for tonight she needed to believe that he loved her.

He wiped the tears from her face with his long fingers, then moved so that she was lying against the pillow his back had warmed.

Slowly, murmuring soothing words, he removed her loafers and long socks. "Such small feet," he said, kissing her ankle. "Soft skin. Nice legs."

Susanna smiled, sinking into the weariness cocooning her. His deep voice soothed, saying words she didn't really hear. His hands were gentle, caressing without seducing, as they worked the buttons of her flannel shirt, then lifted her to slide the soft material from her pliant body.

In the subdued light of the moon, his eyes were very dark, his hair even darker against his muscular neck. His hand moved to the waistband of her jeans, found the metal button. With one twist, the denim parted.

She heard the sound of a zipper, felt the cool air in the room touch her bare thighs as he slid the jeans down her legs, his callused palms wonderfully rough and caressing.

Mat tossed her jeans over the brass rail at the foot of the bed, his gaze devouring the satin smoothness of her skin. Her panties and bra were sheer lace, hiding nothing.

Not that it mattered.

The image of her ripe body, warm and rosy from his kiss and his touch, was burned into his brain. For weeks he had been in torment, watching her, wanting her, dreaming of her in ways that were definitely X-rated.

Each time he was with her, he silently coveted her. Each time he touched her, he remembered the way it had felt to love her. Kissing her had made him come alive inside in a way he'd thought was gone forever. Making love to her had left him hungry for more. Lying beside her, his body still entwined with hers, he'd felt at peace with himself.

More than anything he wanted to feel that way again. He wanted her to love him. He wanted to love her and protect her and give her all the babies she wanted.

But right now she needed rest.

Gently he bent to press a kiss into the tousled bangs that smelled of flowers. Her eyes were closed, the thick lashes casting delicate crescents on her cheeks. Tiny freckles burnished her cheeks with gold, and her mouth was pink and full.

With a gentleness only his children had seen in him, Mat traced the sensuous line of her lower lip with his thumb. When her mouth began to curve into an invitation, his heart stopped.

His hand clenched, his jaw tightened, and his belly burned as he struggled to keep his distance.

"Mat?" she whispered, her voice made husky by the tears she had shed.

Her lashes fluttered, then lifted, revealing eyes as golden as summer grass kissed by the dew. "Don't leave me."

"Not a chance," he whispered gruffly.

"I feel funny. Woozy." Her words were slurred, as though she were sedated. Mat had seen the same reaction in men who had suffered violent trauma during combat.

"I know, sweetheart." Gritting his teeth against the hard throbbing of his need, he sat down on the edge of the bed and pulled off his boots. She needed to rest, and he intended to hold her until she felt safe enough to give in to the drowsiness hovering behind her eyes.

Susanna felt the mattress dip under his weight, and she turned toward him, her knees flexed, her cheek half-buried in the pillow. A strange languor held her in its grip, giving everything a surreal quality, like a dream played out in soft focus.

She watched while he undressed, marveling at the long, clean lines of his back. His torso, defined by sinew and bone, was packed with hard-edged muscle, the kind built slowly through tortuous effort and punishing determination.

His shoulders, bare now that he'd tugged off the khaki sweatshirt, spoke of power and strength in their wide span, strength that she longed to pull over her like a protective shell.

Her heart, pounding slowly, began to accelerate. Her skin, shivered slightly by the cool air, tightened until she felt as though the blood raced just below the surface, every beat of her heart speeding it faster and faster.

She needed him tonight, needed his courage and strength to replace her own. Tomorrow she would tell him everything. Tomorrow would be real.

Tonight was a dream. Her dream. Tonight they were man and wife, the way they should have been years ago. Tonight they would help each other, be strong for each other, love each other.

If these next hours were all that they would have, she wanted to spend them in his arms. "Make love to me, Mat," she whispered, her hand sliding gently over his hip. "Please."

Mat's fingers, busy working the buttons of his jeans, stilled. Slowly he turned to look at her. "Are you sure?" he asked, his voice so husky it seemed to abrade his throat.

Her long thick lashes fluttered, then raised. "Make me forget," she pleaded softly. "I don't need the words, only your body in mine."

Impatient to be in his arms again, she watched as he stood and tugged off his jeans and briefs. Then he returned to the bed where Susanna waited, walking toward her with a loose-hipped stride that suggested fluid, coiled power.

Her eyes devoured the hard muscular length of him. His skin was a variety of textures, smooth where his body had escaped damage, corrugated like hard steel where the scars had formed, covering the terrible wounds. A light dusting of hair covered his legs and arms, but his chest was bare, a broad expanse of burnished copper. A soft black triangle surrounded the potent shaft that was already partially engorged.

In the shadowy light his face seemed too angular, the hollows below his arrogant cheekbones too pronounced. The uncompromising line of his jaw matched the corded strength of his neck and the startling width of his shoulders. Unlike most powerful men she had met, he wore his masculinity easily, without bravado or macho posturing. Her man, she thought. The man she loved.

She moved to give him room, her bare thighs sliding across the crisp sheets like a whisper in the dark. He eased in beside her, taking her into his arms with a rough male dominance that drove darts of sweet anticipation deep into her core.

"You're beautiful when you cry," he murmured, his fingers wiping the last of the drops from her lashes. "And when you laugh. Even when you're glaring at me."

He spoke softly, without inflection, the way a wrangler gentled a nervous filly. He drew her to him, his hands horny with calluses, but gentle where they touched.

His kisses were sweet, tender, healing even as they excited her. Nothing was hurried, in spite of the tension radiating from his corded muscles. Susanna forgot everything but the symphony of sensations swirling through her body, raising her higher and higher.

When his mouth left hers, she whispered a protest that turned to a soft gasp as his teeth nipped her earlobe. His tongue probed the recesses of her ear, trailed moist heat over the delicate whorls, then retreated. She arched her neck, giving him free access to the sensitive skin there.

Her hands moved over his shoulders, his chest, his arms, absorbing the masculine heat, memorizing the various textures. Her desire was born of need and loneliness, tempered to a hot hunger by the potent male energy he projected.

Mat trembled at the possessive way her hands explored him. It had been so long since he'd been touched with gentleness and caring, so long he had no memory of the feelings it had aroused in him.

He kissed her again, more deeply this time, using his tongue to explore the sweetness of her mouth. Her hair tumbled over her shoulders, rich dark silk touched with flame. His fingers threaded through the luxuriant length, releasing the warm, fresh scent of roses.

He slid his mouth along the strong line of her jaw, kissing her, tasting the slight tang of her skin, remembering the set of her small chin even as he touched the tiny dent in the center with his tongue.

His finger traced the lacy edge of her bra, pausing between her breasts. His warm mouth followed his touch, leaving her trembling in its wake.

Another touch, a twist of his wrist, and her bra was loose. With the same slow concentration, he slid one strap, then the other, over her shoulders and down her arms, enjoying the milky perfection of her skin.

He felt her strain toward him, her small body taut with the same need that was taxing his control. He nuzzled her breasts, inhaling the sweet, delicate scent trapped between them.

Had she nursed his child? he wondered, his throat clogging with words he couldn't say, words of admiration and reverence and love, words she wouldn't believe even if he had the skill to utter them.

His mouth did what his voice could not, celebrating the ripeness of each breast with his tongue, while his hands slid under the filmy panties. Slowly, each movement conveying his caring, he slipped them free.

Outside the wind blew against the windowpanes and whistled through the trees. Susanna closed her eyes, sinking into the golden velvet behind her lids, blocking out reality until only Mat's kiss, Mat's strong body and Mat's clean masculine scent were surrounding her.

But that wasn't enough. She needed to be closer, a part of him, with him a part of her. She needed to give herself to him in the same elemental way that she longed to be taken.

The yearning rose in her like a hot wave, erupting in a moan. She arched her back, trying to ease the exquisite tension his fingers were spreading between her legs.

"Soon, sweetheart," he murmured, his hand making slow, sweet circles over the small mound between her legs. Susanna gasped, a long shuddering sound that traveled the length of her body. Her hands burrowed into his soft clean hair, closing and opening in the same spasm of need building deep inside her.

Mat moved lower, his control stretched nearly to the limit. And yet he held back, wanting to make this night, this moment, last.

He levered himself up, parting her thighs with his hand. His fingers found the soft delta, pressing, caressing, enjoying the spun silk that warmed his palm.

A small sobbing sound escaped her throat, and she moved from side to side, stunned by the sensations Mat was arousing in her. She whispered his name, her eyes half-open and kindling with golden fire.

His hand caressed the tender flesh of her inner thigh, arousing small tremors beneath her skin. His fingers curved downward, dipping into the moist heat sheltered there.

Susanna gasped, her every sense exploding into a starburst of sensuality that held her captive. She resisted nothing, exciting him even more, even as it humbled him. Susanna was light and sweetness and beauty—all the things he had missed in his dark, lonely life.

The need to bury himself in her sweetness raged like a fever in his blood as his hands moved to cup her soft round bottom, lifting her toward him. His tongue thrust into her, hot and caressing. Like brandy, her feminine nectar was best savored slowly.

His thumb followed his tongue, pressuring the small bud between her legs until she cried out, her voice hoarse, her breath coming in short gasps.

She was at his mercy, her own will overridden by the wild firestorm of pleasure he was slowly, inexorably fanning with his hands, his mouth, his tongue.

Mat withdrew and took the precautions that would protect her, his body hard and hot and ready.

Through a silky veil of desire, she heard the unspoken plea in his voice. To forgive him, to accept him as he was now, to love him as he would always be. The raw vulnerability around his mouth told her that he would never express those needs, but they were there, inside him, where they hurt most.

Tenderness welled up inside her, even more powerful than the desire shaking her. Shaking with love, she slowly opened her legs, offering all that she was.

His hoarse groan began in the deepest part of him and shook his entire body like a fevered tremor. With a slowness that tested him severely, he eased himself inside her, feeling her body mold around his in a hot, slick welcome. She clung to him, her neck arched backward, her breasts thrusting against his chest.

He held himself rigid, his muscles straining against the savage need to move, absorbing the tremors convulsing deep within her.

Susanna cried out, twisting and turning wildly against his hard body, desperate to be filled by him. Mat lifted her, plunged more deeply until he became a part of her, possessing her with a driving force until she was half-maddened, crying out his name in need and love.

Absorbing her desperate cry, Mat began to move inside her, one slow thrust leading to another and another until the hot friction sent her spiraling into a realm of ecstasy she hadn't known existed.

Mat felt the explosion rip through her. With a hoarse cry, he thrust once, again, his body convulsing with a violence that matched hers, pulse after pulse of hot release flowing from him until he knew only Susanna, only this hot wild need to be a part of her.

He was hers, his heart, his soul, his future held in her small hand. Only she had the power to hurt him beyond his ability to endure. Only she had the power to heal the agony that twisted inside.

"Don't ever leave me," he whispered into the moist shadow between her breasts.

"Never," she vowed on a drowsy sigh.

Her eyes fluttered closed. She was asleep.

Chapter 15

The baby was crying. Susanna struggled to reach him. The room was filled with a thick fog filling her throat, choking off her breath. Her legs burned, but she was running as fast as she could.

The cry came again, louder. She ran faster, her hands searching desperately, her eyes filling with stinging tears.

Suddenly the mist cleared. Ahead was a large white room. Icy white, sterile, brutally cold. A cradle, tiny and empty, stood in the middle of the blinding whiteness, rocking back and forth.

A man with a cruel smile stood next to the cradle, her baby held easily in his powerful arms. His features had been stamped by a kinder hand on the small face nestled in the soft blanket. Father and son.

No! she screamed. *Don't take him. Please don't take my baby.*

She struggled to reach him, but the floor was quicksand, clawing and tugging her back. *Please,* she begged piteously, her eyes pleading with him.

The man turned away, his brutal mouth edged with derision. Before she could reach him, he'd been swallowed by the mist. Gone forever.

"No, no, no."

"It's all right, sweetheart. I'm here. It was just a dream."

Susanna jerked awake, the sound of her cries still hanging in the dark. Her heart pounded erratically. Her mouth was cotton dry.

Mat held her in his arms, his hand stroking her back. He whispered reassurance over and over until the tremors shaking her began to ease. With an unsteady hand he wiped the tears from her cheeks. Susanna huddled close to his solid chest, her heart still beating unnaturally fast.

The room was shrouded in predawn gloom. Everything was gray, except the sheets on the bed, which seemed ghostly white. During the night Mat must have covered them with the blankets that now lay heavily over them.

Had he held her the entire night? she wondered, feeling the weight of his thigh between hers and the warmth of his hand wrapped around hers. In spite of the musky heat cocooning her, she was so cold inside. She shuddered, hiding her face in the curve of his neck.

"Easy, sweetheart. You're safe now." He pulled the blanket close to her neck, then began combing his fingers through her hair, spreading it over her shoulders. His body supported hers, his warmth seeping into her until she felt it begin to absorb some of the chill.

"Were you dreaming about our baby?" His voice carried a rough texture that she now identified as pain.

She nodded, and his arms tightened. Another shiver took her. She had to tell him now, before her courage failed her.

"There's something I have to tell you, something I should have told you weeks ago," she said in a voice trembling with sorrow and regret. She dropped her gaze, shaken by the hope in his eyes. "Something I have to . . . to confess."

His mouth jerked. "If it's about other men, I don't want to know."

Susanna smiled sadly. If only it were that simple. "There have been no other men, Mat. Only you."

Only when she felt relief travel through his powerful body did she realize how tense he'd been. He started to grin, but she stopped him with a kiss. Before his mouth could soften under hers, she buried her face in his neck, her hand curving around his neck to hold him close.

Tears flooded her eyes, and sobs shook her. She clung to him, desperately afraid that this would be the last time she would feel his strong arms holding her with such tenderness.

"Shh," he whispered over and over, trying to absorb her obvious anguish. "Everything will be all right, I promise. There's nothing you can tell me that will make any difference to the way I feel about you."

He'd been awake for hours, staring at the ceiling, Susanna's body nestled against his chest, trying to deal with feelings he hadn't even known existed in him.

More than anything he wanted to cherish this woman, to share his hopes with her, and his triumphs. But more than that, for the first time he knew what it was like to trust a woman enough to share his hurt with her, his insecurity.

For as long as he could remember he had made himself be strong—for the country he loved, the men he was charged with leading, his family. He fought alone, cried alone, even grieved alone. But now, with Susanna, he didn't have to be alone ever again.

He brushed the hair away from her face, then kissed her. In the shadowed light his eyes glittered with an emotion that frightened her. "Did you mean it when you said you wouldn't leave me?"

Her finger traced the vulnerable slant of his hard mouth. "Yes, I meant it."

"That's all that's important, Susanna," he said in a thick voice. "Nothing else."

Slowly, feeling as though she were leaving a part of her behind, she moved out of his arms. The blanket slipped away, exposing her skin to the cold morning air.

Quickly she clutched it to her chin. She had never felt more exposed or more breakable. But this time her pain was self-inflicted. She was responsible for the terrible feelings knotting her throat, not Mat.

"Bobby isn't dead," she said in a torn voice, fighting to keep her chin up.

The shock started in his eyes, then spread like a lightning bolt to his jaw, which tightened until it was edged in white. His son was alive, he thought with numbed happiness. He had another son—a boy Missy's age. He felt hot tears come to his eyes. He sat up, his bare chest dark against the white wall.

Relief shot through him like a rifle slug, leaving him shaken. But on the heels of relief came an explosion of shrapnel-sharp questions.

"You said he died when he was nine months old." Mat tried to make sense of her words, but it was the expression on her face that held him. She looked devastated, like a victim of war who had suddenly lost everything of value.

"It seemed...easier that way." She was clutching the blanket so tightly her fingers hurt.

"Easier? I don't understand how it could be easier, believing that my son was dead when he isn't." With an aggressive gesture that spoke volumes about the things he *wasn't* saying, he raked his hand through his hair.

"Why isn't he here? When can I see him?"

Susanna felt as though she were being sliced to shreds inside. "You...you can't."

Mat heard the bleak note in her voice, and fear twisted his belly. But he ignored it, just as he had been trained to do. First he had to know what he was fighting.

"There isn't anything I can't do if I want it badly enough, Susanna. And I *want* my son."

Shivering more from dread than chill, Susanna climbed from the bed and looked around for her clothes. She saw his, but not hers. Grabbing his sweatshirt, she quickly pulled it over her head. The shirt smelled like Mat, and the soft material molded to her body, covering her in all the places where his body had warmed her in the night.

"He's not yours anymore. Or... or mine. Not legally, anyway." She swallowed the terrible taste that pushed at her throat. "I... put him up for adoption."

Mat went stiff inside. Was this his punishment? To live with the fact that he had a son somewhere he would never know? To know that Susanna had hated him so much she had rejected his son?

"Tell me," he said with a deceptive calm.

Susanna laced her fingers together to keep them from reaching out beseechingly. She rushed into the facts to keep from begging him to understand.

"When Bobby was born, I had to leave nursing school. I was unskilled, with only enough training to qualify as a nurse's aide. The only shift available was from eleven at night to seven in the morning. Still, things were fine for a while. The nurses on staff felt sorry for me, so they let me keep Bobby in one of the empty rooms. My supervisor arranged for me to work weekends, too, and vacations."

She stopped, her breath failing her. Resting both hands on the hard brass rail at the foot of the mattress, she dropped her head, trying to fill her lungs with air. But the band constricting her chest made it hurt to inhale.

Mat clenched his fists against his thighs to keep from reaching for her. He should have been the one working to support his child, not her. He should have been there protecting her, loving her. No wonder she had looked at him with such revulsion when they met again.

"What happened?" he asked, wanting to take the burden of the telling from her, yet knowing he couldn't.

"There was a layoff at the hospital. My supervisor tried, but there were people with more seniority who also had families to support. I got a job as a waitress, but the only way I could make enough money was to work two shifts. That meant child care."

Slowly, as though reciting a story about someone else, she told him about her illness and the social worker who had tried to take Bobby from her. Tears ran down her face, but she let them fall. She had to finish before grief overtook her again.

"I tried, Mat," she said in a sad, small voice when she was done. "But in the end I . . . I couldn't stand seeing him grow up never knowing if there would be enough food in the house or enough money for clothes so that the other kids wouldn't make fun of him or . . . or . . ." She couldn't say more. She had no more strength.

In silence Mat climbed from the bed and pulled on his jeans, knowing for the first time what it was like to hate. But it wasn't fate he hated, or even the woman who had convinced Susanna that she was a bad mother, although he wanted to make the woman pay for what she'd done. No, the lash of his hatred was directed toward the person responsible for Susanna's pain. Mateo Cruz.

Yeah, he'd been some stud, all right, he thought, watching her small face get whiter and whiter. Seducing an innocent nineteen-year-old who had only wanted to comfort and love him. Leaving her to have his child alone. To struggle to take care of him.

He straightened his shoulders and turned to face her. Only a few inches separated them—yet Mat didn't know how to bring them closer.

He'd been so sure he could make her forget what he had done to her. But now, seeing the scars he had inflicted on her soul, he realized that he had no words strong enough or eloquent enough to convince her to forgive him.

"Now...now you know it all," she said, twisting her fingers together. Tell me you understand, she pleaded silently. Tell me you still want me.

"Yes," he said in a voice she had never heard before. "Now I know."

Mat was a man who prided himself on his control. He'd spent more nights than he wanted to count ticking off the seconds until the next pain shot, sometimes biting through his lip to keep from screaming. But he'd never once broken. Never once begged.

But this instant, face-to-face with the man he'd been, the man who had done a terrible wrong, he felt like falling to his knees and begging her to forgive him.

"Susanna, I—"

The phone shrilled, startling them both. Adrenaline flooded Susanna's veins, making her go hot all over.

Mat muttered a succinct curse before snatching up the receiver. "This better be important," he barked into the phone, raking his hair with his hand.

The indistinct rumble of an excited voice filled the air.

"When?" Mat asked when silence fell again.

As he listened, the annoyance on his face turned to a stony look that brought Susanna's hand to her throat in an unconscious gesture of fear.

"Give me ten minutes," he ordered in the coldest voice she'd ever heard. "Find Two Skies and tell her to bring her rifle."

"What is it?" Susanna asked when he hung up.

"A few hours ago Buck Ruiz went back to the Comacho place and threatened to kill Rebecca if she testified against him. Her husband just brought word. Spruce said Ruiz was just sighted near his brother's ranch. I'm going after him."

Susanna heard the savage anger in his voice, and her blood turned icy. "Promise you won't go alone," she pleaded urgently, her mind filled with the image of his battered face.

Mat ground his teeth, the memory of Ruiz's knee smashing into his gut burning like acid in his soul. "Call Grandmother," he said, turning away. "She'll stay with Cody."

Susanna sat slumped over the kitchen table, staring into a cup of tea that had grown cold long before. Mat had been gone over four hours.

She had spent that time trying not to think of the look on his face when he'd left. That was the reason she hadn't done as he'd ordered and gone for Grandmother. When he returned, she wanted to be able to talk with him privately—if he gave her the chance, she thought, pushing away her cup.

When Cody woke up at seven she'd given the little boy his breakfast, each bite he'd taken making her stomach roil. After she'd cleaned away his mess, she'd read him as many stories as he could stand, holding him for what might be the last time. With each hour that passed, each minute, each second, she had grown more anxious.

Her anxiety was worse now that Cody was napping. The house mocked her with its silence. The rooms, filled with Mat's clothes and books and masculine clutter, taunted her with his absence.

Suddenly the front door opened with a whoosh of cold air, startling her from her seat. "Mat?" she cried eagerly, her heart going to her throat as she sped into the other room.

"No, it's me," Missy said with a sunny smile as she flung her overnight case into the nearest chair and closed the door. "Where's Daddy?"

Susanna hung on to the door frame, disappointment making her weak. "He's...out on a call. I'm baby-sitting."

Missy's expression brightened. "Oh boy! Can we play Chinese checkers after I get something to eat?"

"Sure." Susanna's voice came out in a hoarse thread, and she cleared her throat.

She followed Missy into the kitchen and opened the refrigerator. Her hands were shaking so badly she had trouble removing the bread and sandwich makings.

As Susanna worked, Missy perched on a kitchen chair and chattered gaily about the party. With each word she uttered, Susanna hurt more. Was this the last time she would be a part of Missy's life? Of Cody's? Of Mat's?

The ache inside her sharpened until she nearly cried out. "Sounds like you've made a lot of new friends," she managed when she realized Missy had stopped talking and was looking at her curiously.

"Yeah, they're really neat, even if they don't have TV or VCRs or lots of the things my other friends had."

Susanna set the food in front of the little girl, then turned back to the counter to pour a glass of milk.

"Susanna?" Suddenly Missy sounded unsure.

"What, sweetie?"

"Are you going to be here for always now?"

The carton in her hand jerked, splashing milk on the counter. "Would . . . would you like that?"

"I sure would, lots and lots."

Susanna dashed away the tears that spilled from her eyes. During the past few weeks she had begun to think that, in his own way, Mat was coming to love her. But that hadn't been love she had seen on his face when he had left her this morning. In fact, he had looked as though he had wanted to put his fist through the wall. Or her.

With a heavy sigh, she threw the damp towel into the sink. Taking a tighter grip on the milk carton, she poured out a glassful. She was halfway to the sink when the kitchen door slammed open. Buck Ruiz stood there, a knife with a ten-inch blade held ready in front of him.

The glass fell from Susanna's hand, shattering on impact. Jagged fragments flew in all directions, slicing Susanna's bare ankle.

"Don't nobody move," he snarled into the frozen silence. His ratlike eyes darted around the room, then returned to Susanna's face. "Where's Cruz?"

"At the office," Susanna managed calmly, resting both hands on Missy's shoulders. The little girl was shaking so hard her teeth chattered.

"No, he ain't. I checked there."

He advanced into the room, his boot heels clicking loudly on the tile. He was unshaven, and his eyes were bloodshot. Susanna smelled the stench of bad liquor on his breath.

"I heard Cruz had a couple of brats," he said, running his finger along Missy's cheek. The little girl cringed, trying to escape.

"Stop it," Susanna ordered, pulling the little girl closer. "Leave her alone."

His eyes narrowed, and a look of calculation came into the flat black pupils. "Man thinks he can run me off my own land, does he? Sic them parole people on me to do what he ain't got the guts to do. Well, the man's got another think comin'. No one messes with Buck Ruiz and gets away with it."

A drop of spittle formed at the corner of his mouth. "I come to teach him a lesson in respect for his betters before I go, but maybe there's another way to make him remember me." He grabbed Melissa's chin and jerked her toward him. "Cute kid, even if she is a mongrel, like her old man."

Nausea boiled in Susanna's stomach. She couldn't let this animal hurt Missy. "Leave her alone!" she cried, her voice rising. "I know where Mat is. I'll take you to him."

His fingers tightened on Missy's chin, making her cry out in pain. "If you're lying to me, bitch, I'll kill the kid, sure as I'm standing here."

"I'm not lying. I swear." So frightened she could barely breathe, Susanna forced herself to meet his malignant gaze, putting every bit of guilelessness she could manage into that steady look. *Make him believe me,* she prayed silently. *Please.*

For what seemed like forever he stared at her, his body radiating menace. Finally, with a sneer he dropped his hand. "The kid comes with us."

Panic shot through Susanna, settling in her throat. Her insides were jumping violently, and her hands were icy. She took a deep breath. Whatever happened, she had to get Buck away from the children. She had to keep them safe.

"She doesn't know where her father is. I'm the only one who does. But I won't tell you unless the child is safe." She lied with a smoothness that surprised her. Even her smile felt convincing on her stiff lips.

She edged between Buck and the girl. "If it's a hostage you want, you've got me. A terrified child would only be in the way."

Missy began to whimper. Susanna longed to comfort her, but she couldn't afford to draw Buck's attention to the child's helplessness.

An oily look of confidence came into his face. "That's true enough. Maybe you and me'll have us a party before I kill Cruz."

Before she could react, he clutched her upper arm in a viselike grip. "Take me to him, and no tricks. I ain't got much time." He began dragging her to the front door. "We'll take your Jeep. I come by horseback." So that was why she hadn't heard him arrive, Susanna thought as she half walked, half ran at his side.

"Lock the door," she called out to Missy as Ruiz pulled her over the threshold. The child sat frozen in her chair, her eyes so frightened the whites showed all the way around the dark brown centers.

Outside, the sunlight was blinding, making Susanna squint. The air was chilled, and smelled of dust. As Ruiz hustled her toward her Jeep, a jay screeched a warning overhead.

"You drive," he ordered, wrenching open the door on the driver's side.

As she eased into the seat, Susanna desperately searched her mind for a plan. She had to take him away from here, as far as possible. What then? she thought, staring at the knife in his grimy fingers. Wreck the Jeep? Hope that the impact would knock him cold? It wasn't much of a plan, but it was all she had.

"Don't try nothing stupid—" Buck broke off at the sound of a powerful engine. Mat's Bronco was making the turn into the short driveway. Half-hidden by the aspen next to the carport, Susanna watched helplessly as he drew closer.

Ruiz muttered a vicious Tewa curse. "This must be my lucky day," he added in English. His hand grabbed her collar, jerking her from the seat. Holding her in front of him, he waited until the Bronco braked to a halt.

Lost in his own thoughts, Mat didn't see Ruiz and Susanna until they stepped into the open from behind the Jeep. Ruiz was using her as a shield, one meaty arm encircling her waist, the other holding a knife to her throat. It took Mat less than a second to assess the situation. Ruiz had come for him. He'd taken Susanna instead.

An icy calm, more deadly than the most violent rage, came over him. Years of tough army discipline had given him an edge he didn't intend to waste. He knew how to fight, clean or dirty. And he was willing to die to keep Susanna safe. It was all he had left to give her.

Slowly Mat opened the door, keeping both hands where the other man could see them. There was a rifle slung across the back window and a loaded shotgun attached to the dash. Neither would do him a bit of good as long as Ruiz had Susanna in front of him.

He stepped out into the glare, grateful that the sun was at his back. Keeping his hands away from his revolver, he stood perfectly still, letting Ruiz's nerves settle.

All Mat's senses were heightened, his concentration complete. He blotted everything from his mind but the need to keep this man from taking out his revenge on Susanna.

Without seeming to, he tried to gauge the man's mental state. Ruiz seemed jittery, but in control. So far, so good. A man in a panic did crazy things.

"Let her go, Buck," he said easily, ambling toward the Jeep with deceptively lazy strides. Susanna's face was pale, and her eyes radiated a desperate helplessness. Hang on, sweetheart, he told her silently. I won't let you down. Not this time.

"No way, Cruz. You think I'm crazy or what? This bitch is my ticket out of here."

"I won't give you any trouble," Mat said with a shrug. "You have my word."

Buck's arm tightened, pulling Susanna to her toes. She choked, fighting for air. With each step Mat took, the terror inside her grew. Buck had said he had come to kill Mat, and she believed him.

Please don't die, she pleaded silently, helplessly. Don't leave me.

"That's far enough, Cruz," Ruiz called out when Mat was still a good ten feet away. "Unbuckle your gun belt and toss it over here."

"Don't—" Susanna cried out, her words cut off suddenly by the pressure of the knife against her windpipe. Pain seared her throat, followed by the slow trickle of warm blood.

Fury flashed in Mat's eyes, but it was gone so quickly that she wondered if she had imagined it. His hands went to the buckle of the gun belt. Slowly, every movement causing her unbearable pain, he released the belt, holding it out to the side with his weakened left hand.

"Toss it here," Ruiz shouted, his stinking breath hot on her cheek.

Mat kept his gaze riveted on Ruiz's face. The man's cheeks were mottled, his eyes blinking nervously, his lips curled into a triumphant grin.

"Let her go first."

Ruiz tightened his grip on Susanna's midriff, making her cry out in pain. "You got two seconds, Cruz. Then she's a dead woman."

Mat cast a meaningful glance toward the .38 dangling from his hand. "You kill her, I'll kill you."

"Don't give me that. The bitch was in your house. Hell, everyone knows she's your personal whore."

Nothing showed on Mat's face, but inside he went rigid. "What's one woman more or less?" He held his breath. The bastard had to believe he didn't care.

Seconds ticked by while Ruiz calculated his chances. Sweat beaded on Mat's brow and trickled down his back. His thigh began to cramp, but he remained motionless.

"Maybe I won't kill her," Ruiz said, pushing his knee between Susanna's thighs. "Maybe I'll just cut her some so she's as ugly as you are." His laugh snarled between them. "What do you think of that, Cruz?"

Mat eyed him with open contempt. "I think you're as cowardly as the old women who hide in their hogans when the coyotes prowl. Come to think of it, you're not even that brave. You're so yellow you have to hide behind a woman's skirts to feel safe."

Ruiz spat out a curse, the veins in his neck bulging. "Shut up," he snarled, his rage nearly palpable. "I ain't hiding behind no one."

"Then why do you need her? It's me you want." He smiled. "Here I am. Or are you afraid to take on a cripple in a fair fight?" With a violent motion of his arm, Mat flung the gun belt toward the horizon. It landed in a shower of dust in the chaparral, too far for Ruiz to retrieve it easily.

Susanna shut her eyes in a spasm of pain. Mat had made himself completely vulnerable.

"Let's see how tough you really are, Ruiz," Mat challenged. "You think you're man enough to take me, let's see you do it."

Ruiz had the advantage of youth and brute strength, but he was also a bully. Mat knew his only chance lay in goading the man into a fight. Even if he didn't win, Susanna would have time to get the kids and escape.

"Don't do it, Mat," Susanna shouted, knowing exactly what Mat was doing, even if Ruiz didn't. She kicked out wildly, desperate to get to Mat to stop him from sacrificing himself.

With an enraged curse, Ruiz flung her aside. Losing her footing, she slammed into the Jeep, her head smashing against the rear window. Crying out in pain, she crumbled to the ground, reality whirling around her.

Before she came to her senses, Ruiz had landed the first blow.

Chapter 16

"Mat, the knife!" Susanna screamed, trying to get to her feet.

Mat saw the flash of steel in Ruiz's hand and jumped backward, knocking Buck's arm to the side. The knife fell between them, and Mat kicked it under the Bronco. Then, with every ounce of his strength, he slammed his right fist into the other man's mouth. His knuckles split, spattering Buck's face with blood.

Buck staggered, but his bull-like strength kept him on his feet. Lowering his head, he charged, knocking Mat backward and driving the air from his lungs. Pain exploded in his midsection, doubling him over. Ruiz crashed a knee into his jaw, sending him flying backward to fall on one knee.

With a mad bellow, Ruiz came at him again, but Mat rolled away from him, coming to his feet in a move he'd practiced countless times during hand-to-hand combat exercises.

He crouched low, making Ruiz come to him, absorbing the blows he couldn't dodge. His right hand had gone numb with the first punch, but he used his left with a force that sent a stinging shock wave up his arm.

Ruiz refused to go down. He was a brawler, using his fists like clubs, using brute force instead of finesse. His body was strong, but the alcohol he'd drunk made him reckless.

Knowing his endurance was limited, Mat hoarded his strength, trying to make every blow count. His muscles burned, and his head pounded with a pain that sent jagged starbursts of light shooting across his field of vision.

A blow to the stomach drove the breath from his lungs, sending searing agony rippling through him. Sensing victory, Ruiz hammered him, one blow after another.

Mat sank to his knees, his strength nearly spent. But he couldn't give in to the numbness waiting beyond the pain. He wouldn't break his word to Susanna.

Slowly, weaving like a drunken man, he managed to get one foot under him, only to have Ruiz slam the sharp toe of his boot into his side, sending him to the ground. Pain clawed at his ribs, telling him that they had been broken again. Dust filled his mouth, nearly choking him. His breath rasped through his bruised lips. Blood covered his face and ran into his eyes. He shook his head, trying to clear his vision.

Eyes riveted on the battling men, Susanna ran toward the Bronco. Lying flat, she stretched her arm toward the knife, but it lay just out of reach. Tears of frustration and fear rolled down her cheeks. She edged closer, tasting the dust that rose. Suddenly she heard Missy scream her name from the doorway. "Get back inside. Lock the door!" she screamed back.

From a distance Mat heard a woman's voice shouting something. Susanna. Through his pain he saw her white face. Her beautiful golden eyes. Her smile.

A feeling more powerful than the coldest rage, more powerful than lifesaving adrenaline, more powerful than anything he'd ever known, surged through him.

She was his, his woman. His life meant nothing without her. He would kill Ruiz with his bare hands before he would let the bastard hurt her.

Mat surged to his feet, swaying with sickening dizziness. He thought only of one thing—to keep Susanna safe. He dove at Ruiz, bringing him down. They rolled in the dirt, tangled together, their blood dripping into the dust.

Both were nearly spent, their blows clumsy and slow. Desperation gave Mat the strength to blot out the pain. With a final surge from muscles that felt as though they were bursting, he rolled Ruiz to his back. Before the other man could react, Mat landed a bone-jarring blow to the man's jaw.

Buck's neck snapped back, plowing his head into the dirt. With a groan, he went limp, his eyes rolling back in his head. Mat tried to get up, but his legs failed him, and he sank to his knees, his head hanging.

Susanna flew to him, her tears nearly blinding her. "Oh, Mat, my darling, Mat," she cried as she knelt to take him in her arms. "I was so afraid. Where does it hurt? Tell me."

Mat buried his face against her shoulder, too tired to raise his arms to hold her. Her tears bathed his bruised cheek. Her hands were gentle on his battered muscles.

For a long moment he allowed himself to give in to a fierce longing to stay in her arms. He wanted to wake up next to her and go to sleep curled around her small body. He wanted to love her.

Slowly he raised his head, blinking to clear his vision. "Rifle...in the truck. Get...it."

"Yes, I'll get it." Her hands touched his face, wiping away the blood. "Are you hurt? Can you breathe?"

Her face wavered in and out, and a roaring began in his ears, drowning out her voice. He fought to keep the gray fog from enveloping him, but his strength was gone. He tried to say her name, to tell her...

"Bobby...not your fault," he managed to say. "Mine, only mine."

He pitched forward into the black void.

* * *

Flat on his back, Mat floated, moving toward consciousness, from black to gray in slow stages. His body ached. His head was fuzzy, and his throat burned.

"He's coming around." It was a man's voice. Unfamiliar, speaking English.

Mat opened his eyes, feeling slightly disoriented. Steeling himself against the various aches and pains that were beginning to make themselves known, he quickly reconnoitered. He was in his own bed, his nakedness covered by a warm blanket. A stocky, dark-haired man in jeans and a rumpled green smock stood at the end of the bed, returning bandages and gauze to a large black bag. Mat frowned, then recognized the clinic doctor. Greenleaf.

Susanna was closer, perched on the side of the bed less than an arm's length away, her face white, her bangs pushed aside to reveal a wide strip of plastic adhesive. A thin red line slanted across her throat where Ruiz had cut her. Her shirt was dotted with blood, and one sleeve was ripped at the shoulder.

At the sight of her small still face, Mat forgot his vow to clean up his language and swore long and creatively, his fury evenly divided between Buck Ruiz and himself. When he ran out of breath, he sank back on the pillow and tried to ignore the pain in his side.

"Sounds like he's on the mend," Greenleaf muttered with an appreciative grin as he shut his bag with a snap.

Mat inched his shoulders higher on the pillow. He was tired of waking up flat on his back, half-dead and covered with bruises.

"Ruiz?" he ground out impatiently. If the man had gotten away, there wouldn't be enough ground for Ruiz to cover, enough places for him to hide. No matter how long it took, Mat would find him and make him pay.

Greenleaf glanced at Susanna, who answered softly, "After Brad patched him up, Two Skies locked him up in the cell in your office. She said you had to decide what to do with him.''

Mat scowled. ''If it were up to me, I'd put him up against the wall and shoot him, but it's not. It's up to the Tribal Court to decide what to do with the bastard.''

He raised his hand and looked at the heavy thickness of tape binding his knuckles. It was his right, the one he thought of now as his good hand.

''That hand is broken,'' the doctor told him in the same slightly unctuous tone Mat had come to detest. ''Come by tomorrow as soon as you can manage and I'll cast it for you.''

''The tape'll do fine.''

The frustration in his voice tore at Susanna's already shredded nerves. Mat didn't deserve to be hurt any more.

''Not if you want to regain full use of that hand, it won't.''

As he passed by on his way to the door, Greenleaf gripped Susanna's shoulder in friendly support. ''Don't let him do anything strenuous for the next forty-eight hours. Otherwise, he might end up with a punctured lung from those broken ribs.''

''I'll make sure he stays in bed,'' Susanna promised.

''The hell you will,'' Mat muttered, furious at ending up flat on his back in front of Susanna again.

Silence settled between them. Susanna stared at her own hands folded loosely in her lap. One of her nails had been torn to the quick in her desperate scramble for the knife, and two of her knuckles were bruised. She didn't know how that had happened.

''You look tired,'' Mat said after the silence grew thick.

As her head came up, she managed a smile. ''It's been a stressful day.''

Mat thought about the way the day had started, and a leaden fear settled in the pit of his stomach. Paradoxically, in spite of his flawed memory, he remembered every word she'd said to him.

He stirred restlessly, trying not to wince at the pain every movement cost him. "Where are the kids?" he asked, looking past her to the open door.

"Next door with Grandmother."

"Missy okay?"

Susanna nodded. "She's so proud of herself."

Mat raised his one undamaged eyebrow. "She is? Why?"

"As soon as Ruiz dragged me out of the house, she went to the phone and started calling all the emergency numbers you'd put by the phone. Finally she reached John at home, and he . . . he called out the troops."

"Meaning Two Skies and Spruce?"

"Yes, and several of the elders who were at Headquarters for a meeting."

Mat sent a dark look toward the ceiling. "That's just great," he grated with thick sarcasm. "I imagine they were impressed as hell at the sight of their police chief spread-eagled in the dirt."

"More like awestruck, I should say," she told him with a private smile of pride. When he'd pitched forward into her arms, she'd known she would never love anyone as she loved Mat. She only hoped it wasn't too late for them. But the way he looked at her, so expressionless and cold, gave her little hope.

"According to Garcia Crowe, Buck Ruiz once took on three bikers in a bar and knocked them all on their . . . fannies. If you want a raise, now is the time to ask."

"At the moment, that's the last thing on my mind." Gritting his teeth, he eased himself into a sitting position against the piled-up pillows. A dozen different pains shot through him, making him gasp.

"Where was Ruiz taking you?" he asked when he could draw breath again. Her thigh was only inches from his. Her hand was closer, and yet she had made no move to touch him.

Susanna cleared her throat. "Actually, I was taking him."

Mat forgot his aching ribs as he barked out, "You *what*?" Agony exploded in his side, making him suck in his breath. "You what?" he managed more softly.

Susanna cast an anxious look at his ashen face. She was afraid he was going to pass out again. "I told him I knew where you were. That I'd take him there."

A thunderous frown settled between his sooty eyebrows. "To where? You didn't know where I was."

"But Buck thought I did." She twisted her fingers together. "I planned to drive as close to headquarters as I could, then ram into the nearest solid object. I figured he was too macho to use a seat belt, and if I hit the brakes just right, he'd smash his head against the windshield, and then—"

Mat's unbandaged hand tunneled under her hair to curl around her neck. With one swift tug she was in his arms, his mouth hot on hers, his arms crushing her. His kiss wasn't gentle. If anything, it was almost brutal, fired by his realization that he'd almost lost her before he had a chance to make things right.

"You little idiot," he managed against her mouth. "You're enough to drive a man to drink, even after he's sworn off." His mouth settled over hers again, gentler this time, but no less volatile.

Susanna clung to him, her breasts pressed against his pounding heart, her hip angled over his hard thighs. Her senses gloried in the intimacy, reeling from the potency of his not-quite-perfect mouth.

This was the man she loved. The only man she had ever wanted. His strength was much greater than her own, his superior size and rawhide toughness so wonderfully overpowering, and yet she sensed a rough male tenderness in him that was there only when he was with her.

She responded to his kiss with a savage demand that rivaled his own. Whatever happened, she would never be sorry that she had loved him. Nor that she had borne a child from that love. How could she, when Bobby was the one link neither regretted?

She twined her arms around his wide torso, feeling his breathing become hers, his heartbeat dictate the rhythm of her own.

Mat felt her small fingers press his spine, warm and strong and, he fervently hoped, possessive. She was so close, he wanted to believe she was a part of him.

Desperately aware that this might be all he would ever have of her, he took it hungrily, greedily, like a man facing life in solitary confinement.

But when she moaned deep in her throat, he came to his senses. She had just been through a day filled with enough trauma to lay out most men. He had no right to take advantage of her shaky defenses. Not again.

With a control that cost him dearly, he slid his hands to her shoulders and gently pushed her away. Her mouth was full and moist, her eyes glazed with a depth of passion that made him groan silently. But the faint blue crescents under her eyes and the small lines between her arching brows told him that she was near the end of her emotional rope.

"Damn, I didn't mean to do that," he muttered, his voice raw. "But I saw you dead, because of me, and I... It hurt."

"You saved my life," she said in a shaky voice. "No, don't look at me like that. I saw the look in your eyes when Buck's knife drew blood. You wanted to kill him."

Mat clenched his jaw. "I promised you he wouldn't hurt anyone again. But he hurt you." He raised his unbandaged hand and brushed his bruised knuckles over the fragile curve of her cheek. "I kept thinking about you while we searched Diego's place. I kept seeing your face when you were talking about Bobby. I had to come back."

Mat took a deep breath, struggling to find the words to express the fiercely knotted tangle of feelings inside him. "You did the right thing, Susanna. The only thing you could do. Because you loved Bobby, you had to let him go. Sometimes . . . sometimes that's the only thing you *can* do, even though it's the one thing that hurts the most.''

Susanna dropped her gaze, seemingly fascinated with the weave of the blanket beneath her. ''I was afraid you'd hate me.''

Mat swallowed hard. ''That isn't possible.''

Holding his breath against the pain in his ribs, he leaned forward to slide open the small drawer in the stand by the bed. Trying not to wince, he withdrew a tattered notebook and closed the drawer. Without a word he handed it to her.

''What is it?'' she asked, her tone reflecting the same confusion she knew must be in her eyes.

''A journal of sorts. I kept one for each year, until I got out of the habit in Brazil. Read the last dozen or so pages.''

Susanna flipped to a spot close to the end, her stomach fluttering at the familiar sight of his handwriting.

The words were cryptic and blunt, like the man who had penned them. They told of his mother's death, his request for emergency leave. And then the pages were filled with a description of their love affair. ''Susanna asked me about love. Told her I didn't believe in it. Afraid I hurt her, but she has to know I can't make promises I can't keep. Hell of it is, with her I want to believe.''

Her cheeks burned as she read of his desperate hunger for her, his longing to share himself with her in ways that were new to him, his fascination with her laugh and her smile and her spirit. His words painted a picture of a man fighting his own needs in order to behave honorably. Fighting and, ultimately, because of his own desperate loneliness and need, losing.

The man who had written those words was arrogant, yes, and full of himself as young men often are, but he was also as caring and sensitive as she had believed him to be.

Tears came to her eyes as she read of his sadness at their parting. ''Feel guilty as hell because I didn't tell Susanna about Trina. But as soon as I get back to the post, I intend to tell Trina I can't marry her. Not when I know it's Susanna I really want."

Susanna bit her lip, turning the pages now with fingers that shook. "Saw Trina tonight. She's pregnant. Baby due in seven months, she says. Claimed she used the Pill. Not that it matters. Threatened to have an abortion if I don't marry her."

The next entry was dated a week later. "Married yesterday morning. Trina's family came up from Hillsborough, looking anything but happy to have an enlisted man in the family. And an Indian, to boot. Damn, I feel sick inside. Kept seeing Susanna standing next to me instead of Trina. But the thing is done, and I intend to be a good husband to her."

There were gaps in the dates, a few terse entries dealing with his work. And then close to the end she read, "Susanna wrote—she's expecting a child. Read the letter three times, tried to tell myself it wasn't true, but Susanna wouldn't lie. The baby is mine, and there isn't one damn thing I can do about it. If things were different, if I were free, I'd be on the next plane, but Susanna would hate me if I abandoned Trina. A marriage under those circumstances would be hell for both of us. Damn thing is, if the situation were reversed, Trina wouldn't give a damn about Susanna. God, I hate myself."

There was one more entry, on the last page of the book. "Talked to the chaplain. Had to talk to someone. Thinking about Susanna so far away, waiting to hear from me, was driving me crazy. Chaplain told me I had to tell her the truth. Said I had to let her go so that she could get on with her life. So that she could find someone else. Someone who would love her and take care of her and the child. My child. Is this God's revenge for my sins? If it is, He couldn't have found anything that would hurt more."

Susanna was crying openly now, her tears splashing on the black ink. Mat kept his gaze on her face, a feeling of dread crystallizing inside him. If she turned away from him, if he lost her... He clenched his jaw, refusing to think about the possibility.

As she turned the page, Susanna felt Mat's gaze probing her face. But she couldn't allow herself to look at him, not until she knew it all.

"Serving two tours in 'Nam was hell, but writing to Susanna was worse. She'll hate me now, and that's the way it has to be. I can never see her again. It would kill me to walk away again. But I'll never forget her. A part of her will be with me until I die."

The journal ended there. The last page was wrinkled, the cardboard beneath it indented, as though a fist had smashed against it.

"Why didn't you show me this weeks ago?" she asked in a low voice.

"It was packed away with the rest of our household goods." A self-conscious smile softened one side of his mouth. "I had a hell of a time making myself read it. I thought... I was afraid to find out I was a worse bastard than you thought I was. If that was true, I sure as hell didn't want to let you find out."

"Then why did you read it?"

He took a slow breath, hearing the thunder of his agitated heartbeat in his ears. "I had to know what it felt like to be loved by you."

"Oh, Mat," she whispered helplessly, clutching the book to her chest.

"I'd give anything to remember," he said in a low voice that throbbed with sincerity and deeply felt pain. "But I'll never have those years back, Susanna. Just as I'll never really know all the things I felt then. All I know is what you read, that I wanted you, that I would have married you." He raised her hand to his mouth and kissed her ring finger. "I wish I could tell you I loved you then, but I can't."

"It wouldn't make any difference," she said softly. "There's nothing you can say that will change the way I feel about you."

Mat went cold inside. Was this it, then? Had he offered her everything and still lost?

Susanna saw his mouth flatten, saw his jaw clench, saw him prepare himself for the worst. "I love you, Mat. The man you are now."

Mat's breath came shuddering from deep inside, from that private part of him where he locked away his hurts and regrets and insecurities.

"I don't know much about love, Susanna. After a while, with Trina, it seemed like a dirty word, a symbol of all the things that were wrong between us, all the things that she wanted me to be that I wasn't."

"I'm not Trina," she said gravely. "And I'll never try to change you. To me you're perfect just the way you are."

"I'm not perfect, Susanna," he said in a rough voice. "I can only be the best man I know how to be."

"The man I love dearly."

Her hand shook as she touched the imperfect half of his face, her fingers tracing the rough places on his jaw. When her fingers brushed his mouth, it trembled beneath her touch.

His smile was so beautiful, she thought. As though he'd just been given something very precious, something he'd thought he would never have.

He drew a ragged breath. "Think you can teach a beat-up ex-soldier about love?" He asked the question lightly, as though he were teasing. But Susanna heard the note of raw emotion in his deep voice.

"Absolutely," she said, her mouth curving into a smile. "Of course, it might take me years and years to get it right."

Looking into her golden eyes, seeing her smile warm until it blazed with welcome, Mat realized that she already knew all there was to know about love. Love's name was Susanna. And he would never let her go.

Epilogue

"Why do we have to go to Albuquerque now?" Susanna asked for the third time since leaving Santa Ysabel in the early-morning hours. It was Saturday, and traffic was light on Interstate 40.

Mat looked away from the long ribbon of freeway in front of him to smile tenderly at his wife. "Because we do," he said gently, returning his gaze to the road. It wouldn't be long now. Less than an hour. He only hoped she wouldn't hate him for what he was about to do. If she did...

He shuddered inside, where she couldn't see it. After living with her for nine months now, he couldn't bear the thought of losing her.

Beneath the floppy brim of her hat, Susanna's brow puckered into a stormy frown. "I don't know why you're being so stubborn about this. Aurora is already half-frazzled because Morningstar is cutting her first tooth. She doesn't need two more kids to take care of."

Mat heard the soft whisper of maternal concern in her voice and smiled to himself. Susanna hadn't been away from their children for more than a few hours at a time since their honeymoon, and she was as fluttery as a mother owl hovering over her two little nestlings.

"John will be there, sweetheart. And it's only for one night."

With a sigh, Susanna told herself to relax. She'd lived with him long enough now to know that whenever Mat braced his shoulders and set his jaw in that hard obstinate line, nothing changed his mind. Not even her.

"We could have taken them with us. Cody would love a trip to the zoo, and Missy needs clothes."

"You need a break, sweetheart."

"But—"

"And so do I."

Silently admitting defeat, Susanna settled back against the seat and studied his craggy profile through the lace of her lashes. For weeks now he had been preoccupied, wrestling with some private demon, something that had knotted his jaw with tension and returned the shadows to his eyes.

"I'm sorry," she said with the soft smile Mat never tired of seeing. "I know you've been under a lot of stress. It's just that I...I worry about Missy and Cody when we're not there."

"They're in good hands, sweetheart. Missy will beat the pants off John in Chinese checkers, and Cody will trail after Aurora, trying to figure out why Morningstar can't get down and play trucks with him."

Susanna laughed, her amber-gold eyes shimmering with so much love that Mat wanted to stop the truck and pull her into his arms. Instead, he lifted her hand from her lap and settled it on his thigh. After today he might never have the right to touch her again.

Resting her head against the seat, she watched the scenery speed by. It was early September, a fine clear day. The trees were still green, but here and there she saw a wash of fall color covering the aspen leaves.

What did Bobby see when he looked at the autumn leaves? she wondered with a private sad sigh. Did he remember how she used to hold one under his small nose so that he could smell its pungent scent? When he heard a lullaby, did he remember the way she'd crooned to him when his gums were swollen and aching? Or did he feel only hatred for her because she had given him away?

She inhaled a shaky breath. Every time she tucked Cody into bed, she bled a little inside. Every time Missy snuggled against her to whisper one of her desperately important little-girl secrets, she wondered if Bobby had someone to listen to his secrets, to give him advice, to heal his small wounds, to love him even when he was naughty or stubborn or angry?

Deep in her soul she wanted so many things for him. Health, happiness, joy. Most of all she wanted him to know how much she loved him. But she could never tell him. And that was tearing her apart inside.

Closing her eyes, she sank into the soothing motion of the Bronco. Mat was right. She needed a break.

Mat slanted her a worried look, his gut tight with a tension that had been there for days now, since he'd made arrangements for this trip.

With every dawn that broke with her nestled in his arms, he loved her more. With every sunset they watched together, he thanked the benevolent spirit that had brought her back to him. Happiness had only been a word to him before Susanna brought it into his life. His world was perfect.

But not hers.

It wasn't anything she said, or anything she did, really. But sometimes, in the night, he would jerk awake to discover her crying in her sleep.

She claimed it was just the pressure of her job, but with the sensitivity that loving her gave him, he knew it was more than that. In spite of the love she gave unstintingly to Missy and Cody, and the love she gave to him that made his life complete, a part of her was closed off, reserved for the son she missed so desperately.

Mat sighed, then checked his watch. In twenty minutes he would know if he had done the right thing.

"Sweetheart, wake up. We're here."

Susanna sat up and yawned, blinking at the unfamiliar surroundings. "Where exactly is *here*?"

"De Anza Playground."

"De Anza *what*?"

Mat laughed at the befuddled look on her face, but even as he helped her from the Bronco, his gut began to twist with nervousness. Please understand, my dearest, he begged silently as he led her past a clutch of squat adobe buildings to the soccer pitch in the rear.

Susanna stared in rising dismay at the scene in front of her. The game was already in progress. Twenty-two boys, half of them wearing red jerseys, the other half in white, ran up and down the field, forming and reforming into complex patterns that only they understood. On the sidelines, a fair number of spectators—proud parents, she assumed—shouted encouragement.

Was Mat out of his mind? she thought, her temper beginning to simmer. Or was this some kind of a bizarre joke?

"A soccer game? You brought me all the way from Santa Ysabel, made me leave Missy and Cody, to watch a soccer game between a bunch of kids?"

Mat slipped an arm around her waist and pulled her closer. It took all of his considerable strength to voice the words that he had been repeating in his head since they'd left the pueblo.

"I love you more than my life, Susanna. And I can't stand to see you blaming yourself for something that wasn't your fault."

Her heart began to race. Her hands grew clammy.

"Bobby?" she whispered achingly.

He nodded, holding himself very still. This was as painful for him as it was for her, maybe even more so, because this was the only memory he would ever have of his son.

"It wasn't easy, but I called in a few favors with some people I know in the Pentagon and I found him for you. I thought...I hoped that if you knew he was happy, you could let him go."

Susanna's face lit up. "Oh, Mat, which one is he?" she begged in a breathless voice, her nails digging into his arm. The joy in her eyes made him hurt inside.

"Number seven on the red team," he said quietly.

With an eagerness that tore at his heart, Susanna frantically searched the field. "There he is," she whispered hoarsely. "Oh, Mat. He's so big. He's...he's almost grown."

The boy was lean, like his father, with the same imposing shoulders and strong legs. The baby softness was gone from his face, replaced by an angularity that promised to mature into striking good looks.

Tears collected in her throat, making it difficult to breathe.

The coach shouted something, and Bobby looked up, his hair flopping over his brow. "He still has a cowlick," she said through her tears. "He would get so impatient with me when I brushed his hair. I...I remember how he'd jerk his little chin at me and scowl like the very Dickens."

Mat felt the pain settle hard inside him as he struggled to see the baby Susanna described in the half-grown boy streaking up and down the field. But he couldn't, and that would always be his deepest regret.

"He's so beautiful, so perfect." Her voice caught. "He's going to be so handsome someday."

Mat inhaled slowly, feeling as though he were being ripped in two. "I'm told he's the best player on the team. The coach...the coach says he's a natural athlete."

"Like his father," she whispered.

"Yes."

Susanna kept her eyes riveted on the tall boy in red, exulting over each powerful kick, each skillful play. His face was alive with the joy of competition, his black eyes sparkling, his grin flashing again and again.

Suddenly the black-and-white ball spurted away from the shouting, kicking tangle of boys, streaking with surprising speed straight for her head. Before she could duck, Mat moved in front of her, catching it on the fly with one large hand. His left.

A whistle shrilled.

"Red, side out," shouted the referee.

Number seven separated from the others and jogged toward her. Mat hesitated, then took her hand and placed it on the ball. She clutched it tightly against her, warming the leather with the heat of her body.

The boy with the bright, happy eyes stopped a few feet in front of her and held out his hand. Susanna's gaze devoured his features, searching for the face of her son. For Bobby.

She found traces, in the high arch of his black eyebrows, in the jut of the chin, in the sweetness of his smile. But the adorable little baby she remembered was gone.

"Ma'am? Is something wrong?" The boy's smile faltered, and his gaze darted toward the tall, fierce-looking man standing so still and rigid in front of him.

Susanna made herself smile. "You're very good." She couldn't let him go. Not yet.

His grin flashed, going straight to her heart. Their eyes met. Susanna held her breath, searching those dark depths for a glimmer of recognition. Please remember, she wanted to beg. Please know your mama.

The overweight referee came puffing up to them, an impatient scowl on his beefy face. "What're you waiting for, Begay? An engraved invitation?"

"Yeah, let's *go*, Jimmy," shouted one of his teammates.

With shaking hands Susanna passed him the ball. His fingers brushed hers, and she fought down a sob. "Good luck," she whispered.

"Thanks." He turned away, his mind back on the game, already forgetting the small woman with the white face and shaky smile.

Play resumed, and he was gone, charging toward the goal with the same powerful stride that Mat had once possessed. He passed off, shook off two defenders, took the ball again. With one powerful kick, he sent the ball spinning into the net.

That's my son, Mat thought with a thrill of pride, his throat tight. He hugged Susanna closer, offering her silent support. He could feel her shaking, but there was nothing he could do but love her and wait. This was her battle to fight, and she had to do it alone.

The crowd exploded in sound. The boy's teammates crowded around, hugging him, thumping him on the back, hugging each other.

Arms raised in triumph, he ran directly toward a man and woman who stood slightly apart from the others a few yards distant from the spot where Susanna and Mat were standing. She was small and blond, he was shorter than Mat, but with the same Native American heritage stamped on his dark features.

Susanna felt as though she were drowning in sadness as she watched them embrace the boy. Their son. Seeing the pride in their eyes, her own eyes flooded with tears. Hearing the love in their voices as they congratulated him made her heart lurch.

"They love him, Susanna, and he loves them," Mat said in a voice that was thick with the tears he couldn't let himself shed in public. "Be happy for him. Let him go."

She turned into his strong arms and buried her face against his shoulder. "I can't, Mat. He's a part of me. And he's a part of you. Our son. Bobby."

His arms tightened. "No, Susanna. His name is James Frederick Begay, and he's not ours anymore. Or yours. He's a part of the two people who have taken care of him and worried about him and loved him when we couldn't. Just as Missy and Cody are a part of you now."

Susanna took a shaky breath, then another. In her mind she saw Missy's shining eyes when she had introduced Susanna to her classmates as her mother. And she heard Cody's sleepy voice calling to her in the morning, confident that the woman he knew now as Mama would always be there for him.

Gradually, as she listened to the strong steady beat of her husband's heart, a healing peace settled inside her. Finally, after all the years of self-doubt and pain and guilt, she was able to let Bobby go.

Be happy, Jimmy Begay, she murmured in her heart. I'll always love you.

Raising her head, she looked into Mat's eyes. A wave of tenderness overtook her when she saw the unmistakable sheen of tears glistening in their obsidian depths. "Oh, Mat," she whispered. "I love you so desperately. You will always be part of me, even though I have to let our son go."

A lone tear escaped his control and slid down Mat's hard, scarred cheek. Susanna wiped it away gently, her hand lingering against his beautiful, perfect face.

"Take me home, my darling," she whispered. "Our family is waiting."

* * * * *

A Note from Annette Broadrick

Stories about amnesia have always held a fascination for me as a reader. The characters seem to live on in my mind long after I've finished reading their story. *Hawk's Flight* was my first attempt, as a writer, at exploring the possibilities that might occur when a person's memories are erased.

This book adds another element—one I call "when worlds collide." What I wanted to do was to introduce a hero who had his life arranged to suit him, a man who preferred a solitary existence.

In ordinary circumstances, Hawk would never have encountered a woman like Paige. He would certainly not have spent any time with her. Unless...

The words that prompt a writer to create—what if— came to play in my head, and I was off once again in a world of my own.

Welcome to my world.

Annette Broadrick

HAWK'S FLIGHT

Annette Broadrick

This one is for you, Michelle—for your loving
support when I needed it the most—with my love.

One

H awk waited.

When virtues were handed out, Hawk somehow missed out on patience. He didn't handle waiting around well, and today was no exception. He glanced at his watch.

What's keeping Dr. Winston? His office called almost an hour ago to charter a plane.

Hawk stood in the cramped office of Horizon Aviation Service, his elbow resting on the counter. The doctor, whom he'd never met, needed to fly to Flagstaff due to some family emergency. Hawk had been the only one available to take the flight, causing him to postpone his vacation plans for a few hours.

Oh, well. It wouldn't be the first time he'd had to change his plans. Come to think of it, when had any of his plans *ever* worked out as he expected?

Not that he'd minded helping his friend Rick get the charter service going in El Paso, but it had brought him back to the States a year earlier than he'd intended. Now that

Horizon Aviation was solidly established Hawk knew it was time for him to be making new plans.

He never stayed in one place too long. A restless nature and an inquisitive mind kept him on the move.

Hawk was ready for change—he definitely needed the vacation. Eighteen months of long hours and hard work had taken their toll. He pictured himself hiking into the mountains of Mexico's interior, enjoying the solitude and the tranquility of nature.

If the good doctor will get a move on, we'll be in Flagstaff in a few hours. With a good night's sleep, I can be flying south by sunup tomorrow.

Hawk caught a glimpse of a late-model car through the office door and he watched as it pulled in across the street. A young woman threw open the driver's door and leaped out, ignoring the wavering heat waves that rose from the sizzling asphalt of the airport's parking lot. Her rose-colored summer suit, although flattering to her petite figure, made her look overdressed for the hot Texas sun.

She hurried to the back of her car and opened the trunk lid. When she leaned over, Hawk admired the way her slim skirt clung to her curves. It also revealed a pair of very shapely legs. He slowly straightened from his leaning position at the counter. She was a good-looking woman, no doubt about it.

Grabbing a small bag out of the trunk, she slammed the lid and started across the pavement toward him, her high heels sinking slightly in the heat-softened surface. Hawk had to revise his original opinion of her as she came closer. The woman was more than good-looking—she was stunning!

He tried to understand his strong reaction to her. Maybe it was because she wore a look of fragility—she was small with delicate features. Maybe it was her fair complexion that gave her a porcelain-doll appearance. With her soft ivory coloring she was either a visitor to the dry desert air of El Paso or she spent all of her time indoors.

He caught a flash of fiery red in her dark brown hair where the sun picked out highlights. She wore it in a jaunty topknot, with wispy curls framing her face. Hawk wondered about the color of her eyes, hidden by sunglasses.

Her skin glowed and he could almost feel its silkiness as though he'd already experienced the sensation of running his hand along her cheek. His palm tingled.

What's happening to me? he wondered. He'd seen beautiful women before, and she wasn't even his type. Women who looked like she did were notoriously spoiled, and that was a breed he was careful to avoid. *The heat must be getting to me.*

He wondered what she was doing there. He glanced at Rick, who was taking flight charter information over the phone. *Maybe he's got himself a new girl and didn't want me to know. I'll have to tease him about being afraid I'd try to cut in on his territory.*

They both knew that would never happen. Hawk had a standard attitude toward women—he could take 'em or leave 'em. He generally left them—before they decided to discuss a more permanent arrangement.

His gaze returned to the woman rapidly approaching the door. She was different from the women he'd known in a way he couldn't define, and it made him uneasy. He could feel a tightening deep within him, as though warning him to prepare to do battle with his reactions to her.

Hawk deliberately straightened and turned away from the door. He leaned both elbows on the counter. *That's enough ogling for one day,* he reminded himself. *I wish to hell the good doctor would get here if he's got such an all-fired emergency!*

Paige swung open the heavy glass door to the air charter service and stepped inside the refreshingly cool room, pausing to remove her sunglasses and to adjust her eyes after the white glare of the July sun. She looked around the tiny office, wondering if she'd made the right decision.

When her receptionist managed to charter a plane for her, she was so grateful she hadn't questioned her further.

Paige glanced around the room with dismay, beginning to have second thoughts. Large maps, posters and calendars cluttered the walls. A battered desk and two nondescript chairs waited for occupants on the public side of the counter, while another desk and miscellaneous office equipment sat in a crowded jumble behind it.

Two men occupied the office. One was standing in front of the waist-high counter, and the other was talking on the phone in the office section.

She wondered how long the man at the counter had been waiting. She glanced at her watch, then determinedly walked over to the counter, hoping the man on the phone would glance up. She needed to be on her way—now.

"Were you looking for someone?"

Paige stared up at the man beside her. Seen up close, he looked almost intimidating. He appeared to be at least six feet tall, but it was his build she found most disquieting.

He was broad-shouldered, with muscled arms emphasized by the khaki shirt he wore, the sleeves rolled up halfway between his shoulder and elbow. Thick, black hair fell across his forehead, and his face had the high cheekbones and rich skin tones that generally denoted some Indian blood, which wasn't an unusual sight in the southwest. His voice had a full-bodied, rich sound that created a slight tingling within her. She forced herself to meet his black eyes. The man looked tough as well as formidable. Whatever he was thinking, he gave nothing away.

Paige decided she didn't have time to waste, and perhaps he could help her. "Actually, I'm here to charter a plane," she explained.

He stiffened, staring at her with suspicion. "Your name is—"

"Paige Winston."

"*Doctor* Winston?" A note of disbelief crept into his voice.

"That's right." She glanced at the man on the phone, who had yet to acknowledge her presence. "Do you know how much longer he'll be?"

The man shrugged. "It doesn't matter—I'm your pilot. I'm ready to go whenever you are."

"*You're* my pilot?" she asked in surprise.

"Yes. I understand you need to get to Flagstaff right away."

The slight doubt in his tone brought her to her senses. She didn't care who was flying her, so long as she got there as soon as possible. "Yes. Yes, I do. My father's been vacationing near Flagstaff and had a heart attack." She brushed her fingers distractedly through the curls that clung to her forehead. "He's in the hospital there now."

He nodded, then reached over and picked up the small bag resting at her feet. Motioning her to a door she hadn't noticed, he said, "This way."

The blinding sun hit Paige like a furnace blast of heat and glare and she quickly fumbled for her sunglasses. When she got them on she discovered the pilot was halfway to a small plane sitting on the edge of the runway.

Her heart pounded in her chest. She was expected to fly in *that*? It was so small! She glanced around nervously, but saw nothing bigger. The pilot turned around and stared at her, frowning slightly. He, too, had placed sunglasses over his eyes, but his were mirrored and Paige saw only her own reflection as she hurried up to him, breathless from the heat and her fear of the small plane.

He held out his hand, and when Paige placed hers uncertainly into it, he lifted her to the wing of the plane, motioning for her to crawl into the tiny door that was before her.

Paige discovered her suit was not the most practical choice of apparel for the trip, but then, she hadn't given it a thought when she'd rushed home and thrown a few things in a bag. All she could think about was her father.

How serious was his heart attack? What condition would he be in when she arrived? He had to be all right. He *had* to be. Not only was he her parent, but he was her business partner and best friend as well. She couldn't survive without him!

Paige scrambled inside, tugging at her skirt as she slid into the seat next to the pilot's position. She glanced around, bewildered at the gauges and switches that covered the dash. A small steering mechanism was in front of her, and she fervently prayed she wasn't expected to know anything about it.

Hawk followed her into the plane, made sure her seat belt was properly fastened, then settled into the seat next to her, checking that he had all the necessary maps and papers for the flight. He'd already gone through the preflight checklist before she arrived, knowing that saving time was important, but he ran an experienced glance over everything one more time.

He picked up the mike and contacted the control tower, requesting takeoff instructions. Within minutes they were airborne.

Paige watched the brown baked surface of El Paso fall away below their plane as they climbed. Mount Franklin continued to perform its centuries-old sentinel duty overlooking the sprawling city.

"You okay?"

Paige gave a nervous jerk when the pilot spoke. What was there about the man that caused her to overreact to him? He was polite enough, so that wasn't it. It had something to do with the sound of his voice—as though somehow she should recognize it. Yet she knew she'd never seen him before in her life.

Paige glanced at him and nodded. "I'm fine." She cleared her throat. "When do you expect to reach Flagstaff?"

He studied the instruments in front of him for a moment, a slight frown creasing his brow. Then he smiled at her. His teeth flashed white against his bronzed complexion. "We're due in by seven, barring complications."

"What sort of complications?" she asked nervously.

"There's a storm moving in from the north that I'm hoping to avoid. That may mean flying due west, then north. It could mean a longer flight, but it will be a much more comfortable ride."

She shuddered. She'd never cared for flying, even in large commercial planes. This small one made her feel she was barely balanced in the air.

Trying to sound calm, Paige said, "I'm so glad I was able to charter a plane on such short notice." She knew she was chattering, but she needed to get her mind off her thoughts.

"An hour later and you'd been out of luck."

"You mean you'd have been gone on another charter?"

The corner of his mouth turned up in a slight smile. "No, ma'am. I'd have been gone on my vacation."

"Oh!" Paige wondered if he'd been upset about having to take her. She couldn't tell. "I'm sorry," she offered.

"No problem. I intend to spend the night in Flagstaff and leave for Mexico in the morning."

"Do you have family in Mexico?"

"No. A friend of mine has a large hacienda down in the interior. It's got a landing strip I intend to use. I plan to backpack into the mountains and do some fishing."

"By yourself?"

He looked at her in surprise. "Sure."

She couldn't imagine spending a vacation alone. For that matter, she couldn't imagine spending a vacation camping. The Great Outdoors was a total mystery to her and she'd never had any desire to get better acquainted.

"I'm glad I didn't ruin your plans for you."

"Don't worry. You didn't."

"Have you been flying long?" she heard herself blurt out. She hadn't meant to sound so apprehensive, but it was too late to rephrase her question.

He grinned again and her heart tripled its already rapid beat. He had a beautiful smile, one that stirred up all sorts of butterflies within her that had nothing to do with her nervousness.

"About twenty years."

"Twenty!" She stared at him in disbelief. He couldn't be much older than her thirty years.

"I've been flying since I was sixteen."

"Wasn't that a little young to start?"

"I suppose, but I'd been on my own since I was fourteen. I made friends with a pilot and was underfoot so much of the time he finally hired me to work around his aviation service. I think he finally started teaching me how to fly to stop all my pestering questions."

His comments created all sorts of questions in her mind. Where was his family during that time? Why had he left home? It occurred to her that she didn't even know his name.

"I'm afraid you have me at a disadvantage. You know my name but I don't know yours."

"Hawk."

"Hawk?"

"That's right."

She wondered if that were a nickname but didn't want to press. Instead she stared out the window, trying not to think about how far off the ground they were.

"What made you decide to become a doctor?"

His deep voice interrupted her nervous thoughts, although his question didn't particularly surprise her. She'd spent most of her life answering that question in one form or another.

"Several reasons, actually," she admitted. "My father is a doctor—a pediatrician. I can't remember a time when I didn't want to be a doctor as well. And I love children. I've never been sorry for following in my father's footsteps. We have a clinic in El Paso."

"How long have you been a doctor?"

"Four years."

"You must have started rather young yourself. You barely look old enough to vote," he stated with a slow smile.

"I've been old enough to vote for several years now."

He smiled at her prim tone, then picked up the mike and spoke into it. When a disembodied voice responded, he asked for an update of the storm moving in, then listened intently as the voice rattled off what to Paige was incomprehensible data about clouds, winds and air currents.

She knew there was no reason for her to worry about the weather. He was obviously staying on top of things. She just wished she could get her queasy stomach to understand that, not to mention her racing pulse.

"Have you flown much?" His question was a welcome diversion.

"Uh, no, I haven't."

His smile was very reassuring. "Why don't you just relax, lay your head back and close your eyes. You'd be surprised how that helps."

Paige nodded, knowing it would be ridiculous to deny her nervousness. A perfectly good tissue lay shredded in her lap. He probably wouldn't believe an explanation that shredding tissues was a new hobby of hers.

She closed her eyes with a quiet determination, but her father immediately came to mind and they flashed open once more. *Your worrying won't contribute to his recovery*, she reminded herself.

Paige glanced over at Hawk, covertly studying his profile. She found him intriguing—he was different from anyone she'd ever met. He seemed to have forgotten her as he donned earphones. She could no longer hear the radio.

Slowly and imperceptibly, Paige began to relax. The work load at the clinic had been heavy since her father had gone and she knew she'd been overdoing it. *Oh, Dad, please be all right.* Her loving message winged its way to him. She hoped he knew of her concern. *I'll be with you in a few short hours. Please hang on.*

Her long lashes dropped one last time, then stayed down. Paige slept.

It was some time later when Hawk spared a glance in her direction. She really must have been tired to be sleeping through the increasingly rough gusts of wind that grabbed the plane and shook it—like a giant hand wanting to play.

He didn't care for the approaching storm or the way the oil pressure gauge was acting. He'd spent the entire morning working on that oil line and had been convinced he'd discovered and repaired the problem. *So what the hell's wrong with the gauge?*

Paige was jolted awake by a thundering crash. She glanced out the window of the plane and recoiled in horror. Black rolling clouds seemed to engulf them. She looked at Hawk and noted his grim expression as he wrestled the plane through the swirling wind currents.

"It looks like the storm you mentioned earlier found us," she said, trying to mask her concern.

Without looking at her, he nodded. "Right now the storm is the least of our worries."

"What do you mean?"

"I've got to put this baby down in the first available space. We're losing oil pressure."

She looked down, but could see nothing but angry dark clouds. What had happened to the sunlight?

"Where are we?"

"Eastern Arizona," he said in a terse tone.

She tried to remember her geography. What was in eastern Arizona? Hopefully it was desert and saguaro cactus. Or was that the Phoenix area?

Hawk continued to bring the plane down to a lower elevation, praying to break free of the clouds shortly, giving him some visual idea of where they could land.

His prayer was answered almost immediately. The dark clouds began to thin out and patches of green appeared. So far, so good. He glanced back at the oil pressure gauge. It was still dropping.

Paige saw the land and felt her heart leap in her chest. Mountains. Green-covered mountains. Would he find a place flat enough to land?

Once again she stared at the man who held their lives in his hands. He'd removed his glasses, and, except for the slight frown line between his brows, his expression was impassive. She wondered if Indians were taught that look or whether it came to them naturally. She was certain her fear was written in large block letters across her face.

It was too late to ask herself if she trusted the man. Much too late. After all, it was his life as much as it was hers. But she knew nothing about his skills or his background, and she recognized how foolish she'd been not to find out more about him before taking off in the plane.

But would it have made any difference? Her receptionist had tried to find other ways to get to Flagstaff. Chartering the plane had been the quickest, at least it had seemed so at the time.

Paige glanced down again, then wished she hadn't. The ground was coming up closer at an alarming rate. She took a quick breath of relief when Hawk leveled off, skimming the tops of the large ponderosa pine trees that dotted the land. Paige could see no place where he could safely land the plane.

Hawk shared her thought but refused to panic. He'd been in tight spots before. He forced himself to remember landings he'd made in southeast Asia, in Central and South America, when he'd been able to put his plane down in very little space. But those times had been different—his plane had been in good working order.

He checked the oil pressure once again and was heartened to see it was holding for the moment. There was obviously a leak, but maybe it wasn't as bad as he feared.

If he could get the plane down without damaging it, he had enough tools to make some repairs. He mentally inventoried what he had stowed in back—his camping equipment, his AM-FM radio, and the food supplies he'd planned to take to Mexico. It could be worse. All he needed to do was find a place to land.

There it was. He sent up a prayer of thanks. He'd spotted a meadow, lightly dotted with aspen, but relatively clear of the larger pines that would put a quick end to a forced landing. Then he glanced at the oil pressure gauge. Once again it was dropping.

He no longer had a choice. He had to put it down.

"This is it. We're going in."

His deep voice echoed in the small compartment. How could he sound so calm? Paige wondered if this was the time her life should be rapidly flashing across her mind. If so, her thoughts weren't cooperating. All she could think about was her father. Was he still alive? How was she going to reach him? What would the shock of her not arriving do to him? If only she knew his condition.

Her last conscious thought was: *There was so much I still wanted to do in life...*

TWO

Paige groaned.

Icy water trickled down her face. She shifted, and a sharp pain shot through her head. *Is this what a hangover feels like?* she wondered fuzzily. *But I don't even drink.*

Other sensations seeped into her consciousness. She was moving, but not under her own power. The steady thudding that accompanied the pain in her head was coming from the hard wall pressed firmly against her right ear. Steel bands were strapped around her shoulders and knees. She tried to raise her head, but blackness engulfed her once again.

Minutes later, or maybe hours, Paige felt as though she were being held captive by miniature natives, only inches tall. Several held her head while their friends took turns beating on it with their minuscule hammers. Why wouldn't they leave her alone?

She attempted to raise her hand to her head, only to find it firmly tucked under a cover. At least they hadn't tied her down. If she could only free her hand, she could fight them back. One arm swing should swat them away like flies. But they certainly carried a mean wallop to be so small.

"You need to lie still, Paige. You're going to be all right...try to rest."

Where had she heard that voice before? The deep, warm tones comforted her. They were much deeper than her father's voice. Her father.

"Dad!" She tried to sit up. Where was he? He'd needed her for something. What was it?

"It's all right, honey. We'll get you to your father yet." The voice held a quiet authority that soothed her. Who was it?

An arm slipped under her shoulders and brought her forward. The movement caused the sadistic natives to double their efforts. "Please stop," she murmured, wondering if they spoke English.

"I'm sorry, but you'll be more comfortable without these wet clothes."

She wanted to explain that she wasn't talking to the quiet voice murmuring in her ear. It was those blasted natives practicing their construction skills on her defenseless head. But it took too much effort to explain.

A cool wet cloth gently touched her forehead, and she sighed with pleasure. Never had anything felt so good. Soothing strokes bathed her face and a gentle hand pushed her thick hair from her face.

"You have a slight concussion, Dr. Winston, but I don't think it's too bad. I'm sure you'll feel better by morning."

I hope, Hawk silently added.

He sounded so confident that Paige drifted into a natural sleep, content to wait for relief. Maybe the natives had been scattered when she sat up. Serve them right. They were insufferably rude.

Paige shifted in her sleep. At least she attempted to shift, but couldn't move. What was wrong with her? She opened her eyes and decided she had finally flipped over the edge of sanity into a surrealistic existence.

Nothing made sense. Her head rested on a hard, bronzed surface that moved gently. Her body rested comfortably against something large and warm. A canvas surface seemed to surround her, but it was hard to tell in the gloom. Was it night or day?

She attempted to raise her head, relieved to discover her tiny torturers must have given up and gone home, leaving her head with a dull ache. Her pillow shifted, and she focused fuzzily on a pair of black eyes a few inches away staring at her with concern.

What beautiful eyes, she thought dreamily.

"How do you feel?" the man asked, his voice rumbling in his chest. She realized her head had been resting on his shoulder.

"Like I should never have had that first drink," she admitted, and wondered why he chuckled.

Paige discovered she was lying entwined with a man with gorgeous black eyes. *So this is what my subconscious is up to when my back is turned. It has me in bed with a beautiful specimen of virile manhood the minute I slip over the edge. Interesting.* She wondered how long she would be in this condition, but decided she might as well enjoy it while she was there.

Paige discovered her hand draped across his bare chest and she tentatively moved her fingers. They worked. She could feel the warmth of his skin under the sensitive pads of her fingertips. She brushed her hand over his chest and smiled. *Not bad. Not bad at all.*

Other sensations began to impinge on her. She was cozily curled along the man's side, both of his arms wrapped around her. One of her legs was neatly tucked between his, her thigh nestling intimately against him. A warm tide of embarrassment swept through her. Never had one of her dreams been so vivid. Not only could she feel the steady beat of his heart beneath her palm, his soft breath felt like a feather rhythmically brushing against her forehead.

Paige knew that all she needed to do was roll over and look at her clock to come out of it, but she couldn't resist the temptation to enjoy the dream for another few moments.

She absently noted that the only thing each of them had on were their briefs, and yet she was quite warm. The covers fit snugly around them. She raised her head slightly and discovered they were in a sleeping bag.

A sleeping bag? Now where did her subconscious come up with that one? She'd never been camping in her life. The outdoors was a total mystery to her and, as far as she was concerned, would remain that way.

Oh well, a dream was a dream, and she obviously had no control over what was put in it. But a sleeping bag, of all things!

The man shifted slightly, and her thoughts flew back to him. Had his breathing changed? Had his arm tightened around her? His heartbeat had definitely increased.

Then she realized what was happening and jerked her leg away from him. *Okay, time to wake up now. We know what kind of dream this could turn into.* Paige tried to sit up, but was hampered by the man and the covers.

She blinked her eyes, trying to focus on the clock sitting on the nightstand beside her bed. She couldn't even find the nightstand. When she forced herself into a sitting position, the top of her head brushed against canvas.

An ominous feeling suddenly gripped her—a very ominous feeling.

She wasn't dreaming. She was definitely awake, but nothing made sense.

Paige tried to recall the reason why she was there, and the dull throbbing in her head increased its rhythm. She felt along her temple and discovered a large bump just below her hairline.

Panic began to course through her. She searched her memory for her name. Paige Winston. Her age? Thirty. Her occupation? Pediatrician. Her address? Thirteen-twenty-eight La Donna Drive, El Paso, Texas.

So far, so good. *Just take it easy. You've suffered a blow to your head and you're obviously disoriented.* Her medical training was striving to take over and be objective, but she could feel her heart slamming against her chest and she was breathing in short, panting breaths.

Now, then. The next step is to figure out where you are. She gazed around the small area enclosed by canvas, searching for clues. Nothing looked familiar.

Slowly she turned around and stared at the man still lying next to her. She was positive she'd never seen him before in her life. "Do I know you?" she asked politely, a tentative smile hovering on her face.

Hawk blinked in surprise. After only a few hours of sleep, his brain felt sluggish and he wasn't prepared for his passenger's unexpected question. He leaned up on his elbow, his muscled arm flexing painfully where her head had rested for the past several hours.

"Don't you remember?"

That question had to rank as one of the most stupid ones of all times, she decided in disgust. Why else would she have asked? "Didn't anyone ever tell you it's impolite to answer a question with a question?" Paige grumbled. She studied his face for a moment. She did not know this man. Of course she didn't. In which case, she needed to understand why they were in a sleeping bag together under some sort of canvas cover.

She rubbed her aching head, vaguely remembering the constant pounding from the night before. She wondered if this were what a hangover felt like. If so, she knew she'd made the right decision years ago when she decided not to drink.

Hawk watched her in concern. Her concussion must be worse than he'd first thought. He slipped his forefinger under her chin and slowly turned her head until he could see her eyes. Yes, they were definitely dilated. At least the right one was, which wasn't surprising considering the large knot on her temple.

Now what? He had done the best he could last night after they landed. He'd found makeshift shelter for her under the trees until he could unload the plane, set up the tent, and spread out the bedroll. His fear for her had galvanized his actions. He'd never forget the relief he felt when she had come to, even if it had only been for a few minutes.

"Do you remember anything about last night?" he asked, noting her puzzled expression with concern. "Do you remember the plane going down?"

She stared at him in bewilderment. A plane? He was asking about a plane going down.

Paige recalled watching a television news report of a jumbo jet crashing at the end of a runway, going up in smoke and flames. When had she seen that?

Paige rubbed her head thoughtfully. "I don't think so," she finally admitted softly.

Now what? Hawk wondered. Was there any reason to feed her fears by admitting that although they had made it down safely, the plane was in no condition to fly out under its own power?

"It doesn't matter." He edged away from her in the confined bed. "I've got to look for some dry wood to get a fire going. Are you going to be all right if I leave you for a few moments?"

His anxious gaze confused her. What was the matter with her brain? Her thoughts seemed to be sloshing around in some kind of gooey liquid, refusing to form any reasonable shape or make any kind of sense. She couldn't understand what she was doing here when she should be waking up in her own bed, in her own home, and getting ready to go to the clinic.

Hawk couldn't help it. Her anxious frown as she sat in the curve of his arm, the covers modestly tucked around her breasts, leaving her silky-soft back open to his appreciative view, was too much for him to ignore. He pulled her back down to him with some vague idea of trying to comfort her. "It's going to be all right, honey. Please don't worry. I won't let anything happen to you." He leaned over and touched his lips gently to hers.

As kisses go, his was far from demanding. It was almost soothing, and she relaxed in his arms, enjoying the sensation of being held and comforted.

She *had* to be dreaming. There was no other explanation. Maybe it was a dream within a dream, but she'd never dreamed of anyone who looked like him before. His kiss took her breath away.

Hawk pulled away from her slightly, surprised at his actions. He'd only meant to console her, and he found her warm response unexpected.

He forgot who they were and why they were there as, once again, he leaned down and kissed her. Her mouth parted slightly, unconsciously inviting his intimacy. She tasted so sweet, so warm and loving. Hawk soon lost himself in exploration.

What is happening to me? Paige wondered. Never had she felt this way before. Never had a man affected her so.

Who was he?

Paige stiffened and pulled away from him while she studied his features for a clue to his identity. She saw thick black hair that fell across his broad forehead; high cheekbones and rich skin tones; and magnificent black eyes that mesmerized her.

But who was he? And what were they doing in a sleeping bag together? They certainly weren't strangers to each other!

Maybe the bump on her head had been worse than she thought. What if she were more than just disoriented? What if she were suffering from some form of amnesia?

Paige closed her eyes and tried to blot out her surroundings. *Relax. Stay calm. Everything's going to be all right. Don't panic. Try not to panic your companion. He doesn't need to know how little you can remember. Maybe it will all come back to you in a few minutes.*

She opened her eyes and found herself staring deeply into his. "Were we in a plane crash?"

His well-shaped lips formed a small smile. "Not exactly. I was forced to land in a meadow last night."

"Oh." She continued to study him. He was so close she could see her reflection in his eyes. At least she'd learned something about him. He was a pilot. "Where are we?"

He shifted restlessly, moving slightly away from her. "Somewhere in eastern Arizona."

Arizona! What in the world are we doing in Arizona?

None of this made sense. How much of her life had she forgotten?

Paige rubbed her forehead. The pain made her feel as though her head were expanding with each heart beat. She tried to swallow, and her throat felt as though it had experienced a six-month drought. "May I have a drink of water, please?"

Hawk stared at her. Surely, as a doctor she should know a person with a concussion shouldn't have liquids. That was basic medical knowledge. *But she's not a doctor at the moment,* he reminded himself. *She's more of a patient. You can't expect her to diagnose and treat herself.*

He ran his hand down the side of her head, brushing the hair away so that it fell in long waves down her back. "I'm afraid I can't give you anything to drink, Paige." She stared at him in bewilderment. "I think you have a concussion. You mustn't drink anything."

Of course not, she thought. *I know that. I've treated several children with mild to severe concussions. But I had no idea what one felt like.*

I've got to get out of here, Hawk prodded himself. He didn't know what he'd been thinking of, kissing her like that. If only she hadn't looked so bewildered and vulnerable. A strange feeling had swept over him—a need to protect her. *If I don't watch it, the only protection she'll need is from me!* He threw back the cover and reached for his Levi's.

The tent was too small for him to stand up. He wriggled the pants over his long legs, then threw the tent flap open and crawled out. It was still raining.

Swell.

That was all they needed. The storm from the night before appeared to be a forerunner of more to come. He glanced around as he slowly stood up. The sky was heavily overcast, and he wondered how he was going to get word where they were to anyone.

He had flown off course yesterday, trying to get away from the worst of the storm. No one would be looking for them in this area. There had been no response to his repeated calls on the radio. All he'd gotten was static. Somehow he had to get them some help. But how and from where?

He watched the rain beat a monotonous rhythm around him. He was going to have a hell of a time finding wood dry enough to burn.

While he uncovered small limbs and peeled bark from larger ones, Hawk organized his thoughts and sought solutions.

He and the doctor were fortunate in one respect—they had plenty of food and camping equipment, enough to survive for a few weeks at least. He glanced back at the tent, nestled along the edge of a sheer cliff towering above the meadow. It looked as though he and his attractive passenger might be camping there for a few days.

He didn't see how she would be able to reach her father anytime soon. Now that he thought about it, he realized that she hadn't even mentioned her father this morning, which was surprising. Could it be possible she didn't remember why they were flying to Flagstaff? Or did she even remember where they'd been going?

Hawk had seen more head wounds over the years than he wished, and he knew they caused unpredictable consequences. Paige appeared confused and disoriented, and apparently suffered from some form of memory loss. He could think of nothing that he could do for her in that respect. He knew very little about her.

Glancing around the meadow, Hawk was somewhat reassured about their situation. If they had to be marooned somewhere, he'd at least found a location that offered comfortable accommodations.

Uncertain about the possibility of flooding, Hawk had set up camp on the hillside overlooking the meadow and stream that cut through its center. The tent was almost hidden among the boulders and trees, but spotters could see his plane if they flew over.

He winced at the thought of his plane. The damage had been considerable, but any forced landing that could be walked away from was considered an unqualified success.

Only, Paige hadn't walked away. Once again he saw her as she'd been last night. She'd been wearing her hair in some sort of topknot on her head, but it had come down, its mahogany-colored length falling around her shoulders and down her back. Her delicate features and fair complexion emphasized her vulnerability, and he could still taste the fear that had threatened to engulf him when he'd discovered her unconscious. Never had he seen a more beautiful sight than when her eyes slowly opened to reveal their navy-blue color.

Hawk faced the situation head-on. He'd been strongly attracted to her from the first moment he saw her. How else could he explain his insane impulse to kiss her? She'd looked so bewildered—so beautiful—and he'd spent the night holding her in his arms, praying she would be all right. But he would have to ignore his reaction to her. What he had to do was take care of her and get them out of there.

He stared up at the sky. There was a real possibility they wouldn't be spotted anytime soon, in which case their only choice would be to wait until Paige regained her strength, then consider their options. They might have to hike out of the mountains.

In the meantime he might as well try to relax and enjoy their forced camping trip. They certainly weren't in a life-threatening situation as long as Paige continued to show signs of improvement.

The fire finally caught, and Hawk relaxed a little. He would have to make certain he didn't let it go out, after all the trouble he'd had getting it started. He straightened and went over to his box of provisions. At last he could make some coffee.

Hawk heard a movement behind him and turned around in time to watch Paige crawl hesitantly out of the tent. She wore the tailored suit and high-heeled shoes she'd had on the day before.

She stood in front of the tent staring around the clearing with bewilderment. Hawk realized she was swaying, and he dashed over to her.

"Paige, honey, you shouldn't be out of bed." He coaxed her back into the tent. "You need to lie quietly and give your head a chance to heal." She docilely sat back down on the sleeping bag. "The last thing we need is for you to get chilled." Hawk knelt beside her and hurriedly unbuttoned her blouse. "Your clothes are still damp," he explained as he unzipped her skirt and slid it down her legs. Her shoes came off last, leaving her in a lacy half slip and bra. He knew she'd be more comfortable without the constriction across her chest but didn't want to upset her by removing anything more. Hawk tucked her into the bedroll once more.

"Please stay in bed today, all right?"

She nodded her head, looking up at him like a trusting child. He found the cloth he'd used the night before and moistened it with water from his canteen. Gently he placed it on her forehead.

"What's your name?"

Her dark blue eyes continued to watch him. He felt his heart make a convulsive leap in his chest. So she still didn't remember him. Not a good sign. She didn't appear to be upset, just confused. The important thing for him to keep in mind was that she mustn't get upset. Perhaps it was just as well she couldn't recall much at the moment. As long as she didn't remember her father's illness on her own, he saw no reason to upset her with the news under the present circumstances.

He brushed his knuckles across her cheek. "My name is Hawk."

"Hawk?"

"That's right."

"So you're a hawk. I've wondered where a hawk lives. Now I know." Her voice had a little-girl quality, nothing like her normal husky tone. "He lives high in the mountains, in a rainy glen, hidden away from the troubles of the world." Her eyes drifted closed. "I'm glad I'm a hawk, too."

He sat there by her side most of the day, only leaving for short periods of time—to try the radio in the plane again, to make something to eat for himself. He made sure she didn't sleep too long at a time and listened for any sound that might mean someone was looking for them.

The hours passed slowly while he made his rounds between the fire, the plane and the tent. Toward evening the rain stopped and he hoped the clearing skies would bring help, but by nightfall there was no sign of rescue.

Three

Paige dreamed of soaring in the sky, dipping and swooping down through mountains and valleys and over bubbling springs. Sometimes she was alone. Other times a beautiful hawk flew next to her. A hawk with luminous black eyes.

She was hot. Paige pushed against the covers, but they wouldn't move. She tried to sit up and couldn't. Her eyes reluctantly opened, but it was too dark to see anything.

Where am I? she wondered in confusion. Mental pictures flashed across her mind of a man—a campfire—rain dripping from the trees—a tent.

That was it. She was in a tent. She tried to move again and recognized the hard surface at her back was warm, and breathing. She was curled up with a man.

She didn't know any men on that basis. So what was she doing there?

Her head hurt, but nothing like it had been hurting. She rubbed along her temple and felt the large bump there.

That's right. She'd got hit on the head. But how? And when?

A large, muscular arm rested across her waist, keeping her snug against the man who shared her bed. *This is a sleeping bag...I remember now. I'm camping with this man. What did he say his name was?*

She couldn't remember. While she concentrated on remembering—she knew it was imperative that she recall his name—Paige fell asleep once more.

Sunlight filtered through the open flap of the tent when Paige opened her eyes again. She was alone. Raising up on her elbow, she looked outside and saw sunshine. She also could see a man moving around a campfire and smell coffee brewing. It smelled wonderful.

When she sat up, Paige discovered that the horrible pounding in her head she'd experienced the day before was gone. Thank God.

Who was the man who had looked after her? She could remember him coming into the tent, stroking her hair, placing a damp cloth on her forehead, speaking to her, but it all seemed like something she'd dreamed.

Now, however, she had to face the fact that she was not dreaming. For some reason she was alone with a man she could swear she'd never seen before. Not only did they seem to be camping together, they were sleeping together. Why? She could think of only one explanation—she must be married to him.

Paige tried to concentrate, tried to find some memory regarding a wedding. The only thing she got for her efforts was increased pain. If only she felt better, she was certain she'd be able to clear the confusion in her mind.

He had mentioned a plane. She rubbed her forehead distractedly. She remembered nothing about a plane.

Could it be possible she was married? She recalled the intimate way they'd spent the last two nights. She could think of no other explanation. Perhaps if she explained her lack of memory to him, he'd be willing to fill in the gaps for her.

Paige stretched, pleased to discover how much better she felt now that she had some course of action. Surely her memory loss was temporary. She glanced at the man by the fire once more. *It would help if I could remember his name.*

The tent was almost stifling when Paige crawled out of the bedroll. She looked around for her clothes, but all she saw was a backpack in the corner of the tent.

When she opened it, she found men's clothing. Shrugging at the inexplicable details of the trip, Paige dug around until she found a bright red-and-black-plaid shirt. It was much too large for her, but better than nothing. She rolled the sleeve up until she found her hand hidden in the folds, repeated the process with the other sleeve, then hesitantly stepped out of the tent.

"Where are my clothes?"

Hawk spun around at the sound of her voice. His jaw dropped. Paige stood in front of the tent with one of his shirts on. The shirttail hung halfway to her knees in front, but the sides came up high on her thighs. He caught his breath. Her long, well-shaped legs could be the envy of a Las Vegas showgirl. His gaze wandered to her trim ankles and bare feet before he forced himself to meet her eyes. He really hadn't needed a visual reminder of what he'd held in his arms for the past two nights.

She looked as if she felt better and he needed to say something—anything—to let her know he was glad. His tongue, however, seemed to have disappeared.

He strode over to the stack of bags and provisions covered by canvas and partially sheltered by a tree. He picked up her small bag and returned to her side.

"Here you are," he said quietly.

Paige felt shy around him for some reason. She accepted her bag with a nod and disappeared once again inside the tent.

Kneeling beside her suitcase, she threw open the lid, only to stare at its contents with dismay. There were a couple of changes of underwear, one pair of slacks and a few skirts and blouses. A pair of low-heeled shoes were tossed in on top. Outside of her small bag of toiletries, that was all she'd packed.

Paige threw open the flap to ask where the rest of her clothes were and remembered she didn't know her husband's name. The situation was ridiculous and getting worse by the minute.

"Where are the rest of my things?" she asked when he turned around.

Hawk walked over to the tent, concerned. "You only brought the one bag, Paige," he answered with a slight frown.

She nodded, determined not to get upset. Glancing over at the fire, she said, "That coffee smells delicious. I guess it's being out-of-doors or something, but I'm starved."

He lifted her chin and looked into her eyes. They were much clearer this morning. Surely it would be all right for her to eat something. "I'll pour you some coffee while you get dressed. Breakfast shouldn't take long."

When she stepped out of the tent, Hawk smiled reassuringly. Paige's navy-blue slacks and long-sleeved pink blouse looked more appropriate to their present environment than her suit, and the low-heeled shoes were much more practical than high heels.

Paige gave him a hesitant smile and Hawk impulsively walked over and held out his hand to her, much as he would have to a shy child. She brushed her thick hair behind her shoulder and slowly reached for his proffered support. They walked back to the fire together.

Hawk was relieved to have the rain gone, although everything was still soaked. He threw a piece of canvas over a large rock and motioned for Paige to sit down.

She was weaker than she'd realized. Just the small amount of exertion she'd gone through made her head swim. Perhaps she'd take it easy today—maybe take a nap after she ate.

Hawk poured their coffee in silence while he tried to figure out a way to find out how she was feeling and what she could remember.

Paige accepted her cup and took a sip. *Ah, did that ever taste good!* She looked up and caught Hawk staring at her. It was no use. She couldn't remember anything about him and she might as well be honest before anything further developed between them!

"I might as well admit to you that I seem to have a problem." She glanced at him, then abruptly dropped her gaze to her cup of coffee. "I'm afraid the blow to my head knocked out a few rather important memories." She forced her gaze to meet his and was encouraged by the warm look in his eyes. "I not only don't remember your name, but I don't remember anything about our marriage."

Marriage! Alarms began to jangle in Hawk's head.

She nodded, determined to be completely open with him. "I don't even know what I did with my ring," she confessed, holding up her slender hand and revealing its bare condition.

Hawk stared at her, speechless. Where the hell did she get the idea they were married?

Then he recalled sharing the sleeping bag with her during the past two nights. At the time, it had seemed like a sensible idea. The first night she'd been in shock and he needed to get her warm. Body heat was the quickest way under the circumstances, and he'd stripped them both down and hurriedly placed her in the warm cocoon consisting of the two of them wrapped in a down-filled bed.

But what about the second night? Why don't you explain to her that you aren't married but that she's expected to share the only sleeping bag until you're rescued!

"Hawk," he finally managed to say.

She stared at him uncertainly.

"My name is Hawk."

"Hawk? Is that your last name, your first name, or a nickname?"

Her question surprised him. Few people asked, but then, few people cared. If she was somehow under the impression they were married, he supposed the question was understandable.

"My mother named me Black Hawk, but I took my father's name later. My legal papers state my name as Hawk Cameron, but I seldom use anything but Hawk."

She was quiet for several minutes, trying to assimilate the information he'd just given her. "Black Hawk is an unusual name."

He shrugged. "I suppose to most people. But to my mother, who was a Jicarilla Apache, it was a fine name, very honorable."

"How did your father feel about your name?"

"He never heard it. According to my mother, my father never stayed in one place very long. He'd been gone several months before I showed up." He stated the facts surrounding his birth without expression.

She sat there trying to dredge up a mental picture of his mother, but drew a blank. "Hawk," she experimented. *Hawk Cameron. Mrs. Hawk Cameron. Paige Cameron. Paige Winston Cameron.* Why didn't it seem more familiar? For that matter, why didn't *he* seem more familiar?

Paige could feel the slight pressure in her head once more, and she recalled her dream of the miniature natives practicing their skills on her head. "Not again," she murmured distractedly.

"What's wrong?"

"It's my head," she muttered. "It feels like hammers are being pounded on it from all sides."

Hawk stood up suddenly. "Why don't you go lie down again and I'll try to find something light for you to eat. You still aren't recovered."

Paige rubbed her hand across her temple. "Yes, I'm sure I'll feel better once I rest for a while." He followed her into the tent and helped her take off her blouse and slacks with brisk efficiency. It was only when he brushed his hand through her hair, tenderly tucking a lock behind her ear, that Paige experienced an inexplicable feeling of unease. "We *are* married, aren't we?"

He gazed into her troubled eyes. *She needs to rest, and she doesn't need to worry about anything.* Those were the priorities of the moment.

Hawk kissed her gently on the forehead, then straightened, pulling the covers to her chin. Making a sudden decision, he responded, "Yes, Paige, we're married. Try to rest now."

She smiled and closed her eyes. Hawk left the tent and went back to the food cooking over the open fire. *Okay, smart guy, you've got all the answers. What do you intend to do now?*

Hours later he still hadn't come up with a solution.

When he crawled inside the tent to check on her he discovered her gaze following his cramped movements. "There isn't much room in here, is there?" she asked softly.

"No," he agreed. "When I bought it I hadn't intended to share the tent with anyone."

"Have you had it long?"

He smiled. "For more years than I can remember."

"You must enjoy being out-of-doors."

"Yes, very much."

"I don't think I've ever been camping," she said uncertainly. "Or did you already know that?"

"No. But I had already guessed as much."

She shifted restlessly and he picked up her hand, letting it lie palm upward in his larger one. "Are you hungry?"

Paige couldn't get used to her reaction to him. Her skin tingled wherever he touched her. His warm gaze seemed to draw her closer to him somehow, and she had the strangest desire to wrap her arms around him—to be held in his arms.

She gave him a tentative smile. "A little."

"I'll bring you something to eat," he promised. "You just relax and I'll be right back." Hawk abruptly left the confined area.

What is she doing to me? he wondered in dismay. Her eyes seemed to haunt him. They were so expressive of her pain and bewilderment—and her wariness of him. *And why not? How can she be expected to remember a marriage that doesn't exist?*

As soon as she was stronger he'd tell her the truth. If they weren't found in the next few days they could make plans to hike out of the mountains. She'd be better able to handle the news about her father when she was stronger.

In the meantime, he saw no harm in fostering the idea that their trip was in the nature of a vacation. If it made her more comfortable to believe they were married, he'd allow her that fantasy. He'd just have to keep in mind their true status.

For some reason it was important to Hawk that Paige think well of him. Surely she'd understand the reason for his innocent deception once she remembered the reason for their flight.

Paige was asleep when Hawk returned to the tent with her meal. He decided to wait for her to wake up and stretched out beside her, enjoying the opportunity to leisurely study her.

He couldn't understand why all of his protective instincts were aroused by this woman. But she was like no other he'd ever known. Her clear, melodious voice seemed to gently flow through him, and he'd often caught himself absorbing its sound like the parched earth soaked up life-giving rain.

How ironic she thought they were married. No two people could be more different. She was well educated and obviously successful in her field. He, on the other hand, had learned about life the hard way.

Because of his inquisitive nature he'd picked up a considerable amount of knowledge during his travels—and he'd spent time over the years reading about subjects that fascinated him. But he knew he was far from the polished male that Paige was accustomed to.

"Why are you frowning?" Her voice startled him from his thoughts.

"I was just thinking."

Her lips curved into a gentle smile. "Ferocious thoughts, apparently."

He grinned. "Something like that. I'm afraid your meal is cold, but I thought you needed your rest."

She turned onto her side. "I feel as though all I've done is sleep. I haven't been very good company."

"I'm not complaining." He resisted the urge to lean over and kiss her. "I'll be right back with some hot food."

When he returned she was sitting up, pulling a brush through her tangled hair. He handed her a plate, then set a steaming cup down beside her. Once again he left, this time returning with another plate and cup.

They ate in companionable silence. Hawk was glad to see that Paige had a good appetite. Even her color seemed to be improved. Hopefully the worst was over.

"Hawk?"

"Hmm?"

"Could you try to help me fill in some of the blanks in my memory?"

He tensed. "Are you sure you're ready to start probing? There isn't any real hurry, is there?"

She sighed. "I suppose not. I just feel so stupid at the moment."

"It seems to me that's a very understandable reaction. I'm sure anyone would feel the same way." He took their plates and stacked them on the ground near the opening of the tent. "Why don't you rest for a while longer? I'm sure everything will come back to you in time—just don't push it."

"Thank you for taking such good care of me, Hawk."

He glanced over his shoulder and grinned. "My pleasure." His smile caused a distinct disruption to her normally steady heartbeat.

He crawled out of the tent, then paused. "Try to look at this as a well-earned vacation. Relax and enjoy it." He picked up their dishes and walked away.

Of course, he was right. There was very little that could be done. Either her memory would return or it wouldn't.

Paige couldn't help but wonder how long they'd been married. She found him very attractive and from a certain look she'd noticed she could tell that he felt the same way about her.

She smiled to herself as she curled up once again. *Not a bad reaction for a married couple to have toward each other. I must admit I've got darned good taste for picking a husband.*

Four

Hawk disgustedly climbed out of the plane a few hours later. Nothing. He could get absolutely nothing on the radio. He had even tried his portable, battery operated AM-FM radio and got nothing but static.

He jumped down off the wing of the plane and looked up at the mountains surrounding them. He wasn't surprised at the lack of reception.

Walking around to the front of the plane, Hawk winced at the damage. He'd hit a partially concealed rock after they'd touched ground, causing the left wheel to crumple. The plane had gone over on its nose, effectively demolishing the propeller and damaging the left wing. That was probably when Paige hit her head.

At least he hadn't ruptured the fuel line, so they hadn't faced the added danger of fire. He just wished he knew what had gone wrong with the oil pressure.

At least they had been lucky in some respects. The camping equipment had come through relatively unharmed and it was making their forced stay much more pleasant. Paige was as comfortable as possible under the circumstances.

Paige. His thoughts kept coming back to her. He had checked on her several more times since they'd eaten. She'd been peacefully asleep with a slight smile on her lips every time he'd looked in on her.

Why did she have to be so beautiful? Not to mention lovable. He'd quickly discovered she wasn't the typically spoiled beautiful woman. In fact, she seemed unaware of her looks. Where had she been all these years not to know the impact she had on a man?

He hated to be the one to break the news to her that her father was gravely ill—and that at the present time there seemed no way to get her to him. He could only hope she would regain her memory on her own.

Hawk started back toward their campsite. He could hear the small stream as he approached it. He knew that all mountain streams flowed toward larger streams that eventually became rivers. If he were to follow it, the stream would lead him to people who had settled near the rivers. People meant telephones and rescue, but he didn't know how long it would take. He didn't dare try such a venture with Paige until she was fully recovered.

It was time to go check on her, time to plan something to eat again, time to decide what to tell her about their sleeping arrangements. He could feel his body's instinctive reaction to the idea. He wished he didn't find her so damned attractive. Now that she was feeling better, he had no excuse to continue to share the sleeping bag.

The alternative was to be a gentleman and use the extra blanket he'd brought along at the last minute. At this altitude the nights were never warm.

He had to face it—his mother had not raised a gentleman. So where did that leave them?

"Hawk?"

His head jerked up, and he saw her standing by the dying fire. She looked adorable, standing there with his plaid shirt serving as a jacket. She had brushed her hair until it fell in rippling waves onto her shoulders and down her back.

Seeing her standing there looking so young and vulnerable affected him strangely. He wanted to hold her close and protect her from harm. He also had to fight a strong urge to make passionate love to her. Hawk could understand the second urge, but he couldn't understand his fierce desire to protect her.

He took his time walking over to her, trying to get a grip on his emotions. "How do you feel?" he asked, lightly brushing his hand across her cheek.

She smiled. "Much better, thank you." She had trouble meeting his eyes. "Hawk, do you know where my hairpins are? I can't find any of them."

He grinned. "There's no telling. They're probably strewn between here and the plane. But you don't need them."

She looked up at him in dismay. "Of course I do. I can't go around with my hair hanging in my face."

"You could always braid it."

She stared at him for a moment, then slowly smiled. "I suppose I could. Why didn't I think of that?"

He gathered her hair into both his hands, smoothing it, stroking the glossy waves. "I'll do it, if you'd like." She nodded and stood quietly while he plaited her hair into one long braid, tying it with a small piece of twine and letting it fall to her waist.

"You have beautiful hair," he said gruffly, stepping back from her. She turned around to thank him, the words dying on her lips when she saw the look in his eyes. They were blazing with intense heat.

She watched his mouth slowly lower to hers.

His lips felt surprisingly soft as they hesitantly touched hers, and Paige felt a ripple of feeling run through her body. His arms stole around her as though they had a will of their own and knew where they belonged. She felt a stirring deep inside her, a gentle awakening of sensations that she couldn't remember ever having experienced.

Hawk's kiss deepened and the intensity of his searching mouth seduced her into relaxing in his arms. Without a conscious decision Paige discovered she wanted to feel his mouth on hers, his warm, muscular body pressed intimately against her. She slipped her hands around his neck, bringing her even closer to him. Perhaps her mind had blotted out all memory of him, but her body reacted to him with sudden warmth and welcome.

His lips explored her face with gentle, loving touches. He seemed to be memorizing the surface of her face with his mouth—her eyes, the curve of her cheeks, the sensitive length of her neck. When Paige felt certain her knees would no longer support her he returned his mouth to her lips, seemingly starved for the taste of them.

As they kissed, Hawk loosened his hold on her, gently stroking her spine with his hands, learning the contours of her back and increasing the pressure until she felt almost a part of him.

Paige became aware of his body's reaction to her and knew what he expected—what he had a right to expect—and her heart seemed to stop beating in her chest.

No! Not yet! I don't know him. At least I don't remember. It's too soon. I'm not ready.

She turned her head from his seeking mouth and buried her face in his warm neck. "Hawk, please. We need to talk."

The sound of her breathless voice brought him back to his surroundings and what he was doing. Shocked at his intense reaction to her, he abruptly dropped his arms and stepped away from her.

"I'm sorry." His voice was a hoarse whisper.

She stared up at him, her eyes almost purple in their darkened state. "It isn't your fault, Hawk. It's mine. I'm so sorry our trip turned out this way." She backed away from him, watching his face as he stared at her, confused.

Paige tried to joke about it. "It must be tough to look forward to a vacation only to discover your wife suddenly doesn't know you."

"Don't..."

"I'm sure this is only temporary, but you see, I guess I'm still a little shy with you. I'm just not ready to..."

"You don't have to explain to me, Paige. I'm sorry I got carried away just now. You have nothing to feel guilty about."

His eyes glowed intensely, and she couldn't resist resting her palm along his cheek. "I wish we could pretend we just met and get acquainted all over again."

His breath caught in his chest. She looked so wistful, and so very vulnerable. Actually, her suggestion had considerable merit. They had to do something while they waited and he needed to keep in mind not to touch her. He could handle that. He'd better be able to handle that.

Hawk stepped back from Paige and grinned. "Good idea. Why don't we get something going to eat before dark and we'll trade the stories of our lives." He paused, uncertain. "Or do you remember any of the past?"

She gave him a puzzled smile. "It's strange, because I seem to remember who I am and what I am, but I can't remember who you are or what we're doing here together."

Hawk dug through the food supplies and found a package that could be easily cooked in a pot over the grill. Paige sat down on a nearby boulder to watch. She knew she needed to learn more about how to survive in the wilderness.

When he didn't say anything, she finally said, "I've managed to figure out that we are camping, but I don't understand why. Did I dream it, or did you mention something about a plane?"

He glanced up from his meal preparation. "We were in a plane that I had to land during a storm." He stared out over the meadow. "You can't see it from here. I'll take you down there tomorrow, if you're feeling up to it. Maybe you'll recognize something."

"Where were we going?"

Damn. I was afraid you'd ask that question!

The silence lengthened between them. Finally Hawk looked up at her. "Well, I had in mind a camping trip, but not exactly here."

She laughed. "No, I can understand that. So you were flying the plane. Is that a hobby of yours?"

"No. That's how I make my living."

"Oh." In a musing tone, Paige continued, "You know, it's hard for me to think of you as my husband." Embarrassed at the admission, she dropped her gaze to the fire. Finally she forced herself to look at him. "Have we been married long?"

Hawk shook his head but kept his eyes on the stew he was stirring.

"I didn't think so. Otherwise, I don't think I could have forgotten you so completely." She studied the lean build of the man kneeling before her. He looked tough, but surprisingly graceful as he prepared their meal with economical movements. She shook her head ruefully. "I'm having to eat a lot of my words. I always said I would never get married."

That statement brought his gaze up to fasten intently on her. She noticed his surprised expression and blushed. She could actually feel the warmth spread over her neck and face. It was a rather absurd remark to make to her husband.

She knew he needed an explanation. "You see, I grew up watching how unhappy my mother was, married to a doctor. My father was rarely available to take her places. She could never count on his being home at a regular time for meals. Mother ended up having to make a life of her own, independent of my dad. They loved each other, there was never any question of that, but the life of a dedicated doctor precludes a normal married life." She paused, studying him. "Surely I told you all that when you first proposed, didn't I?"

She looked like a young girl sitting curled up on the rock with her braid draped across her shoulder. He straightened slowly and walked over to her. His eyes were on her level and he leaned toward her, kissing her gently on her nose. "No, we never did get around to discussing why you were still single when we met."

Paige was having trouble with her breathing, a condition that seemed to occur whenever Hawk was anywhere near. "Oh. Well, then I was extremely unfair to you not to have mentioned it."

Studying the man in front of her, Paige had a hunch she knew why she'd never mentioned it. Perhaps she hadn't wanted to discourage him. There was something elemental about him that spoke to her. In some respects she felt as though she'd always known him and been a part of his life.

She realized she was sitting there, holding her breath, hoping he would kiss her again. Paige acknowledged to herself that she wanted his arms around her, wanted to feel his strong body against hers. All of her senses pressed to convince her mind that she must love this man very much to have married him. Why fight her reaction to him?

Hawk's hands came up to rest lightly on Paige's waist. His mouth hovered inches from hers. "Are you ready to eat?" he asked softly.

Her obvious disappointment at his prosaic words would have been laughable if Hawk had been in the right frame of mind. He recognized her reaction to him and it didn't help him at all—it only made his strong response to her harder to control. One of them needed to stay in control of the situation, and she had enough to contend with trying to recover from her injury. Hawk couldn't hold her responsible for the misunderstanding of their relationship. He could only try to keep the situation within reasonable bounds.

While they ate they watched the sunlight slowly creep up the eastern cliff overlooking the meadow and disappear.

Evening approached. Hawk became lost in his thoughts of what tomorrow might bring. Search planes should have found them today. Since he'd seen or heard nothing, he had to accept the fact that there was a good possibility they would have to come to their own rescue.

"Are you based in El Paso?" Paige's question startled Hawk from his reverie.

"Yes."

"How long have you lived there?"

"A little over a year."

"You said you were a pilot. Do you have your own business?"

"No. I have a friend in the air charter business, and I've been helping him get it started."

"It sounds like fascinating work."

"I enjoy it."

"I have a feeling we don't have much time to spend together when we're both working." She glanced out over the peaceful scene. "Is that why we decided to go camping? To have more time together?"

He didn't want to lie anymore, but Hawk didn't know what to say. Paige was taking their situation in stride, quickly adapting to the change in circumstances and her loss of memory. He could understand her need for answers, but he hated to continue the deception for any longer than was necessary.

"Paige, I know you're concerned about your memory, but don't push it. Most of your questions will be answered for you when you're feeling better." He stood up. "Why don't you try to get some sleep?" He picked up their dishes and began to clean them.

Paige knew he was right. She was still very wobbly, and the least amount of exertion seemed to tire her. She was surprised to discover how eager she was to learn more about this man. She had gone against a lifetime of strongly held principles in order to marry him. He had to be a very special person.

"Thank you, Hawk."

He looked up from building the fire for the night. "For what?"

"For taking care of me. For being so patient. I know all of this has been a strain on you."

He slowly came to his feet. They stood facing each other, the flickering fire between them. "You're very easy to care for, Paige."

She had an impulsive desire to fling herself into his arms and hold on to him, not a particularly sensible action if she was determined to keep some distance between them.

"I'm sure to feel more like my old self tomorrow."

"I agree. All you need is more rest." He looked down toward the meadow. "I think I'll try the radio again. Who knows? Maybe this time I'll get lucky." Hawk took a couple of steps away, then paused. When he turned around, his face bore signs of strain. "Don't worry about my disturbing you, Paige. I've got a spare blanket. I think I'll sleep out here by the fire."

She tried to see the expression in his eyes, but the light from the fire wasn't bright enough. "Don't you want to sleep with me?"

"That's not the point. You need to get your rest, and—"

"I slept very well with you for the past two nights. Why should I be disturbed tonight?"

"Well, I, uh, you don't know me and—"

"I don't *remember* you, Hawk, there's a difference. You've made it clear you don't intend to push me. Believe me, I appreciate that very much, but there's no reason for you to sleep out here in the cold when we can continue to share the sleeping bag. Is there?"

Good question. Is there? Can you continue to fight the attraction and your reaction to her? Hawk ran his hand distractedly through his hair. *What can I say to her?*

"If anyone's going to sleep with the blanket," she said, "it will be me. I see no reason for you to be uncomfortable because I don't seem to have my head on straight."

They stood there staring at each other, two strong-willed people whom circumstances had thrown together in a bizarre situation.

Hawk sighed. "All right, Paige. We'll continue to share the sleeping bag, if that's the way you want it."

She could feel a bubbly sensation within her which she tried to cover with a formal nod of her head. "That's the way I want it."

She watched him walk away from her, disappearing in the darkness. The dancing arc of his flashlight helped her track his progress down the hill until even the light went out of sight.

Paige shivered, realizing that she was alone. Hurriedly she turned to the tent, glad to have the light from the fire to help her find her way. Her thoughts kept returning to the man who'd just left.

I love him, she told herself. *I must love him or I wouldn't be married to him.* Paige found one of Hawk's T-shirts in his backpack and decided to use it as a nightshirt. She sat down and pulled off her shoes.

He was an easy man to love. She thought of his quiet manner, his knowledge of the outdoors, his kindness to her. She thought of his magnificent build, of his voice that made her feel as though a soft brush had been smoothed across her body whenever he spoke to her. Most of all, she thought of how he made her feel every time he took her in his arms. She was pleased with her choice of a husband. If only she could remember making it!

When she curled up into the sleeping bag, Paige hoped that when she woke up the next day, she would remember everything between them.

Hawk heartily hoped the same. On his way to the plane, he knelt beside the stream and stuck his hand into the icy water racing across the rocks. He tried not to think about the night and the enforced intimacy of their sleeping arrangements.

He'd tried. He'd even surprised himself. Paige was evoking too many unfamiliar emotions within him, and he didn't know how to deal with them. How else could he explain his chivalrous impulse? What had shocked him was the sincerity of his offer. He didn't want her to be uncomfortable around him. What he wanted was for her to accept him. Why? What in the hell difference did it make?

The tent was quiet when Hawk eventually crawled inside. Until now his camping gear had been perfectly adequate for the demands he made on it, but now he found himself wishing he'd gone for extra sleeping bags and a larger tent.

He shone his flashlight briefly around the area, careful not to send the full rays toward Paige. She was sound asleep. Good. She needed her rest, just as he needed his. He sighed, thinking about trying to sleep with her. The last two nights had been difficult. He was afraid tonight was going to be impossible, but he had to try.

She'd been through his things, he noticed. Not that it mattered, but he wondered what she'd been looking for. Was it possible she was trying to find out more about him? He looked at his clothes, tightly packed. Of course not. They would tell her nothing.

He sat down and pulled off his boots, pants and shirt. He carefully lifted the edge of the sleeping bag and smiled. She was wearing one of his undershirts, no doubt as an attempt at modesty. He wondered if she knew how fetching she looked in the soft shirt, her breasts impudently teasing him through the thin material with their provocative tilt.

He flipped off the flashlight, took several deep breaths, then eased his way down alongside her. The only way the two of them fit in the bag was for him to pull her into the curve of his arm and he reluctantly did so. She cuddled next to him as though they'd spent most of their lives sleeping together in that position.

Hawk sighed. It was going to be a long night. He tried to concentrate on the next day. He had to think of anything but the warm, tempting body lying so trustingly against him.

She stirred and murmured, "Good night, love."

His heart pounded in his chest. Was she even aware of what she'd called him? What would it be like to know he was this woman's love?

She said nothing more, and Hawk realized she was asleep. Yet even in her sleep she'd been aware of him, just as he was aware of her. His hand slowly stroked her shoulder, then down her side, where it slid into the indentation between her ribs and hips. She was so small—so delicate—and so precious. He pulled her closer to his side, then determinedly closed his eyes.

Five

Sparkling sunlight warmed the meadow in early-morning splendor. Tiny droplets of water clung to the tall blades of grass and multileafed bushes and trees. A young doe grazed by the stream, pausing to look around the glen for any sign of alien life. She noted only the natural inhabitants—a family of rabbits, a couple of noisy squirrels and a busy racoon, already about their day's business. A blue jay scolded a venturesome chipmunk, and a mockingbird mimicked the lecture.

After three days the natural inhabitants of the meadow had come to accept the unusual presence of the ungainly birdlike structure lying drunkenly in their midst.

Hawk stood on the knoll near the tent, absorbing the scene before him. The place had everything he had intended to find in Mexico, with one addition—the beautiful woman he'd left asleep inside his tent.

He rubbed the back of his neck ruefully. The sleeping arrangements may have become acceptable to Paige, but the forced intimacy was playing havoc with Hawk. Celibacy had never been one of his virtues, particularly when he was continually reminded of the condition by the constant presence of an attractive and intelligent woman. No one who knew him would believe his behavior these past few days. He had trouble believing it himself.

He would have to stay away from her—keep himself busy exploring and fishing. Under ordinary circumstances, that should be all that was necessary. He raised his arms high above his head and stretched, trying to get the kinks out of his back. Unfortunately, these weren't ordinary circumstances.

Hawk strode down the hill. He might as well start making plans to get them out of there as soon as Paige could travel. Glancing around at the cliffs, he decided the first thing to do would be to get up where he could see the surrounding area. Maybe he would spot something—some sign of civilization. If so, he could probably leave Paige alone for a few hours while he went for help.

With a definite plan of action in mind, Hawk felt more in control of the situation. *Someday I'll look back on this episode and laugh. I'll remember it as my closest encounter with matrimony.*

Paige reached for Hawk, her eyes opening when she couldn't find him. Confused, she sat up. The tent gave mute testimony that she was alone. Slowly Paige settled back into the covers.

She barely remembered his coming to bed last night, yet she knew he'd been there. At one point she'd awakened to find herself curled on his chest, her face buried in his neck. She smiled at the memory.

What a set of new experiences she'd encountered in the past few days. She'd never before spent a night out-of-doors, never cooked on an open fire, and never tried to stay clean with the help of water dancing merrily along in a small stream. She was surprised to discover how much she'd enjoyed it. Maybe the bump on her head had changed her entire perspective. She couldn't remember ever feeling so lighthearted, so eager to involve herself in something besides her profession.

Paige had a fleeting thought of her father. She hoped her being away wouldn't create too much work on the rest of them, although her father was always nagging her to take some time off. He believed in periodic vacations as a means of resting the mind as well as the body.

Vacation. What was it about the thought of a vacation that bothered her so? Not her vacation—her father's.

He'd been planning to go to Flagstaff, to do some fishing. Had he gone? Paige rubbed her head uneasily. The pain was never far away, it seemed, and it got worse when she thought of her father. How strange.

She closed her eyes and tried to relax. *Don't push it. Each day you're better than the day before. Relax. Think of something soothing and pleasant.*

Her thoughts drifted, eventually settling on a pleasing subject. Hawk. The name fit him. He seemed to be a part of the outdoors, in tune with nature.

She found him fascinating. Hawk didn't need to call attention to himself—he'd be noticeable in any group. His strength seemed to be an innate part of him, something he took for granted. She found herself watching him whenever he was in sight. He moved with the flowing grace of a large cat. His worn Levi's and multiwashed shirts emphasized his muscular frame, and yet he seemed unconscious of his appearance. He also seemed unconscious of her, treating her more as an acquaintance than as his wife.

Paige sighed, then brightened slightly as she remembered the night before. Hawk might be cool toward her during the day, but at night he held her as though she were part of him.

Was it possible they had quarreled? Perhaps the trip had been planned to draw them closer together. From knowledge of her own nature, Paige had a hunch the problem stemmed from her obsession with her work.

If only she could remember. Because if that were true, she'd need to use their time together to mend the breach between them.

Now that she was awake, she might as well get up. Throwing back the covers, Paige reached for her pants with a frown. They were so hot during the day, but what else did she have to wear?

Digging into her small case, she came up with one of her straight skirts. With a little ingenuity, she could alter the skirt into a pair of shorts, which would provide some welcome relief from the warm, sunny days.

Paige found her emergency sewing kit in her handbag, then sat down crosslegged on the sleeping bag and started ripping out stitches in the skirt. Her small scissors gave her the most trouble, but she finally managed to cut off some of the length of the skirt.

It was almost an hour later when she stepped out of the tent. Her newly-made shorts hugged the curve of her hips, ending high on her thighs. She wore a thin, jade-green blouse with the top two buttons open, the tail tied in a knot under her breasts.

Too bad Hawk isn't here, she thought with a grin. *I could announce to him that he's Tarzan, me Jane.*

The sun was already high in the sky, but Paige saw no sign of Hawk. Should she wait or go ahead and eat without him? She wandered down to the stream and washed her face and hands. Oh, what she wouldn't give for a hot bath, or even a shower. Camping certainly left out a few of the basic amenities she'd always taken for granted.

A shadow fell over her and she glanced up, startled. Hawk stood between her and the sun—and her stomach flipped over. The only thing he wore was a pair of Levi's, hung low on his lean hips, and a scuffed pair of moccasins. He could have posed for one of Remington's paintings.

His chest was wide and muscled, and her fingers twitched with the remembered sensations of touching him there. The muscles in his arms rippled when he rested his hands lightly on his hips. His skin glistened in the sun, and for a moment she thought it was from perspiration, but when she slowly came to her feet she realized he was soaking wet, water forming tiny rivulets through his hair and coursing down his neck and shoulders.

Her mouth felt dry, and she had to swallow before she could speak. Searching frantically for a light tone, she asked, "What happened, did you fall in?"

Hawk noticed with dismay Paige's new outfit, and he knew without a shadow of a doubt his willpower was being tested to its limits. Once again she had her hair in a single braid, and the thin blouse did nothing to hide the jaunty tilt of her breasts. The sleek shorts she wore merely emphasized the beautiful shape of her legs.

What had she just said? He shook his head, and the tiny droplets flew over them both. She backed away with a laugh, her hands trying to shield her face.

"I'd love to have a shower, Hawk, but that wasn't exactly what I had in mind."

She glanced up at him, her eyes sparkling, her skin glowing, her smile causing his heart to pound in his chest, and his feelings for her exploded within him. It was at that moment that he knew he loved her. Hawk had never experienced the emotion before; he had never even come close, and he had no idea what to do about it. He just recognized that what he was feeling for the laughing woman before him was love, and it was slowly driving him out of his mind.

"Are you serious about wanting to take a shower?"

The sun was still in her eyes and she couldn't see Hawk's face clearly, but his voice sounded strained.

"Oh, yes. I'd love to be able to really scrub down and feel clean."

He glanced at the towel and washcloth she carried, items she'd found in his bag along with a bar of soap. "There's a waterfall not far from here where you can shower and bathe. Do you want to go now, or wait until after we eat? The water will be a little warmer then."

She glanced around the meadow, already cherishing the area. Why hadn't she known of the joys of outdoor living, especially if they included a shower? She grabbed his hand. "Let's eat first. I'll show you how much I've learned about cooking over an open fire." She ran ahead of him, pulling him laughingly behind her. Then she made a ceremony of brushing off a place for him to sit down so that he could watch her preparations.

"How's your head?" He studied her face and wondered if she knew about the five freckles that artistically decorated her dainty nose. Only the bruise near her temple marred the delicate softness of her skin.

Paige looked up from stirring the biscuit mixture she intended to bake in the iron skillet. "It's fine. Really."

"Have you remembered anything more?"

She glanced down at the bowl she held, then forced her gaze to meet his. "No. I'm sorry."

"You don't have to apologize. It's not your fault."

"Well, maybe not, but it certainly has put a crimp in our vacation together."

"Uh, Paige, I want to talk to you about that…"

"Good, because I want to talk to you about it as well!"

She placed the biscuits in the skillet, covering them as she'd seen him do, then started mixing the dehydrated eggs with canned milk. She learned quickly, he had to give her that.

"All right," he said quietly. "What did you want to say?"

Now that she had his undivided attention, she was unsure of herself. She'd been rehearsing what she would say, but it was different with him sitting there, half dressed, watching her so intently. "Well…I've been having some uneasy feelings about us." She paused, but couldn't bring herself to look at him.

He didn't respond.

"You mentioned that we hadn't been married long. From what I can tell, you're a very independent person." She glanced up at him and was surprised to see a slight smile hovering on his lips.

"That's very true."

She nodded. "So am I. I'm also opinionated and hard-headed." She waited, but he didn't comment. Their argument must have been worse than she thought! "What I'm trying to say is I feel there's something wrong between us. Did we have a fight about something?"

"No, Paige. That isn't it at all."

Okay. Now is the time to tell her the truth, painful though it might be for her. With calm deliberation, Hawk began. "I met you when you came to the air charter service and chartered a plane."

She looked puzzled. "Why ever would I do a thing like that? I don't even like to fly."

"You said you wanted to fly to Flagstaff to see your father." He watched her and waited for her reaction.

A sudden pain shot through her head. Paige absently rubbed her temple. Her father. Flagstaff. He had planned to go to Flagstaff on his vacation. Had he already gone? He must have. Why else would she be joining him? But why?

"If my father were in Flagstaff, I don't understand why I would go as well. We would be very short-handed at the clinic." She shook her head, bewildered. "It doesn't make sense. Nothing makes sense." She caught Hawk watching her intently.

"Hawk, how long have we known each other?"

Hawk answered her in a firm, deliberate tone. "We just met."

She stared at him with a mixture of horror and dismay on her face. Hawk waited for her to reach the natural conclusion. Only she didn't.

"I can't believe it. I eloped with someone I barely knew!" She stared at him in shock, but she was in no greater shock than he. That was not the conclusion he'd expected her to reach. It was not the conclusion that was going to help him out of the situation he was in. What the hell was he supposed to say to her now?

She sank down beside the fire and abstractedly stirred their breakfast. Almost talking to herself, she muttered, "I must have been under a tremendous strain. My years of constantly pushing myself must have been too much for me." She glanced up at him. "Was I by any chance running screaming down the streets when you first saw me?"

He started laughing, then shook his head.

"Will you be honest with me? I mean, give me a straight answer if I ask you something?" She came over and knelt in front of him.

At last, here it comes, and the charade will be over. Not before its time, he thought.

She stared at him in solemn concentration. "Did I ask you to marry me?"

Bewildered by her intense expression and the tension he could feel radiating from her body, he slowly shook his head no.

"Oh, thank God!" she said, and threw her arms around him in an expression of relief. Breakfast was forgotten for the moment. Hawk found himself flat on his back, with Paige staring down at him from her position on his chest. "Oh, Hawk, you had me so worried. I've never been interested in dating, or getting involved with anyone. I never had the time or inclination for flirtations or affairs. And for a moment I thought you were going to tell me I'd engineered our whole relationship." She stared into his dark eyes, seeing herself mirrored there. "I'm so glad you were crazy enough to propose to someone you barely knew—and so glad I was crazy enough to say yes!"

With those last words her mouth settled contentedly on Hawk's, proving once again she was a fast learner. She traced his lower lip with her tongue, her lips moving lightly over the surface of his firm mouth, while her hands gently explored the wide expanse of his chest.

Hawk's arms came around her. Somewhere in his deepest conscience alarms were going off, but he was obeying instincts older than his conscience. He held her to him, her body resting lightly on top of his, her breasts lying trustingly open to his view. His hand slid into the opening of her blouse, gently touching her. Her body quivered like an arrow finding its mark. He could feel his self-imposed restraints slipping away from him. She felt so good in his arms, just as though that's where she belonged.

Hawk smelled something burning.

He rolled, laying her on the ground, and leaped to his feet. Their breakfast was smoldering on the fire. He managed to rescue the pans, but the ingredients were past saving.

"Lesson number one, young lady. A cook never leaves the kitchen while preparing meals."

Paige lay on her back, breathless, and watched Hawk as he found more food and began to prepare another meal. While she caught her breath she tried to deal with the new information she'd just received. Staid, stodgy Dr. Paige Winston, the dedicated spinster of the pediatrics ward, had so fallen out of character as to meet a tall, dashing stranger and elope with him.

She wondered if her father knew about it. Exactly how long had they been married? Could it be possible they were on their honeymoon? Hawk would have some more questions to answer—but not quite yet. She needed time to think things through. Every new bit of information unnerved her. Paige wasn't sure she was ready to face what their relationship would do to her settled way of life.

I suppose Hawk didn't know how to tell me we had just gotten married. That's why being married seemed so strange to me at first. We've probably never even made love. The thought of the two of them making love seemed to set all her nerve endings tingling.

She watched the sun glisten on Hawk's bronzed back. *It will be up to me to change the situation. He's made it clear he doesn't intend to touch me.* She smiled at the thought

that he was willing to wait for her memory to return before
initiating lovemaking. How could she let him know that
she'd built up enough memories about him since they'd been
there?

Paige trusted her own judgment. Whatever her reasons
that had convinced her to marry him in the first place were
good enough for her now.

Hawk turned to call her over to eat and found Paige staring at him with warm tenderness. He realized she was still
under the impression they were married. Their situation was
becoming increasingly explosive. The safest course for them
both was for him to tell her about her father and the truth
about them, and ask her to forgive him his deception.

I'll tell her right after we eat.

Six

Only he didn't. Instead, Paige convinced him she felt well enough to go exploring.

"Do I have to put on my long pants?" She glanced down at her bare legs.

"Aren't you afraid you'll burn?" Hawk resolutely kept his eyes on her face.

Paige stared up at the sun for a moment, then shrugged. "I'd rather risk it than put on those hot slacks again." With a warm smile she added, "Perhaps we can stay in the shade."

When she smiled at him Hawk had trouble remembering his train of thought. "We won't leave the meadow, so you probably will be all right."

Paige looked out over the pastoral scene. "How big is the meadow?"

Hawk checked the fire, then started down toward the water. "I'd guess it's about a mile long, maybe a half-mile wide." He pointed downstream. "Not too far in that direction the area narrows into a canyon."

"Have you been that far?"

"Yes. I also climbed the ridge behind us, hoping I'd see some sign of civilization. But no luck."

They crossed the stream, and Paige walked over to the plane. It was the first time she'd been up close to it. She studied it thoughtfully. It didn't look at all familiar. She tried to picture herself in it, but couldn't. Flying wasn't one of her favorite things to do. It was ironic she'd married a pilot.

Paige found the view from the valley very appealing—so peaceful and untouched. She felt as though she and Hawk were the only two people on earth.

A sudden thought occurred to her. "There must be a radio in the plane. Have you been trying it?"

Hawk nodded. "I've been trying it for days, but can't pick up anything."

"Do you think anyone will find us?"

"I'm beginning to have my doubts. They would have located us by now, I'm afraid."

"What if nobody finds us?"

"We'll have to hike out of here."

"When?"

He looked up in the sky as though waiting for divine guidance. "I'm not sure. If I were alone I'd leave today, but I don't think you're ready to try it."

"Why not?"

"Because you're still not recovered from that knock on your head." He glanced down at her shoes. "And I'm concerned that you don't have the proper shoes or clothes to take the strain of a trip like that. From what I could see, the going won't be easy."

"So we sit and wait."

"For a while, yes."

"I don't mind. I'm really enjoying the vacation. I just feel guilty being away from the clinic. But it's too late to worry about it. I must have made some sort of arrangements before I left."

Hawk was silent. He didn't know what to do about her continued loss of memory. On the one hand, so long as she thought they were married and this was only a slight alteration of their original plans, Paige was relaxed. Getting upset would be the worst thing for her.

Learning that her father had suffered a heart attack would be a tremendous shock to her, he knew. It was obvious the two of them were very close. She would be frantic to get out of there.

He glanced toward the end of the meadow and wondered how long it would take them to find help. She might be able to take a day's hike, if they took it easy. But what if it took several days, even a week? He hated to take the risk.

"How about my showing you that waterfall I told you about?" Hawk waited for her to join him by the stream before he added, "Would you like to take a shower now?"

"Would I? Just lead the way."

They returned to the tent and gathered up towels, soap and Paige's shampoo, then started down the hill once more.

Hawk led the way, Paige content to follow and enjoy the scenery. A slight path showed through the grass along the stream, and Paige realized Hawk had been along there enough to leave a faint trail. It wound along beside the water, skirting boulders and trees, but always returned to follow the stream wherever possible.

Paige heard the sound of rushing water before she saw it. A large overhang, part of the hillside that appeared to have been eroded by the elements, jutted out over the stream, hiding the waterfall from sight.

Hawk took Paige's hand and helped her over the rocks and dirt that had formed a blockade of sorts to their passage. They paused when they reached the top.

"Oh, Hawk, this is beautiful."

From their viewpoint the waterfall still towered above them at almost a right angle to the previous course of the

stream. The abrupt turn had formed a pool where the water eddied and circled before finding its way downhill once
more. The sunlight caught the water in flashes of brilliant
crystal. Paige could hardly wait to get into it.

She looked at Hawk uncertainly. She just couldn't go in
while he was standing there watching her.

He glanced down at her and smiled. "I think I'm going
to go a little farther upstream for a while. Why don't you
stay here and bathe? I should be back in about a half hour
or so."

Bless you for being so understanding, she thought. She
nodded shyly and began the descent to the water while
Hawk turned his back and started up the higher incline that
created the waterfall.

The area near the stream was strewn with rocks of various sizes. Paige found one that was flat enough so she could
sit down. She pulled off her shoes, regarding them with
concern. The soft leather was scratched and scuffed. They'd
certainly taken a beating during the past few days.

She slipped her shorts and shirt off, folded them neatly,
then laid them in a stack. Standing up, she glanced around
self-consciously before she stepped out of her briefs. Hastily removing her bra, Paige stepped gingerly into the water.
The summer sun had taken some of the icy chill away, and
it felt good.

Moving carefully, Paige waded toward the waterfall, eager to feel its freshness beating upon her. The bottom suddenly disappeared and she let out a yelp as she plunged in
deeper. The sun hadn't had a chance to warm the depths,
and the cold water caused shivers to dance across her skin.

Paige determinedly swam across the pool until the spray
from above started falling around her. She felt for bottom
and eventually found it. The water was up to her shoulders.

Since her hair was already wet, Paige went back for her
shampoo and vigorously scrubbed her head. Never before
had she appreciated the feeling of clean hair quite so much.

After thoroughly rinsing her hair, Paige swam over to the edge of the pool where it was shallow enough for her to stand and soap herself. Now that she was used to the water temperature she found it invigorating. *All the comforts of home.*

Aware of time passing, bringing Hawk's return near, Paige quickly finished and swam to the deeper water. She felt so good. Perhaps she could talk Hawk into taking her on up the trail. She waded back to the side of the pool where her clothes lay. Once again she glanced around shyly before grabbing her towel and briskly drying off. Within minutes she was dressed.

There was still no sign of Hawk, and Paige relaxed by stretching out on the large flat rock and turning her face up to the sun. She lay there with her eyes closed, listening to the sounds of the glade—the twittering of the birds in the trees, the slight rustling of the leaves as a playful breeze flirted among them—and slowly drifted off to sleep.

Hawk watched Paige from his position high on the cliff near where the water fell to the rocks below. He had given her plenty of time to bathe and get dressed—or so he had thought. But when he'd paused at the edge of the drop before following the trail downward, he'd discovered that Paige was at that moment stepping out of the water.

The shock of seeing her nude stopped him in his tracks. He'd undressed her in the dark the night they were forced down. His only concern at that time had been to care for her and to bring her body temperature up.

Now he could see her in the sparkling sunlight, her hair streaming down her back, her shoulders narrowing to a tiny waistline, her hips swelling in a gentle curve that he found utterly enticing.

She was already dressed and stretched out on the rock before he realized he'd been standing there watching her like some sort of Peeping Tom. *Is this what you're reduced to?* he asked himself in disgust. Thank God she hadn't seen him lurking up there as though hoping to catch her. He shook his head, trying to clear it, and started down the steep slope.

A cloud passed across the sun, or so it felt to Paige, and she opened her eyes. Hawk stood there, his shadow across her. She smiled, a sleepy, contented smile, and stretched. "That was marvelous, Hawk. Thank you for bringing me up here."

"No problem," he responded in a gruff voice. "Are you ready to go back?"

She sat up. "Not really. I managed to rest while I was waiting for you." She stood up. "Would you mind if we go up the trail a little farther?"

How could he deny her anything when she looked at him like that? Maybe it would help him to exercise some of his frustrations out of his system.

He held out his hand. "We'll go if you'll promise not to overdo it."

She took his hand and held her other one up in a pledge position. "I promise," she vowed.

Paige was enthralled with the variety of plants, birds and animals they saw as well as Hawk's knowledge of them all. He knew their names, and he knew what plants could be used for medicinal purposes. He seemed to be at home in that environment, and Paige found herself envying him his freedom.

Now that you're married to him, it can be your environment too, she reminded herself. She sighed in contentment.

The climb was more strenuous than Paige had anticipated, and by the time they reached the ridge overlooking the meadow her head felt as though the little natives were back, hammering ferociously.

Hawk took one look at her white face and swore. "I knew better than to let you come this far. Your headache's back, isn't it?"

"A little," she admitted. "I just need to rest for a moment. I'll be okay." She sank down on a rock and tried to let the view soothe her.

Hawk sat down beside her and gathered her into his arms. "I'm so sorry, honey."

She rested her head against his chest. His heart seemed to be racing. "It's not your fault, Hawk."

"I'm responsible for you, and I haven't done a very good job of looking after you."

"You've done an excellent job of looking after me. How do you think I would survive in the wilderness alone?"

"But that's the point. We shouldn't have to be camping at all."

She pulled her head back and gazed at him. "You never intended to take me camping, did you?"

"No."

At least that explained why she didn't have the proper clothes for camping. "You were taking me to Flagstaff to leave me with my father, weren't you?"

"Yes."

What could have happened to their relationship in a few short days that she would have run to her father and he would have made plans to go off camping without her?

She knows most of it now, Hawk thought. *Let her think we've had a fight, at least until I can get her to her father.*

"Do you think you feel up to starting back?" He deliberately lightened his tone. "It's always easier going downhill."

All she wanted to do was lie down, but first she had to make it back to camp. Paige stood up and swayed.

Without a word Hawk lifted her into his arms. She fastened her hands behind his neck, laid her head on his chest with a soft sigh, and closed her eyes. She felt tired, so very tired.

Hawk took his time making sure each step he took was firmly placed. Thankfully he found a more circuitous route back to the campsite that wasn't as steep as the way they had come.

He felt Paige relax in his arms and realized she'd fallen asleep. He pulled her closer to him. She looked like a child being carried to bed, and he felt his heart expand with love for her.

How could he regret their time together—regret the chance to get to know Paige? He glanced down at her once again. She still had mauve smudges under her eyes. Why had he allowed her to coax him into ignoring his better judgment?

Because you become melted butter whenever she looks at you with those wide, pansy-colored eyes.

They reached camp at dusk. Paige had not awakened. Hawk carefully laid her on the bedroll, then returned to the fire and made plans for a meal. Thank God they had sufficient provisions. They could stay there for weeks if necessary. Only Hawk knew he couldn't last that long around Paige without cracking under the strain of wanting to make love to her. His whole body ached, and only part of the pain could be blamed on the hike he'd made that afternoon with Paige in his arms.

Night had drawn its anonymous cloak around them when Paige joined Hawk by the fire. "I'm sorry to conk out on you like that."

Hawk smiled. "No problem. Feeling better now?"

Paige nodded. "I don't understand why the pain gets so bad at times. Whenever I try to concentrate—to remember—my head feels like it's going to explode."

He handed her a plate and a steaming cup. "The answer is obvious, doctor. Don't think. Don't concentrate. Let it come in its own time."

"That's easy for you to say. You don't have any missing gaps in your memory."

"What I'm trying to say is that worrying about it not only isn't helping you, it's actually causing more harm."

She was silent while she thought about what he said. She began to eat. He was right—as usual. They ate in companionable silence while they watched the fire flicker and dance before them.

"Have we ever made love?" Paige inquired abruptly, ending the silence.

Unfortunately Hawk had just taken a swallow of coffee. He choked. In a strangled voice he finally managed to get out, "What on earth made you ask that?"

"I've been thinking about everything you've said. You avoid discussion of our marriage as though it were a mistake. You've admitted we haven't known each other long, so we obviously haven't been married long, and for some reason you don't seem to want to discuss it."

Hawk stood up. "That's right. I don't. Have you finished eating?"

Paige looked down at her plate, surprised to see it empty. "I guess I have."

He took her dishes, then brought her cup back to her full of coffee. Sitting down beside her, Hawk took her hand in his.

"Paige, please drop the subject of our marriage. Forget it. It isn't important at the moment. What is important is for you to relax, quit probing and get well. We're going to be faced with hiking out of here one of these days, I'm afraid. You've got to be ready for that." He turned her hand palm upward and slowly traced her life line with his index finger. "I care for you very much and I promise that I won't ever do anything to hurt you. You're going to have to trust me."

"I do. I've already trusted you with my life. I just don't understand what went wrong between us."

"Nothing went wrong between us. Won't you accept that?"

"I suppose I have to."

"It would help." He stood up, pulling her up with him. "Go to bed now and try to get some more rest. Will you do that, please?"

Paige's gaze searched his face. He looked grim, almost in pain. She wanted to wipe away the look of strain, to hold him close and convince him that whatever their problems, they could work them out together.

"All right, Hawk. Whatever you say." She went up on tiptoe and brushed her lips gently against his. "Good night, love."

He watched her disappear inside the tent. Hawk picked up his coffee cup and for the first time since he'd been forced to land wished for something stronger to drink.

Hawk sat in front of the fire staring into the flames for several hours. Maybe he couldn't control loving her, but he could damned well control what he did about it.

He intended to do nothing. Nothing at all.

Seven

"After I left the Middle East, I was in Southeast Asia for about three years." Hawk sorted through his fishing gear as he talked. He and Paige were by a pool formed by a turn in the stream that ran through the meadow. Hawk was leaning on his elbow as he picked up weights and lures, then carefully separated them into the tiny compartments of his fishing tackle box.

Paige lay flat on her back a couple of feet away. She was enjoying the quiet sounds of the meadow, the shade of the aspen where they had decided to rest, but most of all, she was enjoying Hawk telling her about his life. "Were you ever in the military?"

He shook his head. "No, I did some work for our armed forces, but on a civilian basis."

She watched the leafy shadows form patterns of light and shadow across him. Once again Hawk had dispensed with a shirt, and Paige stared at his tanned chest with unconscious yearning. "Haven't you ever had a place you called home, Hawk?"

He stared off in the distance for a moment, sorting through his memories. "I was born on the reservation near Dulce, New Mexico. For the first fourteen years of my life, I lived with my mother. I enjoyed those years...took them for granted." He gave his head a tiny shake. "But my mother got pneumonia one winter, and died." His fist clenched, the only sign of emotion she saw. "There was no excuse for losing her. I don't think she cared if she lived or not. She felt she'd raised me, I suppose, and wasn't needed." The quiet ripple of the water was the only sound. "She was wrong...but I never had a chance to tell her differently," he finally said in a low tone.

"So you left," Paige guessed. "And you decided you didn't need anyone."

He glanced at her in surprise. "Why do you say that?"

"Because I've seen children react in that manner when they've lost someone close to them. It's a fear of allowing someone else to get close and perhaps losing them as well." She picked up a twig and traced the blade of grass in front of her. "It's hard to lose someone when you're so young. I was eighteen when Mother died of cancer."

"But you had your father," he reminded her.

She smiled. "Yes. He was there for me, and I'll always be grateful for that. He helped me through the healing process that follows grief." Paige was silent for a few moments, then added, "I'd like to think we helped each other." She glanced up at him. "Have you met my dad?"

Hawk shook his head.

"I think you'll like him." Her eyes sparkled as she took in his indolent pose beside her. "I *know* he'll like you." She wrinkled her nose at him. "You're just what the doctor ordered."

Paige rolled to her side and leaned up on her elbow. Hawk had finished with his tackle box and had sat it behind him. Now she lay inches away from him. He could smell the light fragrance she wore, the heat of the summer day enhancing it, mingled with the soft, evocative smell that was her. He took a deep breath, trying to ignore the messages his senses were giving him. "What do you mean?"

"You have to understand that even as a little girl I was always seriously determined to grow up to be a doctor. With that type of dedication, I refused to allow anything to distract me." She ran her finger down his nose. "Even boys."

"You mean you never dated?"

"Some. I went to all the school activities and dances, that sort of thing, but I just wasn't interested in involvement. I wanted to hurry and grow up—to get on with life."

"It looks like you succeeded."

"Too much, according to Dad. He says I haven't taken time to stop and enjoy myself along the way." She gazed out across the meadow. "I'm beginning to understand what he meant."

Her sigh of contentment reminded Hawk that he needed to do something about their situation. He studied Paige, lying so close beside him. Did she have the stamina to hike out?

Their time during the past few days had been well spent. Paige no longer seemed to be suffering from headaches and her energy level was steadily increasing. He wished he had some idea how far they'd have to hike to find help. He'd be better prepared to make a decision.

"Paige?"

"Hmm?"

"Do you think you'd be up to hiking out of here?"

She looked at him in surprise. "I guess so. Are you getting bored?"

He laughed. "No, as a matter of fact, I'm not."

She smiled, and his heart seemed to melt in his chest. "I'm glad. Neither am I."

"What I'm saying is...I don't think anyone is going to find us, so we might better start seeing about rescuing ourselves."

She stretched, raising her arm high over her head. When she brought it down, it landed lightly on his shoulder. She began to draw small circles on his bare flesh. "Are you sorry you ended up having to camp with me?"

Hawk could feel his body tensing at her touch. Dear God, how he wished she would remember the truth. *Do you, really?* an inner voice whispered to him. *Aren't you enjoying your time with her more than you've ever enjoyed anything in your life?*

He sat up. "Not really."

Paige grinned. "I'm glad." She sat up too, and rested her head on his shoulder. "Next camping trip I'll make sure to pack the right kind of clothes."

"Paige..."

"Hawk..." They spoke at the same time.

"What were you going to say?" he asked.

"Nothing important, really. I just wondered if you'd like to go swimming."

"Swimming?"

"Uh-huh. It's really warm today. You know where that waterfall is—where we've been showering. It's deep enough to swim, if you'd like to."

If I'd like to!

Paige jumped to her feet. "Come on. Let's try it—you might even like it." She laughed, a light, happy sound that was Hawk's undoing. He wanted this woman to be happy. He wanted to spend the rest of his life making her happy, but he didn't have the slightest idea how to do that.

She grabbed his hand and pulled him to his feet, leading the way while they followed the stream to the waterfall. The splashing water made a merry sound in the quiet of the warm day.

Paige immediately sat down and took off her shoes. It occurred to Hawk that swimming wasn't a good idea, but he couldn't seem to find his voice to explain why before she took off her blouse and shorts.

The tiny wisps of clothing she now wore hid nothing from view. Her skin turned a rosy hue as she determinedly met his startled gaze. "I don't know why I'm so bashful with you. After all, we *are* married." With a hint of defiance she unsnapped her bra, then stepped out of her tiny briefs.

The past few days had begun to tan her arms and legs, and her tan emphasized the ivory sheen of the rest of her. Hawk could only stare.

His gaze caused her blush to burn deeper, and Paige hurriedly lowered herself into the water. *How brazen can you get,* she admonished herself. *He's been a perfect gentleman, considerate of your condition, and you're flaunting yourself like some sex-starved wanton.*

But she wanted to let him know that her loss of memory didn't have to prevent them from enjoying their idyllic time together. His aloof attitude was no longer necessary, but she didn't know how to tell him. Hopefully he would understand that she was showing him.

She heard a splash behind her and knew that Hawk had joined her, but she didn't quite have the courage to turn around and face him. Instead, she swam to the side of the pool where they had left the soap and shampoo. She began to unbraid her hair, impatiently tugging at the strands. When her hair was free, she vigorously shampooed it, working up a lather, then stood under the waterfall to rinse it.

After diving under the water to make sure all the soap was gone, Paige came up face first, squeezing the water from her hair. Hawk stood a few feet away, watching her with such a tender, yearning expression her heart felt as though it would burst within her.

The water barely covered his hips. He'd followed her example and left his clothes on the large rock beside the stream. The sun on the water shot sparks of light all around him. The water glistened on his shoulders and chest, and Paige knew he was the most beautiful thing she'd ever seen—handsomely rugged, symmetrically formed, his face reflecting his love for her. *Of course he loves me, just as I love him. That's the best reason for marriage I know.*

She moved over to him, watching his eyes dilate as she approached. The water was much deeper on her, it stopped just below her breasts, so that they seemed to be floating. She didn't stop until she was touching him, her breasts lightly rubbing his chest.

"Do you know what I think?" she asked in a husky voice.

It was all he could do to keep his hands off her. He could feel the trembling throughout his body, and he knew that she was close enough to feel his reaction to her.

"No." He had trouble getting the short syllable past his dry lips.

"I think the reason I wasn't interested in anyone, and didn't want to get involved, was because I was waiting for you. Somehow I knew you were out there somewhere and that I'd know you when I saw you." She placed her arms around his neck, pulling her body against his. "I'm so glad I waited."

Hawk's strong self-discipline broke and his arms wrapped around her, pulling her even closer to him. His mouth found hers in a yearning kiss that held all the pent-up emotion he'd been fighting for days. "Oh, Paige, I love you so much," he muttered when he finally paused to take a breath.

She was having trouble breathing. "I love you too, Hawk. I feel that I've loved you all of my life."

The soft call of a bird sounded in a nearby tree, and an errant breeze whispered softly through the leaves. Hawk found her mouth once more and took possession, recognizing that it was time to quit fighting what was between them—knowing this was what he needed, what they both needed—and wanted. The world was light years away. They were in their own special paradise, just the two of them, and they were in love.

He could feel the flutter of her pulse under his hand where it rested lightly across her collarbone. His heart felt as though it would crack the wall of his chest with its heavy thudding. He could no longer resist touching her after all the many nights he'd lain awake, holding her, wanting her, determined to resist. Now his resistance was gone.

Paige felt his light touch shimmer down her body, tracing the curve of her waist and hips. She had never been touched like that and had no idea how much she would welcome it. Perhaps it was only his touch that could make her feel so loved and wanted.

Hawk became aware they were still standing in the small pool. He swung Paige up in his arms and slowly walked to the edge of the stream, his kiss possessing her. When he climbed out of the water he knelt on the grass that covered the flat area nearby, placing her gently on the ground.

His hand rested lightly on her ribs and slowly smoothed across her stomach, her abdomen, then lower. He paused. She was so delicate, so beautiful.

Hawk stretched out beside Paige, determined not to rush her. He leaned over her, his hair brushing against her shoulder while his lips traced a line across the soft swell of her breast. His mouth settled briefly on the darkened tip, then carefully caressed its mate.

A languorous feeling flowed through Paige, her thoughts seeming to float away like the soft wisp of cloud overhead. She could only feel. She felt the touch of his mouth so intimately pressed to her body; she felt his hand gently stroke across her thigh and hip. The moist heat of his body radiated his special scent and she found it heady.

Her tentative fingers tried to imitate what he was doing. He'd been her teacher all week. It was time for a new lesson—this time in the art of loving.

Her hand brushed down his chest and she felt the muscles of his stomach and abdomen. Her fingers lightly brushed against his arousal, and his whole body jerked.

"I'm sorry," she whispered.

"Don't be. It's just that I'm not sure of my control where you're concerned. You've tested it to its limits, I'm afraid."

She looked deep into his eyes and saw the love and desire within them. Her voice shook as she said, "You don't need to have control with me, Hawk. Just love me."

"I do. Very much."

Hawk began to show her how to express her love in physical terms, and Paige responded like a flower bud opening to the sun in full maturity. She had waited for years for this man and it scared her to think she might not have recognized him when they first met. But she had. She hadn't let convention, different life-styles, or different backgrounds sway her.

Now he was hers.

Hawk carefully lowered his body over hers. She was so small and he didn't want to hurt her. His mouth claimed hers once again and his hand gently brushed across her upper thighs. He pulled back slightly to see her face, to watch her reaction as he took her for the first time, but he hoped fervently, not for the last.

She lifted drowsy eyelids to gaze dreamily at him, and Hawk felt as though a giant hand grabbed his heart and squeezed. How could he make love to her while she believed they were married? How could he take advantage of what she felt for him without telling her the truth?

He cupped her face between his hands, his weight still on his elbows. "Paige, darling, listen to me..."

Her smile was heartstopping. "I'm listening. Is this where you tell me you're a virgin?"

He choked, a chuckle almost strangling him. "No, I'm afraid not."

"I figured as much. Most thirty-six-year-old adventurers I've met have the same problem."

How could she joke when everything was so serious? *But she has no idea what I have to tell her.*

"How many thirty-six-year-old adventurers have you known?" he murmured, unable to resist the temptation to kiss her once more. He tried to ignore how well their bodies fit together. He was so close to taking her, so very close.

She kissed him back. In a breathless voice she managed to say, "Oh, dozens I'm sure. I just can't recall their names at the moment."

"That's good. Oh, baby, you feel so good, and I want you so much."

"But you're afraid it's going to hurt me, aren't you? Please don't worry. If I'm willing, you shouldn't mind."

"Paige. There's something I have to tell you. I can't make love to you without your knowing."

His grim tone caught her attention. Then she realized how still he was, how full of tension. The lazy seductiveness of a few moments ago was gone. "What is it?"

"Paige, the day of the crash you hired me to fly you to Flagstaff because you'd heard your father was...ill. The plane went down a few hours later."

He could feel her stiffen beneath him, and he rolled away from her, coming up on his side to stare down at her. He watched the myriad emotions flashing across her face and he wished he could protect her from them. But it was too late.

Somewhere deep inside her Paige could feel the pain starting. Confused emotions darted at her from several different directions at once. Hawk was telling her they didn't know each other. He was telling her he was only a man hired to fly her to her father. He was telling her...

Paige sprang to her feet, frantically searching for her clothes. She spun around, hastily pulling them on, refusing to face the man who still lay where she'd left him, seemingly unconscious of his nudity.

When she was dressed she spoke without looking at him. "So this whole scene has been a complete farce. Not only am I not married to you, I don't even *know* you."

"That's not true, Paige. We may not have known each other when you hired me, but we've had several days together, and I think we've learned a great deal about each other. I know I've told you more about myself than I've ever told another living soul."

She finally forced herself to look at him, then flinched. He was making no effort to cover himself, a reminder of what had so nearly happened.

"Would you please put on some clothes?" Her tone was icy and his heart sank. She was taking it as badly as he'd imagined. But then, what could he have expected?

"Paige, I think we need to talk about this."

"About what? About the fool I've made of myself? That really isn't necessary. I'm well aware of it. The frustrated spinster finds the man of her dreams and decides she's married to him. That makes all those fantasies acceptable, doesn't it? I'm sure you've had a hard time not laughing in my face!"

"I haven't been laughing, Paige. I've been falling in love with you."

"Stop it! You don't need to continue the charade now. I understand. The only other thing I need to know is why I was flying to see my father. Surely you can tell me that. You said he was ill. My father is never ill."

By this time Hawk had pulled on his Levi's and stepped into his moccasins. He combed his hair back with his hands. When he walked over to where Paige stood, she backed away from him. He stopped, resting his hands on his hips.

"You told me that your father had a heart attack. That was why you were in a hurry to get there."

Paige felt faint and she sank down on the large rock where she'd had her clothes. The news was fresh to her, and the shock was every bit as severe as the first time she'd heard it. "A heart attack..."

"Yes."

"And you've kept me here all this time when I needed to be in Flagstaff!" Her voice rose in agitation.

He waved his arm. "Well, as you can see, I don't have a magic carpet that will whisk you away. Otherwise, I would have sent you right on."

"But why haven't we hiked out?"

"Because I thought you needed to recover. I didn't know if you had the strength and the stamina for what will probably be a very grueling trip." He dropped his hands. "I kept hoping someone would find us."

Distraught, Paige looked around the peaceful meadow. "You're an Indian. Why haven't you sent up smoke signals?"

"Very funny."

"I'm not *trying* to be funny. I'm trying to get out of this place."

"What do you think *I've* been doing?" he demanded.

"Seducing me."

They stared at each other in anger, in hurt, and in despair. Their paradise had disappeared, along with any dreams of a possible future.

Hawk stared at her for a long time, his face grim. Finally he spoke. "If I'd been trying to seduce you, Paige, we wouldn't be having this conversation. I would have gone ahead and made love to you." His mouth turned up in a sardonic smile. "You certainly weren't doing anything to stop me."

He disappeared upstream, heading away from their camp.

Eight

Paige didn't remember returning to the camp, but she found herself sitting in front of the tent. Their tent. They had spent several nights together, nights wrapped in each other's arms, nights when she'd wondered why he didn't make love to her.

Now she knew.

The pain had grown and blossomed within her until it seemed to consume her. Her whole body ached and she shook so hard it was almost as if she was undergoing a chill.

Shock. I'm in shock. My dad is ill. My marriage is nonexistent.

There was no Hawk in her life. There never had been—there never would be. Hawk was a mirage that had lingered longer than most.

He didn't make love to you. He could have. He knew it—you knew it. But he didn't. A sob escaped her.

How can I face him again? How can I pretend that nothing has changed? Everything has changed. Nothing will ever be the same. I can't face him. I just can't.

Paige glanced around the meadow. She remembered all she had learned from Hawk during the week. He'd pointed the way downstream that would be the best direction to go if they had to walk out. She hadn't cared. She hadn't wanted to leave. She hadn't known about her dad.

Oh, Dad, please don't die. I need you so much. Never more than I do now.

A growing determination seemed to grab her, forcing her out of her misery. She had to get to her father and she had to get away from Hawk. Standing up, she looked toward the stream. She didn't know where he'd gone and didn't care. He knew she wanted to leave here. She glanced around at the tent. There was no way she could stay there another night.

Once her mind was made up, Paige wasted no time gathering some supplies, taking the extra blanket and changing into her heaviest clothes. She wrapped everything she'd gathered in the blanket, then folded it as small as she could and tied it around her waist with some of Hawk's twine. It was bulky, but it left her hands free.

She stared up at the sun, trying to figure the time. She had no idea, but it seemed to be early afternoon. There must be several hours of daylight left. Perhaps she could find someone before dusk. It was better than sitting there waiting to face Hawk.

Hours later Paige wondered if she'd made a mistake. She was hot, tired and hungry, and the terrain had become increasingly rugged. The stream had left the pretty meadow and dropped at an alarming rate through giant boulders and tumbling rocks. She could no longer follow the waterway and was forced to fight through the underbrush, hoping not to lose track of the stream, the only guide she had.

Paige was glad she'd taken the time to rebraid her hair. It had snagged on an overhanging limb, but would have been so much worse loose. As it was, she felt as though a giant had tried to pull her hair out by the roots.

The soft mauve of twilight was touching the mountains around her when Paige slipped and fell, rolling down a rough incline until she landed in a heap at the bottom. Luckily she'd been deposited once again by the stream that had grown into an energetic river since leaving the meadow. She lay there, too sore to know if she were truly hurt or not.

Eventually Paige forced herself into a sitting position. Her clothes had saved her from abrasions but they'd paid the price with several rips and tears. She gingerly tested each ankle. They seemed to be all right, and she breathed a quiet prayer of thanks.

She looked around and discovered that she was sitting on a slight overhang above the river—not a bad place to camp for the night. She wasn't too far from the water, but far enough not to be bothered by any of the forest inhabitants who might want a drink. She hoped. Hawk had described some of the animals that lived in the area, most of which she'd only seen in a zoo. She would just as soon leave it that way.

If she were going to spend the night there, she needed to gather wood for a fire. With fresh determination, Paige limped into the underbrush, dragging out dead limbs. She didn't have anything to chop them up, but she had matches and she'd watched Hawk start a fire by peeling off the dry bark of the dead limbs.

He'd taught her a lot.

She sat back on her heels and thought about him. The hard physical exercise she'd experienced during the past several hours had taken away some of her emotional pain. In fact, she'd been able to identify part of the pain—pride and anger at being fooled. After all, he *had* lied to her. She had specifically asked him if they were married, and he had said yes.

She wondered why. What had he gained out of the charade? If he'd made love to her that first night, or any night afterward, she could better understand the lie. She shook her head. None of it made sense.

Once Paige had the fire going, she quickly pulled out the packets of food she'd brought, glad she'd decided to bring the small pot despite its bulk. She dumped the food in the pan, adding water, then watched it come to a boil. Never had she been so hungry. Never had she been so alone.

Alone. Paige had never really thought about what that meant before. She'd always been so busy with her life, snatching moments for herself to catch up on reading or writing, taking her solitary life for granted.

What if she were lost? What if she never found another person in all of this wilderness? What had made her think she could blithely take off and find her way out of there when Hawk had been hesitant to try?

She was a fool. Her pride and hurt feelings had compounded the problem, and now she'd taken an action she couldn't change. She wasn't even sure she could find her way back to the meadow, even if she tried. And she was too tired to try. Her head was throbbing for the first time in days, and she knew she'd overdone it.

Hawk had been right. She wasn't strong enough, and she didn't have the stamina—but she had to keep going.

Tomorrow. She would get a good night's rest and start out again tomorrow, and the next day, and the next. She had food. She would stay close to the river so she'd have water. She had a bed of sorts. She would make it because she had no choice.

Hawk knew he had to return to camp and face Paige sooner or later, but he wasn't looking forward to it. The strenuous hike upstream had done him good. It had helped to clear his brain of the fever Paige created within him whenever he was around her.

He hadn't realized how isolated he'd been from people until Paige appeared in his life. Since his mother's death, he'd never formed a close relationship with anyone. He'd never had any responsibilities to anyone else; he'd never concerned himself over another person; he'd never felt protective toward another person—until Paige.

Of course she was upset. He'd spent the afternoon thinking about how he would have felt in her place and knew he'd have been mad as hell at the deception. He hadn't really faced until now how hurt she'd be—or maybe he'd been so wrapped up in what he was feeling that he hadn't given a thought to her feelings.

He'd hurt her, and she was the one person whom he wouldn't have hurt for the world. He'd spent the afternoon trying to figure out a way to ask her forgiveness, to explain his reasoning for allowing her to think they were married.

He'd also come to grips with the problem that had been eating at him for days. They had no future together. He'd allowed himself to live in the world created by Paige's misunderstanding of their relationship. He should have known better. She had her life, had even explained to him the heavy demands made on a doctor and why she never expected to marry.

He knew marriage was not part of his plans, just like they'd never been a part of his father's. It was bred into him; he was too restless to stay in one place for long.

So where did they go from there? What could he say to Paige? *I love you, but you wouldn't fit into my life-style, so it's just as well we aren't actually married?*

It was late afternoon when a grim-faced Hawk returned to their camp, determined to face Paige and be as honest as possible with her, only to find her gone.

He had no trouble reading the signs of her activity, and noted with unconscious approval what she'd chosen to take with her. Then the realization of what she had done hit him. She was going to try to make it out of the mountains alone!

"Paige!" His bellow echoed around the meadow, startling the small animals and birds. Of course, she couldn't hear him. He tried to determine how long she'd been gone. She must have left hours ago. He glanced up at the sun. He had to find her. He had deliberately omitted some of the

stories that might have frightened her—that frightened him just thinking about her being on her own. Not all the animals in the mountains were friendly. There were pumas and other wildlife that were aggressive predators.

Hawk broke camp in his usual, thorough manner, packing the tent and sleeping bag in their small cases and stowing them on his backpack. He gave only fleeting thought to his plane, wondering if he'd ever find it again. Right now he had more immediate concerns.

He started downstream at a slow trot, following her trail.

Hawk found himself cursing under his breath, the first sound he'd made during the past several miles. From her tracks he could tell she was tired. Of course she was tired. There was no trail to follow and the rugged area where the stream fell to the lower slopes of the mountain range was treacherous.

Daylight was fading and he still hadn't caught up with her. The sensible thing to do was wait for daylight, then pick up her trail again. Not that he needed to track her. She was staying as close to the stream as she could. She must have remembered what he'd told her.

Would she remember that he'd also told her he loved her?

He knelt by the water and drank, trying to decide what to do. He'd gained on her; her tracks weren't but a couple of hours old. But could he keep going without possible injury to himself?

I can't sit here and wait, he decided. He dug into his pack for a small flashlight and started down the incline. It was going to be a long night.

Hawk lost track of time. He didn't seem to be making much progress, and having to watch where he was going by the small light was even more time-consuming. Then his luck began to turn.

The moon appeared over the rim of the surrounding hills. Thank God for a full moon. Within minutes the landscape was touched by a ghostly hue. He still had to be careful. The light could be deceptive, and he didn't need to step into a hole that he'd mistaken for a shadow.

He paused at the top of a long slope and spotted her fire. He hadn't realized how frightened he'd been for her until he saw the light and her small shape huddled nearby. Then his knees almost buckled with relief.

She was all right. He took his time coming down, taking care to place each foot on firm ground. He was over half-way down when he came to the place where she had fallen. The rocks and brush showed that she had rolled. His heart leaped, then settled painfully back in his chest. She had to be all right. Otherwise, she couldn't have set up camp. He could see that she had chosen well. Despite everything, he was proud of her.

Paige kept waking up, then dozing back off. She had built a large fire, not only for warmth but to keep any animals away. Hawk had assured her that most of the wildlife was more afraid of her than she was of them, but she didn't want to take any chances.

She lay there remembering how well she'd slept with Hawk. Already she missed him so much. Her wounded pride and bouts of self-pity were small comfort to her now. She wondered what he was doing. She pictured him sitting beside the fire in the meadow, watching the moon come up. It was beautiful tonight. Would he miss her? He was probably relieved to have her gone.

Paige cringed at some of her memories; she'd behaved like a wife in love with her handsome husband. Hawk had handled her so well. He hadn't encouraged her, but he had been careful not to hurt her feelings. He'd also told her he loved her.

She had a feeling he didn't admit that to many people. From what he'd told her about himself, he let very few people get close to him. But he'd been gentle with her, teaching her how to camp, how to read trail signs, how to fish. He'd been so patient with her lack of knowledge about his world. Would she ever see him again?

"Paige?"

She bolted upright, wondering if she were dreaming that he'd called to her. Glancing at the fire, she saw Hawk standing at the edge of its light. Or was it her imagination? She blinked her eyes, and when she opened them again he was striding across the clearing toward her.

"Hawk!" Forgotten were the hurts of the day, both physical and emotional. Paige was aware of only one overwhelming thought. She loved Hawk as she had loved no one before in her life. It no longer mattered that he had lied to her. The important thing was that he'd followed and found her. Paige flew across the small space that separated them and into Hawk's arms.

She feels so good in my arms.

I'm so glad he's here.

I wasn't sure I'd ever see her again.

I was afraid I'd never see him again.

Dear God, how I love this woman.

How can I hide my love for this man?

"You okay?" Hawk rasped past a tightened throat.

Her head was buried in his chest, but she nodded vigorously. "I'm fine, now that you're here."

He smiled, holding her close. "You know, all you would have had to do was tell me you were bored. We could have hiked out together."

She laughed, her voice shaking slightly. "Now why didn't I think of that? It *was* a rather lonely hike."

He let go of her reluctantly, then swung the heavy pack off his shoulders. "I brought you your bed. Thought it might be a little more comfortable."

"I haven't really been cold. The fire was nice."

"You did a good job of building it. I'm proud of you."

She tried to see his eyes in the flickering light from the fire. "Are you?"

He nodded. "More than you can possibly imagine."

"I'm glad."

A strong current flowed between them and their minds seemed to touch, to recall another place, another time, when their love and their need to express that love had almost overwhelmed them.

Hawk broke the tension between them by turning away. "Let me get the tent up and you can have the sleeping bag. I'll sleep by the fire." He became very busy as he continued to explain. "We can take off at daylight. It shouldn't be much farther to some sign of civilization." His matter-of-fact words were given away by the gruffness in his voice.

Paige silently helped to spread the canvas, the two of them working together in unspoken harmony. Within minutes a new camp was ready.

"Have you eaten?" she asked, breaking the silence at last. The unspoken communication was tearing at her emotions.

"I had some jerky and leftover sourdough bread," he admitted. "I didn't want to stop and heat up something."

"Do you want anything now?"

The multiple meaning hung in the air between them, daring him to give her an honest answer.

"No, I'll wait until morning. I need to get some rest." He sat down near her blanket and began to tug off his boots.

Paige watched him uncertainly. What did she expect from him? She realized that whatever she wanted, she would have to let him know. He was not the kind of man to take advantage of a situation, no matter what she'd accused him of earlier in the day.

What did she want? She crawled into the tent and found the sleeping bag open and waiting for her. She slid out of her shirt and slacks, glad to have the privacy of the tent and the freedom away from the constricting clothes. Then she stretched out in the bag and sighed. Its padding was heavenly after the hard surface she'd been lying on—that Hawk was now lying on. She sat up, wondering if he were already asleep.

She lifted the flap. He was stretched out on the blanket, his hands behind his head, staring at the fire. The move-

ment from the tent caught his attention and he glanced over
at her.

"You okay?"

She smiled. That was a familiar question with him. Was
she okay? She wasn't sure. She wasn't sure about anything.
All she knew was that she loved him and she wanted to be
with him.

"Why don't you sleep in here?" she asked.

His slow smile disarmed her. "Don't tempt me. I'm afraid
I'm fresh out of willpower this evening."

She swallowed, trying to dislodge the lump in her throat.
"I'm inviting you to share the sleeping bag with me, Hawk.
I'm not insisting your willpower accompany you."

Surprised, he stared at her across the intervening space.
There was no way he could misinterpret her suggestion.

Like a sleepwalker Hawk came slowly to his feet. He
leaned over and methodically picked up his boots and blanket, then padded softly over to her.

Paige scooted back from the door, giving him room to
crawl in. The only light inside the tent was the reflection of
the brightly burning fire through the canvas. She crawled
inside the bag and waited.

For a moment, Hawk made no movement. Then he
slowly began to undress. She heard the rustle of his clothes,
and her heart kept up its steady thumping to the harsh
sounds of his breathing. She felt him reach for the cover,
and she raised it, guiding his hand inside. She heard his
breath catch, and then he was lying beside her.

Never had the sleeping bag seemed so small. They had
only been able to share it because she'd slept practically on
top of him. It took only a moment for her to find the position she'd grown used to—her head on his shoulder, her
body snuggled against him, her leg tucked between his. But
the tension between them now was almost unbearable.

Hawk tried to control his breathing and his heartbeat. He
tried to think of every unpleasant chore he'd ever had to do.

He tried to forget the woman in his arms. Then she shifted, and he was lost.

"Hawk?" she whispered.

"Hmm?"

"Teach me how to love you." She felt the heavy thudding of his heart beneath the palm of her hand. Paige raised her head slightly until her lips rested softly against his.

Hawk tightened his arms around her and deepened the kiss. He had waited a lifetime for this woman, and for whatever reason she was now in his arms. He had tried to resist her, but could no longer fight what they both wanted to happen.

Paige had learned a great deal about making love that afternoon by the waterfall. For the first time she'd discovered her sensuous nature and learned something about Hawk's. She wanted to give him pleasure, to express her love for him in every way she could.

Paige was only a shadowy figure in the darkened tent, but Hawk's memory of the afternoon told him how she looked as she lay in his arms tenderly kissing him along his jawline. He could feel the slight perspiration on his forehead, caused by the restraints he'd placed on himself. He didn't want to hurt her by rushing their lovemaking, but his pent-up emotions were taking their toll.

Slowly he turned her over, then carefully lowered himself to her. Her arms snaked around his neck in an eager embrace, reassuring him of her lack of fear. Hawk slid his hands under her hips, carefully positioning her. Then his mouth found hers once more. This woman was his; he knew that in some deep, fundamental way. He found her waiting for him, and he took her with warm tenderness and loving patience.

Paige trembled with the force of her feelings. *I belong to him now,* she thought with a sense of rightness. She felt surrounded and consumed by him, swept up in the wonder of his possession—and in the tingling of desire that raced through her when he began the gentle rocking movement deep within her.

She held him closer, ever closer, learning to meet his rhythm, to join it, to experience the inexplicable joy of physical union between two people who have already merged their emotions.

She could feel the hard muscles of his back beneath her fingertips; his hands caressing her sides, then sliding to her breasts; his mouth as it memorized the contours of her face. Most of all, she could feel a tension inside of her, as though a spring was being wound, tighter and tighter, and she gasped as it suddenly seemed to project her straight up into the moonlit sky, a cascade of stars spreading its brilliance around her.

Hawk made one final lunge, then held her in a grip so tight she could scarcely breathe. He rolled over, still holding her, and gasped for air. Resting on his chest was like trying to float on a tidal wave, and Paige chuckled.

Hawk growled, "That is not a proper response to my lovemaking, I'll have you know. I think my heart is going to quit on me any minute, and all you can do is laugh!"

She stroked his jaw. "Not at you, love. Never at you. I was just thinking about what an active pillow I've found to rest my head on."

She could feel his grin against her palm. He shifted so that she could lie by his side and he sat up, reaching for his backpack.

"What are you doing?" she asked with relaxed interest.

"Getting a towel. I feel like I've been in the shower."

"You mean making love to me is like taking a shower?"

"Hardly." He relaxed back beside her, pulling her close. "Did I hurt you?"

"If you did, I wasn't aware of it." She leaned up to try to see his face, but it was too dark. "Hawk? Is it always like that?"

"I have no idea. It's never been like that for me before."

"I just wondered. Because if it was, I've got many years to regret. I had no idea making love could be so beautiful."

"Neither did I. You see, that's the first time I've ever made *love*." He sighed. "I may never recover."

Paige placed her head on his shoulder with a contented smile. If she had her way, he never would.

Nine

Paige's dream was delightful—full of light and color and happiness. She and Hawk were together, loving each other, on their honeymoon—honeymoon? Her eyes flew open, and it was as though her dream continued.

She was curled against Hawk's chest, her head resting against the soft movement of his breathing, her hand resting over his heart. Her body was tucked neatly by his side, her thigh intimately nestled between his. Overhead a bright sun beat down on the canvas so that she felt as though they were gingerbread people baking in an oven.

Hawk stirred beneath her, pulling her closer against him. There was a satisfying familiarity about the scene that Paige found reassuring. It was the slight differences that caused her heart to race.

This morning there were no clothes to separate them, and the slight soreness Paige experienced was new. Hawk's hold on her was much more possessive. His hand covered her breast as though for protection.

She glanced up at his face. He looked tired. She realized she'd never seen him asleep. In the past, he'd already been gone by the time she woke up. Now she studied him with a newfound possessiveness.

She studied the thick line of his brows that almost touched across his nose and noted the way his skin glistened in the warmth of the tent. Dark lashes rested against high cheekbones that gave him an autocratic, almost arrogant appearance. Her finger lightly touched his wide, strong chin, then traced the firm jawline to his ear.

He jerked his head suddenly and captured the tip of her finger between his teeth. She yelped.

"Is that any way to treat your tired old Indian guide when he's trying to catch up on his sleep?" he complained in a husky voice.

She leaned over him, watching him with suspicion. His eyes remained closed. "Why is it my fault you're tired?" she asked with interest.

His hand slid around the back of her neck and coaxed her mouth to within a couple of inches of his. "Honey, if you can't remember that, you've got a bigger problem with your memory than we guessed." His mouth captured hers in a lazy kiss that effectively ended their teasing.

Of course she remembered. She remembered waking up during the night to Hawk's erotic touch as he gave a strong impression of a man determined to memorize every inch of her body. How could she forget?

His lovemaking had been slow and very thorough. She felt that she could spend the rest of her life in his arms and never grow bored.

"Shouldn't we be leaving?" she managed to whisper when his kiss finally ended.

"We should have left several hours ago," he admitted ruefully.

She started to shift her leg and his thighs clamped down on her like a vise, effectively holding her prisoner—a very willing prisoner. From that position she could tell the effect she had on him. Even as inexperienced as she was, she'd had the ability to respond to him, to satisfy him—and to keep him still wanting her. Paige sighed with fervent pleasure.

He pulled her over on top of him. She grinned. "Is this what is considered the view from the top?"

"Could be. What do you think?"

"I think I could become addictive."

His mouth found the soft spot at the base of her neck where her pulse quivered. His tongue explored the area until she shivered, then he pressed his lips along a trail to her chin, tipping her head down until he found her mouth.

Time no longer mattered. They were lost in the pleasure of learning more about each other. Hawk introduced her to new sensations, new intimacies, that carried Paige to a dimension where she could share the intense love she felt for Hawk by expressing it in arousing and exhilarating ways.

This morning Paige set the rhythm for their lovemaking. From her position on top of Hawk she discovered how to tease and torment him until his greater strength finally forced her to accept his hard length within her, a most satisfactory conclusion for both of them to her teasing. She slowly built the spiraling emotional structure that led them to the top, where they soared together on a mindless plane of sensation and pleasure, slowly circling back to earth, wrapped in each other's arms. Then, limp from her exertions, Paige lay quietly on Hawk's chest, content to rest.

Because her ear was pressed against his chest, she heard the rumble of his voice as the words left his lips. "We need to be moving, love."

She raised her head and stared at him in bewilderment. "I thought we were."

His smile lit up the small tent. "I mean we need to get down the trail...what there is of it, anyway."

"Oh." She dropped her head and thought about her father. She and Hawk had been together for almost a week. That meant he'd had his heart attack seven days ago. Seven days. If he'd survived the initial attack, he would have passed the crisis stage by now. Had he made it?

She sat up, sliding off Hawk in one graceful movement. He pretended overwhelming relief that he could now breathe again, but she ignored him. She also ignored her lack of clothing when she threw the flap of the tent open and stepped out of the tent. It was another beautiful day.

She glanced down at her shoulder and discovered a long scratch, no doubt picked up on her travels the day before. Walking over to the edge of the swollen stream, she knelt down to wash off the scratch and rinse her face.

Paige only had a moment's warning before hands grasped her around the waist and she was propelled into the river, securely held against a large, warm body.

They hit the water with a resounding splash. Her squeal of shock was due as much to the unexpected push as it was to the temperature of the water. She came up sputtering, discovering she was little more than waist-deep in the clear running river. Hawk was sitting so that the water came almost to his neck.

"That was rude!" she declared in her most haughty, well-bred tones.

"Was it?" His look of repentance needed a little work to be convincing.

"I could have drowned."

"Not while I was holding you."

His infectious grin totally destroyed her efforts to solemnly discuss the deficiencies of his deportment as reflected by his recent behavior. She resolved the matter by splashing water in his face and an olympic-sized water fight ensued, scaring the wildlife around their campsite.

Paige couldn't remember when she'd ever acted so childish—certainly not as a child nor as an earnest adolescent. When they discovered, to no one's surprise, that Hawk could outmaneuver, outswim and outguess Paige, she conceded defeat and proceeded to bathe herself, as though getting into the water had been entirely her own idea.

By the time she crawled out of the river to dry her hair in the sun, Hawk had their meal prepared. Paige was surprised to discover how unself-conscious she was with him. She grabbed his shirt to put on after drying herself, and ate unconcernedly, oblivious to the side glances she received from Hawk. She was modestly covered. It wasn't her fault that he was aware of what she didn't have on underneath that shirt.

"I never thought I'd ever be envious of a piece of my clothing," he said after finishing his cup of coffee. He stood up, staring down at the cleavage revealed by the loose shirt.

In the carefully modulated tone of a professional doctor, she inquired, "Tell me, sir, how long have you noticed having this insatiable sexual appetite?"

He leaned over and picked up her empty dishes and shrugged. "Only since being around you, doctor."

"I see. Then the cure is obvious." She stood up and headed toward the tent.

"Is it?" His gaze followed her graceful body as she walked away from him.

She stopped and looked back over her shoulder. "Of course. Remove the source, and you remove the problem." She disappeared inside the tent.

He washed up their dishes and deftly packed them away. "Isn't that a rather drastic solution?" He raised his voice so that she would hear him.

A few minutes later she stepped out, chastely covered in her own rather bedraggled clothes, a little worse for the wear they'd had the day before. "Drastic, perhaps, but certainly effective."

They pulled the tent down in companionable silence. When he had everything back in his knapsack, giving Paige a smaller pack to carry, Hawk finally admitted, "I'd prefer a less effective cure, if you could arrange it."

Following the river, Hawk started off and Paige fell in step behind him. She admired the width of his shoulders and the seemingly weightless way he carried the pack that she

knew must weigh at least sixty pounds. "Well, it might take
some experimenting, trying various concepts, to find a
suitable cure."

Without turning around, he answered, "Whatever you
say, doc. I know I'm in good hands, so you have my permission to experiment to your heart's content."

My heart will be content only when you're around, she
decided, but thought it more politic not to mention it.

Hawk set a steady pace that seemed to eat up the miles.
He was an expert at picking the easiest path, Paige discovered, and wished she'd managed to control her feelings
enough not to have struck out on her own the day before.

When the way was rough, Hawk helped her, and Paige
discovered her most exhilarating feeling came with his silent look of admiration when she determinedly stayed up
with him.

It was midafternoon when their good luck seemed to run
out. The river disappeared underground through a hole in
the canyon wall.

Hawk stood there, his hands on his hips, and studied the
rugged terrain around them. They were in some type of
canyon and there didn't seem to be a way out. "Why don't
we stop here? It's a good place to eat and get some rest," he
finally said.

Paige sank down gratefully. Her body had been protest-
ing the unusual treatment for the past two hours, but she'd
been determined not to ask Hawk to stop. They were hiking out because she'd insisted. She refused to admit it was
too much for her.

Hawk was right. There was shade here, and the water was
still sparkling clear. With some stiffness Paige knelt by the
river and scooped it up in her hands to drink. Then she
splashed it on her face to cool off. Was it only that morning that they had played in the water? It seemed years ago.

Their entire time together seemed to have lasted forever.
She could scarcely remember her life before Hawk and she
refused to think about what it would be like when they re-

turned to their daily routines. All she had was here and now. It was enough, because it had to be enough.

Hawk handed her a large piece of sourdough bread and a piece of jerky. A cup of cold water was in his other hand.

"Thank you," she murmured, seating herself cross-legged under a shade tree a short distance away.

Hawk stared at her, concerned. Had he pushed her too hard? She sounded different—as though they were barely acquainted, as though they knew nothing about each other, or as though she cared nothing for him.

That was the difference. From the time she was aware of him after their forced landing, she had been warm to him. Wary, perhaps, but she'd projected a strong vibration of caring. Now it was almost as though she'd erected a shield between them. He wondered if it were to protect herself or him. He sat down next to her, biting into the bread and staring into the distance.

Perhaps she was trying to protect him. She'd had time to come to terms with their new relationship, or rather, their lack of a formal one. Yet she had given herself to him—totally, without reservation. What did it mean?

Had she finally found a man who could arouse her and she'd decided to further her education? What did he mean to her? What could he mean? She was a career woman—he was a maverick.

Hawk finished eating, then stretched out in the shade and closed his eyes. He refused to worry about it. He had nothing to offer her and they both knew it. He'd learned at an early age to take what life offered and not question it. As a philosophy, it wasn't a bad way to survive. The secret was not to want something you could never have.

Paige studied Hawk's relaxed position and envied him his ability to fall asleep immediately, to wake up alert, and to be in control of his emotions at all times. Her problem was that he had stirred up emotions within her she'd never known existed. Now that they were alive and well and clamoring to be used, she didn't know what to do with them.

Trying to deal with emotions on an intellectual basis was impossible. Emotions were like errant children, bounding out of control at the least provocation. No matter how much time she spent reasoning with them, they proceeded to go their merry way, ignoring the consequences.

What she had to keep in mind was the importance of getting to Flagstaff. Up until now, her father and her profession had been her entire life. She could only pray that her father was all right.

She mentally listed all the positive items in his favor—his relative youth, the fact that he did take care of himself, and that he knew the importance of good health. Paige had to leave him in God's hands, but she prayed that God in his mercy would grant her a few more years with him.

For the first time in her life, Paige faced how much she'd taken her father for granted. Although she'd loved her mother, her thinking processes had been more like her father's and she'd had trouble relating to her maternal parent. She understood her mother's pain at being on the outskirts of her father's life, but she couldn't relate to it, because she had made herself a part of his life as soon as she could.

Instead of sitting around wishing for something, I've always gone after what I wanted, she realized in surprise. The sudden insight into her own character surprised her. Paige had never been one to spend much time in self-analysis.

"We need to go, Paige..." Hawk's deep voice brought her out of a surprisingly deep sleep. She hadn't meant to sleep, only to rest her eyes. Hawk stood over her with one hand outstretched. She grasped it and pulled herself up. He increased her momentum so that she fell against him. With calm deliberation he found her mouth with his and gave her a leisurely, but very thorough, kiss.

Damn him! Her new resolution to hold herself aloof from him disappeared, and she could feel her body melt against him. *It just isn't fair.* She returned his kiss with fervor, until he pulled away from her, his expression strained.

"I'd like to get out of this area before nightfall. Hopefully it levels out down a little lower. There's a possibility the river will return to the surface and we can find it."

Once again Hawk led the way, and Paige followed. She couldn't help but wonder what would have happened to them if she'd had another kind of pilot, one who didn't know how to survive in the wilderness. She shook her head impatiently. *Don't think about it. Just be thankful for Hawk.*

She had reason to reiterate that thought several times as the rugged miles continued to unroll beneath their feet. The river no longer guided them. They scrambled up one side of a hill, then down the other. Paige wondered how Hawk knew which way to go. She was turned around in her directions. She was also exhausted.

Twilight was beginning to place its mystical touch around them when Hawk finally halted. "We'll camp here."

Paige wearily looked around. The place looked no different than many other places they'd passed, but she asked no questions at all. Instead she helped Hawk put up the tent, spread the sleeping bag, gather wood and prepare a simple meal.

They were both too tired for conversation. They spent little time in front of the fire after eating. Instead they both stripped down and crawled into the sleeping bag, immediately falling asleep.

It was light outside, but the sun wasn't up when Hawk gently shook Paige awake. She groaned, trying to find her comforting pillow. "We need to get started, love," he said in a low voice that brought her out of her dream-filled sleep.

Paige sat up groggily, feeling aches and pains in places she'd never known existed. She'd thought she was in good physical condition, but this little outing was rapidly convincing her otherwise.

Hawk felt as though a hand was tightening around his heart as he watched her painful movements. He'd been

amazed at her stamina and the valiant effort she'd been
making. But they couldn't afford to waste time now. They
were away from water, and their food supply was dwin-
dling. He had to do everything he could to find a settlement of some sort that day.

Paige reluctantly pulled on her clothes, vowing to burn
them as soon as she found a place to buy more. She was sick
of them, sick of walking, sick of trying to keep up with the
robot she was with who never seemed to get tired, or hungry, or thirsty. She glared up at him and froze. The tender
look in his eyes caused tears to form in her eyes.

She slipped her arms around his neck. "Oh, Hawk, I love
you so much. I'm sorry to be such a tenderfoot."

His arms came around her in a fierce hug. "I love you,
too. And you're doing fine, just fine. We should be out of
here today."

She pulled back from him in surprise. "You think so?"

He nodded, unwilling to make a more emphatic statement on such an uncertainty.

She hugged him back. "Won't that be great? Just think
how it will feel to have a hot bath for a change, and eat
something besides jerky and dried fruit, and sleep in a nice,
comfortable bed, and ..."

"But madam, you paid an incredible amount of money
for this special safari into the wilds of eastern Arizona. I
thought you wanted to get your money's worth." His fake
British accent was very well done.

"That's true, young man, very true. However, you didn't
mention the exercise program in your brochure, or I might
have had second thoughts."

He scratched his head thoughtfully. "Perhaps we should
revise the brochure, do you think?"

"Definitely. But don't expect an overwhelming amount
of people to sign up."

He drew himself up to his full height. "But madam, we
only cater to the most elite clientele. Surely you recognized
that."

She looked at their clothes, white with dust, ragged and torn, and at the battered camping supplies that had kept them going, and she laughed. "I'm glad to hear it. I want nothing but the best. I thought that was understood." Her gaze turned back to him. "I'm so glad I got it."

She was irresistible in that mood, and he didn't even try to resist. Instead he gathered her into his arms and kissed her with all the fervency he possessed.

A few minutes later he let her down with a sigh. "We still need to leave."

"I know."

"I could stay here all day and make love to you, you know that, don't you?"

"I'm glad," she whispered, in awe of the miracle that had brought them together and caused such similar strong feelings to occur in each of them for the other.

Hawk firmly set her aside and left the tent, and Paige hurriedly repacked what they had taken out of the back-pack the night before, then efficiently rolled up the sleeping bag. She was getting almost as good at packing as Hawk. Almost.

A little hero worship never hurt anyone, she decided. Wearily she crawled out of the tent to begin a new day.

Ten

The river reappeared about midmorning but was nothing like the one they'd been following. This one seemed out of control, raging along in a rolling frenzy.

Hawk found a small pocket of shallow water that had already been heated by the sun and suggested they take time to bathe. Paige hadn't realized what a luxury water could be. It felt so good to feel clean again. She took her hair down and washed it, luxuriating in the cool water.

It's amazing how different your outlook is when you're clean and well fed, Paige decided, looking for Hawk to share her bit of philosophy. But when she spotted him, all previous thoughts flew from her head. He stood under a rocky overhang where part of the river gushed over the side, taking a vigorous shower.

She could only stare at his unconscious male beauty. His bronzed skin glistened in the sunlight and water, and she visually traced a path from his broad chest to his waist and hips, down to his thighs and well-developed calves. Only his feet were hidden in the swirling water.

Paige slicked her wet hair back from her face, then started swimming toward him, ignoring the pull of the current. The bubbling water broke over her head several times, but her gaze never left the man ahead of her.

Hawk had turned his back to her, his face raised to the hard-driving water, and didn't hear her approach. She waded out of the deeper water until he was close enough to touch. He couldn't have heard her with the rushing water all around him; he could only have sensed her presence. But he turned as though knowing she were there.

The message in her eyes was unmistakable, and it fanned a flame within him that had never gone out since the first time he saw her.

Without a word he scooped her up in his arms and strode out of the water. Their things were packed, but he spotted the blanket she had made into a small pack for her, and without breaking stride he reached for it, shook it out and lowered her on one side of it. She watched as he flicked the other half open.

Still without speaking, Hawk reached for her, his need obvious. Their communication was more basic than words, and when she flowed into his arms an explosion of desire swept over them.

There was no gentleness between them. Instead theirs was a fierce enactment of possession. They belonged to-gether—they belonged to each other—and they used the act of love to reinforce that statement. Hawk took her in a powerful, surging drive and she was with him all the way. Her arms locked around his neck and her legs wrapped around him, encouraging the savage swirl of emotions that gripped them.

You're mine, you're mine, you belong to me, only to me—his rhythm matched the litany of phrases running through his head. She responded to him as though she had heard the refrain and affirmed it.

Paige found herself once again in that other world of pleasurable sensation, her body flexing convulsively as she toppled over the edge of the sky. Hawk's harsh breathing filled her world when he made his final plunge, then collapsed in her arms, his chest heaving.

I feel that every part of me has melted and remolded itself around him. She enjoyed the weight of his body pressing against her; knew that he'd lost control this time, and she was reassured. He hadn't been able to completely hide from her what he was feeling.

They lay there, bodies intertwined, as the world began to impinge once more on their consciousness. Hawk shifted, rolling free of her and sat up. His folded arms rested against his raised knees and his head dropped against his arms.

"I'm sorry."

Paige felt too limp to move, but she forced herself into a sitting position. "For what?"

"For being so rough."

"It's obvious I'm beyond redemption, then. I enjoyed it. Thoroughly."

He raised his head and stared at her smiling face. Then he rested his forehead against hers. "Oh, Paige, you're a constant surprise. You never say what I expect. You're not like anyone I've ever known." He sighed. "What am I going to do with you?"

She tried to sound light and cheerful. "Love me?"

His black eyes glistened with emotion. "Is that enough?"

She stared at him, feeling his uncertainty as though it were her own. And perhaps it was. "It will have to be."

Midafternoon found them facing a dilemma. They needed to cross the river, but the rushing water had widened to a dangerous degree. There were no fordable spots that Hawk could find.

He toyed with the alternative. They could stay on this side of the river in the hope it would continue toward civilization. But crossing was the quickest way to get to help. He had spotted their first sign of the twentieth century over the last rise—a towering antenna standing tall on the next ridge over from them. That antenna had to have a power station nearby, which meant there was a road to follow. It was time to leave their guide, the river. But first they had to cross it.

Hawk planned carefully. He made them stop and eat first. Then he built a small raft to carry their provisions. They stripped down to essentials, so that the heavy drag of water wouldn't catch in their clothes. He was thankful the bedroll and tent were in waterproof containers.

The care he took in making the crossing would have placed them safely on the other side, except for one unforeseen detail, and that detail made a mockery of all his precautions.

They laughed when all of their provisions and clothes were neatly strapped to the small raft. "Do you realize that if we lose that raft, we'll never dare come out of hiding?" Paige stood there in her brief shorts and blouse tied under her breasts. Hawk had dispensed with everything but his briefs.

"Now's a lousy time to ask, but how good of a swimmer are you?" he asked with a slight smile. The smile didn't reach his concerned eyes.

"Better than average," she assured him. "I haven't won any gold medals or anything, but I can stay afloat."

He glanced over at the water that was moving swiftly past. "It's hard to tell how deep it is along here, but there's no way to cross either upstream or downstream from here, so this place wins by default." A limb came floating by, then disappeared in the suction of the water. "The rains up in the mountains must have caused this heavy flow. Normally by July the mountain streams are quiet and subdued."

"I guess somebody forgot to point out the date to this one."

"A definite oversight, but it can't be helped." He stepped off the bank into water up to his knees. Dragging the small raft alongside him, he motioned to her. "I'm not going to hang on to you. It would be more of a hindrance than a help." He pointed to the other bank about 150 yards downstream. "That's where we'll end up, hopefully. When the current catches you, keep swimming as straight as you can." He watched as she slid into the water beside him.

Just one more adventure to tell my grandkids, she decided with characteristic resolution.

Hawk gave her a head start, wanting to keep her in his line of vision. He pulled the raft along beside him, keeping it upstream of him so that he would have better control—which is why he didn't see the tree stump suddenly churn up to the surface right beside him.

He didn't have time to evade it. The long roots caught the raft, flipping it high into the air, and the tree trunk slammed into Hawk, carrying him down the river in its curling grasp.

Paige was concentrating on putting as much power into each stroke as she had. She was wondering how long she could keep it up when she heard a loud, crashing sound behind her. She jerked her head around in time to see the raft go tumbling and Hawk disappear beneath the tree stump.

"Hawk!"

Water sloshed into her mouth and she sputtered. She fought to keep her head out of the water and began to swim furiously after the twisting, turning stump. The swirling water kept washing over her, and she couldn't keep up with the stump.

She had to find Hawk. He had to be all right. She closed her eyes for a split second, frightened at the thought that he might not be all right. Not Hawk. He was too strong. He'd been through too many things and survived. He was tough. He'd make it. She knew he'd make it.

At first she thought her foot had caught on something in the river. Then she realized she'd found bottom. With her last remaining strength Paige pulled herself through the dragging water until she reached dry land and collapsed in a heap. She lay there, gasping for air, praying for strength. She had to get up and find Hawk—he needed her.

When Paige opened her eyes she knew too much time had passed. The sun had moved into the west. Shaking, she got to her feet and looked around. The ridge where the antenna stood was no longer visible. She wasn't even sure which direction to look. She only knew it was somewhere on this side of the river.

The river continued to rush by, but there was no sign of Hawk. She felt a burning and looked down at her legs, absently noting they were raw with scrapes. She ignored them.

Hawk had gone downstream. Therefore, she had to go downstream. It was a fundamental decision, one that took no effort at all. She couldn't afford to waste her energy—she had to find Hawk.

Paige stumbled along the river, but saw no sign of anyone. It was as though she were completely alone in this strange world. *Maybe Hawk found the tree stump provided faster transportation.* She forced her shoulders straight and continued walking.

It was only when she spotted their raft, innocently floating along the edge of the river, that she cried. She cried all the while she tugged it from the water and spread their clothes and provisions out to dry. She wasn't even sure why. So much had gotten wet, maybe that was it. Or maybe it was because Hawk had taken so much care to protect her and their belongings, but had not taken enough care of himself.

I'm not going to let you leave me, damn you, or our things. I'll find you, if it takes all night.

It didn't take all night.

The sun had set, casting its last scarlet rays into the sky, when Paige saw something lying in the water. She couldn't run; the pack she carried weighted her so that she was forced to place each foot carefully in order to keep her balance. She wasn't even sure she wanted to find out what it was.

Hawk was draped over a large rock protruding near the center of the river. When the stump sweeping him along downstream had connected with the rock, the stump had catapulted into the air, freeing him. But by that time he was barely conscious.

He'd hung on to the rock until he found the strength to crawl up on it, but didn't have the strength to make it to shore.

Paige dropped the pack and stared at him. He looked so pale and still, but he was breathing. One side of his face was bloodied and bruised, but he was alive. His side looked as though he'd been kicked by an angry bull.

If she could just get to him.

Then she remembered the raft. How far back was it? She couldn't remember, but it didn't matter. She had to find it. Paige dropped the backpack and hurried back along the way she'd come, fear lending speed to her failing body.

The light was rapidly fading by the time she returned. Hawk hadn't moved.

They would need a fire, but she didn't want to take the time to build one until she could get him to dry land. At least the large rock he had found was big enough to take his full length, so he hadn't been subjected to the continual pounding of the water.

She slipped into the water, surprised at how much colder it felt, and pushed the raft ahead of her. The current wasn't too bad on this side of the large rock, and she only had to go a small distance where her feet wouldn't touch bottom.

"Hawk?" she pulled herself up beside him, struggling not to lose her grip on the raft. "Hawk, please answer me." She dipped her hand in the water, then brushed it across his face.

He groaned.

"We need to get you out of here, Hawk. Can you help me?"

His eyelids fluttered, then were still. She didn't have time to waste. By gently shoving on his unhurt side she managed to shift him until he began to slide into the water. Paige quickly grabbed the raft and maneuvered it under his head. If she could just keep them afloat, they would make it.

Paige never remembered the details of that nightmare journey back to shore, or how she managed to get him out of the water. But she did it. She rolled him onto the blanket and then dragged him next to the fire she managed to build. Once again Hawk's precautions had helped—the matches had stayed dry in their waterproof pouch.

Her next priority was to examine his wounds. From the flickering light of the campfire she could see that one side of his face was bruised, swollen and scratched, although most of the bleeding had stopped. His side was scraped raw from his armpit to his hip.

His pulse was strong and steady—a reassuring sign—but he had an angry welt across his forehead, which could explain his unconscious state. *This seems to be our trip for head wounds. I wonder if you'll know who I am when you wake up.*

She needed to get him warm. She warmed the blanket by the fire, making sure it was dry before wrapping him up in it once more.

When his eyes opened, she could have wept with relief. Instead she stroked his cheek and asked, "How do you feel?"

He stared up at her, his eyes dulled with pain. Then they seemed to focus on her face and brighten. "I'm not sure," he whispered. "Kinda like I've been in a barroom brawl." He touched the side of his face and winced.

"As a matter of fact—" she tried to keep her voice steady and unconcerned "—that's what you look like." She brushed his hair back. "How does your side feel?"

Hawk drew a breath, then abruptly stopped, pain obvious on his face. "Like hell."

"I can't be certain without X rays, but you may have a cracked rib or two. You took quite a jolt."

"What happened?"

"What do you remember?"

A gleam appeared in his eyes that could have been amusement at their reversed positions. "I remember swimming across the river and something hitting me. What was it?"

"A tree stump. You got caught in the roots and were dragged downstream."

He lay there, staring at her. "I could have drowned."

"Yes."

"How did you find me?"

She forced a smile. "Easy. You were sunning yourself on a rock in the middle of the river when I came along."

He frowned. "I remember that—I remember trying to hang on so I wouldn't be swept back into the water."

"You did a great job of hanging on. When I found you, you'd crawled up on top of it."

He looked at her, disbelief plain on his face. "You found me on the rock?"

"Uh-huh."

"How the hell did you get me off it?"

"I used the raft. You should be pleased with your construction skills. It took quite a beating today, but it's still intact."

She placed her hand on his forehead. He felt warm. Too warm.

Paige nonchalantly came to her feet. "I think I'll put the tent up now. I'm very glad to report the waterproof cover kept the sleeping bag from getting soaked. You could write all kinds of endorsements for your camping gear after this trip."

Hawk tried to respond with a smile, but the pain and swelling in his jaw stopped him. Paige tucked the blanket tighter around him, then left his side. Within moments he was asleep.

The tent was much tougher to put up by herself, but Paige managed. The sleeping bag was warm from being spread in front of the fire by the time she arranged it inside the tent.

Hawk was still asleep when she returned to his side. "Hawk? Can you walk to the tent? Your bed is ready."

He roused himself, staring around the area as though trying to get his bearings. With Paige's help he made it to bed, then dutifully drank the hot soup she brought him.

Paige could see his pain, and fear clutched at her. He wasn't going to be able to go any farther—not on his own.

What were they going to do?

Afraid that she would hurt him if she shared the sleeping bag with him, Paige wrapped up in the blanket and stretched out by his side. Never had she felt so helpless to care for someone.

She checked on him several times during the night. He was restless and feverish, but never awakened. Paige made sure he stayed covered, fearing complications due to exposure. It was almost dawn when she dozed off, and later she thought she was dreaming because she heard voices. They were speaking in a language she didn't recognize. Paige woke up with a start, realizing that someone was outside.

She jerked open the flap and crawled out of the tent. Two men stood there, staring at her as though a Martian had landed in front of them demanding to find their leader. She felt the same way. They were dressed in Levi's and plaid Western shirts, but their hair was long and tied at the nape of their necks. Their Western hats shaded bronzed faces. Unsmiling bronzed faces.

"Did you know you're on posted property here, lady?" one of them finally asked.

She burst out laughing, almost hysterical with relief. "Are we? Well, you see, we really aren't camping, even though it looks like it. Our plane was forced down up there... She waved her arm over her shoulder and they looked up at the mountain range behind her, then back at her with twin expressions of disbelief. "My...uh, friend was hurt yesterday when we crossed the river. Is there any way we can get him to a doctor?"

She knew better than to explain that she was a doctor. She could tell she'd stretched her credibility with them to the outer limits.

One of them stepped inside of the tent. When he came out he spoke to his companion, but not in English. His friend nodded and disappeared through the trees.

"Where's he going?" she asked in alarm. Didn't they care that Hawk was hurt?

The remaining man answered, "He's gone to bring a truck up here. It's too far to carry him."

"Oh."

"He's Apache, isn't he?"

Surprised, she said, "I believe so. Why do you ask?"

The man grinned, changing his austere expression into a friendly one. "Are you aware you're on the Apache Reservation?"

She shook her head.

"I don't recognize him. Is he from around here?"

"He said he's originally from Dulce, New Mexico."

"Ahhh. A Jicarilla." He nodded, seemingly satisfied.

Paige looked around. "How long will it take your friend to get here?"

"He should make it in about an hour."

She went over to their supplies and found the coffeepot. "I thought I'd make some coffee, then try to get Hawk to drink some water."

"Your friend's name is Hawk?"

"That's right."

"You don't hear those names much anymore. My name is John Anthony. My friend is Roger Thomas."

"Oh." Why did she feel as though she'd stumbled into an Alice in Wonderland scene?

They'd made it. They'd found their way out of the wilderness and down to civilization. She glanced at the man hunched over, feeding the fire. Yes. Civilization. *Oh, Hawk, if you could only enjoy this with me. We made it, thanks to you. Please get well for me.*

Paige sat back from the bed, pleased to see Hawk resting naturally. They'd been brought to a mobile home by their rescuers, who'd explained they were almost a day's drive from the closest town. They'd put Hawk to bed and she'd begun to bathe him with cold water, trying to get his temperature down.

His fever had finally broken. She'd been afraid of pneumonia, but she was beginning to hope the worst was over. After two days of vigil by his bedside, Paige felt limp with exhaustion.

Deciding that it was safe to leave him, she walked down the short hall to the kitchen. A young woman was stirring something that smelled delicious in a large pot. She smiled when Paige paused in the doorway.

"Hi. I'm sorry I wasn't here when you and your husband first arrived. I'm Alicia, John Anthony's daughter."

She was the picture of youthful freshness, Paige thought with a smile. Her tight faded jeans emphasized the shapely length of her legs in knee-high leather boots. A red T-shirt enhanced her dark skin, and her short haircut accented her large black eyes. A real beauty. She looked to be in her late teens.

First things first. "He isn't my husband. My name is Paige Winston. Hawk Cameron was flying me to Flagstaff last week when we had to make an emergency landing."

"Oh." Alicia's eyes lit up. "I went back to introduce myself when I got home, but you'd fallen asleep in the chair. Hawk looks like he's been in a fight."

"He was. With a tree stump. If you think *he* looks bad, you oughta see the other guy," she said with an exaggerated drawl.

They both laughed. Alicia's eyes sparkled. "He's very handsome, isn't he?" she asked shyly.

Paige could feel her reaction to Alicia's innocent words somewhere deep inside. "Yes, he is."

"Have you known him long?"

"No. Just since our mishap."

"So you don't know if he's married."

"I think it's a safe bet to guess he isn't."

Alicia's smile became even brighter. "Well, if there's anything I can do to help, please let me know."

"As a matter of fact, there is. Your father told me you didn't have a phone. Can you tell me where I might find one?"

Alicia thought for a moment. "The nearest one is about twenty-five miles from here." She grinned. "Twenty-five long miles—it takes hours to get there. I'm sure my father would be willing to give you a ride, though."

Paige sat down at the small kitchen table. Her brain seemed to be as sluggish as molasses.

Alicia dished up a steaming bowl of stew. "Here, have something to eat. After that why don't you take a nice, relaxing shower and get some sleep." She sat down across from Paige and looked at her with concern. "You look exhausted. If Hawk needs anything, I can either take care of him or call you." She reached over and softly patted Paige's hand. "You can sleep in my room if you'd like."

Paige could feel tears prickling at the back of her eyes and knew she'd been pushing herself too hard if a young girl's thoughtfulness could make her feel weepy.

"Thank you, Alicia. You and your dad have been great, taking us in like this."

Alicia's smile lit up the kitchen. "We've enjoyed having you. I'm just sorry we can't help out with a phone—your families must be frantic for some sort of word. You both were tremendously lucky."

"I know. Hawk made most of our luck. I wouldn't have made it without him."

Alicia's smile was very understanding. "He's really special, isn't he?"

"Yes," Paige murmured, "he really is."

When Hawk woke up the next morning he was surprised to see a young Indian girl sitting by his bed.

"Good morning," she offered shyly.

He tried to smile, but one side of his face felt like it was made of plaster of Paris. He felt along his cheekbone and discovered bandages covered half his face.

"Where am I?" He heard himself and almost groaned aloud. Not the most original question, but dammit, he seemed to have misplaced a few things—like a river, a raft and a companion. Before she could answer, he interrupted with, "Where's Paige?"

"Oh, she's asleep. She sat up with you until quite late last night. I told her I'd check on you if she wanted to go on to bed."

He mentally digested that, feeling better to know that Paige wasn't far away.

"This is my father's home," the young girl explained. "I'm Alicia Anthony. My father and a friend found you and Dr. Winston camping near the river day before yesterday, so they brought you here." She gave him a very sympathetic smile. "Dr. Winston said you were running a temperature."

He took a few minutes to consider the information Alicia gave him. So they'd been here for two days. He only had vague memories of warm hands caring for him and a soft voice. Paige. He smiled. It had been her turn to look after an invalid.

Hawk felt a tightness on his forehead and touched it lightly. A large bump sat above his right eye. "I must have really gotten a blow to my head to make a knot that big." He looked at the young girl who was watching him so intently. "I'm pretty hardheaded."

"Dr. Winston was quite concerned," she admitted. "You were very lucky to have a doctor with you."

"You know, I never thought of it that way. I guess you're right." He grinned, a lopsided grin to ease the tightness of his swollen jaw and face.

Alicia stared at him for a moment, her gaze admiring. Then, blushing, she rushed into speech to cover her confusion. "Dr. Winston was also trying to find out how she could get to Flagstaff. She seems most anxious to leave."

*Of course. He'd forgotten about her father. They needed
to leave right away.*

"She explained that you were her pilot and she didn't
want to leave you until she was sure you were going to be all
right."

Her pilot. She doesn't want to leave...until I'm all right.
He stared at the young girl. *Of course. Now we're in the real
world and we revert back to our former roles. She's Dr.
Winston and I'm just the pilot.*

Hawk tried to sit up, and a pain shot through his chest.

"Oh, Hawk, you shouldn't be moving around. Dr. Winston said she's almost certain a couple of your ribs are broken." She leaned over and pulled his pillow higher. "Why
don't you lie back and I'll bring you something to eat? I bet
you're starved!"

He glanced up into her glowing eyes, full of admiration.
He ignored the pain in his side, and in his head. He ignored
the pain of knowing that whatever he and Paige had shared
was over. That was yesterday. He had to live with today. He
smiled at the girl hovering anxiously beside him. "That
sounds fine, just fine."

He would deal with his pain later, as he always did—
alone.

Eleven

The sound of Alicia's light, tinkling laugh settled like a feather in Paige's sleep, tickling at her consciousness, taunting her with its subtle sensuality.

When Paige had finally fallen asleep, she had succumbed to the deep, healing rest of the exhausted. Hawk's fever was down; she'd managed to tape up his ribs and to clean up the contusions and abrasions on his face and head. He was going to be all right.

She'd left him sleeping peacefully, but from the sounds in the other room he was not only awake but enjoying company. She heard the deep rumble of his voice, then Alicia's clear, delighted laughter.

Paige tried to ignore the twinge of pain that shot through her. He wasn't her personal property, after all. There hadn't even been the most rudimentary of commitments made. *Hadn't there?* she asked herself. *Perhaps not on his part, but you know very well you would never give yourself to a man if you hadn't made a commitment of love to him.*

She dug through her small supply of clothes and decided to try one of the skirts and blouses. They were sadly wrinkled but she took them into the small bathroom with her and hung them while she showered, hoping the wrinkles would disappear in the steam.

Has he asked for your commitment? Has he asked anything of you? Her inner voice continued to probe. She reviewed their time together, all of their conversations, and his lovemaking. He'd convinced her he'd never before experienced the feelings he'd shared with her. *That was something, wasn't it?* Perhaps, but what? Where did she stand with him now? Where did they go from here?

Paige had never before been faced with her own vulnerability, and she was afraid of what the future might bring.

After her shower, Paige dressed and did her hair carefully in the topknot she generally wore in the summer. Feeling much more like her old self, she went down the hall to see Hawk.

She found him sitting up in bed sipping a cup of coffee. A tray of empty dishes on the table nearby attested to the fact he had eaten, and well.

Alicia was seated by the bed, but hopped up when Paige walked in. "Your patient is doing much better this morning, doctor," she announced brightly.

Paige smiled at Hawk. "I'm certainly glad to hear it."

He did not return her smile. In fact, his glance was one he might have given a casual acquaintance. "I'm surprised to still find you here, Dr. Winston. I figured you'd be on your way to Flagstaff by now."

Dr. Winston? Then Paige glanced at Alicia's interested expression. *He wants to keep up appearances, does he? I wonder why?*

Suddenly shy, Paige walked over to the side of the bed and reached for his forehead. "Any fever this morning?"

He flinched away from her hand. "Of course not. There's nothing wrong with me but a few scrapes and bruises." His voice was brusque.

"And a couple of broken ribs," she added.

"You don't know that for sure," he insisted.

"True. Without X rays, I can't be positive. But there's every indication."

He shrugged, then winced. "Maybe so. But they'll heal."

She grinned. "And you're tough, right?"

He stared at her, his expression giving nothing of his thoughts away. "Tough enough."

Tension grew in the room, and even Alicia became aware of it. She picked up the tray and said, "Well, I'll go wash these up." She paused at the door and gave Hawk a dazzling smile. "You behave now."

For the first time since Paige had walked into the room Hawk's face relaxed into a soul-wrenching smile. "I don't have the strength to do anything else." His smile widened to a grin when she laughed.

"Why aren't you gone?" Hawk asked Paige in a careless tone after Alicia disappeared down the hall.

"Because I didn't want to go off and leave you," she explained patiently.

He shifted restlessly in the bed. "There's no reason for you to stick around here. I'm sure Alicia's dad will give you a ride into the nearest town and you can find some kind of transportation to Flagstaff."

"Do you intend to go to Flagstaff?"

His eyes suddenly veered away from her and he looked out the window as though intently studying the scenery. "I might, later. There's no rush for me. I've got to figure out if we can salvage the plane. That might be quite a project."

She sat down by the bed and placed her hand over his. She could feel him tense. "Hawk, what's wrong?"

He rolled his head slowly on the pillow so that he was facing her. Without expression he said, "You are the one who just told me."

"You know that's not what I'm talking about."

A nerve began to jump in his cheek, and she realized his teeth were tightly clamped. He shrugged.

"I guess I'm having trouble knowing how to thank you for saving my life...then telling you goodbye." His gaze dropped and he studied her hand still lying on top of his.

"Oh, Hawk, is that what this is all about? Can't your macho self-esteem accept a little help from a tenderfoot female?" she teased.

He grinned, and it was close to his natural, humorous expression. "Oh, my macho image might have been knocked around a bit, but I think it's going to survive."

She cocked her head to one side and asked, "Why do we have to say goodbye?" She hoped he couldn't hear her heart pounding in her chest. The answer to that question held all the hopes for their future.

Once more his gaze met hers and the sadness in his eyes caused her throat to tighten in despair. *No!* she protested silently. *Don't say it!*

But he did. "No matter how we got here, and who saved whom, the fact remains that my job is over. I'm sure the insurance will cover all your costs. I'm sorry I didn't get you to Flagstaff."

"But what about us, Hawk?"

He jerked his hand away from under hers. "There is no *us*, Paige. What did you expect? I'm not some tame lapdog that you can come home to each evening. I'm too restless to stay in one place, anyway. But even if I could, I wouldn't want to live on the fringe of your life. I'd want all of you, not just the leftovers when you were through with your work each day."

He was putting into words what Paige had known all along. So why did it hurt so much to know that he recognized the futility of trying to prolong their relationship as much as she did?

Because I wanted to believe in happy ever after and love overcoming all obstacles and that love will find a way. She could feel the tears sliding down her cheeks but refused to try to hide them. "I love you, Hawk."

His impassive expression threatened to completely break her composure. *Damn his stoic Indian heritage!*

"What we shared was very special," he finally said in a low voice. "Nothing can ever change that."

"But I want more than just a week with you, Hawk," she pleaded.

A lopsided smile appeared on his face. "You've always existed in an environment where you got whatever you wanted, Paige, but life isn't always like that for everyone. You and I live in two different worlds. We've always known that."

They both heard the sound of a vehicle on gravel drive up and stop outside the trailer.

"That's probably Alicia's dad. She said he was going to come back to take you into town." His eyes were level and without expression when he added, "You'd better go with him."

She nodded, defeated by his polite, calm attitude. There was nothing for her to say—he'd said it all.

Paige paused at the door to the bedroom and turned. For a moment she thought she saw anguish on his face, but it was gone and he continued to meet her gaze without flinching. "Goodbye, Hawk. Take care of yourself."

"You too."

She was thankful she didn't see anyone as she hastened back to the room she'd shared with Alicia. She gathered up the few things that had survived the past week and walked out to meet John.

Paige felt as though she'd been bouncing in the front seat of the pickup truck for years. Sooner or later she was bound to reach Flagstaff.

John had taken her to a little settlement where she found a pay phone and called the hospital. The news was good. She'd even been able to speak to her father and to explain that she was on her way to see him. He'd sounded fine—

much better than she felt, as a matter of fact. *Just remember, Paige old girl, nobody's died of a broken heart.*

John had taken her to his brother's house and explained that his brother was going into Flagstaff that day and could give her a ride. She thankfully accepted their help and began her lonely journey back to her old life. She tried to plan what she would do when she reached Flagstaff—find a motel; go shopping; try to forget Hawk; take a hot, soaking bath; try to forget Hawk; go see her father; eat dinner; try to forget Hawk.

Paige rested her head against the back of the seat and closed her eyes.

Try to forget Hawk. That would be the hardest thing to do. There was so much to remember...

"How would you like to learn how to fish?" Hawk had asked Paige the second day they were together.

"Are you sure fishing is part of the curriculum?" she managed to answer. Her head was still sore and she hadn't felt like doing much.

"Wellll..." He ran his hand through his already rumpled hair. "It's the least strenuous thing I can think of for you to do, under the circumstances." He lightly touched the side of her head.

"Good point. I hope I'm not being graded on my performance as a camping mate. Otherwise, I'd have flunked by now."

Hawk laughed. His eyes were so beautiful—they sparkled when he laughed. She loved to say things to amuse him. "You're in luck. You aren't being graded this week. You've been put on the sick list and relieved of all duties."

She gave an exaggerated sigh of relief. "In that case, let's get on with this serious business of fishing."

By the end of the afternoon, they realized she had a long way to go to get the hang of it. Paige had managed to snag a bush, a limb, two rocks, and made a rat's nest of the line before admitting defeat.

"You're giving up?" Hawk asked with simulated surprise.

"Before you fire me. Yes, I am."

"You mean you don't like to fish?"

"How would I know? I haven't had a hook in the water yet. Is there a chance there *are* fish somewhere besides the water?"

"'Fraid not."

"Then we cannot consider that I have been fishing."

Hawk found some shade by the stream and suggested they rest after their strenuous afternoon. Paige was more than ready to comply. The least bit of exercise and her head tended to swim.

He pulled her head into his lap and softly stroked her hair from her face. "Have you ever been deep-sea fishing?"

"Uh-uh. Can you imagine what I'd do with one of *those* lines?" She relaxed, soothed by his gentle touch.

"Oh, you probably wouldn't have any problem at all. They have everything rigged up for you on the boat so that all you do is cast out, then sit and wait for a strike." He smiled at his memories. "Boy, can that be exciting."

"Do you go often?"

"Whenever the mood strikes me."

"It must be nice to do whatever you want, whenever you want."

"It has its advantages...and its disadvantages. It can get a little lonely."

"Not anymore. Or have you already forgotten you now have a wife that will tag along?"

He'd changed the subject, Paige remembered now, pointing out a bird, then suggesting she go to sleep to rest her head. He'd had several opportunities to tell her the truth, but Paige reluctantly faced that they were during the time when she was still suffering from her concussion.

He hadn't wanted to upset her. Instead he'd allowed her to believe they were married, giving her time to fall in love with him.

The pickup slowed, then turned onto the highway. The relief from the jouncing was tremendous. Paige rubbed her head. She no longer had pain of any kind, but she'd never remembered her lost hours.

From what Hawk told her, she'd only forgotten the call about her father, and the plane ride. If only she hadn't assumed she was married. What had made her assume such a thing?

Because you would never have shared a man's bed without being married, her inner voice pointed out implacably.

Oh, that.

Yes, that.

But I ended up making love to him, anyway, she pointed out.

Only after you recognized how deeply you were in love with him. The need to express that love was stronger than thirty years of inhibitions.

Paige could find no answer to that.

It was dark when they reached Flagstaff. Paige had John's brother drop her off at the mall so that she could find something decent to wear to the hospital. He refused payment for the ride, explaining it hadn't been out of his way.

By the time she found what she needed, it was after nine o'clock. She checked into a small motel near the hospital, called to find out the latest news regarding her father, and decided to wait until morning to visit him. The trip into town had taken more out of her than she'd expected. Paige wondered how long it would take her to recover from her experiences during the past week.

Eight weeks later she was still asking herself the same question.

Her father was more to the point. "What are you trying to do to yourself, Paige, have a coronary by the time you're thirty-five?"

Paige had stopped off to see Phillip Winston at his home. At fifty-four, Phillip looked ten years younger, though his russet-colored hair was freely frosted with silver.

"Dad, please don't fuss. We've been over this before. I am *not*, repeat *not*, working too hard. I am eating enough, I am sleeping enough, there is nothing wrong with me. I'm working the same hours I've always worked." She leaned over and kissed him as he sat in the shade out on his patio. "Besides, I stopped by today to check on *your* health, not to discuss mine."

"You never want to discuss yours," he grumbled.

"That's because there's nothing to discuss."

"If you say so."

"Good. I'm glad to have that out of the way." She settled comfortably in the chaise lounge next to his and sipped from the tall, frosted glass of iced tea that Sarah, Phillip's indomitable housekeeper, had brought out to them. "Your problem, dear doctor, is that you're bored, so you're letting your imagination have a field day."

"I *know* I'm bored, Paige. Why the hell wouldn't I be? I could have been back to work two weeks ago."

"Of course you could have," she agreed smoothly, "and been back in the hospital the week afterward."

"I am not an invalid and I'm tired of being treated like one."

Paige couldn't conceal the amusement in her eyes. "Oh, I don't think Sarah and I treat you like an invalid. I think we treat you more as a child having periodic temper tantrums. That's because that's the way you've been behaving." She enjoyed another swallow of her refreshing beverage while she watched that thrust hit home.

Phillip stared at her, startled. The Paige he was used to wouldn't have been quite so caustic, but he ruefully acknowledged to himself she might have some cause.

"Have I really been that bad?"

"Let me put it this way—I've got patients in the hospital right now who are handling their convalescence with more maturity than you've been showing."

"Temper tantrums, huh?"

"Close."

Phillip sighed. "Okay. I'll behave."

"Oh, we don't expect miracles, love, just a little more effort on your part. Believe it or not, we all want to see you back at the clinic just as badly as you want to be there."

He reached over and patted her hand. "Yes, little mother hen, but please don't patronize me."

Paige's eyes glistened with pain. "Dad, I don't mean to sound patronizing, but you scared all of us with that heart attack. We don't want it recurring."

"Amen to that."

"Look, I've got to run. There's a young patient I want to check on. He went home three days ago, and I promised to visit him."

"Aren't you staying for lunch?"

She glanced at her watch. "Not today. I'll grab something later—and I'll be back to see you tomorrow." She stood up. "Would you like me to bring you a coloring book and some crayons?" He threw a small pillow at her as she opened the sliding-glass door into the house. "That's strange. All my other patients are generally delighted with the suggestion."

With a fond smile, Phillip watched her leave. He was inordinately proud of his daughter and didn't care who knew it. He'd always felt they had a good, close relationship—until recently.

Something was definitely bothering her. Her excuse that she was busy at the clinic made sense, but she'd always stayed busy and had seemed to thrive on the hectic pace. That was no longer true.

He could tell she wasn't sleeping well, and she'd lost weight. Paige had always been slender, burning up calories relentlessly as soon as she consumed them, but now her appetite was practically nonexistent.

Phillip had a strong hunch all of her behavior could be traced back to her week in the wilderness. Whenever he tried to discuss it with her, she changed the subject.

He didn't like to see himself as a nosy parent. In fact, Phillip took pride in the fact that he'd always allowed Paige the freedom to make her own decisions without his influence. So why was he feeling the need to confront her with her recent behavior and demand some answers, like the father of a recalcitrant teenager?

He was worried about her—not only because she was his daughter, but because she was his partner and his friend. Phillip suddenly recognized that had one of his other partners or associates been behaving in a similar manner he would not have hesitated to sit down with them and try to find out what was wrong. That's what friends were for.

The next time Paige came over, he'd approach her as a friend rather than a father to see if he could get her to open up to him.

It was plain that she needed someone, but he had a sneaking hunch it wasn't her father!

The late-August sun continued to beat down on the city of El Paso. Wisps of hair stuck to Paige's forehead and she decided to stop and have lunch somewhere quiet and air-conditioned rather than drive through a fast-food place.

Her young patient was doing nicely and she was glad she'd taken the time to check on him. His corrective surgery was healing satisfactorily, and she was pleased with his progress.

She took the next exit off the freeway and saw a Luby's Cafeteria sign. Just what she needed. With her lack of appetite these days, a delicious array of attractive choices would encourage her to eat.

She remembered the meals she'd shared with Hawk. Hawk. Sooner or later her thoughts always returned to him and to their time together. Paige wondered if he ever thought of her. Oh, how she wished she could quit thinking about him!

It was unfortunate for Paige's peace of mind that she'd no sooner found a small table and begun to eat than Hawk walked into the cafeteria with three other men.

They were all dressed in colorful coveralls, and she realized the cafeteria wasn't too far from the airport. Why had she picked this particular place to eat today?

She watched him hungrily, making a mockery of all of her determined efforts to forget him. The four of them were all laughing and joking with each other and the people behind the counter. It was obvious they were regular customers.

He looked marvelous. *At least you know he hasn't been pining away for you.*

The men took their loaded trays to a table across the large room. She discovered she'd been holding her breath, waiting for him to notice her. He didn't. He sat in profile to her and she had an opportunity to prove or to disprove her theories. For weeks she'd tried to convince herself he had only seemed attractive to her because of the environment they'd shared. Paige had to concede that she found him devastatingly attractive regardless of his environment.

Two women walked by the table occupied by the men and stopped. Paige watched Hawk glance up at them and smile—the warm, sensuous smile that accelerated her pulse rate.

Hastily finishing her glass of iced tea, Paige stood up abruptly. Whatever interest he'd shown in her before, he had none now, and she was making herself needlessly miserable by dwelling on what they had shared.

Ignoring the temptation to go over to him and say hello, she made herself walk out of the cafeteria without a backward glance. They had already said all there was to say to each other.

* * *

Hawk glanced toward the door and watched a woman leave the cafeteria. She reminded him of Paige, but that wasn't unusual. Everywhere he went these days, he was reminded of Paige.

He couldn't forget her.

It had taken him several weeks to recover from his injuries, including the ribs. Paige had been right about them. It had taken him several more weeks to get his plane out of that meadow.

He'd also found out why no one had found him and Paige. The control tower had lost track of him in the storm and he was nowhere near where he was supposed to be when they were forced down. They could have stayed there for six months and probably not been spotted.

A tiny curve appeared on his lips at the thought. *That might not have been so bad. Maybe I could have gotten her out of my system in that length of time.*

Who was he kidding? He'd already discovered how difficult it was to forget her. He would welcome a nice case of total amnesia about now. He could remember everything she had said to him, everything they had done together, and at night he dreamed he was making love to her. His memories were driving him out of his mind.

Now he thought he saw her everywhere he went. He shook his head.

"Where've you been, Hawk? I've asked you to hand me the salt three times. You tryin' to save me from sodium poisoning or something?" His friend grinned at him.

"Sorry. I was thinking."

"Yeah, we noticed. Our conversation must be too boring for you, right?"

"You got it."

They finished their meal heckling each other, and once again Hawk tried to put Paige out of his mind.

A few days later he decided that the best thing for him to do would be to look her up—go see her—maybe take her to dinner. No doubt his imagination was building her up too much. If he saw her in her natural environment, he'd be reminded of why they had no future together.

He found her number listed in the telephone book, but when he called he discovered he'd reached her answering service. An answering service. What other woman of his acquaintance had a damned answering service? He refused the offer to have Paige return his call, but he couldn't get her out of his mind.

When Hawk saw the mention in the local paper of a hospital benefit being held he thought about attending. It would give him a chance to see her, maybe speak to her—find out if she was all right. He could treat it as a casual meeting between acquaintances. If he could see her one more time, he was sure he'd be better able to deal with his feelings.

Ten days later he realized how big a fool he'd been. Hawk leaned against the marble pillar of the mammoth hotel convention room, watching the cream of the city's society dancing by, decked out in all their finery. The glittering decorations had turned the room into a magical fairyland. Unfortunately Hawk had never believed in fairy tales. He felt ridiculous in his rented formal wear, unaware of the admiring glances he was receiving from several of the women in the room. Why had he ever thought going there was a good idea?

What if Paige didn't come? Why had he thought she would? Were doctors obligated to attend these affairs?

Hawk slowly straightened as he spotted her at the entrance to the ballroom. Paige wore an ivory gown that flowed around her petite form with flattering attention to her feminine shape. She wore her hair loose around her shoulders, and Hawk suffered a sharp pain as memories assailed him.

Her hand rested lightly on the sleeve of the distinguished man who stood by her side, tall and slim. The resemblance was strong. Paige's father. Hawk felt a slight easing of tension. At least her father was all right—one question answered. He watched them circulate around the room, greeting the dignitaries, making conversation, and the gulf between them had never been more apparent to him.

She was like a fairy-tale princess holding court. Several men stood around her, vying for her attention. Why had she made her life sound so lacking in social contact? She appeared comfortable and at ease, totally in her element.

He'd seen enough. More than enough. He recognized that more than the room separated them. He'd never be comfortable in her environment. He wouldn't want to try.

Paige accepted the lighthearted teasing regarding her appearance with a smile.

"How come you never dress like that when you're at the hospital?" Rob Hartman asked.

She glanced down at her gown. "Because I'd probably trip over my skirt halfway through making rounds."

"No. I mean wear your hair down like that."

Paige knew why she'd worn her hair loose. She'd been thinking of Hawk, remembering how he'd enjoyed running his hands through it. Her father had noticed the new style when he came to pick her up and commented on how attractive she looked.

"Sorry, Rob. It isn't practical to wear it loose during the day." She smiled and absently glanced around the room. A tall, attractive man in superbly tailored clothes strode toward the exit. *He looks like Hawk,* she thought. With a small gasp Paige realized it *was* Hawk—and he was leaving.

"Excuse me for a moment, will you?" she murmured. Without waiting for a response, she hurried across the floor.

Of course it was Hawk. No one else had that indefinable air of authority and arrogance he carried—nor walked with the lithe grace of a jungle cat.

People stopped her repeatedly while she tried to catch up with him. By the time she reached the door he was no longer in sight.

Why had he come? To see her? If so, why hadn't he spoken to her? She could make no sense of his behavior, but long after the evening had been forgotten by others, Paige remembered Hawk's presence at the gala event.

She could think of only one reason why he'd attended—to see her.

Twelve

Paige shook her head at the proffered plate of food. "I can't eat another bite, Dad. I'm stuffed."

Phillip glanced at the plate in front of his daughter. She had only taken a few spoonfuls of food on it, and he shook his head. "Paige, you aren't eating enough to keep a bird alive."

She laughed. "Remember when you used to tease me about eating like a bird—a vulture?"

He grinned. "So you did, as a teenager. But you burned it off before it turned into fat. Now you're burning calories you can't afford to lose." He bit off his next thought, determined to choose a better time to discuss his concerns with her.

Sarah came into the dining room with a pot of coffee and poured them each another cup.

"Sarah, your meal was delicious, as always," Paige told her.

The older woman smiled. "I'm glad you enjoyed it."

Phillip stood up. "Why don't we have our coffee in the den, Paige, so we can stretch out and get comfortable."

Paige had fallen into the habit of spending Friday evenings with her father years ago. Nothing had broken that routine. It gave them a chance to catch up on personal news as well as professional problems they might have. Paige had long since discovered that although they worked in the same clinic, they rarely had time to see each other, except while passing in the hall.

Paige settled back in one of her dad's recliners with a sigh. She couldn't remember when she'd felt so tired. A fleeting image of hiking through rugged mountains flashed before her, but she determinedly shoved it away. That happened in another lifetime—to someone else.

"Paige?"

"Hmm?"

"I'm worried about you."

She glanced up at her father in surprise. He was stretched out in another recliner, looking well and rested. He had been given permission to work in the clinic on a part-time, consulting basis for the next few weeks, cheering him up considerably.

"What do you mean?"

"You've lost weight—you aren't eating—I don't think you're getting enough rest—and it bothers me. I thought you and I were friends."

She stared at him. "We *are* friends."

"But not close enough to share our troubles?"

Puzzled by his serious tone, Paige replied, "Dad, I don't know what you're talking about."

He shrugged. He couldn't force her to talk, not if she didn't want to, but he could read the signs. She needed to talk to someone. Desperately. His eyes were filled with love and concern when he said, "Paige, have you thought about getting professional counseling?"

Was she that bad? she wondered with dismay. Was it so obvious that she was suffering? She'd made every effort to

forget Hawk and their time together. She'd managed to put
him out of her mind for large blocks of time during the day,
but he invariably showed up in her dreams at night until she
thought she was losing her mind.

Maybe she was.

She sat up in her chair so that she faced Phillip. Maybe it
would help to talk about it.

"Do you remember when you had your heart attack and
I flew to Flagstaff...or at least I tried to fly?"

He nodded, unwilling to interrupt now that she seemed to
have started.

"Being marooned with another person for a week gives
you a chance to know him better than if you'd known him
for years." She searched for words to explain what happened between her and Hawk. She wasn't even sure that she
herself understood.

"I'm sure it would," Phillip murmured.

"I've never known anyone like Hawk Cameron. He's as
different as any alien that might have landed from another
planet." She looked up and met his quiet gaze. "I found him
fascinating."

She waited for his comment, but he made none. He
seemed to be waiting for her to continue.

"Hawk is a loner. He's been on his own since he was
fourteen...traveled and worked all over the world...and is
content to continue his wanderings. I doubt that he'll ever
settle in one place."

Phillip was beginning to understand, more by what Paige
wasn't saying than her actual statements. "You fell in love
with him," he stated quietly.

Her head jerked up from studying her fingers twisting
together in her lap. She stared at him in confusion. "I don't
know what I feel anymore. I can't seem to forget him. I can
recall every conversation we ever had, everything we ever
did together..." Her slight blush gave Phillip enough information to draw his own conclusions. "He taught me so
much about how to survive in a wilderness, how to rely on

myself and nature's provisions, even though he'd brought enough equipment to keep us in comfort." She shook her head. "I don't understand why I miss him so much."

Her dad smiled. "It certainly sounds like love to me."

"How do you get over it?"

"Why should you want to?"

She shrugged. "I don't have much choice. He made it clear we come from two different worlds."

"You already knew that."

"Yes."

"But it doesn't make any difference to you."

Her eyes slowly filled with tears until Phillip was only a blur. "No. It doesn't."

"So what do you intend to do about it?"

"Not a thing. It takes more than one person loving to make a relationship work."

"Ohhhh," Phillip drew out. "Now I understand. Although you fell in love with him, he showed no interest in you."

Paige could feel the heat in her body at the memory of the amount of interest Hawk had shown toward her. In a low voice that Phillip could scarcely hear, she murmured, "He said he loved me."

"Maybe he does."

"But not enough."

"Now I'm not sure I understand what *you* mean. What sort of measuring stick are you using?"

"He told me he wasn't some sort of tame lapdog to wait around until I had some time to give to him." Her hurt and pain echoed through the words.

It was unfortunate that Phillip laughed. Her eyes widened with pain at the sound.

"Paige, honey, you wouldn't be interested in a tame lapdog that sat around and waited for your attention. Why does that comment upset you?"

She thought about his question for a long while. "I guess because I felt he was criticizing my dedication to my profession. I had already told him I didn't have time for a personal relationship in my life."

"Then I don't blame him for his remark. You had already made it clear you weren't willing to change anything in your life to accommodate a relationship with him."

Surprised at his insight, Paige stared at her father with dismay. "That's right, I did."

"So what did you expect him to do...or say? If he's half the man you've described to me, he would want more than bits and pieces of your life."

"That's true, but that's all I have to give."

"Is it?"

"You're a doctor. You know how demanding a profession it is."

"Yes, and I know that I made some serious mistakes in choosing to let it take over my life."

She'd never heard her father talk that way, and when she saw the pain in his face she realized he had some painful memories of his own.

"I loved your mother more than you could possibly imagine, Paige. She was everything I'd ever wanted in a wife...or a lover. And wonder of wonders, she felt the same way about me. Those kinds of shared feelings are very rare and should be appreciated and treasured. They should never be taken for granted." Phillip paused and swallowed, as though his throat had been constricted.

"In my arrogance I took our love for each other for granted. I was young and ambitious—" he gave a rueful shrug "—and very shortsighted. I assumed we had forever together, but in the meantime I had a practice to build, a living to make, demands on my time to fulfill..."

He faced Paige, the pain in his eyes almost more than she could bear. "Then it was too late to change the habits I'd set up. Too late to arrange my schedule so that I could stay home with your mother." He shook his head. "She never complained, although I knew she felt that she came second in my life. But she was wrong. So wrong. I just assumed that we'd have time together later...always later...at some mystical point in life. I didn't realize that I needed to realign my priorities at the very beginning, because some of us aren't given enough time for all we want to do.''

Tears ran down Paige's face as she listened to her father. She had memories of her own that confirmed what he was saying. She remembered her mother's joy when her dad came home early and spent any time with them. Her mother counted the days to his vacation when they were off together, away from the heavy demands of his profession.

Paige had always known how much her mother had loved her dad. She'd never understood until now how much her father had loved her mother.

He had given Paige a great deal to think about.

Paige stared up at the ceiling above her bed late that night, thinking of all she'd learned. Life was full of choices—almost too many. Sometimes one choice wiped out many equally fulfilling ones.

Is that what she'd done by choosing medicine as a career? She'd never cared before. Her dedication was all-encompassing and satisfying. She'd never needed anything more to make her life complete—until now.

She needed Hawk. She needed his calm, levelheaded attitude toward life that seemed to keep things in perspective. She needed his love and affection, his teasing, his enjoyment of his surroundings—and his steady warmth in her bed each night.

But how did he feel? He'd made it clear he didn't want to be tied down, hadn't he? He enjoyed his present life-style—free to come and go as he pleased.

What if he didn't want her?

She recalled the day they'd found the river again and saw him once again standing under the hard-driving water pouring over the lip of the falls. She saw the look on his face, the love and desire shining in his eyes when he had turned around and had seen her standing there before him.

She remembered the urgency of his lovemaking, the fierce possession, his loss of control with her. He had wanted her then. Was there any way she could make him want her now? Even if he wanted her, would he be willing to share her life?

A sudden thought struck her. A thought so foreign that she was shaken. Was she willing to share *his* life?

Paige spent many days and sleepless nights facing that thought-provoking question.

The late-September sun beat down on the metal hangar where Hawk was working on the engine of his plane. He could feel the perspiration trickling down his back, underneath his mechanic's coveralls.

He rapped his knuckle against one of the parts deep inside the engine and colored the air with a few pungent statements regarding the engine, the plane and El Paso's hot weather.

Straightening, Hawk rubbed his back, tired from the bent-over position he'd held for so long, and glanced out the hangar door. The blue Texas sky looked like a backdrop to Mount Franklin, sitting there like a crouching cat overlooking the city. He walked over to the water fountain and took a long, reviving drink.

Hawk knew he was in bad shape, but he wasn't sure what the hell to do about it. Not that he hadn't tried—he'd almost killed himself trying.

He still couldn't forget Paige. Seeing her at the formal benefit had convinced him they could never make a relationship work, but it hadn't helped him to forget her. That was the first night Hawk had gone out and deliberately drunk himself into oblivion. Unfortunately it hadn't been the last.

He'd tried to replace her memory with other women. He knew several in El Paso and he began to call them. Only, they seemed different to him somehow. Their conversations were boring. Had he ever bothered sitting around talking with them before? Probably not. He decided he probably wouldn't find anyone like Paige to talk to, but he could certainly replace her in bed.

After the third attempt, he'd quit trying. The damn woman had turned him into a eunuch. Embarrassed, he'd had to explain to his dates that he'd had too much to drink. After he'd left them he'd made damn sure that was the case before he finally went to bed.

Damn her.

Rick walked into the hangar just as Hawk picked up a small wrench.

"Uh, Hawk..." Rick was never sure how to approach Hawk anymore. He was worse than a grizzly with a thorn in its paw. Rick didn't think Hawk would be any too pleased with the news he had for him.

"Yeah?" Hawk was already reaching for the troubled insides of the engine.

"There's somebody here to see you."

Hawk raised his head in surprise. No one ever came out to the airport to see him. "Who is it?" The frown he wore wasn't encouraging.

"Well, I only saw her once, but I think it's the same woman who chartered the plane last summer to go to Flagstaff." He shuffled his feet. "I didn't ask her for her name."

Hawk felt like Rick had just picked up a sledgehammer and swung into his midsection. He could scarcely breathe, and the pain in his chest made him realize his lungs had quit working.

"Paige?" he said faintly.

"Yeah, I think that's her name. Dr. Winston, isn't it?"

"Paige is here?"

Rick nodded, surprised at the stunned expression on Hawk's face. He had no way of knowing that Hawk was certain his mind had finally managed to conjure her up in the flesh since he'd been thinking of her for so long.

"What's she want?" he asked gruffly, staring down at the forgotten tool in his hand.

Rick scratched his head. "Well, she said something about wanting to charter a plane or something...said she only wanted you for the pilot."

What the hell? She needed a plane so she'd looked up her old pal, the half-breed pilot? What kind of game was she playing?

"Tell her I'm busy."

"I did."

"So?"

"So, she said she'd wait."

Once again the air was full of Hawk's invective as he discussed the vagaries of certain women who could take off in the middle of the day and wait around indefinitely to see someone.

Rick waited. "What do you want me to tell her?"

Hawk stared at his friend. He and Rick had met in southeast Asia more years ago than either cared to admit. They knew each other too well for him to try to fool Rick now.

He groaned, knowing he was going to have to see her one more time. "Send her out here."

Rick looked around the large hangar in surprise. "Out here? She'll get dirty around all these greasy parts."

"That's just too damned bad, isn't it? If she wants to see me, she can come out here. I'm not going to get cleaned up to talk to some society dame."

Rick backed away. "Okay, no need to take your bad mood out on me, Hawk. Just back off, will you?"

Hawk stared at his friend in alarm. "I'm sorry, Rick. I didn't mean to come across so strong."

Rick waved his hand. "No problem. The trouble with you is lack of a good love life." He laughed as he walked away.

If only Rick knew just how accurate his teasing comment had been. Hawk didn't need Paige's presence to remind him that he hadn't been with a woman since he'd been with her.

Hawk grabbed a rag and began to wipe the grease off his hands. He stood there, facing the door where she would enter, bracing himself to deal with her one more time. At least he'd make sure this would be the last time.

The door hesitantly opened and Paige peeked around, then walked into the hangar. She wore a sleeveless dress made of some type of sheer material, the skirt swirling around her knees. The style drew attention to her beautifully shaped legs and highlighted her slim ankles. Sandles with high heels accented the delicate arch of her small feet. Hawk felt his body react to her.

Just what he needed—visible evidence that she still had a strong effect on him.

She walked toward him as though unsure of her welcome. As she drew closer he realized she'd lost weight. Her air of fragility was even more enhanced. He stood where he was, forcing her to come to him.

When Paige opened the door to the hangar she was shaking so hard she was certain she'd be unable to walk through it. Then her attention was drawn to the foreign-looking garage area of the charter service. She'd never seen anything like it. The building was huge, sheltering three planes and several engines, all partially broken down.

At first she didn't see Hawk—until he moved. He wore greasy coveralls, bright red, and a grease smear across his cheek. The force of her heartbeat seemed to shake her entire body when she spotted him. He stood there watching her, unsmiling.

Paige had thought about this meeting for weeks. She and her father had discussed the possible outcomes and how she might deal with them. What if he refused her? How could she survive without him? It didn't bear thinking about.

She reminded herself that she'd never been one to sit and wait for something to happen, and she couldn't wait any longer for Hawk. She had to face him once and for all. As she neared where he stood she suddenly wished she'd waited a while longer. She wasn't ready for this!

"Hello, Hawk."

"Why aren't you at the clinic?" were his first words.

"I have Wednesday afternoons off."

"Oh."

He looked down at the rag he held, then continued to clean his hands as though removing the grease from his fingers was the most important thing in his life at the moment.

"How have you been? Are your ribs all right?"

"Fine. I'm just fine. How about you?"

She smiled. How honest dared she be? *I'm miserable, Hawk. I haven't had a decent night's sleep since I last slept in your arms. I haven't enjoyed a meal since the last one we cooked out on an open fire.* "Okay, I guess."

He stared at her, waiting, but when she didn't say any more he impatiently asked, "What brought you out here?"

She tensed at his abrupt question. Being close to him, she caught the slight scent of his after-shave—the scent that had haunted so many of her dreams. What she wanted to do was throw herself into his arms, but he made it obvious she wouldn't be welcomed.

Maybe she should leave. She'd already received her answer, in his tone, his speech, and his body language. She meant nothing to him.

Or he's hiding his feelings. Remember—he's good at that. You always had trouble trying to figure out what he was thinking.

Paige took a deep breath and then slowly exhaled. "I wanted to charter a plane to go camping...and I was hoping you'd be willing to pilot me."

Go camping! Was she out of her mind? Hawk's glance fell, and he noticed her hands. They were systematically shredding a tissue. A slight smile formed on his lips, then was quickly gone. *She's nervous. I wonder why?*

He shook his head. "Sorry, Paige, but I'm not available to fly you anywhere. Didn't Rick tell you I'm leaving El Paso?"

Paige couldn't have been more shocked at his words than if he'd slapped her across her face. In all of her fantasies the one constant was that Hawk would somehow be nearby.

"Where are you going?" Her lips were so stiff she could barely move them.

"A Peruvian landowner I met a few years ago called and asked if I'd be interested in coming to work for him. He's got extensive landholdings and decided having a plane and a full-time pilot on hand would make his life much simpler."

"When will you be leaving?"

Her words hung between them, slowly dissipating in the continued silence. Finally he shrugged, then motioned to the plane behind him. "Whenever I can get this thing running again. It hasn't acted right since I cracked up in that meadow in Arizona."

Paige looked closer at the plane behind him. "You mean this is the plane we were in?"

"Yes. It's the only one I have, but I'm thinking of selling it and buying another one before I go to South America. I'm not sure I really trust this one anymore."

He leaned against the wing and patted the side of the plane. It was an affectionate pat, effectively negating his words.

"How did you get it back here?"

"It wasn't easy. I flew a helicopter in and worked on it. Finally had to get some help to get it out of there, but we managed."

"Hawk?" She couldn't hide the trembling in her voice.

His eyes met hers in a calm stare. "Yes?"

"Would you like to come over to my place tonight for dinner?"

His expression never changed. "Why?"

"Because I want to see you again...and talk to you."

"What about?"

She fought to keep from saying *us*, because she knew the answer to that. He refused to accept there was a chance for the two of them. But she was ready to fight for the love they shared. A couple of times since she'd entered the hangar Paige had seen past the stoic facade he wore. He'd missed her. Just as she'd missed him. Somehow she had to convince him to give them a chance, but she needed more time to plan. His intention to leave El Paso threw all of her thoughts out of kilter.

"Do we have to have a reason to spend an evening together?" she finally asked.

"Not really. I just don't see the point myself."

"Please, Hawk. For me."

When she looks at me with those waiflike blue eyes pleading, I'm lost. All of my willpower deserts me. This has to be the dumbest thing I've ever done. I must get some sort of pleasure out of making myself miserable. There's a name for people who enjoy being miserable.

"What time?"

Her smile made him flinch—it was so beautiful. If he hadn't still been holding the grease rag he would probably have dragged her into his arms and kissed her silly, but he managed to restrain himself.

"Why don't you come at seven." She fished around in her purse and found a pad and pencil. She wrote something down and tore off the sheet, handing it to him. "Here's my address." She seemed to be memorizing his features. "I'll let you get back to your plane. I'm sorry to have interrupted you." She backed up from him. "I'll see you tonight at seven." Paige left quickly, before he could change his mind.

Hawk continued to stand there, staring at the door she'd closed behind her. He was going to have dinner with her. He was going to her home to see where and how she lived. In other words, he was going to collect more memories of her to try to forget.

"I've got to be out of my ever-loving mind," he muttered in a gruff voice, turning back to the engine.

Thirteen

Paige hurried to the door when she heard the bell. She didn't care if Hawk knew she was eager to see him. She had rushed home from the airport and industriously planned a menu to dazzle him, then realized what she was doing and laughed. They were so very far past that stage in their relationship. Yet he'd never been in her home. For that matter, she had no idea where he lived, either. None of that was important, she thought as she swung open the front door.

Hawk stood there waiting. He looked wonderful to her, wearing tailored chocolate-brown slacks, a creamy beige shirt that emphasized his dark good looks and a look in his eyes that was the most encouragement Paige had received from him all day!

"Come in," she said with a smile, and stepped back from the door.

Hawk stared at her in confusion. Gone was the doctor image he'd tried to focus on all afternoon. In its place stood a gorgeous woman in a caftan of swirling autumn colors.

Bright earrings dangled from her pierced ears, peeking through the riotous curls that surrounded her face and shoulders.

Not fair. Not fair at all, Hawk decided. She ushered him into the living room, where he found more surprises. The place was nothing like what he had pictured. Her home was small, tucked within one of the many subdivisions in El Paso. Her living room looked comfortable and well used—nothing like the picture-perfect place he'd conjured up in his mind. Scatter pillows dotted the room with color and candles scented the air with the subtle smell of spices.

"I'm so glad you came over," Paige said breathlessly. He glanced down at her so close by his side. "I've missed you—very much."

Once again his body betrayed him as it responded to the woman only inches away from him. He turned slowly to her, gently stroking her hair behind her ear. "I've missed you too," he finally admitted to them both.

She slid her arms around his neck, going up on tiptoe to reach him. Hawk needed no more encouragement. His arms snaked around her waist and he pulled her tightly against him. His mouth found hers and his kiss left no doubt that he was hungry for her.

For the first time in months Paige felt as though she had found her rightful place. Her home would always be in Hawk's arms.

Hawk's reaction to Paige made a mockery of all his fine intentions. He'd spent the afternoon steeling himself for the evening, determined not to give away any of his feelings for her. He'd decided to show them both that he could spend one last evening with her and they could part as friends.

As a matter of fact, he was feeling quite friendly toward her. Any friendlier and he would explode! Hawk reluctantly placed his hands at Paige's tiny waist and gently pushed her away from him.

Just as reluctantly Paige dropped her arms from around his neck. It felt so good to be near Hawk once more. She

had felt his arousal and was reassured even more that her
evening might have a happy ending. He certainly couldn't
pretend to be indifferent to her.

"Are you hungry?" she asked, then realized how that
sounded. Her face flushed.

Hawk started laughing. He hadn't laughed in months, but
the release of his feelings felt great—wonderful. What was
the use of denying it? He loved this woman to distraction.
He might as well enjoy the little time he had with her.

"As a matter of fact..." he drawled, his eyes dancing.

Paige unconsciously placed her hands on her cheeks to
cool them, then discovered what she'd done and dropped
them to her side. He rubbed the back of his hand against her
cheek. "It's good to see you with some color."

"Yes, well, uh, why don't we go into the dining room?"
she asked nervously, and turned away.

The table was beautifully arranged with long tapered
candles casting a glow to the room. A delicate bouquet of
flowers added color.

"I'll go get the wine," she explained, and disappeared
into the kitchen. She took a few minutes to force herself to
relax, then found the wine in the refrigerator and returned
to the other room. "Would you mind pouring?"

"Not at all." He took the bottle and the corkscrew from
her. Paige returned to the kitchen and began to bring out
their meal.

By the time they were through eating, both of them were
more relaxed. They had quickly fallen into their former easy
camaraderie. Paige asked him many questions; she wanted
to know everything that had happened to him since she'd
left him.

"I'm sure Alicia was upset when you left," she finally
offered over the rim of her wineglass.

At least he has the grace to squirm at the reminder, she
thought, watching him.

"Alicia was a nice kid. Very helpful."

"I can imagine."

"But she was just a kid. Hell, I'm old enough to be her father!"

"A very precocious father, but I suppose that's true."

"Speaking of fathers, you haven't mentioned how your dad is doing."

Paige sensed a deliberate change of subject. "He's doing great. Chomping at the bit to get back to a full-time routine."

"I suppose you've been pretty busy too."

"Yes, the clinic has been going through some major upheavals."

"How's that?"

"Well, we've hired three more doctors, and I've been cutting back considerably on my hours."

He stared at her in disbelief. "Why would you do that?"

She smiled. "Because that's what I want to do."

A sudden suspicion grabbed him, causing him to tense. "Are you pregnant?"

The look of worry and concern on his face almost decided Paige to put him out of his misery at once, but she couldn't quite resist stringing him along for a moment. "Funny you should ask."

He leaned across the table, studying her intently. "You are, aren't you? You've been sick, haven't you? That's why you're so thin."

"And if I am?" she asked with interest, folding her fingers together and resting her chin lightly on them.

Hawk stood up abruptly and began to pace the room. He'd never given it a thought. Not once. All the women he'd ever known had been experienced and knew how to look after themselves. But Paige hadn't been experienced. He'd recognized that immediately. And he'd done nothing to protect her.

What a bastard you are, he told himself. *In every sense of the word. You were going to go off to another country without even finding out—without even discovering if a child was on the way. Just like your father did.*

Paige stood up and began to clear the table. She'd taken all their dishes to the kitchen before Hawk followed her.

"We're going to get married," he stated firmly as soon as he walked through the kitchen door.

Paige turned around from the sink and stared at him. Never had she seen him so serious. "Why?"

He wasn't prepared for her question. The reason was obvious enough, wasn't it?

"Are you saying that you'd be willing to marry me because I might be pregnant?" she asked.

"Of course."

"But what about our different life-styles, our different worlds?"

A very stubborn expression appeared on his face. "Then we'll have to work something out between us...some sort of compromise. I know I'm not the type of person you'd ever marry, but I'm not going to let a child of mine come into this world not knowing its father."

Paige walked over to where Hawk stood in the middle of the kitchen floor and gently stroked his jaw. "Hawk, you're the only type of person I could ever imagine marrying. I spent almost a week thinking I was married to you, and I've never been happier." She leaned up and kissed him on the cheek. "I willingly accept your most romantic proposal," she whispered.

Fierce joy flooded Hawk at her words. She was going to marry him. He couldn't believe it. They were going to be married! Forgotten were all his plans to spend his life alone. Forgotten were all of his vows not to get involved. Dammit all, he *was* involved! He became involved the first time he made love to Paige.

"When is the baby due?" he asked.

Paige took him by the hand and led him back into the living room. She gently pushed him until he sat down on the sofa, then she draped herself across his lap, her arms curled around his neck.

"Hawk, do you love me?" she asked, staring straight into his eyes.

He'd lost the battle—with himself and with her—but for some reason he felt as though he'd won all the jackpots ever offered. He nuzzled her neck, tasting her, smelling her soft flowerlike scent. "Very much."

"That's good, because when we get married I'm all you'll get...at least for a while."

He raised his head and stared at her, bemused.

"I'm not pregnant, Hawk," she whispered.

"But you said..."

"No, *you* said, and I let you think it." She settled more comfortably into his lap with a little wriggle that created havoc with Hawk's concentration. "You see, I've spent the past several weeks trying to figure out a way to convince you that we could have a fine life together."

He opened his mouth to speak, and she placed her fingertips gently across his lips.

"I discovered that you were the most important thing in my life. More important than my career, even though I enjoy it very much. And I couldn't figure out a way to convince you." She dropped her head to his shoulder so that she no longer had to face him. "I'm ashamed to admit that when I discovered I wasn't pregnant I cried for hours. I had so wanted your baby, Hawk. I was even despicable enough to consider using a pregnancy in the hope you'd be swayed into giving us a chance together."

She kissed him lightly in front of his ear, then followed the strong jawline to his chin, her soft kisses creating chills along his spine.

"I love you, Hawk, and I want to marry you. But I'm not pregnant."

When she glanced up at him she couldn't speak. His eyes glistened with moisture, the tenderness and love in them causing her to catch her breath.

"Paige, love, how can I resist you?"

"I was hoping you couldn't."

He dropped his head on the back of the sofa. "So what now? I suppose I need to call the landowner in Peru and tell him I'm not coming..." he said, as though thinking aloud.

"Not necessarily. Why don't you call him and ask if he could use a medical doctor anywhere on his staff."

Hawk's head snapped forward. "Are you serious?"

"I've never been more serious in my life. What is that old saying? Whither thou goest?" She smiled softly. "I don't want you to change, Hawk. I fell in love with the man you are. All I want to do is become a part of your life. Is that so hard to understand?"

Hawk couldn't believe what he was hearing. "But you're a doctor. You're already established here. Why would you want to move?"

"That's simple—to be with you. Hawk, I'll always be a doctor. Nothing can change that—it's a basic part of me. But there are sick people everywhere. If you're too restless to stay in one place, fine. We'll both move on."

"I think you've lost your mind."

"No, just my heart."

"I can't let you do it."

"Does that mean you're withdrawing your proposal?"

"No, but—I mean, maybe we need to think about this for a while..."

"That's all I've thought about for months. I have to be honest with you and admit it took me a while to work out all of my priorities. But I have them in order now. That is, if you want me."

"Want you! You've haunted me for months. I tried everything I knew to erase you from my mind." He bitterly recalled some of his more resounding failures. "I just want you to be sure."

"I love you, Hawk."

"Oh, dear God, Paige, I love you too. I just hope we're doing the right thing," he said in a husky voice. He kissed her, and Paige knew it was going to be all right. Love really would find a way.

Her thoughts scattered as Hawk deepened his possession of her mouth, his hands sliding down to the hem of her caftan, then slowly climbing once again. Everything was going to be just fine.

Three years later Paige was still convinced. Everything was just fine.

She turned over in their roomy, double sleeping bag and studied the sleeping man beside her with deep-seated love. She'd discovered a fascinating phenomenon—the longer she was with Hawk the more she loved him. Her love seemed to grow like a prolific plant that had been pampered and fed with the finest nutrients.

She watched him quietly, not wanting to wake him. He looked so tired. He'd been working too hard, which was the reason for their vacation.

Only, this time she'd known what to pack for a couple of weeks in the great outdoors. When they'd arrived back in the States last week, Hawk had borrowed a helicopter from Rick and explained they wanted to go camping—in eastern Arizona.

They'd found a lake fed by underground streams and decided to stay for a few days. During their exploring Hawk had even found them a waterfall.

Peru had been an education Paige wouldn't have wanted to miss. She had grown to love the people in the village near their small home, and fortunately they had come to accept her. She'd been able to teach them how to care for their young ones, and found the experience very satisfying and fulfilling.

Hawk turned over, effectively pinning her into place by throwing an arm and a leg over her. "Move over, you big ox. You don't have to take up all the room," she complained, chuckling.

"Who's a big ox?"

"You are," she muttered.

"Is that any way for you to talk to your dearly beloved?"

"It is when your dearly beloved weighs almost two hundred pounds."

"I see. Does this mean that the honeymoon is over?"

"Of course not. We've only been married three years. Honeymoons are supposed to last up to twenty-five years. After that, we'll be on our own."

He tried to hide his smile, but was unsuccessful. "Are you warm enough?"

"Yes. This new camping gear is great, and so roomy."

Hawk stared up at the ceiling of their tent. It was a six-man tent, large enough so they could move around comfortably. He would never try to do any backpacking with it, but then, he didn't need to.

"Do you want to go fishing?"

She looked at him with suspicion. "I thought you said you weren't going to fish with me anymore when I caught more yesterday than you did."

He smiled innocently. "I changed my mind."

She digested his remark. "Why?"

"Because I love to watch you make all those faces when you bait your hook."

"Oh, Hawk, don't make fun of me."

"But darling, I love to make fun of you, and to love you, and to laugh with you. I love to do everything with you." His actions soon followed the example of his words.

With easy familiarity he touched her in all those places that fanned the flame of her desire, and she was soon lost to everything but him. The years had also taught Paige how to love Hawk, and she delighted in causing him to lose his iron control.

"Oh, honey, you feel so good," he whispered some time later. The only peace Hawk had found in the world was there in her arms. He lay there, trying to catch his breath, while she stroked her fingers through his hair.

"Hawk?"

"Hmm."

"Is it definite we're moving to Alaska after our vacation?"

He lifted his head, then dropped it on her breast once more. "Uh-huh. The letter was waiting for me in El Paso, confirming the date we're due up there. I forgot to show it to you."

"So now we're officially partners. We'll be flying supplies and medical attention to people who are isolated."

"Uh-huh."

"Hawk?"

"Hmm?"

"I have a confession to make."

He raised his head. "You talk too much?" he offered with a straight face.

"That too. But it may have more serious consequences."

He shifted slightly, so that he was lying beside her. "What's wrong?"

"Maybe nothing, but then again..."

"Paige..." he said in a warning voice.

She stared at him uncertainly, then decided to come right out with it. "I forgot to pack my birth-control pills for our vacation." She waited, watching his face apprehensively.

His impassive expression fell into place. *Damn*, Paige thought with vexation. *He can still hide what he's thinking and feeling from me when he wants to!*

"I find it interesting that you've waited almost a week to inform me of that little bit of vital information."

"I know. I'm ashamed. I really am."

"But not enough to have said anything about it before now."

"No, because...well, because I didn't get pregnant the other time we were camping and we didn't take any precautions then either."

He studied her anxious expression for a moment, then grinned. "I take it you're ready to start our family, even if it means in Alaska."

She nodded her head. "Oh, Hawk, it wasn't a conscious decision, but I'll admit that when I discovered I didn't have them, I wasn't sorry."

"You are a sneaky, scheming woman, you know that, don't you?"

She nodded slowly.

"Because if you weren't a sneaky, scheming woman, I would be doing all of this traveling on my own, with no one to keep me warm and keep me company and keep me well taken care of." His tone of voice finally convinced her he was teasing. "So why should I expect the choice of when to become a parent to be left in my hands? Now I know how it feels to be henpecked."

"You henpecked? Hah!" Paige sat up, then discovered her legs were still entwined with Hawk's.

"And I love it," he murmured, rolling over onto his back and pulling her down onto his chest. He pulled her face down to his. "I hope you *are* pregnant," he said in a fierce undertone close to her ear. "In fact, if you aren't, I'm most willing to spend whatever time necessary to see that you do become pregnant as soon as possible."

She sighed, relaxing her head on his chest. "It's that sort of devotion to duty that makes me love you so much," Paige said, closing her eyes with complete contentment.

Silhouette

SPECIAL EDITION

TM

SPECIAL EDITION

Stories of love and life, these powerful
novels are tales that you can identify with—
romances with "something special" added in!

Fall in love with the stories of authors such
as **Nora Roberts, Diana Palmer, Ginna Gray**
and many more of your special favorites—as
well as wonderful new voices!

Special Edition brings you
entertainment for the heart!

New York Times Bestselling Author

PENNY JORDAN

Explore the lives of four women as they overcome a

CRUEL LEGACY

For Philippa, Sally, Elizabeth and Deborah life will
never be the same after the final act of one man. Now
they must stand on their own and reclaim their lives.

As Philippa learns to live without wealth and
social standing, Sally finds herself tempted by a man
who is not her husband. And Elizabeth struggles
between supporting her husband and proclaiming
her independence, while Deborah must choose
between a jealous lover and a ruthless boss.

Don't miss CRUEL LEGACY, available this December
at your favorite retail outlet.

 MIRA **The brightest star in women's fiction**

SILHOUETTE® *Desire®*

Do you want...

Dangerously handsome heroes

Evocative, everlasting love stories

Sizzling and tantalizing sensuality

Incredibly sexy miniseries like **MAN OF THE MONTH**

Red-hot romance

Enticing entertainment that can't be beat!

You'll find all of this, and much *more* each and every month in **SILHOUETTE DESIRE**. Don't miss these unforgettable love stories by some of romance's hottest authors. Silhouette Desire—where your fantasies will always come true....

DES-GEN

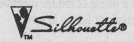

INTRODUCING...

A collection of award-winning books by award-winning authors! From Harlequin and Silhouette.

Falling Angel
by Anne Stuart

WINNER OF THE RITA AWARD
FOR BEST ROMANCE!

Falling Angel by Anne Stuart is a RITA Award winner, voted Best Romance. A truly wonderful story, *Falling Angel* will transport you into a world of hidden identities, second chances and the magic of falling in love.

"Ms. Stuart's talent shines like the brightest of stars, making it very obvious that her ultimate destiny is to be the next romance author at the top of the best-seller charts."
—*Affaire de Coeur*

A heartwarming story for the holidays. You won't want to miss award-winning *Falling Angel*, available this January wherever Harlequin and Silhouette books are sold.